Mission

Mesquite

By

Diane E Tatum

Winged Publications
PO Box 8047
Surprise, AZ 85374

ISBN-13: 978-1-0880-1364-9

Amazon Review for *Mission Mesquite*:

5.0 out of 5 stars Great read!!-

By Brenda C Griffin on January 20, 2017

Stayed up way to late enjoying this book! I could not wait to get home from work to finish it!!!

Mission Mesquite Beta Reviewers' Remarks:

Katherine Pasour: I have completed my review of Mission Mesquite ... I LOVED IT! Tyler is my hero and it was a joy to see Kate mature spiritually and emotionally.

Rose Delancey: SUPER cute story! I'm not a huge fan of the romance genre, but even *I* got into this one! Kate and Tyler were just adorable, and you handled your characters excellently ...

I can't wait to see this book published! As I was reading this, I kept gushing to my mom about how impressed I was with your skill. ... Miguel was just the cutest thing, and nothing was really cheesy or oversimplified or flat. Great work, Diane! You are a master of your craft. ☺

Kathy McKinsey: I love this story. The people are so fun. [After seven chapters], I can't wait to see what happens next. :) [After finishing], this is very touching. Excellent work.

Amazon Reviews for *Gold Earrings*:

5.0 out of 5 stars Great insight into human relationships

By W. Horner on October 30, 2011

Diane Tatum's characters are realistic and complex, not simple heroes and villains, as are their interactions and conflicts....

Tatum in similar fashion illustrates in these pages the tension between forgiveness and judgment, mercy and high moral standards. Life is full of such seeming contradictions, but as this book demonstrates, a God-pleasing love story can arise out of the midst of them.

You'll enjoy this book.

5.0 out of 5 stars Beautiful historical romance!

By K. Fugate on December 13, 2011

Author Diane E. Tatum is a natural storyteller, and her novel is an engaging, moving, historical romance that I devoured in one sitting. The story is wholesome, charming and well-researched, and full of colorful, well-rounded characters. I highly recommend it!

To my husband, Ken, who shows me agape love every day since we met in church on December 11, 1977.

Jeremiah 31:29
"For I know the plans I have for you,"
declares the Lord, "plans to prosper you and
not to harm you, plans to give you hope and
a future." (NIV)

Chapter 1

The smell of manure and earth accosted Kate's nostrils as she entered the arena.

Washington may have some stinky deals, and the Metro might be stale at times, but DC never smelled quite this 'aromatic'. She looked around in curiosity. She couldn't believe she was actually at a rodeo.

Cows lowed in closed cages. Horses pranced and whinnied with excitement. Cowboys and cowgirls strutted around the inner ring in jeans, Justin boots, and Stetson hats. In the general admission seats, would-be cowboys and cowgirls mimicked the fashion *au rigueur*. A bandanna be-decked cowgirl with fringed vest twirled toy lassoes in hope of a sale from a parent wanting to please an eager child. Hawkers called their wares - cotton candy, popcorn, lemon chillers. The country jazz band played loud western music over the low-key bedlam. It was the first weekend in June, the start of Rodeo Season at Mesquite Arena.

What was she doing here anyway? Kate shook her head in disbelief. What in the world did she know about any of this?

An usher dressed in denim shirt, jeans, and boots showed her to her seat in the front row of the box section of the arena. He smiled a bright smile and tipped his hat. Her Liz Claiborne jeans were obviously new, and the silk shirt was more like Saks Fifth Avenue than the local tourist shop. She knew she stuck out like a sore thumb.

"If I can help, just whistle, ma'am." His drawl reminded her she was in a foreign land called Texas.

"Thanks." Kate smiled tightly. "I'll remember that …"

"Wayne. I'm Wayne Justus."

Kate nodded curtly, and the usher took his leave. She settled into the seat, arranged her macramé sling-sack underneath her, and flipped through the program with disinterest. Calf-roping, bronc-riding, bull-riding, barrel racing, and Tijuana stud poker? Tonight would definitely be an education like none she had received at college.

"Kate! There you are. I'm so glad your flight landed in time for the show."

The smallish woman who had called out was her mom. She ran to Kate's box and hugged her tightly. "I knew you would come if we asked."

"I love you, Mom. Of course, I would come to see you whenever you ask. What's the problem?"

"No problem. I just wanted you to finally understand the life that your dad and I have chosen. Coming to Dallas and the rodeo is the best way to see it firsthand. Plus we haven't seen you in years."

Kate brushed her curls behind her ear and wiped the unexpected tears from her face.

"I've missed you, Mom. And you're right; I really don't understand."

Conversation ceased when the rodeo announcer began calling the names of the band members and sounding like a square dance caller or auctioneer. Kate's mom waved and ran back to her place amid the rodeo participants. Kate sighed as the crowd rose to their feet for the parade of rodeo contestants and the American flag. The crowd buzzed with excitement as the spirited horses galloped into the ring with their riders wearing spangled, multi-colored clothing.

As the announcer led the crowd in prayer for the safety of the contestants, Kate wondered about the last time she had truly prayed. How had she fallen so far away from all the things her parents had taught her? Why had she created such a different life – a life without her parents or her parents' deep faith?

She covered her heart with her hand and sang the "Star Spangled Banner" with the crowd and the closed-circuit monitor.

More tears. Drat. Why was she so emotional tonight? Must be because she was reconnecting to her parents again. She dug in the macramé sling bag for a tissue.

"Hey, missy. It's not too many people who cry at the National Anthem."

Kate quickly wiped her eyes with the tissue in order to more clearly see the cowboy on horseback who addressed her from the other side of the box wall. Kate smiled a shy smile, hoping the man would ride off and leave her alone with her thoughts.

"I'm Tyler Hawkins, ma'am."

"Pleased to meet you, sir."

"You must be Kate. Miss Sarah has talked for weeks 'bout you comin' out for a visit. I coulda picked you out of the crowd even without having seen her with you."

Kate looked squarely at the man on horseback then. He wore a black felt Stetson – not a cheap accessory Kate had contemplated in the gift shop. A loose, soft cotton white shirt tucked neatly into his black jeans. Hugged around his waist rode a leather belt adorned with a huge gold buckle. Huge chaps covered his legs with the Dodge truck logo plastered on them. Blond hair curled lazily out from under the black hat. His bright blue eyes were trained on the numbered gates, not on her, she was surprised to discover. Suddenly he turned his boyish, bronzed face toward her and grinned as he caught her eyes.

"Gotta go earn my pay, milady. They don't call me the 'pickup guy' for nothing, ya know." Tyler tipped his hat and rode off toward the middle of the arena.

Kate wasn't sure whether to be offended, pleased or what.

"Pickup guy?" She'd met plenty of his kind on the DC subway, cowboy hat or not. "What nerve."

Suddenly a bull shot from gate number one.

The announcer began his patter. "The bull to watch is Dangerous Dan and the rider is Murray Mullion from chute number one. If he can stay on the bull for eight seconds, he has a shot at the day's pay. To earn points, he must sit upright with one hand in the air and show poise on the back of the bucking bull."

A horn sounded the end of the time period. Murray Mullion slid off the angry bull and scurried away from danger while a clown distracted the snorting beast. Tyler Hawkins circled the outer perimeter of the ring, eyes trained on the rider's exit to safety. Dangerous Dan continued his rampage around the arena, chasing the clowns, and exciting the crowd.

The clowns and Murray Mullion climbed the gates to safety while Tyler and his partner guided the bull to the appropriate exit.

"Give a good hand to our Dodge pickup guys for the night, Tyler Hawkins and Stan Moran. They'll be assisting the riders to safety all evening."

The crowd rose and clapped for the two men on horseback with the red and white chaps. Both tipped their hats to the applause. Kate thought she detected a tinge of red below Tyler's black hat and a nervous acceptance of the crowd's attention. He seemed relieved when the next bull shot out of chute number two, and the attention shifted to a new cowboy. The second rider hit the dirt immediately. While the clown distracted the bull, Tyler raced to the injured man, pulled him up onto the horse, and carried him to safety.

"See that pickup guy, Tyler Hawkins." The voice came from two rows above her. "He used to be the best – roping, bull-riding, bareback, and bronc riding- he did it all. He was even best all-around cowboy one year. See that gold belt buckle?"

"So what's he doing a pansy job of pick-up riding for?" The second voice was gruff.

"He was thrown and trampled by a huge bull. Near died. The pickup guy was flirting with a gal in the stands and didn't do his job. When he recovered, he swore that no other rodeo sweat would be hurt by a lazy pick-up guy. So he gave up the glory and prize money for a pittance riding pickup two nights a week here at Mesquite Arena."

The crowd drowned out the rest of the conversation as another rider risked life and limb against a bull. Kate watched with fear and fascination at the raw courage and strength of the men, young and old. And she watched Tyler and Stan work as a well-oiled team to quickly reduce the danger to all.

"Not at all like the suits and pickup guys in DC." She smiled to herself at her own cynicism at the supremely heroic effort being performed before the crowd. But most of the applause was for the riders and bulls. The pickup guys worked without much recognition.

As Kate watched the action in the ring, an older man settled in beside her carrying popcorn and Coca-Cola.

"Refreshments, Katie?"

"Daddy!" Kate flung her arms around the tall, thin man, knocking his hat into the arena ring.

Tyler rode over and deftly scooped up the hat. The crowd cheered as he delivered it to the man.

"I believe you lost this, Rev. Ryan."

"True, true, Tyler. But I found my baby girl – worth all the ten-gallon hats in Texas."

Tyler touched his hat and smiled at Kate. Whoops came from the crowd that made Kate blush with anger and embarrassment. Why was it that she was already embarrassed by her family and their choices again?

"Something wrong, Katie?" asked her dad. "Don't worry. It's all part of the show – and carried by The Nashville Network to the world. You're the unknown socialite with the dried up old codger."

"Oh, Daddy." She grinned back at him and accepted the treats. "My favorites were always popcorn and Coke. So much for my diet!"

"Diet, Katie? You're hardly a scrap now. You're even thinner than the last time I saw you. You're not having that problem again, are you?" His face screwed up in worry.

"No, Daddy. It's just a stubborn five pounds I gained when I went to Martha's Vineyard with Doug over Easter. You wouldn't believe the seafood I put away. And it made these jeans a little snug to wear tonight." She frowned ruefully.

"How is Doug? How are the wedding plans?"

Sadness enveloped Kate. "We'll talk about that later, Dad."

Kate resolutely turned her attention to the ring and munched a handful of buttery popcorn with relish. Those five pounds were more consolation chocolate than seafood, but that discussion needed a different venue.

***

When the show turned to bronc-busting, Tyler and Stan went into action in earnest.

The first bronc burst from the chute with the cowboy holding on with one hand. The horse bucked this way and that trying to throw the man. As the horn sounded, Tyler and Stan became a well-oiled work team. Tyler grabbed the rider, then swung him over onto his horse. Meanwhile, Stan released the strap under the horse to cease its bucking.

"Call that pansy work, do ya?" asked the voice from two rows up. "I'd like to see you do it!"

The gruff voice growled a response as the crowd cheered the rider, Tyler, and Stan.

The next horse threw the rider before they'd got into the arena properly. The cowboy curled up in a ball to avoid the horse-shoed hooves of the enormous beast. Tyler rode over to the man and pulled him up out of the dirt onto his horse. Stan trapped the bronc against the wall to release the strap, then led him away once he'd calmed down.

"Wow, that's amazing." Kate offered some popcorn to her dad. "I mean the pick-up operation that Tyler and the other guy are doing. They really do rescue these guys."

He declined the popcorn. "The other guy is Stan. Their role out there is dangerous and unrecognized. Tyler's injury happened because the pick-up guy wasn't doing his job."

Kate nodded. "I can see how important that is. 'Course I don't know anything about the rodeo. It looks like a lot of macho guys trying to prove something."

As though proving her point, some girls hung out over the wall waving bandanas at the cowboys in the gate.

Her dad gave her that father sigh and looked over the top of his glasses at her. "It's their living, Katie. Without the rodeo, most of these people would be homeless and purposeless. It may look simple or ridiculous to you, but it is deadly business for rodeo people."

Great. I've already offended him.

"Think of it as just another culture group. That's why there's a mission here. To reach the needs of this specific culture." He settled back in the chair and drummed his fingers on the armrest.

They were silent while the rest of the bronc riders took their turn on the magnificent, energetic animals. A few finished their rides. The rest took a dirt bath. Tyler and Stan helped them all.

"Well, I gotta go, Katie." Her dad scooted to the edge of his seat. "At intermission, I help out with refreshments for the riders and hold a prayer rally for the injured and the rest of the folks. I'm glad you're here. Want to come over, meet the guys and gals, and participate in the prayer rally?"

"No, that's okay, Dad. I'm fine right here. I probably need to check in at the office during intermission."

Her dad sighed again and slid his hat onto his balding head. "I love you, Katie."

Kate smiled. "I love you, too, Dad."

Her father, Reverend Ryan Lawrence, stood. His eyes scanned over the white, empty space around her left-hand ring finger. Kate moved her right hand over her empty finger. He nodded and hurried away leaving Kate alone, again, to do his missionary work. She noticed how much older he'd become in the five years since her last visit. His face had wrinkles she'd never seen before, and he had a slower step. Was it her imagination that he was stooped ever so slightly?

Kate drew the macramé sack from under her seat and extricated her cell phone. She slung the sack over her shoulder and headed for the outer corridor to call the embassy.

***

"Kate all right?" called Tyler. "She rushed out after you left her."

Ryan Lawrence shook his head and sighed as Tyler tied up his mount. Pandemonium reigned around them as the contestants groomed horses and prepared for their performances. Miss Sarah, Kate's mom, prayed with the lady barrel racers who would be on right after the intermission. Bull riders, bronc busters, and clowns gathered around Rev. Ryan for his brief devotional and prayer service. Many voiced numerous prayer for man and animal alike. Rev. Ryan cleared his throat.

"You know that for the last few years I've been here to help you and pray for you. Tonight I'm asking you to pray for us and our daughter."

Hoots went up around the circle from the cowboys. Tyler shushed the rowdy crowd to silence, so Rev. Ryan could continue. Tears filled the minister's eyes, and he sniffed.

"Katie is like the prodigal son I tell you about from time to time. She decided a long time ago that the missionary lifestyle didn't suit her. And that was fine, except that she's left God out of her life, too." He paused to accept a bandanna from one of the cowpokes. "This is the first visit we've had from her since we returned to the states from the Ivory Coast or the *Cote d'Ivoire*. Pray that God will touch her while she's here."

With that, Rev. Ryan sobbed openly. Tyler stepped forward in his big boots and hugged the older man while he prayed for Kate and for the performances to come. After the crowd dispersed, Tyler turned to go back to his horse.

"Ty." A hoarse Rev. Ryan called to him. "Thanks. Think you could help show Katie the town while she's in Dallas? I'm sure she wouldn't enjoy it half as much with her mom and me."

"Sure thing, Rev." Tyler tipped his hat and grinned.

"Come on over after the show for coffee, then, and we'll arrange it with Kate."

"Yes, sir."

***

Kate located her section to find her mother seated beside her empty designated space. She brushed her auburn curls back and buoyed her strength.

"Mom, don't you have somewhere else you need to be than baby-sitting your grown daughter?"

"Oh, no. I can't wait to show you my ladies. These barrel racers are something else, Katie. They're pretty and fast and can sweet talk the speed right out of their horses. We have a Bible study each morning of the rodeo and get to know each other really well. They're like my own daughters."

Kate blushed. *Since your own daughter is such a disappointment.*

She dropped into the seat beside her mother as the show began again.

A racer started out of the entrance, around the barrels in a cloverleaf pattern and sped across the electric eye counting the time of the lap. Her mother narrated the race as well as giving commentary on the rider.

"Susan is a sweet young lady who just accepted Christ as her Savior this morning. Her parents were killed in a car accident when she was a teenager, and she was raised in a foster home on a ranch. That's where she learned to ride. She never went to church much 'cause she was always working the ranch on Sundays and doing horse shows and rodeos. She brought me a flower this afternoon and said I was her spiritual mom. Isn't that sweet?"

Kate listened respectfully as her mom described each successive racer, their life stories, and their spiritual condition. She'd learned a long time ago not to interrupt.

As the last racer entered the arena and rounded the first barrel, the horse brushed it, and bucked her rider off under the falling barrel.

"Tara!" Kate's mom jumped to her feet and ran off around the arena to the gateway to the ring.

Stan and Tyler spurred their horses into action. Stan grabbed the hanging reins of the horse and led the kicking hooves away from the injured rider. Tyler dismounted in a single leap to move the heavy barrel off the young lady as the Dodge truck crew drove into the ring. Her mom and dad rode in the back of the truck. Her mom jumped out as the truck stopped. Tyler gently picked up the girl and carried her to the pickup as Kate's mom held her hand and spoke words of encouragement to her.

Kate leaned over the box rail, sharing the terror with the rest of the audience. It was then that Kate noticed Tyler's limp. No, not just a limp, but a jarring motion when he walked. One boot stuck out at an odd angle as he lurched along with the injured Tara. The sight raised as much fear in Kate as the limp girl in his arms.

Is this limp the result of that accident that happened to you, Tyler Hawkins? You're so perfect on the horse, but on your feet like everyone else; you're so imperfect.

She watched Tyler arrange the unconscious figure in the back of the truck with her mom and dad by her side. He whistled for his horse, and he galloped over to his master like an obedient Irish setter. In one fluid motion, Tyler was again on horseback and the vision of imperfection was gone.

"Isn't he just so gallant?" asked a feminine voice behind her.

"You bet," replied another. "And available."

"Wish I was," came a third voice wistfully.

Did I imagine the limp? Or is it just not noticeable to those who know him so well? Kate sat down slowly as Tyler rode up to her seat.

"Don't worry, Kate. Your mom said she would go to the hospital with Tara, but she'll be back to tuck you in later tonight at the mission."

"The mission?"

"That's what the sign says on the trailer where your mom and dad live." Tyler pushed his hat back to the back of his head. "Mission Mesquite. I'll show you over there after the rodeo if you'll wait by the east ticket box for me. I'll let your dad know that you have an escort, so he can stay and talk to the guys afterwards. Later."

With that, Tyler rode off to prepare for a round of bareback riding without giving Kate a chance to protest.

The lady behind her sighed. "I'd wait for him all night if I had to."

Kate shot her a look of indignation and hunkered down in her seat in embarrassment. How dare he? Why am I here anyway? Mission Mesquite? What kind of corny name is that for a mobile home?

Chapter 2

Thrills and spills. Animal and human pitted against each other and the clock. Glitz and glitter on beast and rider. But after the main event, after the cameras stopped rolling for TNN, the ordinary cowboys in jeans and ragtag shirts tried their best to beat the previous star contestants. Kate watched as thirty or more horses and riders rode around the ring to loosen muscles tired from waiting their turn at the prize money. Many of the spectators had already headed for the parking lot when the announcer told the crowd they could stay for an hour or more to watch the rest of the untelevised portion of the rodeo. Kate sank back into her seat for it was clear that her parents and Tyler were not through for the evening.

Her parents had grown old in the five years she'd been at the State Department after her posting in *Cote d'Ivoire*. Five years since the fight they'd had over her choice of career. Couldn't they see that she was helping people, just like they did, even alongside them in *Cote d'Ivoire*? She just didn't try to force religion down their throats while she offered bread.

Hopeful cowboys and cowgirls tried their hand at the tasks previously demonstrated. But none received a better time or score than the televised events. As the rodeo Zamboni smoothed the earth for the next day's performance, Kate picked up her belongings and trash and headed for the east ticket office to meet Tyler for their rendezvous. Small children giggled and laughed as they lingered at the livestock cages to pet nervous calves. The calves bleated and licked the boys and girls before being loaded into the trailers. Popcorn boxes and cotton candy wrappers littered the arena. That foreboding sense of loneliness settled down upon her as she rounded the near-empty parking lot and headed toward the ticket office.

Lord, I'm almost afraid to pray. I know I've made a mess of it. The relationship with Doug was not what you wanted for my life, but it fit so well with what I'd already done ... But then that's the problem, isn't it? What I've done, not what You've done.

Kate sighed. She always got that far with her desperate plea, but no farther. Her prayers always seemed to bounce back to her off the ceiling, even when the ceiling was star-lit.

"Katie!"

The deep man's voice brought her out of her reverie. The pickup truck drove up to her, spinning gravel every which way.

"Where's your car? We can get your luggage on the way to the mission rather than coming back for it later. That way I can help you now and just bring you back to the car later."

"Tyler, my luggage is at the hotel."

She pointed to the brand-new sixteen-story hotel adjacent the arena parking lot. She climbed into the truck and pulled on the shoulder belt across the silk shirt. Tyler stared at her as though she'd slapped him.

"What?" Annoyance crept into her voice. "I got a hotel room because I know these 'missions' my parents end up in. They're always too small for the family, much less for guests. I'll be more comfortable at the hotel, and my parents can keep on with their own busy schedule while I'm here."

"Okay, but I think Rev. Ryan and Miss Sarah are gonna be plenty disappointed. They've been fixin' up the guest room anticipating you being there."

"Thanks for the warning."

Even though it was June in Texas, the air in the truck cab turned chilly between them. Kate pulled a sweater from the macramé bag and slid it around her shoulders. The truck slowed as it approached a trailer park village across the parking lot. Light, music, and activity poured from the RVs and mobile homes as rodeo guys and gals prepared for sleep after a full and exciting evening. Dim street lamps lit the graveled path into the park. The truck bumped over speed bumps and graveled holes until it pulled up into the well-lighted Lawrence home driveway.

"Mission Mesquite." Kate read the words aloud with disdain from the hand-carved wooden plaque above the door.

"Hey, don't knock it. This place is the best for these people to go to when they're hurting, angry, frustrated, and spiritually broke. Rev. Ryan and Miss Sarah are the best, and the people here think they're amazing. I don't know what your story is, but your parents are an island of calm amidst this bedlam."

Kate winced when Tyler slammed the door harder than necessary and lurched around to the other side to open the door for Kate. Her sweater fell to the ground as she whipped the seat belt off. In a swift motion, Tyler gathered it from the dust and presented it back to her. She took it with a jerk and strode to the door without a thanks.

"Katie, I knew it had to be you when I heard the door slam. Isn't she the most frustrating thing, Ty?"

Her dad opened the screen door for them. The porch light lit the doorway.

"Hey, Katie. Where's your luggage?"

As Kate opened her mouth, Tyler answered for her. She saw the full effect of his words upon her father's countenance. All he said was "Oh."

The three sat around the kitchen table.

"Coffee, anyone? I'm brewing a fresh pot. Thought we'd be up half the night anyway catching up."

"What type you have? Cappuccino? Mocha? Hazelnut?" Kate was eager to see a smile return to her dad's face.

His countenance dropped instead. "Just coffee, I'm afraid. How about hot chocolate?"

"That's fine, Daddy."

The screen door slammed as her mom entered the trailer. She slipped off her loafers and laid them on the mat by the door. She ran her hand through her disheveled hair. All at the table waited to hear how Tara was, but Kate knew not to rush her when she was this tired.

"Tara's fine. A few bruises and a bump on the head, but she'll be okay. And the judges have said she can redo the ride tomorrow if she's up to it."

"That's great news, Miss Sarah!" Tyler smiled a winning smile. "Is she home?"

"Just dropped her off. I smell the coffee, but no one's drinking anything here. You slipping, Ryan?" Her mom placed her hand around his chin and kissed his lips gently.

"No, ma'am. I just offered it. But Kate would rather have hot chocolate."

Kate winced at her dad's use of her proper name. She'd offended him again.

"Coffee's fine. Two sugars and cream is great."

Tyler asked for it black. Her mom brought over the milk carton for Kate. Not even cream or half 'n' half.

"Have you already got settled in your room? We managed to fix it up just like you'd like. You can even see the Dallas skyline from your window. I know it's not DC, but I thought you'd like seeing the city everyday anyway."

"She's set up at the hotel, Miss Sarah."

Her mom looked at Kate and at her husband. Tyler's resolute face looked back from the other side of the table.

"That's just fine for tonight. Save your money, Sweetheart, for the wedding. Tyler can help you get checked out in the morning, then you can stay here the rest of your visit."

Kate winced at the reference to the wedding and rubbed her naked finger. She managed a "Yes, ma'am" just the same.

***

It was two a.m. when Tyler drove her up to the lobby entrance of the hotel. Neon lights cast odd shadows around the building. Kate pulled out her room key to open the secure entrance. The humidity of the day settled as a damp chill in the dark.

"Can I walk you up to your room, Katie?" Tyler leaned against the building beside the door.

"No thanks, Tyler. I'll be fine. You've done enough already. No need for you to have to walk all that way and back with your ...." Kate stumbled over the word 'disability.'

"It's no problem, Katie. I'm used to it. I do just fine. See you in the morning then." He turned to leave.

"By the way, only my parents call me Katie."

14

Tyler turned back to her. "Katie suits you. Kate is too harsh for such a sweet thing, even if you do enjoy hurting your parents."

Kate opened her mouth, but Tyler held up his hand at her protest.

"I'll see you in the morning. Your explanation is your own business."

Tyler Hawkins limped back to his pickup and drove off in a cloud of dust from the parking lot entrance toward the trailer park and Mission Mesquite.

As she crossed the carpet to the elevator, Kate realized that her car was still parked at the Mesquite Arena. She sighed in frustration. What could have been a delightful evening had ended like so many of them had with her parents since college. They were hurt and perplexed at her values and dreams, and their lack of understanding of her need to belong in another world than theirs had wounded her again. She kicked off her flats as she stood waiting for the elevator to take her to the sixth-floor room where she'd dumped her luggage earlier that evening.

"I'll think about it tomorrow," she drawled in pronounced Scarlett O'Hara fashion. "Right after a hot shower and a good night's sleep."

***

The ringing of the phone woke her to a brilliant morning peeking through the heavy hotel drapes. Its incessant appeal finally moved her to the phone, which promptly fell to the floor as she grabbed for it in a groggy haze. A man's voice was already speaking into her room as she fell out of the bed trying to reach the receiver on the floor.

"Hello."

"Having a little trouble, Katie dearest?"

The voice belonged to Tyler Hawkins.

"What do you want at this time of the morning?"

"Your parents tell me you're a diplomat. I guess all those meetings occur after noon since you sure aren't up for diplomacy in the morning."

Kate crawled back into the bed and plumped the pillows behind her back and looked at the clock.

"Is it really ten o'clock?"

"You betcha. You've slept away the morning, Sweetheart. And checkout time is at eleven."

"Where are you, Tyler?"

"In the lobby. They've started to put away the breakfast already. Can I save you something? They've got a machine for Cappuccino. Shall I fix you a cup?"

Kate rubbed the sleep from her eyes and grasped the immediacy of the situation.

"Please do, Tyler. And toast an English muffin and spread it with some low-fat butter stuff. And maybe a glass of orange juice. I'll be down just as soon as I dress and pack things up. Get yourself something, too, if you like."

"I can do it, Katie. I'll be waiting in the lobby with your breakfast."

"Thanks, Tyler."

Twenty minutes later, Kate emerged from the elevator struggling with her bags. She'd pulled her auburn hair into a loose ponytail and pulled on a poet's blouse and slacks. Tyler jumped up to help her. She turned away to the desk clerk as he lurched toward the pile of luggage. Tyler gathered up the bags and carefully headed out the door to his pickup parked just outside. After checking out, she sat down at the table where she'd seen Tyler as she entered the lobby and sipped the lukewarm cappuccino. Her cell phone began to ring, bringing stares from the other late risers in the lobby.

"Kate Lawrence. ... Yes, that's correct. ... No, it will be next Friday when I'm in. ... The ambassador said what? ... I understand. ... Can John cover for me? ... Well, I'll change my tickets then. ... Yes, I'll let you know when I'll be landing. ... Thanks."

"In demand, Katie?" Tyler took a seat during the call.

Kate nodded as she took a bite of the muffin. "Hey, this is good. It's not low-fat, is it?"

"Nope. Life's too short not to taste the real thing once in a while. It is your vacation, right?"

"I don't need to go back heavier, Tyler. I've got to wear a ball gown Friday at an embassy bash. I don't have the time or the inclination to shop for a new one when I get back."

"We have stores here, you know. Dallas has some fabulous shopping. Even Neiman Marcus, if you've got the money."

Kate threw a napkin at him as he smirked. "That's not the point, Mr. Hawkins."

At that, Tyler threw back his head and laughed a great roaring laugh. "So it's not really the dress. It's keeping that anorexic figure that concerns you."

"Not funny, Tyler. Have my parents told all my secrets to you? Are you CIA under cover as a rodeo jock?"

Tyler sobered swiftly. "I'm sorry. I didn't know you had a problem with food."

"Most of my problem with food is people who try to make me eat it. Let's get going."

Kate shoved her chair back and grabbed the rest of the muffin and coffee and trashed it before the gallant Tyler could carry it out for her, too. She stalked out to the truck and jumped in the passenger's side without watching Tyler's pronounced "swagger" from the hotel lobby.

Tyler got in the truck and started it up. They drove in silence across the parking lot to her rental car.

"Why don't you follow me to the mission, and you can park your car at your parents' house for the day? I have orders to show you the town."

Kate jumped out of the truck and wrenched open the door to the Camry.

"Great, just great. What a fine day this is turning into," she muttered as the car roared to life.

***

Kate discovered that her parents were already off on some unknown errand of mercy "just like old times." While depositing her luggage in the cramped little bedroom prepared for her at the mission, Kate heard Tyler answer the phone in the kitchen. Since he was occupied, she noticed what her parents had done to prepare for her.

The curtains were sky blue novelty cotton with Eiffel Towers, Big Bens, Notre Dame, and other recognizable travel destinations. The walls looked freshly painted to match the blue in the curtains. Framed travel photos of her and her parents hung around the walls including one of the last time she'd visited her parents when she was posted with the State Department in *Cote d'Ivoire*. The quilt on the bed had been handmade, no doubt by her mother, with patches of similar sites on the curtains.

That's when Kate spied two old friends on the pillow, souvenirs from two different visits to *Cote d'Ivoire*. One was Ellie the Elephant. Kate had taken Ellie to boarding school when she had been banished from Africa to France in favor of an education without her parents. Ellie had been her connection to the mission field in which she'd grown up. The second stuffed animal was Leo the Leopard. Kate had purchased Leo after arriving in Abidjan to work at the US Embassy there.

Kate curled up on the bed with the stuffed animals. She'd been so excited to be back on the mission field with her parents. Her job was part of the "U.S. Mission of Abidjan." The embassy's Public Affairs section offered aid to the Ivoirians: girls' education, cultural and educational programming, economic recovery, technology, and health programs to help with poverty, water, and HIV/AIDS. Kate's position had been part of that effort.

Her parents had disapproved of her job choice. True, Kate wasn't in Africa to spread the gospel. But hadn't Jesus said to "offer a cup of cold water in His name"? One of her old Bibles was on the nightstand. She checked the concordance. Mark 9:40-41.

"…[F]or whoever is not against us is for us. I tell you the truth, anyone who gives you a cup of water in my name because you belong to Christ will certainly not lose his reward." [NIV]

If Jesus saw ministry that way, why was it so hard for her parents to see that she was on the mission field just like they were?

Kate looked up to see Tyler poke his head in the door.

"Who are your friends?"

"Ellie the Elephant and Leo the Leopard. Last time I saw them was also the last time I saw my parents, on the mission field in *Cote d'Ivoire*. I was there on mission with the State Department. I was so excited to be going home, where my parents had ministered for most of my life."

"Can I ask what happened?" Tyler sat down in a chair from the desk.

"You know my parents. They are passionate in their vocational calling." She hugged Leo tighter. "They didn't think I was doing the right thing with my life. They couldn't see that I was also on mission there, doing some of the same social ministry they were doing, but through the State Department."

"So that's the reason you've been estranged?" Tyler's earnestness was visible in his brilliant blue eyes. "I'm sorry that happened. Why don't we get out of here and away from the sad memories?

"You don't need to babysit me. I'd be happy to unpack and settle in here."

"I promised to show you the sights. Come on."

The gracious Tyler wouldn't take no for an answer, so soon they were in the cab of his pickup once again.

"What would you like to see first, downtown, South Fork, or the countryside? Or would you like to see my ranch? I need to check in with my foreman to make sure things are going okay."

"Use my cell phone."

Tyler grinned. "He doesn't have one out on the back forty. No signal there anyway."

"Fine with me, Tyler. Whatever you need to do. I'm a captive audience."

Tyler muttered under his breath and headed off onto the Dallas freeway. Even on Saturday morning, the road was congested with the suburbanites of the large city running errands or trying to find recreation for the day. Tyler carefully but deftly managed the pickup truck in and out of the traffic the way he'd handled his horse the evening before. But before they'd gone very far, he pulled off at the next exit.

"I thought we were going to the ranch."

"Well, we are. But you need the right apparel to go riding across my back forty lot. So let's go ahead and make the required trip to Shepler's Western Wear and get you fixed up with the tourist duds."

"You are so presumptuous."

Tyler smiled an innocent grin back at her. "Just don't want your pretty clothes ruined, Katie. All the tourists come here. You need some souvenirs to take back to DC. I hear they have some western theme night spots back east where you can reminisce about your Dallas visit in your cowgirl clothes and do the two-step."

"I don't think so, Tyler."

"We'll see."

***

An hour later, Kate was laughing and getting back into the truck. Tyler stashed her bag in the truck bed with her poet's blouse and slacks. Instead she wore dark blue cowboy denim jeans, a white cotton shirt with a tatted lace over-vest, and a cowboy hat that matched Tyler's.

"I still say, you should have bought the boots, too."

"Tyler, I've gone far enough. My loafers are just fine with this."

"Don't say I didn't encourage you. They looked great on you."

"The hat was over the top as it was, Ty."

Soon the truck was skimming out of the Dallas congestion into the outer reaches of the city where fingers of new subdivisions sprung up like new grass.

"There's South Fork." Tyler pointed out. "You know, the one from the TV show."

"Never watched it."

Finally, Tyler pulled up to a green expanse of land. The gravel entrance was canopied with trees and a wrought iron gate lettered with the words "Green Pastures."

"Could have been Green Acres - like the TV show."

"Never watched it." Tyler grinned. "It's named for the 23rd Psalm, Katie. You know, 'The Lord is my shepherd, I shall not be in want. He makes me to lie down in green pastures, he leads me beside quiet waters, He restores my soul. He guides me in the paths of righteousness for his name's sake. Even though I walk through the valley of the shadow of death, I will fear no evil, for you are with me; your rod and your staff, they comfort me.'"

Tyler fell silent. He surveyed the land stretching out before him as he drove past the whitewashed cottage toward the pasture land. The stables and corral appeared on the horizon. Activity buzzed around the corral.

"'You prepare a table before me in the presence of my enemies. You anoint my head with oil; my cup overflows. Surely goodness and love will follow me all the days of my life, and I will dwell in the house of the Lord forever.'" Tyler finished the recitation solemnly as he parked the truck next to a van labeled "Mission Mesquite" at the corral.

"Tyler! Tyler!"

Children's voices rang out, chattering and whooping, around the corral. Some on horses, some on the fence, some on the hood of another pickup truck. Soon Tyler was swallowed by a crowd of short, hungry admirers, and Kate was forgotten in the front seat of the truck. She climbed out slowly and relished the scene of the disabled man amidst his adoring fans. He climbed the fence with one stride. He helped one child with the reins, another with a stirrup, someone else up onto the back of a beautiful chestnut horse. In fact, all the horses were an auburn hue and meticulously groomed. Kate perched on the fence and pulled the new hat down over her eyes to block the sun. She watched the blond enigma at play with the children and the horses from under the shady brim. She wondered who enjoyed this more, the children, the horses, or Tyler Hawkins?

"Quite a sight, isn't it?" Her father's voice broke into her reverie. "He provides the horses and the land, and we truck in the children from the city to learn to ride. A really simple idea, but only possible through Tyler's generosity."

"So here you are." Her mom called out to her as she joined them at the fence. "Tyler said he'd take care of you. I didn't really expect to see you here. He must have taken you to Shepler's first."

"Yes, he did, Mom." Kate pulled the hat back to see her clearer. "He just told me he was showing me the ranch. I never dreamed there was a 4H project in progress."

Her dad laughed. "Every Saturday, we load up fifteen kids in the van over there and bring them out. Joe, Tyler's foreman, and Tyler are always here to help the kids saddle up. They also provide lunch for the kids."

Just then, the dinner bell at the house rang. Kids flew off the horses and raced across the blowing grass to a large picnic shelter behind the white cottage. An older woman served hot dogs and beans to the children while Tyler and Joe put the horses back in the stables. Kate tiptoed across the corral to get a closer look at the horses. Kate stroked the nose of a red and white mare as the horse whinnied softly her approval.

"Here, give her this sugar cube for a job well done." Tyler tossed her the treat.

"I rode some at boarding school in France, but I never was very comfortable on the back of a horse. They always seemed too mysterious and powerful to trust completely."

The horse nibbled the sugar cube out of her hand and licked the crumbs away as Kate giggled.

"This is Ariel. She looks like she likes you. Maybe she thinks you'll take her out later for a look at the big house. Whatta ya think, Joe?"

"She's probably in need of a stretch, Ty. After lunch, I'll saddle her up for your lady."

Kate blushed and tried to protest, but Tyler waved her blusters aside.

"That'd be fine, Joe."

***

As the children prepared to leave after lunch, they all gathered around Tyler and hugged him. Then they bounded onto the van labeled "Mission Mesquite" and waved until the van was out of sight. Tyler and Kate drove back out to the corral to pick up their mounts for the afternoon. Kate awkwardly mounted and settled onto the horse Tyler called Ariel. As awkward as Tyler was on foot, Kate felt on horseback. They set out across the waving prairie once Kate settled comfortably on Ariel.

A large structure rose in the distance. The closer they got, the bigger the house got. Soon Kate could appreciate the fine details of the big house: rubbed wood entry doors with triangular cut glass in an oval pane, white gingerbread wood work in the gables, polished windows in dormers, white porch columns, a wooden suspended swing, azaleas in bloom around the front porch, a tire swing hanging from a huge live oak. Tyler swung down gracefully from Asher, his steed, and tied his reins to the porch rail. He helped Kate down from her mount and tied the reins next to Asher.

"You two be good while we're inside." Tyler winked to the horses. They each whinnied a soft reply.

"What a beautiful house." Kate climbed the steps to the wide front porch. "Who lives here?"

"I do." Tyler offered no more than that simple reply.

He opened the massive wood door and invited her in. They hung their hats on a wood coat tree in the foyer. Their footsteps echoed on the polished wood floor. The first rooms held very few furnishings, returning the echo of their walk through the grand hallway. In the back of the house was the kitchen and a den. The kitchen focused around a wood trestle table with eight ladder back chairs. A bowl of fruit accented the table. Pristine white walls showed off the bay window of Texas scenery. The den was sparsely decorated with a red-brown leather recliner, oak occasional tables, and an oak entertainment center. A fan spun lazily from the center of the ceiling. Everything was spotless as though no one lived here at all but kept as though awaiting a special guest.

"It's just beautiful, Tyler." Kate spoke in a hushed awe.

"Rose keeps it clean for me. She and Joe live in the cottage by the corral. The master bedroom's down here off the den, for obvious

22

reasons." He slapped his gimpy leg. "Three more bedrooms upstairs. You can go look while I fix us a soda."

Kate nodded and ran up the polished wood staircase. Her footsteps echoed through the empty upstairs. Three huge bedrooms held picture windows with window seats looking out across the prairie. One held the Dallas skyline. One overlooked the corral. The other featured a pond shaded by an old climbing tree. She sat on the window seat in the last room and soaked in the peace.

Lord, you are so much a part of this place and of this man. Help me find just a small measure of the peace he has found in Your plan.

She felt a ray of light enter her darkened soul. She'd finally found a place where her prayers didn't hit the ceiling, but went straight to the Father.

Chapter 3

Kate was startled from her reverie by the ringing of the phone. For a change, it wasn't her cell phone. She heard Tyler answer in his deep bass and realized she needed to finish her tour and make an appearance downstairs.

"Well, I don't care if it will cost $20 to fix it. ... I need that saddle for tonight's performance, so go ahead and do it. ..."

Tyler motioned Kate out to the deck where two frosted glasses of soda sat under the patio umbrella. She breezed out into the sun and took a sip. Not diet. But cold and good.

As she looked around the deck, she noticed French doors off the end leading toward another room. She carried the cool drink with her and tried the door. Unlocked. The doors opened into a large airy bedroom. The color scheme was neutral, but the furniture was classic polished oak, reminiscent of the front doors. The dresser held a tri-fold vanity mirror. A few male accessories and change lay scattered across the dresser, boots sat by the bed, and the gold belt buckle gleamed from the bureau top.

"So what do you think?"

Kate startled. "I'm sorry. I'm a sucker for French doors. It's beautiful. The whole ranch, the whole house is just beautiful."

"That's good to know."

"But Tyler, there's one problem. It's so empty. You really need to hire a decorator and furnish the place properly."

Tyler led Kate back onto the deck and collapsed into a patio chair. Kate followed suit.

"You're right, of course, but I could never see decorating it and having my future wife hate it. So I figured once I married, we could choose what we both liked best."

"So who's the special woman?"

Tyler stood abruptly. "Time we got you back to Mission Mesquite, and I got to head to the arena to groom Jake and get that saddle fixed. Let me call Joe to get the truck and take the horses back."

Tyler left her alone on the deck with her empty glass.

Kate was stunned. What did she say? Whatever it was had struck a deep nerve.

"Come on out to the front porch and let's wait for Joe."

The chill was palpable. Kate followed him obediently, placed her glass in the sink, and grabbed her hat on the way to the porch. She sat down on the swing. He perched on the steps after making the call.

"They're beautiful horses, Tyler."

"Ariel and Asher are soul mates. They've been together ever since they were born. They've given me a foal every spring. That's what I want in a woman."

"A baby every spring?"

He blushed. "No, a soul mate. Someone who shares my faith and my life. Someone who doesn't look at my disability, but at me as a person. Someone faithful and loving."

"And who'll play catch and snuggle up beside you at night? Sounds like you need a dog, not a wife."

"So what does your fiancé want in a wife?"

"Someone who'll sleep with him before marriage and pick up his dry-cleaning."

Tyler looked shocked.

"That's why we're not engaged anymore. I haven't had the guts to tell my parents yet."

The pickup came roaring up. Tyler gave Joe some instructions about the horses, and he galloped off on Asher with Ariel in tow. Kate and Tyler headed for town.

***

"So, Mom, what is the story about Tyler Hawkins?" Kate cut the carrots for the salad. "He's an enigma to me. He's got a beautiful empty house, a stable full of chestnut ponies, and a heart as big as Texas, but he seems sometimes like the loneliest guy in the world. He's gorgeous, but disabled; gracious, but very private. What's the scoop?"

"Ask Tyler. He'll tell you."

"You tell me so I know what to ask. I already offended him today when I asked about his future wife."

"Okay. Tyler was engaged before he was hurt. His fiancée dumped him while he was still recovering from surgery. It was a very hard time for him."

Kate scraped another carrot thoughtfully. "By the way, Mom. My wedding's off, too. Doug and I have broken our engagement."

Her mom sank into a chair opposite Kate.

"What happened? I thought you were so sure of Doug."

"Well, he just wanted more than I was willing to give before marriage. I told him I didn't feel that it was in God's laws to have sex before marriage."

"Surely he understood."

"Sure he did. What he didn't understand was why I would suddenly stand up for being a Christian when he said I didn't live it any other time. That's what I couldn't forgive. It's better this way."

"It's best that you found out before the wedding, I suppose."

"Mom, you never liked Doug, so you should be relieved."

Her mom nodded and placed the mashed potatoes on the table. She pulled the roast out of the oven. "True, but I never like to hear of you being hurt."

Kate changed the subject abruptly. "So what happened to Tyler's leg? I overheard someone last night say that he was trampled by a bull."

"True." Her mom whisked the flour paste into the meat juices. "He was best all-around cowboy the year before the accident. That's what the gold belt buckle signifies, if you've noticed it."

Kate nodded but didn't interrupt her mother for fear she'd ask more questions about Doug and the canceled wedding.

"Anyway, he did it all: bull-riding, bronc-busting, bareback riding, calf-roping. To be all 'round cowboy you only need two, but Tyler was a champion in all of them. He drifted from town to town in the circuit besting all the cowboys. They say he also made the most money that year, which he invested in Green Pastures, though he didn't call it that back then."

Her mom stopped and stared out the window as the gravy bubbled.

"It must have been hard for him to give all that up after the accident." Kate prompted her.

"Tyler was a different man in those days than the man you've met. He caroused with the best of them. He drank into a stupor after rodeos and had groupies following him out to his trailer at night. He got engaged to one of them and swore it was the start of the real thing. He built the house for her in the off-season, mostly by himself."

Her mom poured the rich, brown gravy into the chipped gravy boat and carried it to the small kitchen table.

"And?"

"Well, the following spring at the first Mesquite rodeo, Tyler was tossed from the bull almost as soon as the ride commenced. He was knocked unconscious when he hit the ground. The clowns did everything they could to distract that bull, but it just kept goring him and running over him. The pickup guy was flirting in the stands with some sweet young thing when it happened. If he'd been available to rescue him, things might have turned out different."

Her dad entered the small kitchen. "Who we talking about now? Mr. Hawkins, I presume."

"Yes, Daddy. I'm just trying to understand where he's coming from."

"Well, he nearly died." He picked up the story. "I sat by his bed for hours that week while he went in and out of coma. But the Lord used that experience to change Tyler's life. Guess he was so bull-headed it took a bull to knock some sense into him."

"He got saved as a result?"

"Yep, he helps us out a lot at Mission Mesquite. Why don't you go get washed up while I help your mom with the iced tea?"

Kate scraped the last of the carrot into the big salad bowl and went down the hall to wash the orange carrot juice from her hands.

***

After Kate had safely left the room, Sarah whispered. "Ryan, you didn't tell her all of it."

"What? The part where he went back to school at the seminary and got his divinity degree? The part about how he's our assistant pastor here? The part about his application being at the mission board to take over here as pastor so we can retire?"

"You know very well what I mean."

Ryan grinned at his wife. "I want her to like him, Sarah. If fact, I'd like nothing better than to get rid of this Doug character and have Tyler as my son-in-law. But Kate has already rejected the mission field. I don't want her rejecting Tyler just because we like him and because he's part of the mission field picture."

Sarah kissed him playfully. "That's not telling the whole truth."

"I never said that I was, Sarah. And she never asked."

The two hugged conspiratorially and sat down to dinner as Kate returned to the table.

***

Kate decided not to attend the rodeo that night. Horse riding had definite side effects that did not allow sitting in a metal seat for three hours. She opted for the recliner and the TV. TNN carried the show. True to form, the pickup guys got very little show time. She never saw Tyler's face through the whole show. When her mom and dad got home, Kate was fast asleep in the recliner in front of the droning television.

***

"Mom, have you lost your mind? You're wearing jeans to church!"

Sarah turned and smiled at her dressed-up daughter.

"You'll need to change, Kate. We have church at the Arena. Our participants are cowboys, cowgirls, clowns, and their families. Most of them have never seen the inside of a church building. They won't because they don't stay in one place long enough, and they put all their money into their horses, livestock, and costumes. They're uncomfortable with non-rodeo folk. So we dress like them."

"Okay. No lecture about not understanding the culture of the mission field, Mom. I've heard it before. I guess I thought America was America, and we all did things the same."

Kate caught her mom's smile as went back to change into jeans.

The threesome walked across the parking lot from Mission Mesquite to the Arena. Kate was surprised to hear calves and horses on this morning.

"They pull out today for the next rodeo." Her dad answered her unasked question. "Most of them are staying long enough to hear a little Bible and sing some songs together. It makes the rodeo seem like family for them."

As they reached the entrance to the Arena, they heard gravel crunch under truck tires. They turned in time to see Tyler climb out of the truck cab and limp across the short distance to the entrance.

"Good morning, Rev. Ryan, Miss Sarah, Katie." His smile lit the morning. "What's the word this morning, Pastor?"

"Be available to God's call, Tyler." Her dad bantered back.

"I'm doing the best I can, Pastor." Tyler protested. "Except for that one item of discussion."

"Let's discuss it again soon, Ty." Her dad smiled. "I really think it would help you in the long run to get that job you've been wanting so bad."

Kate watched the faces of the two men in the brilliant sunlight. They seemed to be speaking in code. Code to exclude her? Fine, she didn't need to know anyway. She had no interest in the man. Kate grabbed her mother's arm and steered her toward the restroom.

***

The two men watched the ladies go.

"What are we hiding from Katie?" asked Tyler.

"That you're a minister and the soon-to-be pastor of this mission."

Tyler arched his eyebrows in a question.

"Oh, you'll know soon enough, I guess. Katie was a missionary kid from the time she was born. She was born in France. French is nearly her mother tongue. In fact, she's got a dual citizenship birth certificate. And while we were in France, that was great. Then Sarah and I moved to Cote d'Ivoire. When Katie turned twelve, the mission board felt the schools in Africa were not up to Katie's level of achievement. We put her in a boarding school in France for 7th to 12th grade. She felt abandoned. The boarding school was full of other MKs, all of whom seemed to get on just fine. But not Katie. She hated the board for separating us. She hated us for allowing them to separate us. She hated the school."

Tyler greeted two cowboys as they swaggered past. Both clasped his outstretched hand and clasped him in an embrace as they met.

"I still don't get it, Rev. Ryan."

"Katie's had many boyfriends in school. As each of them felt a call from God to the ministry, she dropped each one cold. She attended the American University in Paris and studied World Affairs."

"Which is how she got the job at the State Department and met Doug." Tyler nodded with understanding.

Rev. Ryan shook his head as they entered the arena stands. "She needs a good man to lead her back to God, Tyler. Doug sure wasn't it."

"They're not engaged anymore?"

Rev. Ryan nodded. "That's what I hear."

Tyler mused as he sank into the first row of seats in general admission.

"You think I'm the man to do it? I've broke a few too many broncos and bulls. I don't know that I can tame your Katie."

Rev. Ryan shrugged and went over to the musicians to make last minute arrangements. Tyler stretched out his bad leg and rubbed the ache from the muscles. *Could I tame her?* He laughed to himself. *Do I really want to try and be hurt again?*

***

The service started with a steel guitar player leading a rousing chorus of "This is the Day that the Lord hath Made." The small crowd in the stands sang loudly from a copied handout. Kate barely recognized two of the clowns without their makeup. The other cowboys seemed humble compared to the spirited exhibition she'd witnessed on Friday and on television.

With pain and stiffness, Tyler rose and made some announcements.

"In case you haven't made her acquaintance yet, this pretty stranger among us is Katie Lawrence, Ryan and Sarah's girl. Be sure and say a howdy to her before y'all leave."

Kate blushed as the crowd whistled and hooted and hollered, "Howdy."

Tyler winked at her.

He continued, "It's good to see Stan among the living this morning."

Stan tipped his hat. "Thanks to you, good buddy."

"Tara is better, but still sore. Pray for her, too. Also pray for the rodeos going on this next week, 'cause lots of us will take chances we shouldn't with the body-temples God gave us."

A sinking feeling hit Kate as she listened to the tall bronzed cowboy go over the prayer concerns for this unusual congregation.

"Let's pray. Hats off." Tyler sank to a kneeling position on the cold concrete floor with his hat hung on his bent knee. "Lord, you know our hearts and minds. You know our needs. You know the needs of those around us. God, make us mindful of the things you are calling us to do and help us do those things willingly and swiftly. Just as the calf comes out of that chute and hopes to escape the rope, we're like that when you call us. We hope we'll escape. Slow us down so we will know Your will and do it. Bring those who need it to salvation and others back into relationship with You. In Your Son's Name, Amen."

Kate watched with horror as he struggled to his feet and limped to the seat. The horror was not so much for the handicap, but for the realization that Cowboy Tyler Hawkins was also Minister Tyler Hawkins. She'd been deceived.

After the unusual service, Kate stalked out of the Arena toward her parents' trailer. Anger seethed in her soul.

"It's a set-up. They knew all along that Tyler was the assistant pastor at Mission Mesquite, but they managed not to tell me straight out. Well, an omission's as good as a lie. That's what you always taught me, Daddy. How dare you try to fix me up with a minister." She mumbled to herself as she went.

She was barely aware of the pickup truck that rolled up beside her.

"Need a ride where you're going, Katie?" asked Tyler. "You seem in a hurry to get there."

Kate turned on the innocent-seeming man, shook her head, and continued her stalk.

"Look, Katie, it would be better to get in the cab, so we can talk about the problem instead of letting it eat you up inside."

"You are the problem," she shot back. "You and your horses and your empty house waiting for a wife to fill it. You thought I'd fall into your arms and into this mission like I'd never notice that I was breaking my oath to myself. You and your white knight image."

Tyler chewed on that one for a few minutes as he drove beside her.

"I'm wrongly accused, Sweetheart. I only offered to help entertain Rev. Ryan's daughter while she was in town since the Mission takes so much of his time. Nobody told me you'd be so beautiful."

Kate stopped in her tracks and faced the truck.

"What's your title at the Mission? Assistant Minister? Associate Pastor? Minister of Ministry?"

"Assistant Pastor."

"Aha! The cowboy is a minister. Reverend Hawkins." Kate shouted and restarted her stalk across the dusty, hot gravel.

"Well, not officially. I've never been ordained. I only got the seminary degree so I could help your parents at Mission Mesquite. Most of the cowboys don't know I'm a trained minister. 'Reverend Hawkins' would cramp my style."

"Great. Another missionary." Kate muttered as she reached the trailer and slammed the screen door.

***

"So, she has a temper to match the red hair." Tyler spoke to himself as he sat in the truck and waited for Rev. Ryan and Miss Sarah to arrive so they could all go out to a cafeteria lunch.

Chapter 4

The ringing cell phone greeted Kate as she slammed into the trailer.

"Yes? Kate Lawrence."

"Kate? It's Cindy."

"What is it, Cindy? We still don't work on Sunday unless there's a state emergency, right?"

"Hey, cool down girl. I'm just calling to ask a personal question."

"Sorry, Cindy. My parents are already driving me crazy. What is it?"

"Should I give Doug your parents' number?"

Kate switched ears with the phone.

"Let me get this straight. You want to know if you should give that rat my number while I'm on vacation. Have you lost your mind? Only if we are threatened with impending nuclear winter will I take a call from that man. Absolutely not! It's bad enough that he knows my cell phone number. Luckily my display tells me who's on the line so I can ignore him."

"That's what I thought, Kate. He seems to think that the 'absence makes the heart grow fonder' adage will work with you, and you'll jump into his arms when you arrive home. How's Dallas?"

"Dallas is complicated. Let me go now. I've made a huge scene here, and I've got to smooth over it somehow. See you Friday."

Kate shoved the cell phone back down in her purse and brushed her hair. Her mom's image appeared in the dresser mirror beside Kate's.

"You okay?" Kate nodded shortly as her mom ran her hand through Kate's curly tresses. "It's not like you have to marry Tyler. We only thought you two could have a good time while you're here. Like you said, he's lonely. You've just broke up with Doug. Just enjoy some friendship with Ty. He's such a sweet man."

Kate nodded. "Whatever you say, Mom."

***

After lunch, they came back to Mission Mesquite. The four of them settled into webbed patio chairs and an uncomfortable silence. They gazed up at the clear blue Texas sky. Kate shifted uneasily in the creaky aluminum frame.

"I'm sorry I've spoiled everyone's day. I obviously made too much of the whole thing. Will you forgive me, Tyler, for acting like a spoiled brat?"

Tyler swept his hat from his head in a mocking bow. "Anything wouldst I do for you, milady. Your entreaty is accepted with great honor."

Kate squeaked a laugh from her serious face.

"Mom? Dad? I accused you unjustly." She had a hard time speaking between the giggles that threatened to overtake her.

"Of course, dear. You're just still sensitive about your breakup with Doug." Her mom patted her hand.

Her dad rolled his eyes. Her mom elbowed him in the ribs. All four broke into uncontrolled laughter after the tension of the morning.

"Okay! Enough sitting around staring at the sky. It's time for miniature golf. Who's in?" Tyler announced.

Kate watched in alarm as her dad raised his hand.

"What about not working on Sunday?" she asked.

"Man was not made for the Sabbath, but the Sabbath for man," Tyler quoted loosely. "This man declares mini-golf as rest on the Sabbath."

"Here! Here!" agreed her dad to Kate's utter surprise.

"Not me." Her mom begged off. "Rest means nap to me."

The phone rang in the trailer. Kate jumped to answer it.

"This one's mine, Katie. Sit and help Tyler make our plans for the day." Her dad jumped up and rushed inside.

"What do you say, Katie? All the cards are on the table. No ulterior motives. Just friends playing mini-golf."

Kate eyed Tyler curiously. Her mom rose from the chair and left the two alone.

"But, isn't it a little difficult for you to play mini-golf with your handicap."

"As long as you don't add points for how long it takes to climb and descend the mountain, I don't have a handicap for mini-golf."

Kate grinned back at his pun.

"Okay, I'm in, too."

The screen door creaked as her dad joined them on the patio once again.

"But I'm out. It seems Tara's been taken back into the hospital for observation. She may have some internal bleeding they didn't catch Friday night."

Tyler struggled to his feet.

"Do you need me to go instead?"

"No, you and Katie have a good time. I'll go hold the pretty girl's hand this time."

Her dad winked as he slipped his hat on his head and headed around the trailer.

"It's just you and me, kid." Tyler attempted his best Bogey voice.

Kate laughed. "Another set-up, I'd suppose."

Tyler put on his innocent face, shook his head, and offered Kate his arm. Kate laughed and took his arm.

"Let me get my bag, and I'll join you in the truck."

***

"I still can't believe you beat me, Tyler. You didn't tell me you were a mini-golf pro."

They sat at a table outside the arcade with dripping ice cream cones. Mynah bird calls shrieked overhead. A Texas breeze cooled the summer sun around their faces. Kate shoved back her wind tossed hair with her free hand and laughed.

"And I did very well climbing and descending Mount Golf over there."

As he gestured a drip ran down the cone and onto the concrete. He swiftly licked the offending stream of sticky fluid. Kate laughed and nodded.

"Tell me about your injury," Kate asked, suddenly serious. "How bad is it? Will it get worse? Is there any cure or surgery to help it get better? Mom told me some about the accident."

Tyler examined the melting mound of ice cream and frowned. He looked at Kate and down at his lap.

"Okay. All the cards on the table, right? The bull incident was the best thing that ever happened to me."

Kate nearly dropped her cone. "You're serious?"

"Yes. Because before that bull bucked me off and tromped all over this fleshly body, I was living my own life the way I thought I wanted to live it. I had a new girl every night. I drank everyone else under the table after my rides were done. I kept my body in shape - lifted weights, did chin-ups on the stable door frame, drank those high-energy drinks and muscle builders. I was the best anybody could be on their own. Even won that gold belt buckle for being the best."

Tyler stopped and licked the cone thoughtfully.

"God blessed me. I didn't get HIV or AIDS, though I deserved to and had all the inappropriate behavior to get it. I didn't hit anyone or anything when I drove drunk. I didn't end up in jail for disorderly conduct. Lots of my pals experienced one or all of those. But I was the golden boy; I was untouchable. And when I got that belt buckle, I knew I had done it all by myself. No one else could claim credit."

Tyler stared off into the distance.

"Where were your parents?" Kate interrupted his silence.

"They died when I was a kid. I grew up in an orphanage. One of my uncles would take me out for the summer to work on his ranch. That's where I learned to ride. But at the end of the season, he'd take me back to the children's home for schooling and safekeeping. The state helped buy me a college education, but when I graduated, my uncle convinced me that real men worked with their hands, not their minds. So I went to work on his ranch for my room and board and a little drinking money until my uncle died."

"And then?" Kate prompted.

"The ranch was sold to pay all the gambling debts Uncle Richard had amassed. I was left with nothing but Jake and the rodeo. Alone again." Tyler looked around at the setting sun. "Let's continue this at the ranch. I need to check on the horses."

On the way out to Green Pastures, Tyler continued his story.

"The only wise thing I did before I was injured was save the prize money I didn't drink away, enabling me to buy Green Pastures, Asher, and Ariel. Then I fell for Tina and built the house, too, because she said she could never live in the cottage Joe and Rose occupy."

"You must have made a lot of money." Kate quickly calculated and felt new wonder about this man.

Tyler laughed. "Oh, yes. More than I'd ever dreamed of seeing in my whole life. And I tucked it away carefully. Budgeted what I could spend and drink. Bought Tina a huge diamond and still stuck some away for the future. I just didn't realize that the future was so close at hand."

Tyler pulled into the stable lot, conversed with Joe, and greeted each of the horses in the stable while Kate lagged behind him.

What he's accomplished from the ashes of his life, Kate marveled. Ashes? Of course! That's why he named the sire Asher. And Ariel was a water spirit. There must be a reason for her name, too.

"Why Ariel?" she asked. "I can see where you get Asher, but how does Ariel fit into this story?"

"Asher represents the old man, ashes to ashes, dust to dust. But in the Bible Asher means happy. Ariel is the rebirth through water, washing away the old life," he answered solemnly. "Let's go up to the house so I can check the machine for news on Tara and call the hospital."

When they arrived at the house, Kate perched in the swing in the near-dark while Tyler went into the big house. She swung in the silence of the summer night. Chirps of insects, croaking of frogs at the pond, and the twinkling of lightning bugs calmed her as she swayed on the front porch swing. An odd tick, tick, tick sound followed the swaying of the swing. She emptied her mind of all the pressures of Washington and foreign affairs. She thought about Tyler and his life. She thought about her lonely life and how it compared to his. And she thought about what God wanted from her. She shivered in the cool evening breeze and pulled her legs up under her in the swing.

"What next, God?" she said to the stars. "What should I have done? What should I do now?"

"Well, Tara's in surgery, Katie." Tyler's face mirrored the grim report. "They're not sure she'll make it."

Tyler took a seat next to Kate and stretched his arm on the back of the swing. Kate snuggled up to his warmth. He hugged her in a friendly way.

"Need a jacket?"

Kate nodded. Tyler went back into the house and came back with a wool rodeo jacket. He draped it over her shoulders. It swallowed her whole. They laughed.

"What about the bull accident?" Kate prompted. "Unless you need to go."

"No, your dad's there. I'll go over and relieve him after I take you back to Mission Mesquite." Tyler ruffled his hair. "So where was I? I guess after I won the gold buckle and established the ranch, right?"

"Sure."

"Well, I was the reigning champion of rodeo when the season opened. And I was cocky. I had a beautiful woman, a ranch, horses, fat bank account. I decided that I was so good that I could afford one beer before the show. I knew I was invincible." He laughed. "I guess it's true that pride comes before a fall because I fell hard."

"Mom said you nearly died. How did you survive?"

"I survived because your dad confronted me with the sin in my past life and told me that Jesus would forgive me for it." Tyler's voice was low. "The physical pain was bad, but the spiritual pain was unbearable. Tina left me while I was in the coma. When I woke up, I realized I was broken, physically, emotionally, and spiritually. I have scars all over my torso and legs, and my left leg was crushed. It's been put together with pins and wires. Makes it impossible to get through metal detectors when I fly."

Tyler grinned at Kate in the dark. She hit him.

"But is there anything else they can do for it?"

Tyler shrugged. "I get by, and it reminds me that I serve at God's command, not my own."

A loud chirrup interrupted their soft discussion in the dark.

"What was that?" Kate asked.

"It's a katydid. Relative to the grasshopper. Common to the southern and western United States. In fact, that's a Texas bush katydid, I bet."

The chirrup sounded again, followed by a dozen more.

"Did you hear a tick, tick sound earlier?"

Kate nodded.

"As night falls, the male katydids change their song. It starts as a tick, tick sound. As it gets dark, the song turns into a chirp that sounds like 'Katy-did, she did'. Listen."

They listened closely as several males sang their moonlight serenade.

"Question is, what did she do?"

"Actually, only the males sing. They warn each other of their territory. If another male comes too close, they scream at each other. And they call to the females."

"What do the females say back, then?"

"She ticks back as though to say 'come on, then.' The male can tell if the female's ready for love by how many times she ticks. When she ticks three times, he flies over to have a rendezvous."

They swayed in the wooden swing, listening to the katydids and watching the stars in comfortable companionship. The night became loud with ticks and chirrups, croaks and bird calls.

"I think they're saying it's time I got you home, Katydid. I need to get to the hospital to relieve your dad, too. Tomorrow I'd like to take you to see downtown Dallas and Los Colinas. We can see the Farmer's Market, if you get up early enough, and two fabulous sculptures. Bring your camera. Let's go, so you can get up, sleepyhead."

Chapter 5

The week flew by for Kate. On Monday, Tyler took her to downtown Dallas. First stop was the Farmer's Market. He bought her flowers; she bought him fruit. They each purchased a cinnamon roll from a vender with steaming coffee.

They went to see the Herd sculpture in front of the Convention Center. She took pictures of him on the back of one of the bronze longhorns and one of him riding with a long-ago cow herder on his horse. He insisted on taking her picture in front of the stampede. He pointed out all the sights downtown: the Kennedy Memorial, the Pegasus on the skyscraper high above the city streets, the underground shopping, and the nightclub district.

After buying a Coke and hot dog from a vendor, they hit the freeway to Los Colinas to see the famous sculpture of the Mustangs. Kate rode a sculpted mustang for the camera with fountains springing up beneath its hooves. The sculpture was breathtaking - the free ranging wild ponies "splashing" through the granite courtyard. She took Tyler's picture holding one by the mane and "bronco-busting" the wild pony.

Tuesday, her dad had tickets for the Rangers' baseball game for all four of them. They started the evening at Houston Steakhouse with ribs and spinach dip and ended at a local pizza place after the game.

Wednesday, Tyler surprised her with tickets for Six Flags Over Texas where they rode every ride and wore a sunburn into the evening fireworks display.

"Tyler, I've never had so much fun. But I really should have worn sunblock. And I really should NOT have eaten that fried chicken for dinner."

Fireworks burst above them in blues, reds and golds. Loud cracks and sizzles punctuated the night sky. Tyler wrapped his arm around her shoulders, and she leaned her head back on brawny muscle. He bent down and kissed her lightly on the lips.

"You positively glow, Katydid," he said. "Is that the sunburn or the fireworks?"

Kate stretched up to him and kissed him back.

"One tick," he said.

She untangled herself from his embrace and raced toward the park entrance, darting to and fro through the crowd. She left Tyler limping through the crowd behind her. She was sitting on the hood on his pickup truck when he caught up with her in the parking lot.

"Need keys? Easier to get in that way." His face wore a dazzling grin

"It's your truck. I'm only along for the ride."

"Would that the ride was longer, Katydid." He unlocked the passenger door and held it open for her. "We've only one more day of fun and games."

Her impulse was to slide over beside him and hug his neck, but she was afraid he'd say "tick two." She wasn't ready for that yet. Instead, the silence between them was punctuated by her cell phone ringing.

"Who could that be, this time of night?" She flipped the phone screen open.

"It's for you, Tyler. It's Dad."

"Yes, sir," answered Tyler. "I see. … When? … What can I do, Ryan? … We're on our way back now. … We'll see you there."

Tyler handed her the phone silently and cranked the engine. Gravel spun out from beneath his tires as he pulled out hurriedly toward the park gate.

"What's wrong, Ty?"

"It's Tara." Tyler choked on the words in the dark. "She's dead."

Kate watched Tyler throughout the ride back to Mission Mesquite. Tears coursed down his face, and he was silent. She respected the silence and thought about the dead girl and the game-turned-deadly she had played, racing the pony around a barrel. She thought about Tyler and how close he came to death in his ride on a bull.

There are no certainties in this rodeo world. These people need God to be in control or there's no tomorrow. She thought about her own life and her insistence on control. She thought about the battle with anorexia she had won by her own determination. But she thought about the closet full of size 2s and 4s that she could still wear at times during the past year and realized that she also walked a fine line between control and her own destruction.

Oh, God, help me learn to release control of my life to You.

As they pulled up in the yard of Mission Mesquite, clusters of rodeo folk were scattered across the lawn, praying, crying, and embracing one another. Tyler hustled from the truck to join the impromptu wake taking place at the Mission for Tara. Kate hopped down on her own and watched as Tyler went from group to group, adding a word here, praying there, wiping tears, and hugging fellow mourners. She also saw her father walk to Tyler's side and gather the crumpling bronze man into his arms. Tyler cried like a baby in her father's arms. She looked away, for fear of embarrassing him. Kate made her way from the pickup to the trailer avoiding each prayer gathering as much as possible. She still caught the familiar entreaties to the Lord on the breeze. She slipped into the trailer, unnoticed. The living room was also full of western-garbed people, praying and crying. Her mother held court in this room from the worn swivel rocker. The aroma of freshly brewed coffee permeated the air. She slipped through the narrow hall to her room.

***

"Ryan, I didn't do all I could for her. I should have gone back one more time and talked to her about Jesus. I should have stood up for the gospel more. I was so concerned about saving her physical life, that I didn't place as much significance on her spiritual life. I just knew she had another day to be saved. I failed her, Ryan. I failed God."

Rev. Ryan settled the big man into a chair on the porch. He placed his arm over Tyler's shoulders while he wept. Tyler surveyed the scene before him, the church at Mission Mesquite in mourning for one of the rodeo's own, taken by the sport they all knew, loved, played, and feared.

"They need you, Tyler, to help them process this pain. No one knows better how they feel, how they hurt, how they live from day-to-day better than you."

"You're right, Ryan." Tyler wiped the tears from his sunburned cheeks. "It's time I took a stand for what God's calling me to do here at Mission Mesquite. When can you do my ordination council?"

Ryan grinned. "As soon as I can gather the appropriate folks all in the same room, Tyler. I don't think you'll regret it."

"I may, Ryan. You see, I've fallen in love with your daughter. But I don't think she'll be too thrilled with me as Reverend Tyler Hawkins, Pastor, as opposed to Tyler Hawkins, cowboy/Assistant Pastor."

Ryan nodded thoughtfully. "But, perhaps it's what God is calling Katie to do, too. Bide your time with her, Tyler. She may just come around someday soon. She's been running from God's call for too many years. I fear He's going to need to get her attention in a major way soon. She's as stubborn as you."

Tyler chuckled and rose. He embraced the older man.

"Thanks, Rev. Ryan. Let's attend to this gathering of folks."

"You bet, Rev. Tyler."

Tyler groaned, and it was Ryan's turn to chuckle.

***

In the bathroom, she flipped on the light and looked squarely at the sunburned reflection in the mirror. "Oh, Kate, you are in trouble deep here. Tyler's too appealing. These people are so in need of his strength. With Tyler comes Mission Mesquite."

The little quiet voice inside her, the one she'd tried to drown out for so many years, spoke to her. *And is that such a bad life, Kate?*

She turned on the tap to cover the stirrings within her soul and splashed cool water on her hot face. She gently toweled the droplets from her nose and chin and surveyed her image again.

"I've definitely lost control here." She critically surveyed her body image in the mirror. "That black sheath formal will never fit over this body Friday night."

She sighed. But it had been fun and relaxing. She'd never been happier than eating a hot dog with Tyler at the baseball game. Or eating Cajun shrimp at lunch at Razzoo's with Tyler. Or savoring the ribs at Houston's without a tiny bit of guilt about her possible weight gain.

"Maybe I'm finally at the weight Doc Anderson set for me." She tried to dispel the fear of losing control and to convince herself that this was all a very good thing. "To the mall with you tomorrow, Kate Lawrence. Buy new clothes in a new size. Be happy. Tyler, Mom, and Dad will be busy tomorrow, anyway."

She smoothed lotion onto her glowing burn and brushed her hair. A rap at the door interrupted her pep talk.

"Kate? Are you in there?" She opened the door to Tyler's face.

"I just wanted to say good night. I'll probably be tied up a lot of the day tomorrow with funeral arrangements, but I wanted to let you know that we're still on for Medieval Nights tomorrow evening, if you want to go, that is."

Kate grinned back at his serious face and embraced him.

"I'm sorry about Tara, Tyler. I hope everything goes okay tomorrow. I'll have Mom point me to the mall, so I can buy some new clothes to accommodate my spreading figure."

Tyler shook his finger and hushed her. "You're beautiful, Katydid. You're radiant and what little weight you may have gained only makes you more beautiful."

"Are you sure that's not sunburn?"

"I'm sure." Tyler took her chin in his hand and kissed her gently. "I'll see you tomorrow about five."

Kate closed her eyes as he lurched off down the hall and ducked beneath the door frame. She willed her heart to slow its pace and her knees to hold her upright. She exhaled slowly and then continued getting ready for bed.

***

It was nearly four o'clock when Kate burst into the trailer with a sea of packages.

"Why, Katie, I thought the mall had swallowed you whole." Her dad looked up over his glasses from his Bible study. "But I see you brought it all home, too."

"No, Daddy." She laughed. "Only a part of it. I have to stuff this in a suitcase to go home tomorrow, remember?"

"Look at this one, Mom," she said as she pulled a soft pink gathered western blouse from a bag. "And I got this yoked denim skirt to wear tonight with it. Won't I be in Texas fashion? And a vest to match my hat."

Kate laid the ensemble on the bed. Then she tore into another bag. "Here's the tote bag I bought to take all this stuff home in. But here's the best part."

Kate pulled a garment bag from one of the bags. She carefully unzipped the store bag and removed the ball gown from the hanger. She held it up to her and twirled around the room.

"Oh, Katie. It's beautiful. Put it on so we can see it on you."

Kate shooed her mom from the room, clipped tags and redressed quickly in the rose-colored satin gown. The sweetheart neckline showed off her décolleté. The puffed sleeves held onto the edge of her shoulders, and the skirt flared to a full hem, skimming over the new curves in her figure. She quickly located the heart locket her parents had given her for graduation and suspended it in the neckline. Barefoot with hair flying every which way, Kate swooped into the living room and twirled, creating a rippling effect in the full satin hem.

When she came to a dizzying halt, she was face-to-face with Tyler Hawkins. Her parents applauded and cooed. The smoldering look deep in Tyler's eyes left Kate speechless.

"So this is how you go out in public in Washington DC?" His voice sounded throaty and hoarse. "I think I'm jealous of every man you'll greet, speaking French, at that party tomorrow night. You'll be very hard to resist, Katydid."

Kate stumbled over the hem of the gown as she unconsciously backed away from the handsome cowboy standing in front of her. He reached out to steady her and sparked a static charge. She felt the slight jolt. Her knees weakened and a hot flush colored her already red face.

"I'll go change. I won't be long."

She gathered up the long skirt and rushed from the room while Tyler sank down into the swivel rocker and watched her go.

***

It was late when Tyler and Kate returned from dinner at Medieval Nights.

"I couldn't believe it, Dad." Kate began her tale. "They gave me half a chicken to eat. Half a chicken! And no silverware at all to eat it with."

Tyler laughed. "Same thing with the potatoes and greens."

"I mean, I thought the dark ages were somewhat civilized."

"And if you think the rodeo is tough, you should see this type of rodeo, Ryan. Those spears were sharp." Tyler casually looped his arm around Kate's waist. "Makes bull riding look sane."

Kate playfully escaped his grasp. "Don't get any ideas, Tyler Hawkins. The Mesquite Rodeo is dangerous enough. Don't go volunteering to rescue anyone with a lance in his hand."

The two laughed. Her mom and dad held hands as they looked at the happy couple.

"I'll walk you out to the truck." Kate opened the door. "Be right back, Mom, Dad."

Kate held the door as Tyler negotiated the front stairs. Once at ground level, Tyler reached back and pulled Kate down the stairs into his strong arms. Kate thought she saw the curtain move in the living room window. She pushed against his hard chest.

"No, Tyler. I'm just not ready for this. It's too fast and requires too much from me."

"Life's short, Katydid, and none of it is guaranteed. Don't waste our time together without good reason."

Kate pulled away from his embrace and walked toward the pickup. She swallowed hard as he trapped her against the truck.

"I can't give up control of my life that easily, Tyler. There's still a lot you don't know about me and a lot I don't know about you." Kate's voice trembled as she spoke. "And then there's Mission Mesquite in the bargain."

Tyler released his hold on her and turned away.

"There's something you need to know." Tyler cleared his throat. "One more card to add to the stack on the table."

Kate turned him around to face her.

"How do you know I don't know?"

Tyler cleared his throat. "I have applied to the mission board to take over Mission Mesquite from your parents when they retire. I'm going to be ordained in a couple of weeks. Lord willing, I'll be the pastor of this motley crew sometime soon."

"My parents are planning to retire?" Kate was stunned. "They never said anything to me about it."

"Your dad's health isn't so great, Katie. That's one reason I think God called me to work with them in the mission. He's okay right now, but the doctor wants him to slow down on some of the stress and responsibility for Mission Mesquite. I guess I'm the heir apparent."

Prickles ran up Kate's arms and down her spine. She rubbed the goose flesh to warm it against the chilly night air. Tyler grabbed the wool rodeo jacket from the back of the truck, wrapped it around her, and held her tight against his broad chest. Kate rested her head on his chest. She knew the tingle wasn't just caused by the breeze.

Tyler released his grip and opened the truck door.

"I'll be here at 5:30 AM tomorrow. Your dad has to be at the funeral home early, so I told him I'd go with you to the airport."

"What about the rental car?"

"I'll follow you."

Tyler climbed into the truck and backed out onto the gravel drive. Kate stood wrapped in his wool jacket saturated with his scent and watched him go. She blew a kiss toward the back of the truck as he headed out of sight.

Her mom and dad were already in their bedroom when she came in. She turned off the light in the living room and went back to her room to pack her things.

***

Kate used her State Department ID to get Tyler through security.

"Flight 202 departing Dallas-Fort Worth for Atlanta and Washington-Dulles will be boarding in 10 minutes at gate 12," the public address blared. "All passengers holding tickets for Flight 202 should prepare for boarding."

Kate handed the wool jacket back to Tyler. "I think this is yours."

"Keep it as a souvenir. I've got another. I've got something else for you."

He reached down in the deep pockets of his windbreaker and pulled out a small stuffed armadillo dressed in a cowboy hat and bandanna. Kate laughed and stroked the furry little critter.

"Thank you for everything, Tyler. It's been a great vacation. I almost hate to go back."

"That's what I'd hoped you'd say." Tyler pulled her close. "Stay."

Kate searched the cowboy's face for the tease she expected to find. Instead she saw an earnestness that was hard to resist. She set her carry-on bags on the floor and draped the ball gown over the pile. She stretched up to place her arms around his neck.

"Tyler, I can't. Not now."

"Flight 202 is ready for boarding. Passengers in first class and requiring extra assistance may board now through gate 12."

"I understand, Katydid. Two ticks are all you can give me now. But I'll keep calling, Katie. I'm only one tick away."

They kissed long and hard in the middle of the terminal. People around them began to clap when the hat fell off Kate's head. Flustered, she hastily picked up her hat and things and headed for the gate. Tyler waved a small wave when she turned around.

"Adieu, Tyler," she mouthed to him as she entered the gate.

"I love you, Katydid," he mouthed back.

And then she was gone.

Chapter 6

The whine of the plane's engines and the short squeaks of the wheels touching down at Dulles awakened Kate from her nap. She stretched and caught the pillow the flight attendant had provided as it slipped from behind her head. She finger-combed her auburn tangles and gathered her hat and other belongings as the plane taxied into the gate.

"Sleep well?" asked her seat mate.

"Better than I have in a week. It's good to be home."

Placing the cowboy hat on her head, Kate freed her hands to grab the rest of her possessions. She carefully extracted the ball gown from the hanging compartment where it was crushed between overloaded suit bags and juggled her dress bag and carry-on luggage as she tromped down the jet way to the terminal.

"Kate! Over here, Kate!" A man shouted to her, waving a huge bouquet of roses.

Kate wasn't sure if she was happy to see Doug waiting for her. He took her in his arms as they met and hugged her tightly.

"Cindy called and told me you'd be coming in earlier. It's so great to see you. I hope you don't mind that I came to meet you. I really want to talk and try to change your mind. There. It's out, so let's grab your luggage and get lunch somewhere."

"Doug, don't you have a job you're supposed to be doing?"

"Kate, picking you up *is* my job this morning. John was concerned about you getting in on time. I have strict instructions to deliver you home as quickly as possible so you can get changed for the embassy ball later."

"Oh." Kate felt a little deflated by his explanation. *So it's just a work thing.*

"Texas must have been wonderful, Kate; you're positively glowing. But I think you ate a little too much Tex-Mex. Looks like you gained more weight while you were there. Being un-engaged has taken a toll on your figure. What is it now? Fifteen pounds over fighting weight. That black skinny number you usually wear to these events may not fit. That could be a state crisis, you know."

Kate looked at him to see if he was joking. It was the kind of thing Tyler would have said with a laughing twinkle in his eye. Doug was dead serious, however.

"Not to worry, Doug. I bought a new gown in Dallas for tonight. It's a killer, and it looks great on me...."

"Well, it's back to diet sodas and salads for you. Guess a salad bar is all you get for lunch."

Kate stopped dead in her tracks.

"Excuse me, Doug. Who are you to decide what I eat and what I wear and what I weigh? We're not married. We're not even engaged. I really don't need all this unasked-for criticism."

"Hey, sorry. You just always didn't seem to mind my little reminders about your weight. You should be thanking me for keeping you as rail-thin as you've been the last five years. And it's done wonders for your career, you know."

Kate nodded. "So I see. For your information, I feel good about the extra weight. I can get to the embassy on time by myself. And I can get myself a cab. Thanks for the help, but no thanks."

She slammed the roses into Doug's chest, grabbed her carry-on from him, and headed for the luggage carousel.

"I didn't say you didn't look good, Kate," Doug called after her. "And the hat is a cute souvenir. Just don't wear it to the party tonight. The French ambassador might get the wrong idea about his interpreter."

She didn't turn around to see if he was following her. Part of her was mortified by the public scene she'd just created. But another part caught herself smiling a "Texas" smile.

At least I made the right decision about canceling the wedding. She stalked through the interminable terminal. Doug is definitely out of the future picture.

She noticed some interesting looks from other passengers as she grabbed for her luggage in her black cowboy hat and the tight skirted black suit. While most of them had been on the same flight, they had not all originated in Dallas.

"Suits," she muttered. "Loosen up."

***

The cab and tip cost her a fortune by the time she arrived at her Georgetown townhouse, but at least she didn't have to share the ride with Doug Hastings. Mail, slipped through the brass mail slot in the door, covered the foyer floor from her week's absence. She scooted up the stairs to her familiar bedroom, placed the luggage in the floor, and hung the gown on the door hook. The doorbell summoned her back to her front door.

"Doug, I don't want to talk to you right now." She opened the door without looking through the peephole.

The delivery man looked perplexed. "Flowers for Katie Lawrence."

"Oh! That's me, thanks. Sorry."

She pulled a tip from her pocket, handed it to him, and swiftly shut the door. The bouquet of wildflowers and daisies smelled sweet in their green florist vase. She carried them back to her tiny kitchen to fill the vase with water. Once watered and arranged on the kitchen bar, she removed the card.

"Dearest Katydid, Have a blast at the bash! Hope the trip home was safe and wonderful. Hope you see Dallas as home, someday. Yours, Tyler"

The card made her smile.

"What a sweetheart of a man." She spoke aloud in the too silent room.

The grandfather clock in the hall chimed three. Kate gathered the mail from the floor and dumped it on the table for later perusal. She rushed up the stairs for a shower and transformation from Dallas cowgirl to Washington diplomat.

***

"Your keys, *Mademoiselle Katerine*?" The valet held out his hand to Kate as she pulled up in front of the French embassy. "You look especially lovely this evening. A new dress or hairstyle, perhaps?"

"*Merci, Henri.*" She flashed him a brilliant smile. "New dress." Also a new attitude and a new figure. Anything else? Oh, yes! A new freedom! "Don't park it too far back, Henri. I may not stay too long this evening."

Henri winked back at her as he shifted her little black BMW into drive and drove it into the monitored parking lot beyond the gates. She adjusted her shawl and smoothed her hair as she readied herself for a long evening of small talk and socializing. Her parents were at the rodeo. Tyler was at the rodeo.

The rodeo would be a whole lot more fun.

"Kate, you did make it back." Her boss gave her a long glance. "That's not exactly State Department formal attire."

"I told you I would be back, John. And after all, it is a *soirée*, isn't it?"

"Doug said there was some kind of problem at the airport. I couldn't get all of it because his cell phone was out of range."

"John, the only problem was Doug. I'm fine, and I'm here."

Kate swirled around in the new gown to find the ambassador. Stefan found her first.

"*Très magnifique*, Kate! I like the new you. The dress is stunning and the, how do you say, the figure in the dress is unbelievable. Vacation must have been most good for you."

Kate felt the red heat of her blush. Frenchmen! Always direct and flattering.

"You are too kind, Ambassador."

"Hardly. Every eye in the place is on you. I am delighted to have you at my side for the evening."

"*Merci*, Ambassador, but I will need to leave early tonight. As you know, I 've just arrived, and have some things I must do before I can rest."

"*Mais bien sûr, cherie.* I am honored with your presence, then, for as long as you can stay. I understand you cut short your time away for my benefit. I can certainly honor your request. Shall we join the others in the dining room?"

Kate took the Ambassador's arm and joined the other diplomats at the dinner table.

Three hours and lots of lemoned Perrier water later, Henri met Kate at the curb with her car.

"This look, *Mademoiselle Katerine*, it is so chic. You must keep up whatever you've done to create such a grand image. Monsieur Doug must be most pleased."

Kate laughed. "We're no longer engaged, Henri. I'm a free woman."

"Then, perhaps, tomorrow night, we could …"

"*Non, merci, Henri.* I'm looking forward to a quiet evening at home, and Madame Henri would not be pleased."

Both laughed as Kate drove off toward Georgetown.

***

Kate heard the answering machine as she let herself into the dark foyer in time to hear the click off. She raced to the foyer phone to answer it, but the caller had just hung up. She kicked off her heels and scooped them off the floor as she headed to check caller ID and answering machine in the kitchen.

A Texas number, in fact, Mesquite Arena. She replayed the messages on her tape.

"Beep! Hi Katie. It's just Dad. We're hoping you had a good flight and are home safely. Call when you get a have time. … Beep! Kate, it's Doug. Give us another chance. Maybe tomorrow we can go jogging on the mall to start your slim down program. … Beep! Katie, it's Tyler. I just thought I'd call and see if you made it in okay. Hope you like my Texas reminder I sent. That's all. Call if you ever want to talk."

Kate picked up the receiver and hesitated over the call back button. She placed the receiver back firmly and went upstairs to change. The light continued to blink on the machine.

As she slipped into bed, she reached for the phone again. She dialed the area code, and then finished with her parents' number.

"Hello, Rev. Ryan at Mission Mesquite."

"Dad, it's Kate. I hope I'm not too late to call."

"It's fine, Katie, we just got in from the show. It was exciting as always. Stan Moran, Tyler's partner, was pulled off his horse and run over tonight. He's okay, but bruised pretty good."

"And Tyler?"

A pause punctuated the phone line. "He's fine, Sweetheart. Rescued Stan as fast as he could and got him to safety."

"Good." Kate frowned. *What difference should it make to me if he was hurt? He is just an acquaintance I'll probably never see again.* "Just wanted to let you know I was home. Good night, Dad."

"Good night, Katie. We love you."

"Love you too, Daddy."

Kate hung up the phone gently, wiped her eyes, and slid out of the bed. She slipped back downstairs and flipped on the kitchen light. She dialed the number on caller ID.

"You have reached the Mesquite Arena, home of the Mesquite Championship Rodeo. For ticket information, dial 1. For days of operation, dial 2. To speak with an operator, hold on the line."

Kate waited nervously for a live voice to answer the phone.

"I'm sorry. Our office hours are from 9 to …"

Kate hung up and went on back to bed.

***

"Not that one either". She scowled as she tried on clothes for church Sunday morning. "Obviously I've been buying my clothes too small. Something should fit over such a minor weight gain."

Blouses gaped in front and zippers refused to zip. Clothes were scattered everywhere. Finally, she picked up the white blouse with the tatted lace over-vest and slipped it on. It fit perfectly. Another perusal of the closet found a little-worn shirred black skirt. It fit, too. She picked out the silver jewelry she had bought in Dallas, grabbed her bag and Bible, and rushed out to the car.

"I haven't been to church in years. I'm not going to be late today."

***

Just as she opened the door, the phone rang. Kate listened as the answering machine picked up, "*Bon jour*. This is Kate Lawrence. I can't come to the phone right now, but if you leave your name and number and a brief message, I'll get back to you as soon as possible. *Merci beaucoup. Au revoir.*" Beep!"

"Katydid, this is Tyler. Just wanted to remind you to visit the Lord this morning. I've been thinking and praying about you since you left Friday morning, well … If you want, give me a call back. You've got the number."

54

With sheer force of will, Kate closed the door and headed out for church. She'd have to catch him later.

***

Kate pushed open the front door with a load of bags and packages.

"I know, Lord, it's Sunday; and I shouldn't be shopping. But I have to have something to wear to work tomorrow morning!"

She smiled at her reflection in the hall mirror.

"There's nothing like shopping for new clothes to make you happy, is there Kate? Even if they are a size larger. That's okay, 'cause the others were old and boring anyway. And, besides, some men think I look better with a little curve."

She recalled the admiring glances she'd received at the French embassy party on Friday night and Henri's remark at her departure. Several handsome young men had made a point of speaking to her at church that morning. Her eye caught sight of the cowboy hat on the hall tree. She placed the black felt hat on her head and cocked it at an angle.

"Tyler Hawkins did, too."

The clock chimed four. The answering machine alerted her to new messages. She headed toward the kitchen, tossing the hat back on the hall tree and leaving her bags at the foot of the stairs.

The number on the caller ID was Tyler's "big house" number. Kate listened to the message and then played it again. She scooped ice into a glass and filled it with water deliberately. After squirting lemon juice from a plastic lemon onto the ice, Kate swirled the mixture then took a long, slow sip. Kate then picked up the phone and dialed the number displayed on the caller ID.

"Howdy, this is Tyler Hawkins. I'm not in, probably at the corral. Call there or leave a message. Remember, this is the day the Lord has made, REJOICE! Beep!"

Kate hung up before leaving a message. She'd try again later.

***

Monday morning, she chose one of the new outfits she'd purchased and modeled it in front of the full-length mirror. Instead of her usual tailored business look, she'd opted for softer clothing. Full a-line buttoned skirts in floral prints and solids. Pastel and white blouses with gathers and soft draping sleeves. Sweater vests with embroidered flowers. A new black suit with turned-up silk under-sleeves. A camel brown jacket with black velvet collar. As she turned in the mirror, the soft skirt twirled out from her legs and the sleeves of her blouse shimmered.

"It looks just fine, but I really don't have money to buy another new wardrobe, so this gaining weight thing has to stop." She chastised the image, pointing a finger at the new, soft, feminine version of herself. "Salad for lunch today."

DC traffic was horrible as usual, but her reserved parking space was always open, so she made it into the State building just before starting time.

"'Morning, Kate. There's a press release on your desk. You need to read it and pass it on. Hope you had a great vacation, because now it's back to the grind."

"Thanks, John," she said to the fleeing back. "I like your outfit, too, John."

"What?"

"Nothing." She turned her mind to other things. People hurried past her cubicle, just like any other Monday. She dealt with the press release and started sorting through the pile of mail on her desk. The picture of Doug and her at his family's cottage on Martha's Vineyard last Christmas mocked her. The gaunt, hard-angled Kate in the picture looked frail and dependent. She turned the picture on its face. She jumped up to answer a summons to John's office. A few meetings and phone calls later, she settled again at her desk to take care of overseas e-mail requests.

"I hear you made quite a smash at the party Friday."

"Cindy! How are you, girl Friday?" Kate jumped up to hug her assistant.

"Hey, Kate; I see what the fuss was about. You look great. The skin and bones routine was getting really old anyway. The guys down in the mail room are betting on whether that's a Miracle bra or you!"

"Cindy, that's totally inappropriate." Kate scowled and then slowly smiled. "It's me."

"Kate, I must know the diet you're on."

Kate shrugged. "Just real food over vacation. No diet, artificial, or low-fat anything."

"Well, I'm for that, except I'd look like a blimp in a week's time, not like a playboy pinup." Cindy rolled her eyes. "Doug stopped by earlier and asked if you were in. By the look on his face, I figured you weren't. Oh, and some guy named Tyler Hawkins from Dallas called this morning while you were in that meeting with John. He said he'd call back later if you were too busy to call him. Something about he'd wait till you were available." Cindy screwed up her face. "That's what he said, but it sounded more like code or something. Who is he?"

"Oh, a rodeo jock who works with my parents at their mission." Kate hoped she sounded unaffected, but her heart was racing. Three phone calls in one weekend? "It may be about my parents; maybe I should call him back. Did he leave a number?"

"No. He said you knew how to reach him if you needed to." Cindy looked at Kate oddly and grinned. "Is he as handsome as he sounds long distance?"

Kate leaned back in the creaky office chair and nodded. "And more."

Cindy shrieked and all the work in the office came to a halt. Kate stood, shushed her, and said, "She thought she saw a mouse, but it was just this beanie thing on the floor."

Shocked faces eased and went back to work. She assisted Cindy to a chair and handed her three packs of pictures.

"Vacation pictures, but no shrieking."

"Aren't you going to call him back?"

"No, but I am going to call my parents to make sure they're okay."

While Cindy looked at pictures, Kate ascertained her parents' welfare and got the number for "the big house" and the corral at Green Pastures.

"This is Tyler?" Cindy pointed to a photograph. "He is dashing. Why are you here? You should have extended this vacation. And poor old Doug was waiting for you at the airport. He didn't stand a chance."

"Hush, Cindy. Don't talk nonsense. We're just friends, so far. And I'm here, and he's two-thirds of the way across the country." Kate looked out the window facing west. "Not much chance of more happening."

The mail cart rolled down the aisle, and the mail boy appeared at the cubicle entrance.

"Your mail, Ms. Lawrence." He handed her mail from the whole last week. "Could I ask you a question?"

"Sure, Arnold, shoot."

"Well, I don't know exactly how to ask, but given your sudden change of appearance, we were wondering if ... well... you were working out or something on vacation."

"No, Arnold. It's just me in there."

Arnold blushed to his toes and hustled the cart away. Cindy and Kate laughed until the man in the next cubicle looked over the wall and stared at them over his glasses. Cindy handed Kate her pictures and rushed back to her desk. Kate chuckled under her breath and smiled.

"Lord, how long has it been since I smiled at just being me?"

She picked up the picture from its face and gazed into the formal smiles of the couple in the picture. The picture- perfect couple. The diamond ring on the woman's hand sparkled under the photographer's canopy. Kate pulled the picture from the frame and tossed it into the bottom drawer of the desk. She chose a picture of herself with her parents and Tyler on the last day of her visit, taken by Joe, the foreman. The smiles in this picture were real, despite the lack of a diamond. She slid the picture into the frame and adjusted it to sit on the desktop properly. She smiled at the people in the picture and then at the numbers her mother had given her. She picked up the phone, but her intercom buzzed before she could dial the number.

"Kate. I need you in my office, posthaste."

"Yes, sir." She rushed off, leaving the phone numbers on the desk.

Chapter 7

It was after eight when Kate opened the door to the dark foyer of the townhouse. Mail lay scattered on the floor once again. She sighed, leaned against the closed door, then squatted down to retrieve the mail. Kate stood and picked up the rest of the mail she'd placed on the hall table. She carried it back through the darkened hallway to the kitchen and turned on the overhead light and ceiling fan. Washington was already hot and humid, even though the air-conditioning was running at full tilt. Kate grabbed a diet soda from the refrigerator, popped the top, and downed a swallow.

Gag! This stuff is so awful.

She set it aside and began combing through the pile of mail. As she sorted, Kate found a postcard or two in each day's mail from Texas: The Mesquite Arena. Shepler's Western Wear. Southfork Ranch. Mission Mesquite with Tyler's corral. The mini-golf place. The Herd. The Mustangs. Ranger Stadium. The Farmer's Market. Pegasus above the Dallas skyline. Six-Flags Over Texas. Medieval Knights. And Monday's mail held one from the airport. Each was addressed formally in a bold hand. None held a message, save the date they had visited each site, except the last. The last one said, "I miss you already, Katydid" and was addressed to "Katie Lawrence."

"Tyler." Kate closed her eyes as the salty tears ran down her face. "I miss you, too."

The phone began to ring. Kate wiped away the tears with a napkin from the island and picked up the receiver, hoping her hello would be strong and not misty.

"Kate, it's Doug. Don't hang up on me."

Kate looked at the message on the airport card, smiled through her tears, and hung up the phone without regret. She fished through her purse and finally found the scrap of paper that held Tyler's phone numbers. She dialed the big house first and got the machine.

"Tyler, it's Kate. I just want to thank you for the flowers and the cards. I also would love to actually hear your voice instead of playing phone tag. Call me whenever. Don't worry if it's late. I'll be up a while."

She left her number and then tried the corral number. It rang a long time before Joe answered the phone in his gruff way.

"Yeah?"

"Joe? This is Kate Lawrence. I've been trying to reach Tyler. Is he around?"

"Well, Katie, he's been out for a while on Asher. Not sure when to expect him back. Call up to the big house and leave a message on that infernal machine of his."

"Thanks, Joe. I already did. Tell him I called."

"You bet I will."

"Oh, and Joe, tell Rose 'hi' for me, too."

"I'll tell her fer ya."

The line went dead. Kate laughed at the gruff man's few words and missed him, too.

***

Tyler rode the red steed hard across the ranch, dodging through the vales and under trees. He checked every inch of fencing and gave Asher a drink at every puddle and brook. They practiced roping techniques and jumping over hedges until the sides of the horse were soaked in lather. Tyler stopped beside a pond and gave Asher his head to graze, drink, and cool down. He lurched over to a nearby tree stump and gingerly slid his crippled body down onto the ground, using the stump as support and back rest. Removing his hat, he ran his hand through the wet blond hair underneath. He leaned his head back against the stump and prayed aloud.

"Father God. Paul prayed in Second Corinthians for his thorn of the flesh to be removed three times. You know I've prayed more than that about this gimpy leg and the ugly scars that run all over my body. I know You spared my life. But, Lord, I lost Tina; and I lost the competition of the rodeo. I lost the respect of the other participants. I lost the opportunity for a wife and family because what woman worth salt would want this disabled man? Even Katie couldn't look at me when I had to walk somewhere. I don't want a pity party. I just want someone to love me. I thought maybe it was her."

Tyler pulled a worn New Testament from his hip pocket and read the underlined verses in 2 Corinthians 12:8-10 yet again:

"But he said to me, 'My grace is sufficient for you, my power is made perfect in weakness.' Therefore, I will boast all the more gladly about my weakness, so that Christ's power may rest on me. That is why, for Christ's sake, I delight in weaknesses, in insults, in hardships, in persecutions, in difficulties. For when I am weak, then I am strong."

He rubbed his face and ruffled his hair.

"Lord, if I can't have my strength, give me my Katydid. She took my heart with her to Washington DC. I can live the rest of my life as a cripple if only Katie is by my side to love me and laugh with me."

A bird flew into the edge of the water and fluttered in the shallows. It flicked water onto Tyler's boot, chirped mightily, and flew away. Tyler laughed at the little bird and watched as the sun set on the prairie.

***

When Tyler returned to the corral, Joe was sleeping in a leaned back chair. He nearly toppled over when Asher nudged the older man. Tyler laughed as Joe startled awake.

"'Bout time you got back. Where you been, boy?"

"Out on the ridge at the pond. Been praying and thinking."

"Mooning is what you been doing. Over that Katie lady. She called whilst you was out mooning."

Tyler slid off the horse and steadied himself against the steed while he unhooked the saddle and gear.

"She called?"

"Yeah, said she'd left a message at the house. She was real sweet, too. You better not let this one go, Ty. She's a keeper, if you know what I mean."

Tyler began grooming the horse in slow deep strokes. Asher whinnied softly in reply. Ariel answered from the next stable stall. Tyler grinned at their attachment for one another. He could count on another love child from the pair this spring, too. Their love was permanent and strong. His auburn lady would fit right in at Green Pastures.

***

His boots thudded on the wood floor as he entered the dimly lit hallway of the big house. He found his way back to the master bedroom and the answering machine. The lit alarm clock read midnight.

Too late to call her back tonight. "Guess I shouldn't have been 'mooning,' Lord."

He settled onto the bed carefully, but the old wrenching pain came anyway. He caught his breath until the pain reduced to a dull ache. He reached over to play the message. Then he dialed her number, even though he knew it was 1 a.m. in D.C.

***

Kate rolled over and looked at the time as the phone rang. She closed her eyes and buried her head in the pillow.

Not Doug again.

The incessant ringing finally roused her from sleep. She grabbed the phone.

"Doug, I'm not talking to you. Don't call me. Don't see me. Don't send me messages. Don't send me flowers. Don't talk to Cindy. Can't you get the message?"

Just as she was ready to hang up on Doug for the tenth time that evening, she heard a bass voice say with a laugh, "But I'm not Doug."

"Tyler?"

"In the flesh, ma'am," he said with bravado. "What can I do to serve you, fair maiden?"

"Just don't change, Tyler. Be just who you are."

Tyler snorted. "Gimpy leg and all, huh?"

"Gimpy leg and all," she affirmed softly. "Just so you're always the sweet man that you are."

She could picture his soft blush under his bronzed tan.

"Wish you were still here, Katydid."

"You and me both. I had to buy a whole new wardrobe for work. I think you'd approve, Ty. I'm making a big splash at the office and the embassy. But Doug is driving me crazy."

62

"I don't need to approve your wardrobe, Katie. Doug's just sorry he lost such a prize catch, I bet."

"No, he wants me to go jogging to lose all my excess baggage, so I can fit his image of me." The anger in her voice shocked her. When had she become angry with Doug and his manipulation? "Sorry. I didn't mean to go off like that."

"High time, I'd say."

"Tyler, have you always been this good at comforting women on the rebound?"

She heard his broad smile in his words. "Trust me, Katydid, there are no women falling around my crippled feet, rebounding or otherwise."

"They should be, Ty. They don't know what they're missing."

Kate frowned. Was she a little too transparent? Was her banter too close to her true feelings? Was she being pushy? But more important, was she falling in love with him?

"Katie? Are you still there?"

"Yes, Ty. How are the horses?"

"They miss you. I miss you."

"I miss you, too, Tyler Hawkins. *Bon nuit, cheri.*"

"Good-night, Katydid."

Kate hung up the phone and curled her arm around her pillow. Her heart ached to hold him close and kiss him good-bye.

***

Tyler cradled the phone and looked at it before hanging it up.

This situation will not do. I need to see her again, if only to know that there's really hope. She could be just being nice to the cripple. He undressed for bed and then called the airline.

It was early morning when Tyler knocked on the screen door at Mission Mesquite. Pans rattled in the kitchen.

"Coming!" Miss Sarah appeared at the door wiping her hands on the orange dish towel. "Tyler, come in! You're up early this morning."

"Yes, ma'am. I'm always up this early, but I'm usually still attending to the horses now."

Tyler took off his hat as he entered the trailer. The screen door slammed behind him. He twisted the brim of his hat, trying to put the words together in his mind first.

"Can I speak with Rev. Ryan alone? I need to talk man to man with him."

"Sure, Ty. He's out on the patio doing his quiet time. Go on out. I'll put the coffee on and fix you both some eggs."

Tyler nodded his thanks and headed after her to the back screen door. He awkwardly descended the treated timber steps to the concrete patio behind the trailer. Rev. Ryan was deep in prayer and didn't seem to notice his approach. Tyler took a seat in the lawn chair opposite the minister's and waited quietly.

"Good morning, Tyler." Rev. Ryan greeted him without opening his eyes. "Anything I can tell the Lord for you before I close?"

"No, sir. He already knows my heart this morning."

Rev. Ryan nodded and opened his eyes. He closed the Bible in his lap and set it on the plastic patio table.

"What can I do for you, Tyler?"

"I need advice, Rev. Ryan, and a request. But I'm not sure where to begin."

"Begin at the beginning, son."

"Okay. This leg of mine. On horseback, nobody can tell it's gone. In the truck, it makes no difference. But on the ground, I'm a sight. Lurching here and there. What woman would choose a cripple for a husband? Why would God cripple me? Isn't it enough that I can't compete anymore? Isn't it enough that I can't walk up the stairs in my own house without stumbling? Isn't it enough that I lost Tina because of the accident? What use am I to God or to a wife?"

Rev. Ryan took the twisted hat from Tyler's grasp and smoothed the brim. He gently placed it back on the blond man's head.

"Scripture tells us of another man with a limp. Jacob wrestled with God. But he was so stubborn, that when morning came, the angel of the Lord touched his hip socket and wrenched his hip. And from that day forward, Jacob was called Israel and walked with a limp. The limp was a mark of his encounter with God and a physical reminder of the spiritual change that had occurred in Jacob's life. You remind me of him, Tyler. So stubborn that God had to fling you under a dangerous bull and deliver you from death to get your attention. When I see that limp, Ty, it reminds me of the miracle of your survival and spiritual salvation."

Tyler nodded. "I think of that often. How God saved me both physically and spiritually because of that bull. But I still have a life to live. And it gets lonely. I want to ask her to marry me, but I don't know if it's fair to her to even ask her to give up her life for a gimpy old cowboy on a horse ranch, playing at being a cowboy two nights a week."

"Do you love her?"

"Yes, that's the whole problem. I love her enough to let her live the life she loves so much without complicating it with … me."

"Does she love you?"

"I don't know. Maybe. If that's even possible. I look at you and Miss Sarah, and I want what you have - a lovely woman who wakes up every morning beside you. A woman who'll stand by you, no matter what. A woman who loves me regardless of a limp. I think I found that woman. But I'm not sure I should change her life because of what I want."

"Ask her anyway, Tyler. You are a wonderful person, limp or no limp. She probably loves you just because you are who you are. Who's the lucky lady?"

"Well, that's the other part of the request, Rev. Ryan. Can I ask for your daughter's hand in marriage?"

A skillet clattered to the floor inside the trailer. Rev. Ryan dashed up the stairs by twos. Miss Sarah met him at the door.

"The eggs are all over the floor, Ryan." Tears spilled down Miss Sarah's face.

"Are you hurt, my love?" Rev. Ryan took her hands in his and kissed the palms gingerly.

"No. But if you don't tell this dear man 'yes,' I may have to hurl that skillet at your head next time."

"You were listening?" Tyler eased his aching body from the rickety chair.

"Hard not to when the windows are all open. Well, Ryan. Yes or no?"

Rev. Ryan looked back at the tall blond man. He clapped him on the back and hugged him tightly.

"Tyler, I have loved you like a son ever since you hit the dirt in the arena. We've loved you, and you've served the Lord with us here ever since. I discipled you and sent you to seminary. I endorsed your application to the mission board even though they first turned it down due to your health. There's nothing I'd love more than to give my Katie to you. But she's her own woman, Ty. That's a decision she'd have to make on her own - with the Lord, I hope. But I'll back you thoroughly. Yes, you may have her hand if she allows you."

Miss Sarah hugged him tightly. "Just remember - she's more stubborn than you. And there's no bull in her future that I can see. Somehow God's going to have to get that girl's attention. I'm afraid it'll be as rough a ride before she turns her life back over to Him."

"That just makes me love her more, Miss Sarah. She'll need somebody to help her when that time comes."

"Well, come help me scrape your eggs off the floor; and I'll start you a whole new batch."

"Here, here." Rev Ryan held the door for Tyler to climb the stairs. "It's too early for all this serious talk without breakfast."

Chapter 8

Kate sat at her desk, doodling on the blotter pad. Outside her window, the Beltway became a parking lot as the world attempted to leave the city for the Fourth of July holiday. Traffic flowed slightly faster as tourists entered the nation's Capital for the patriotic celebration. Silence pervaded the State office as the few diplomatic workers straggled out for the three-day weekend. Only those with nowhere to go remained. Like Kate.

"It's steamy out there." Cindy entered Kate's office, took a handful of M&Ms from the globe candy dish on Kate's desk, and perched on the windowsill. "Clothes coming off all over. The subway will be interesting tonight. Lucky you got A/C."

Kate shuffled papers over the floor plan on the blotter. "Hey, you made a choice. Remember, you're saving the planet by not using gas and Freon. 'Mass transit is the answer to the pollution/oil shortage/ozone failure/global warming.' Pick one. The rest of us lonely capitalists get to sit in traffic listening to traffic reports, overheating our engines, and cranking our A/C."

Cindy scowled.

Kate tried to look busy by scanning international incident reports on her PC. "What about this airport thing? Does John know about this?"

"Yeah, he's seen it. Turns out the guy, an ugly American, decided to make French security jokes. He missed his plane, lost his luggage, and claims he was abused by the air marshal. No story here. He got what he had coming, the jerk."

Kate glanced up at her secretary/friend. "You're in a lousy mood. Is this the heat or your love life?"

"And PMS/global warming/mass transit. Pick one."

Kate laughed. "Want to do dinner at the Bistro? I'll take you home in the sedan."

"Are you buying, too?"

Kate shot back, "'Course not. You buy your own poison. And more M&Ms for the globe, too, since I don't eat them."

Cindy grabbed the remaining red and green candies and spied the floor plan. "Whatcha drawing?"

"I'm ashamed to even say, Cindy. It's a floor plan actually."

"Oh yeah? Are you taking up architecture or is this someplace you've been … recently?"

Kate felt the heat crawl up her neck and across her cheeks.

Cindy pointed at her nose as though playing charades.

"His house?" She pointed to the picture of Tyler and Kate's parents.

"Right again. The sad thing is I've been doing this all afternoon."

Cindy sauntered around Kate's desk to admire the blueprint.

"Kate, you're arranging your own furniture in this theoretical floor plan. Is that your French armoire in the master bedroom? And your grandfather clock in the foyer? And I thought you said the upstairs was empty. What's this bunk beds notation?" Cindy shot Kate a knowing look. "You're more than smitten, girl. You are hooked on a cowboy. Unbelievable."

Returning to the chair, Cindy sank back into it and smiled. "Love is a wonderful thing." She sighed.

"So why does it hurt so badly?" Kate shot back, out of sorts. "Why isn't it a little more convenient? Like to the ever-dogged Doug for whom I have embroidered towels? Or to the man who lives across the street and walks his dog every evening at seven? Why does it have to seek and destroy my entire life?"

Kate tossed the pen at the desk and walked over to the window.

"Oh my …"

Cindy stood and looked out in the direction of Kate's shocked stare.

"Now there's a sight you don't see every day. Besides the former president, when's the last time you saw a 10-gallon hat get out of a cab in downtown DC?"

The man in the hat paid the cabby and stared up at the State Department Building. The tall man wearing boots, jeans, sport coat, and cowboy hat walked jaggedly down the sidewalk staring up at the federal buildings and down at a scrap of paper. A blond curl had escaped the hat, and the Washington humidity had plastered it onto his forehead.

"It's him, isn't it? That's pretty convenient."

Kate continued to stare at the familiar lurch as he approached her building. He took off his hat and seemed to look up at her window. Kate pulled back from the window but watched him turn and enter the foyer.

"I can't believe it." She dropped into her desk chair. "I never expected him to come here."

"Must be love. And he's drop dead gorgeous. What a hunk," teased Cindy. "Security will have to call you to let him in."

She pointed to the phone as it rang.

"Ms. Lawrence, you have a visitor in the lobby. A Tyler Hawkins from Dallas. Would you like to come and escort him up to your office or shall I send him away?"

"I'll be right there, Lennie."

Kate scattered paperwork back over the floor plan and found a brush in her purse to tame the wildfire in her auburn tresses from twisting them around her finger all day. She straightened her hose and skirt and freshened her makeup.

"Bet this means dinner's off and mass transit for the girlfriend. But I want to meet Mr. Right … I mean Mr. Hawkins. Don't forget to bring him by my cubicle."

Kate shoved Cindy out of her office as she headed for the lobby. Kate discovered that her knees were wobbly and her hands were shaking when she attempted to walk. She took the stairs hoping her nerves would settle before she reached the ground floor. She was wrong; they only got worse the farther she descended.

As Kate emerged from the stairwell, Tyler stopped in mid-sentence with the security guard. Kate smiled as their eyes met. Tyler grinned a huge grin and crossed the lobby in two limps to embrace her.

"Surprise," he said in her ear. "You know the male katydid always hops to where the female is."

Kate was sure she glowed from the blush she felt as she guided him toward the elevator. A look back at Lennie yielded a knowing wink from the security guard. The hot flush rose again into her cheeks.

"I didn't know you were coming, Tyler. I'm really overwhelmed. I'm just about ready to leave work. How did you get here? Do you have a car parked somewhere? Do you have a hotel? How long can you stay?"

Tyler pulled her into the elevator. As the doors shut, he kissed her passionately.

"I couldn't stay away, Katydid." He completed the kiss. "I had to see you again to see if the memories were figments of my imagination or truth. They were truth."

He tried to kiss her again, but Kate shoved him aside as the elevator door slid open. A thin man stepped onto the elevator in between them. Doug.

"So, Kate. What are your plans for the weekend? Obviously you're not leaving town or you'd be gone like the rest of the people in this place. How about dinner at my place?"

Kate glanced at Tyler as he hid a smirk. Her look warned him to keep quiet.

"I'm sorry; I have unexpected company for the weekend."

"Lose the company. It's rude to arrive unexpectedly. Point them to the nearest Hampton Inn and let's make up. After all, I know you still have towels with an H on it."

***

Tyler could stand it no longer.

"That works mighty fine for Hawkins, too, sir," he said in an exaggerated Texan drawl. "Tyler Hawkins, sir; pleased to meet you."

Doug gave Tyler an astonished look as the door slid open to Kate's floor. Cindy was waiting at the door.

"This must be Tyler that I've heard so much about. Not too many people in DC wear cowboy hats and boots. At least not since the last Bush administration."

Doug disappeared down the hallway as Tyler grasped Cindy's hand in both of his. Kate collapsed in a chair beside the elevator.

"Nice to meet you, Cindy. I heard about you a lot while Katie was in Dallas. You called her frequently."

'Yeah, that would be me," she acknowledged. "You know; I hardly notice the limp at all."

Kate groaned and made a beeline for her office. Tyler winked at Cindy, who laughed behind her hand.

"Thanks for the directions, Cindy. I really appreciate you playing along with my little plan."

"My pleasure." Cindy dropped a little curtsy.

Tyler loped down the hallway after Kate's sprint. He looked into offices until he found Kate slumped onto the desk. He crossed the office and looked with awe at the Capitol mall and accompanying sights.

"Unbelievable, Katie. I've only seen this in books and pictures. And to think you see it every day. I'm glad I came. I hope it's not a bad weekend to show me the sights and eat a few meals with me. You don't handle the food thing very well, ya know."

"Amen!" shouted Cindy from the office door. "Just leaving, Kate. Need anything else?"

Kate lifted her head from the desk and shoved her hair back into place.

"Go home, Cindy. I'll call you later in the weekend."

***

Cindy winked and flounced out of the office. Kate looked at the handsome cowboy gazing out her window. Her nerves calmed as she saw him as her friend, someone who really cared for her. Warning bells still rang in her head. He still had one fatal flaw: Mission Mesquite. He caught her gaze in the reflection in the window and turned around.

"It's okay that I'm here, isn't it? I didn't really conspire to embarrass you in your workplace."

Kate grinned up at him. "It's okay. I know you didn't. I'm not really embarrassed, just a little confused and very surprised that you would come all this way not knowing what my reaction might be. I hope, well, I hope you're glad to see me anyway."

Tyler nodded and shrugged into her desk chair. He swiveled it around to survey the office. He reached out and turned the picture around on her desk.

"I'm glad to see this here. I was afraid I'd find your dear ex-fiancé, Doug H., on your desk."

"No, I needed happy people to look at me all day."

She reached into the bottom drawer and tossed the engagement picture toward Tyler.

"These two people are not happy. These two people look 'satisfised.' They didn't have anyone else, so they thought they could have each other. Luckily, I realized it in time to stop a disaster. Doug still is trying to schedule a voyage on the Titanic II with me."

"The guy in the elevator, right?" Tyler looked at the photo with interest, especially at how pale and lifeless Kate seemed in the photo and how dominating Doug seemed.

"You're right, Katie. As wimpy as he seems in real life, he's obviously someone who would try to run your life without your input. This photo is a perfect example of an unhealthy relationship. What about this photo?"

Kate turned the photo of her parents, Tyler, and herself around and looked into it. As though it were a crystal ball, she gazed into that other world in Texas in that rodeo subculture.

"What do you see, Madame Katydid?"

"The photo intrigues me, Tyler." Kate used her best gypsy/psychic inflection. "These people are all bound up in a mysterious relationship. The man is tall and handsome but hides scars beneath the surface. The older couple have taken him into their family as though a son, and yet still not legally a son. They have provided hope for the young man to exorcise the demons of his past and a hope for his future."

"What about the woman?" Tyler asked.

"She is a mystery. While she has a blood tie with the couple, her relationship is strained to strangeness due to hidden scars. Her future is unclear because she has difficult choices to make about who is in control of her life. Is it the young man in the other picture or the mysterious cowboy in this picture? Is it her parents or will she take control of her own life? Will she yield to the calling of the God of the universe or choose a path of least resistance and be a slave to convenience?"

Kate looked up at him, smiling in congenial fun.

"Or will she take box number three in exchange for what's behind the curtain?"

They both laughed as the phone rang.

"Kate Lawrence. ... Of course, Ambassador. ... I'm sure you are aware that this is a holiday weekend. ... *Oui, monsieur.* ... *Mais bien sur, monsieur.* ... I'd be delighted, Ambassador. ... Yes, I think there is someone I'd like to bring with me. Let me check with him."

Kate covered the phone with her hand.

"When are you going back? Will you still be here Monday afternoon? Would you like to go to a barbecue on the lawn of the French embassy?"

Tyler nodded, and Kate firmed up the details for the barbeque, French-style.

***

Kate and Tyler found her Beemer in her reserved slot in the parking garage. Tyler removed his hat as he folded his long body into the tiny black car.

"Guess these yuppie mobiles aren't made for arthritic cowboys," he said as his blond head brushed the header. "I took a cab from my hotel. It's near your place in Georgetown."

Kate started the Beemer and gunned the engine as she backed out of her spot in the nearly empty parking garage. She shifted into drive, and the powerful engine roared to life. She waved at the guard, and he waved back. She zipped out into the rush hour traffic and maneuvered skillfully through the maze of streets.

She finally found a comfortable spot in the traffic. "So what do you want to see while you're here?"

"You, Katydid; that's the only reason I'm here now. I've completed my business. Now it's time to woo milady." Tyler adjusted his seatbelt and turned to face here. "I wanted to see where you were when you weren't with me. After all, you saw my spread."

He grinned an infectious smile, and Kate couldn't stifle her laugh. She was so glad he had come after all. She wove through traffic to her favorite Thai restaurant. She helped him order and laughed at him as he grimaced at the unfamiliar variety of foods. She then took her turn to grimace as he told about the previous weekend's spills and chills. He also described fervently the work of Mission Mesquite and his role in it.

Finally, he pulled a burgundy velvet jewelry box from his jacket pocket.

"What's this?" Kate asked with trepidation. "Your personal gold toothpick?"

Tyler laughed. "Open the box, Katydid."

Kate opened the burgundy box carefully and gasped as its contents became visible. A solitaire diamond pendant on a platinum chain winked in the light. She turned questioning eyes on Tyler.

"I know we haven't known each other long. This diamond has a twin, set in a platinum engagement ring back at the ranch. It's waiting for you to be ready to accept it."

Kate stared, dumbfounded at the handsome cowboy and the sparkling diamond necklace.

"God has told me that you're the one. He's also told me that you're not ready to hear that or to commit to me or to Mission Mesquite because, yes, we come together in a package. So consider this a promise and a reminder of God's promise. No matter where you are in the world, someone loves you. And I promise that someday you'll be Mrs. Tyler Hawkins for the rest of our lives."

"I can't accept this," Kate stammered. "I'm so conflicted over the whole Mission Mesquite thing."

"I know," he stated patiently.

"No, you don't understand. I've been running from being the missionary's kid all my life. You're asking me to choose this for the rest of my life as well as for my children."

"Our children. Take the gift. The only strings attached are to my heart. I'll wait until you're ready to say yes, the third tick, Katydid. Forever, if necessary."

Kate did not know what to do. The Asian waitress brought fortune cookies. Kate set the box down and accepted a cookie that Tyler offered her. He took the remaining cookie.

"'Wise investments yield future rewards,'" Tyler read from his slip of paper.

Kate crumpled her fortune. Tyler scooped it from the table and smoothed it out.

"'Take opportunities offered by those close to your heart,'" he read. "Hey, maybe these fortune things are on the level." He reached for the burgundy box and slid the fortune into the top. "Another reminder, Katydid."

Kate smiled a reluctant smile and accepted the velvet box from his outstretched hand.

"This in no way commits me to anything? It's just a gift, right?"

Tyler nodded and smiled. "It's just a remembrance that a broken-down cowboy loves you."

***

Katie pulled into the Georgetown alley behind her condo. Tyler tried to jump from the car to open her door, but the catch in his leg hindered him from jumping out of the car. He succeeded in bashing his blond head into the edge of the top of the car. Katie spilled her purse rushing to his aid.

"Are you hurt, Tyler?" Katie brushed his head with her lips.

Tyler blushed and blundered his way out of the car. "Guess chivalry is dead."

"Nonsense." Katie grabbed his arm to steady him. "It's like Christmas. It's the thought that counts."

Once she was sure he was okay, she slammed the Beemer's door, scooped up the contents of her purse, and guided Tyler to safety. She unlocked the back door to the kitchen, threw her purse and briefcase onto the table, and hustled into the foyer to get the mail and check the answering machine. The grandfather clock in the hall chimed eight.

***

Tyler followed in her wake. The kitchen was small, white, and sterile. It needed a checkered tablecloth or a bowl of flowers to make it look welcoming. A small stack of mail clutter waited for attention in the corner desk area. Otherwise the kitchen was barren. As he passed the refrigerator, he opened it to see what she had. A few diet drinks, a wilted salad in a takeout box, and several condiment jars were the outstanding features.

"Help yourself to a drink, Ty!" She called to him from the foyer. A beep and a male voice sounded after her call. "Tyler, I need to return this call upstairs. Make yourself at home. I'll be right back."

Tyler closed the refrigerator door and meandered into the small living room. Or was it a parlor? The love seat was cream and blue. The rocker was Early American. The occasional tables were formal. The room was cozy in a formal way, like someone had tried to pull off eclectic with the details. He tossed his hat on the back of the couch and wound his way to the foyer. The grandfather clock reigned in the hallway. A hall tree held a raincoat, a straw hat, an umbrella, and a leash. The high table in the hall held the answering machine and the phone. Newly arrived mail scattered around the phone and machine, daring to be forgotten amidst the newer communications devices.

Tyler heard Katie's voice rise upstairs. It was tense and stern sounding, nothing like their evening's conversation.

"Doug, I have said all I have to say in that matter. I'll not marry you. I'll not date you. If I can at all influence it, I'll do my best not to work with you ... I am being reasonable, for once in my life. You're not good for me. You reinforce the things I try to get out of my life and my negative self-image. That I can do for myself, thank you... I'm sorry, Doug, but I'm hanging up now... No, I have company so don't try to call back. I'm getting on with my life."

The phone slam made Tyler grin in spite of himself. *And am I part of that life?* He asked himself. A door slam accentuated his thoughts and he smiled.

"You okay up there, Katie?"

A mumble answered his question. He smiled and settled into the love seat to wait on her return.

***

Katie grinned despite her anger. She had told him off. She had Tyler in her home. She was confident in a way she had never felt before. She washed her face and brushed back her hair. She slipped out of her suit and pulled on a sweatshirt and jeans. She checked her image in the mirror, and the sweatshirt reflected at her backwards, emblazoned with the American University of Paris. She slipped on the diamond pendant with her sweatshirt and jeans. She tried a smile and was pleased with the results after all.

She padded down the stairs in her bare feet and peeked around the corner to see Tyler snoozing on the love seat. She grinned and snuck up behind him.

"Guess who?" She covered his eyes.

"Better be my Katydid." He reached up and pulled her over the seat back and settled her easily in his lap. "You're wearing my diamond."

"And it's lovely and that's all it is right now: a lovely gift from a very special friend."

"It looks great, Katie. Actually, you look great, and I love your place. But it needs some life, Katydid. If you'll stop at the store after you drop me off at my hotel, I'll come over and cook breakfast in the morning. Waffles, if you've a waffle iron, or pancakes if not."

"You've got a deal."

Kate scooted off his lap and into the seat beside him. They talked for hours as though they'd not seen each other in years until both were yawning and clearly done for the night. Kate cranked up the Beemer and took him to the store where he bought eggs, Bisquick, milk, and strawberries for Belgian waffles.

After check out, Kate drove him to his hotel near her townhome. After a sweet, lingering kiss at the car, Kate drove home to put the groceries away.

***

Tyler took off his hat and smiled up at the stars twinkling in the heavens despite the light pollution from the District of Columbia. Then he turned into the hotel for the night.

He took the elevator to the fifth floor and used the entry card to open the door. The light beside the bed was on, and the covers were turned back. He rummaged through his bag to find his Bible to spend time with the Lord.

Chapter 9

Thunder rumbled in the distance. Kate looked at the clock and groaned. Tyler had said he'd take a cab over about 8, and it was 7:30 now. If she planned to get a shower before Tyler arrived, she'd better get herself out of the bed. She rolled over and stretched as she forced herself to a sitting position in the four-poster bed. Shoving aside the pink rosebud comforter and sheets, she dangled her feet over the side of the tall bed. The back doorbell rang as she stood on the air-conditioned chilly floor.

Kate reached for her robe and flew down the stairs to the kitchen. She tried to smooth down the tangles as she peeked through the curtains on the door. Tyler smiled back at her. She opened the door and hid her face.

"You're early, and I'm not dressed."

Tyler took her hands down from in front of her face and kissed her. "You look lovely. Go get ready, and I'll start the waffles."

Kate showed him where to find the supplies and waffle iron and headed upstairs. She called to him from the stairway. "Don't burn down the kitchen. The condo association frowns on kitchen fires!"

Tyler laughed in reply.

***

As Kate descended the stairs, the heavenly aroma of coffee and rich Belgian waffles wafted up to greet her. She suddenly felt ravenous – a condition she rarely felt since before, well, then. She checked the mirror in the foyer on the way to the kitchen. Her auburn curls were damp but semi-under control.

Ripe, red strawberries luxuriated in sugar and milk. Waffles steaming with melting butter awaited her. Tyler had opened her paper and was reading the comics. Outside the kitchen door, rain poured down with rumbles of thunder and flashes of lightning.

"So much for a picnic on the mall today." Kate alerted Tyler to her presence. "Guess we'll have to do something indoors. The Smithsonian maybe?"

"Good morning, Katydid. If I'm with you, I care not what the weather holds. You look lovely."

"Better than your first glimpse, I hope." Kate slid into a chair. "I don't remember buying orange juice or syrup last night."

"Oh, I liked the fresh-from-the-bed look." Tyler grinned as he looked up from the paper. "You didn't. I had the cabby take me to the store for the finishing touches."

Kate glanced around the kitchen. The cooking dishes were already washed. The counters were wiped. The pitcher of juice sat ready for seconds on the counter, and the coffee was freshly brewed.

"This is probably the most excitement this kitchen has ever seen. I could get used to this."

Tyler leaned over and kissed her cheek. "That's the idea," he whispered in her ear. "By the way, Doug called. He was quite put out when a man answered the phone."

Kate giggled as she poured the steaming coffee. "I'll bet. He's wanted me to let him spend the night for the past year. Do you think that's what he thought happened last night?"

"Well, he may have, and I didn't say one way or the other. He's quite a pest, isn't he?" Tyler teased. "Will you call him back?"

"Not when the waffles and coffee are hot, and I'm this hungry. Let's eat."

"After we bless the food, Katie." He took both her hands in his. "Father, thank you for this food and the chance to share it together. Bless it to our strength. And give us a day of fun, laughter, and love. Oh, and a little help with that project we've been discussing would be great, Lord. Amen."

Kate looked at him questioningly.

"Katydid research. Let's eat."

Kate and Tyler ate the strawberries, waffles, orange juice, and coffee with relish. They cleaned up the rest of the dishes together over laughter, towel swatting, and sweetheart kisses. When the phone rang and the caller id identified the caller as the rejected Doug, it went unanswered.

"Look, the storm is clearing." Kate looked out the window, seeing a robin-egg blue sky. "I'll gather some sunscreen, a blanket, and a Frisbee in a tote bag."

Tyler wrapped his arms around her. "Sounds great as long as we're together."

Kate felt the burn of the blush. He really was too good to be true.

Kate parked the Beemer in her reserved slot at the State Department secure parking garage, then they headed for the Mall like all the other 4th of July tourists. Steam rose from the concrete and asphalt promising a humid Washington DC 4th of July weekend. Puddles were already evaporating into the hazy sunshine. Kiosks for hot dogs, souvenirs, and ice cream were opening in time for the lunch crowd. Children climbed on the triceratops model, Uncle Beasley, in front of the Natural History Museum. Music blared from boom boxes on beach blankets under the shade trees, oblivious of the national treasures around them.

"There's so much to see and do. How can one ever do it all?" Tyler turned to take it all in. "The Lincoln Memorial on one end of the reflecting pool and the Washington Monument on the other, the Smithsonian Museums, the National Archives, the Capitol, the Holocaust Museum."

"There's a new one too. The Newseum." Kate pointed out an assortment of monuments honoring heroic, historic figures in United States history, including The Vietnam War Memorial Wall, jutting from the earth as well as.

"What should we do first? It's overwhelming."

Tyler looked into her eyes. Kate's heart skipped a beat.

"The American History Museum is my favorite." Kate pulled Tyler across the Mall and into the cool A/C of the museum.

After exploring the exhibits, they ate lunch in the cafeteria in the basement. Then they found a shady spot to warm up from the chilly A/C in the museum.

They tossed the Frisbee a while before others invaded the green, historic space. Then they trundled off to see the dinosaurs, the Hope diamond, the Constitution and Declaration of Independence, and finally, the aeronautical wonders of the Air and Space Museum. Kate was a knowledgeable tour guide since she had often taken diplomatic visitors, especially those requiring a French language version, on tours of the amazing sights of the District of Columbia.

By five o'clock, both were exhausted. Kate drove the Beemer back to the Georgetown townhouse to order pizza and relax in front of a chick flick video from Kate's collection. In the flickering darkness, leaning in Tyler's strong embrace, Kate looked up into his face, blurting out her question.

"Why aren't you already married?"

"I told you about Tina already."

"Sure, but that was then. This is now. Why hasn't someone else caught you by now? You're handsome, spiritual, stable, rich, and athletic despite your handicap. You have a lot going for you, Tyler Hawkins. Surely there are still groupies and wily women trying to catch your eye. Why hasn't some young lady saddled and tamed you for her own?"

Tyler paused and chose his words carefully. "Katie, I'm sure there have been women who would have liked to add me to a trophy shelf. And even some who have been genuinely interested in me as a person, not just a piece of horseflesh to tame. But since Tina, I've been, well, cautious. Almost skittish, you could even say, for four basic reasons."

He held up a finger. "One, I was afraid of being hurt and rejected again. Two, I was afraid of being lured back into a promiscuous lifestyle again. Three, I've been busy getting my seminary training and helping your dad with Mission Mesquite. Four, I didn't feel a reason to get involved with any woman until God told me she was the only one. Because, face it: What's the point of having a relationship, dating, if the woman isn't the one I would, should, or could marry?"

Kate nodded her understanding as she mused over his words. He must feel very strongly that she was worth pursuing. Who was she to question the source of his assurance in her? After all, how could she fight God? And why had she fought Him for so long already about everything in her life?

Tyler broke into her thoughts. "What about you? Why is such an intelligent, beautiful, and all around lovely lady as you still available?"

Kate rose swiftly from the couch. "Popcorn? I think I have some microwave popcorn in the pantry."

Tyler gently pulled her back onto the couch. "Don't change the subject. I can tell there's something you're running from. It's not just God or your missionary parents. Why is it so hard for you to trust? And why did you choose an egomaniac when you did make a choice? What's up with you?"

Kate pulled her legs up under her, scooting back into a corner of the couch and bear-hugging a throw pillow.

"My anorexia counselor says I have issues with control. I never felt I had any control over what happened to me on the mission field. Whether I was in France or Africa, I never knew when we'd be uprooted."

Tyler moved closer and stroked her arm. "Go on."

"Doug is stable. He's going to be here with me always. I do recognize that he feeds the anorexic impulses in me though. On some level, I know that's not a good thing."

Tyler moved closer and reached an arm around her. "I'm not going anywhere, Katie. I have my ranch, my horses, and Mission Mesquite. My location is fixed." The doorbell rang just as he leaned in to kiss her.

Kate bolted from the sofa and flew to the front door with cash for the pizza.

"Pizza? Anybody? I knew you had company and thought Tyler could use some food. I'm sure Kate hasn't a thing to eat here." Doug pushed his way past her carrying a pizza box. He placed it on the coffee table and plopped himself onto the couch. "Got some plates and napkins, Kate?"

Kate stood at the open door. "No. No. No. Doug, leave."

"She said 'leave'. Pretty sure that's what she meant." Tyler stood at the end of the couch and pointed toward the open door.

"Are you sure, guys? We could play a game or watch a movie. It'd be fun until you need to return to your hotel. You are staying at a hotel, aren't you?"

Before Tyler could answer, Kate shouted, "Not your business. I'm not your business. If you don't leave, Tyler could calf rope you and leave you on the hood of your car."

Doug stood quickly then. "Seriously, you would do that, Tyler? Hey, we're all friends here, aren't we?"

Kate shook her head and pointed toward the door. "Take the pizza with you. We can always order more food."

"Sorry, Doug. Nice effort, though. Do they teach that strategic maneuver in the diplomatic corps?" Tyler clearly was having a hard time maintaining a straight face.

"Keep the pizza and the cash." Doug straightened his shirt. "I'll be going then. Just trying to help. I know how hard unexpected company can be on the budget. Kiss?"

Kate shook her head and tried to hand him the money for the pizza.

Doug waved off the cash. "Well, enjoy the weekend then. If you need anything, just let me know. I can be here at a moment's notice."

As Doug backed out, he stumbled over the threshold. Kate slammed the door. Tyler began laughing. Kate joined him.

**

The next morning Kate was hit with a wall of humidity as she left the condo. "Not a cloud in the sky. 'Gonna be another scorcher of a day."

Kate arrived at Tyler's hotel at eight, as arranged. She found him in the lobby holding an intense conversation with a man who, based on the luggage at his feet, undoubtedly was a guest as well. Kate opened her mouth to speak but realized the two men were in prayer.

"… and bless Dan as he travels. Thank you for your saving grace for him this morning. Amen." Tyler finished his prayer and hugged the man's shoulders. "You will not regret your decision today. When you get home, join a church that will help you become the disciple God wants you to be."

The two shook hands. Kate caught Tyler's attention.

"Katie, come meet our new brother in Christ, Dan Waring."

Tyler pulled her into their small circle. She smiled and shook Dan's hand.

"Thank you. You have changed my life today, Tyler. You must tell me if you're ever in southeast Texas. You are always welcome in Beaumont." He handed Tyler his card.

"I will remember that."

Dan Waring picked up his luggage and headed for the waiting shuttle to the airport. Tyler guided Kate toward the hotel restaurant for an overpriced buffet brunch.

***

After worship at Kate's new church and lunch, Kate drove them into Virginia to the Manassas battlefield. Both were silent as they stepped out of the Beemer. They entered the National Park visitor center.

"Welcome to Manassas Battlefield. Two Civil War battles were fought on this land." The ranger handed them a flyer and a map. "If you have any questions, feel free to ask a park ranger."

Tyler paid the entrance fee for them both. He took Kate's hand and electrical charges went off all over Kate. She squeezed his hand back. They continued to hold hands as they browsed the display of pictures and artifacts from the battles of Manassas/Bull Run. They spoke in funeral whispers only, respecting the memorial of those who gave their lives in a fight for freedom.

When they finally reached the door onto the battlefield, Kate felt as though they had stepped into history itself. A hot wind ruffled the grass and Kate's hair. She clamped her broad-brimmed hat on and tied it down with a sheer scarf.

"Can't you just feel it?" Kate looked up into Tyler's face, avoiding looking into the sun. "Men died here. Lots of men died here."

Tyler's faraway gaze returned to her. "Blood-soaked soil is always sacred."

They used the map to explore the grassy plain, the small buildings, and the historic markers. Kate sensed the reverence Tyler held for this place and restrained herself from idle chatter. The grip of his hand grew tighter the more they discovered in this place. When her hand was numb, she escaped his grip to point out a bird. Once she'd grabbed his attention, he took her hand back.

"You're not getting away that easily."

His smile and touch brought goosebumps to her skin regardless of the July heat and humidity. She smiled back and squeezed his hand again.

"What's for dinner, Madame Diplomat? I think I've about walked enough for today." Tyler rested against a cannon. "My hip and leg are yelling at me."

"I never thought about that. I'm so sorry." Kate tried to pull away, but he pulled her closer.

"It's fine. I'm just ready to sit down with you somewhere. Let's look at souvenirs at the gift shop and then go get food." He stood and pulled her after him.

"I have no food at my house." Kate hurried to catch up with his long stride, despite his limp.

"I know; I ate the leftover slice of pizza while waiting for you to change after church. You don't even have condiments, no mustard, ketchup, or pickles. Do you ever eat at your house?"

Kate pulled away. The burn on her face was not from the sunburn she no doubt had acquired. "No. When I do, it's takeout. I usually don't plan to eat."

Tyler turned around and took both her hands. "I'm sorry. I didn't mean to bring up a hurtful subject."

"Let's stop at 5 Guys for burgers on the way back to the house." Kate pulled her hands back. "I'm fine. Forget it, Tyler."

She walked away, leaving Tyler to limp back to the National Park station behind her. She entered the gift shop and browsed the history books while Tyler caught up.

"Hey." Tyler stage whispered in her ear. "I didn't mean to say something insensitive. I need you to explain why what I said hurt you. I would never do so intentionally."

Kate turned to look at his puzzled face. "It sounded like something that would send me in a spiral toward collapse. Just when I thought you were safe."

He took her shoulders as she turned to leave. "I just need to understand."

"You know I have an eating disorder. Why would I need condiments if I don't eat?"

Tyler wrapped his arms around her and pulled her into an embrace. "Haven't you figured out that I love you, Katie. You can trust me to never hurt you intentionally."

"Did you say you love me?" Kate looked into his eyes. "And that I can trust you?"

"Yep. I love you, Katydid. And I will wait as long as it takes until you can love me, too."

Kate felt the stare of the gift shop patrons and workers. She pushed him back, causing him to stumble backwards into a bin of stuffed animals. She grabbed his hand and pulled him up.

"I'm getting this book. It's a Civil War romance *A Time to Choose*. I like to read before bed." Kate swallowed hard. Letting him in would be difficult after Doug. Learning to trust would be the big problem. But wasn't it always?

They went by the grocery for condiments and pantry staples. After picking up burgers, Kate and Tyler returned to her condo to eat and watch a movie.

She sat in his arms all evening, mulling over what he'd said. *Haven't you figured out that I love you, Katie. You can trust me to never hurt you intentionally.*

Kate drove Tyler back to the hotel. She pulled up under the covered area at the doors to the lobby.

"Good night, Tyler. We have one more day together."

Tyler leaned over and kissed her. "Promise me you'll think about coming to my ordination in two weeks. I know it's a hard thought for you, but I would want my future wife there, for support."

"I have a lot of work to do here. I doubt I can take any more paid vacation for a while." Kate felt nauseous. How could he be a missionary pastor? The one guy that loved her the way she was and that she loved. Some kind of cosmic joke, God?

"I'll see you in the morning then." Tyler got out, grabbing his hat. "Good night, Katydid."

***

Tyler checked out and waited with his bags for Kate to turn up to go to the barbecue at the French Embassy. He'd not slept most of the night after his declaration of love and holding her through the movie. It had been hard to say good night when Kate had taken him back to his hotel. Tyler pulled his hat down to shade his eyes and leaned back against the hotel.

The sun glinted off Kate's BMW as she pulled up.

"Good morning, Tyler. Hop in. You can see where I do most of my work today."

He threw his bags in the trunk that she had popped open, then settled into the low riding seat. After putting his hat in the back seat, he leaned over and kissed her.

Kissing her was like being bucked off a bronco, the jerk in your heart just before you hit the ground. She was definitely the one worth fighting for.

"You know I'll never let you go, right?" Tyler rested his hand on her shoulder as she pulled onto the street. "Wow, that sounded kinda creepy."

Kate flashed him a smile. "It's okay. I knew what you meant; I think."

A few blocks later, Kate pulled the Beemer into the French Embassy drive.

"*Bon jour*, Henri. Will you have a chance to enjoy barbecue with the rest of us?"

He shrugged his shoulders. "Only if someone arrives to take my place, *mon amie*. Introduce me to your friend."

Tyler leaned down to make eye contact with Henri. "Tyler Hawkins, sir."

"Tyler Hawkins! *Mon Dieu*, I watch the rodeo on TV all the time since coming to work in America. You are All Around Cowboy." Henri hurried around the car to shake Tyler's hand. "I saw the rodeo on the night you were hurt. I'm proud that you are still helping people avoid the same fate, sir."

"Call me Tyler."

A honk from behind reminded them that others still wanted to enter the drive.

"A pleasure, sir. *Mademoiselle* Kate is one of the best young women I know. You are happy to be with her, *n'est-ce pas?*"

Kate reddened at Henri's words and jumped from the car, so the valet could park it for them. Tyler grabbed his hat and unfolded himself from the car with pain. Kate ran around the car in her high heeled sandals, flouncy sundress, and broad brimmed sun hat. She took his arm.

"This is a working event. Whenever we're invited to a social event at another embassy, we're expected to turn up and have a good time." Kate stumbled in the gravel. Tyler pulled her back to safety. "Nice catch," she mumbled.

Tyler met all of the big shots on embassy row including Stefan Dremond, the French Ambassador.

"So glad to meet you. You must be the cowboy that all the gossip is about." Stefan slapped him on the back. "Sorry to have brought Kate back from Texas early."

"Still standing here, men." Kate tapped her foot in what might have been construed as impatience.

"And what a lovely flower she is, *n'est-ce pas*?"

"Yes, she is. I also think she needs a drink or food." Tyler shook hands warmly with the ambassador. He then steered Kate toward the drink table where Tyler ran into a flurry of napkins requesting his autograph.

Henri had informed all of the guests arriving after Tyler that a real American cowboy was in attendance, and his hat was a tip off to those interested in an autograph.

"I cannot believe that you are the hit of the barbecue." Kate shook her head. "Some of these people do not speak English, but they sure do speak cowboy."

"You're annoyed." Tyler finished signing yet another napkin.

"Well, yes. I have to take you to the airport after this party. I had hoped we'd have some time together."

He sat down on a patio bench and pulled her down next to him. He swirled his lemonade. "Well, sweetheart, fans pay the bills."

Kate slugged him in his upper arm. He leaned down to her and gave her a gentle kiss.

***

Kate parked in the Dulles Airport parking garage and hurried to the check-in counter after dropping Tyler at the curb with his bag. He was just finishing checking his bag as Kate hurried into the terminal.

They lingered outside the security line.

"Thanks for coming, Tyler. I had a great time." Kate placed a hand on his arm.

"Is that a tick, Katydid?"

Kate shook her head. "Not yet, Tyler. I'll admit that you are a much better choice than Doug."

"Seriously. If he continues to call and show up unexpectantly after I'm gone, consider an order of protection. He seems a little stalker-ly to me."

"Doug's a pest, but I have to work with him. An order of protection would mean one of us would have to quit a job."

Tyler nodded. "I checked. There's a French Consulate in Dallas." He raised his eyebrows.

"Good to know, but not ready yet. Who's stalker-ly now?"

Tyler leaned down and kissed her. "Guess that's my cue to leave. It'll take forever to get through security with the metal in my leg, even with a doctor's notarized statement. I should start now."

"Call me when you get home."

Tyler smiled a dazzling smile. "You bet I will, Katydid darling."

Chapter 10

Kate waited in the office of the French Ambassador. Her phone dinged a calendar reminder: Tyler's ordination, end of the week, at four on Sunday. She switched the phone to silent and replaced it in her jacket.

The phone rang on the office assistant's desk.

"I see. Yes, she's here. I'll tell her." She hung up and turned to Kate. "You can go in now."

The assistant jumped up to open the door into the opulent office of the French ambassador.

"Ambassador."

"Kate, *mon cherie*, your Tyler was the hit of the picnic last week. Join me for breakfast. A croissant, perhaps?"

A vision of the scales on her bathroom floor said, "Yes, eat. You're losing weight again!" The thought of the calories in that one croissant nauseated her.

"*Non, merci*, Ambassador. Too rich for my stomach this morning."

Stefan placed a pastry on her plate anyway with a few strawberries and grapes.

"Coffee?"

"*Oui, monsieur, si vous plait.*"

"Come, come. Call me Stefan. We've known each other for years." A look at her face sobered Stefan's attitude. "Not a social call, Kate?"

"Stefan, I'm here on official state business."

Stefan sighed and speared a sausage link, fruit and a croissant for himself.

"You are an emissary for the Secretary, I presume, regarding the farmers' strike."

"That's correct. The President of the United States is quite concerned about the residents of Paris. The news is that the roadblocks have effectively kept fresh food from entering Paris for a week."

Stefan's assistant brought in the rich mocha he knew she preferred from her favorite café near the French Embassy. She sipped the foamy top and set the cup down.

Stefan settled in his huge leather executive chair and laced his fingers together.

"The *Presidente* will not give in to terrorists, Kate. We must wait these farmers out. You have lived in the French countryside …"

"Half my life, Stefan," she confirmed.

"You know these men are quite… how do you say…obstinate."

Kate leaned forward in the antique French chair.

"Like most French men I've known, Stefan."

Stefan roared with laughter and popped a grape in his mouth.

"*Touché*, Kate. We will wait them out. There is nothing anyone can do."

Kate shredded the end of her croissant.

"Then I am to ask your permission, Ambassador, for the United States government to airlift food into Paris. Americans in Paris are beseeching the US embassy for help."

Kate plucked the greenery from a strawberry and licked the tart juice from her fingers.

"The US government does not need France's permission to feed Americans, Kate. You know that. There's more to this, *n'est-ce pas?*"

Kate sipped the hot mocha and relished the warmth it gave to her empty stomach. She knew she held the trump card and waited to play it as long as she could.

"The President plans to feed all of Paris, if necessary, Stefan."

Stefan rose from his chair and looked out the embassy window down onto Washington, DC.

"That would start a riot, Kate, and cause my *Presidente* to lose face. I cannot allow it."

Kate leaned back in her chair and sipped the mocha. She bit a grape in half and swallowed it.

"Then I am to tell you that we shall present our case to the United Nations. We are the last link in the diplomatic chain, Stefan. Children have no milk or bread."

Stefan walked around the desk and perched on the edge in front of Kate,

"What would you do, Kate?" he asked solemnly.

Kate felt the vibration of her beeper in her jacket pocket. She reached in casually and turned it off.

"My opinion? Stefan, surely you jest."

"Hardly, Kate. I know you to be a very wise woman, especially in satisfying the politicos. You see we are at an impasse, but we can neither one afford to be there today. What's your solution?"

Kate stood to look the ambassador in the eye.

"Compromise, Stefan. Compromise with dignity."

Stefan threw his hands in the air.

"Then we are lost because the *Presidente* will not compromise his position."

Kate sauntered around the room.

"But if he pleads mercy to allow the U.S. to provide the food, or meet with the farmers to stay the strike in exchange for negotiation, or meet their needs provided the food is brought to market immediately, then your *Presidente* becomes a savior for the city, a humanitarian, and the farmers' friend. It's a win-win if he plays his cards right."

Stefan shook his head. "The *Presidente* will not go for it."

Kate pointed her finger at the phone.

"You don't know until you ask, Stefan. This croissant is made from flour and butter. The wheat farmers and the dairymen cannot enter Paris to get to the baker. Grapes come from a vineyard and strawberries from a dirt farmer outside Paris. The sausage comes from a pig farmer. None of these things are available in Paris. If we were having this discussion in your capitol, you could offer me none of these luxuries this morning."

Stefan nodded. "I see your point, Kate. Very wise indeed. I will speak to the *Presidente* immediately and call you at your office." He offered his hand which she shook warmly.

"Before noon, Ambassador. The children will go to bed hungry tonight," she reminded him. "Let's be sure they can get breakfast tomorrow morning."

Stefan eyed her suspiciously. He wrapped a fresh croissant in a napkin and handed it to her.

"You need breakfast, too. Eat, Kate. You're losing weight again. The world can't afford to lose you."

Kate felt the bold rush to her face, accepted the croissant, and carried the cup of mocha with her. She greeted the embassy workers on her way out to the black Beemer and headed back to the office. She ate the tip from the croissant as she drove back to the State department. The phone vibrated again in her pocket.

"I'm almost there, Cindy. Chill." She turned her car into her reserved space.

***

As Kate breezed through the hall, Cindy waved to her frantically. Kate waved back and continued on to her office to catch the ringing phone.

"Kate, it's Stefan. You are a miracle worker. The *Presidente* intends to make a grand show of concern over the starving citizens of Paris and concede to the farmers' demands in principal to allow the food to flow into Paris. He has already set a time to meet with the leaders to iron out further details. As we speak, the roadblock is being dispersed, and the trucks are bringing food."

Kate grinned, leaned back in her chair, and bit into the croissant.

"I will tell the Secretary. You are a wise and persuasive man, Stefan."

"How do you think I got this position in America?"

Kate rang off and headed down the hall to the Secretary of State's office. When Kate returned, a huge fruit basket sat in the middle of the desk on top of the hot pink Post-it notes that Cindy used for immediate attention.

"Great job, Kate." John swaggered into her cubicle. "I see someone has already expressed their appreciation.

Kate laughed and read the card aloud, "To Kate Lawrence, a most wise and persuasive woman who will go far in diplomacy. Eat the fruit of your labors. Your humble servant, Stefan."

"It's nearly lunch, Kate. Let me treat you to the café across the street."

"I can't turn down that offer from my boss, John. I'm suddenly ravenous."

Kate and John headed out for lunch.

After placing their orders at the café. Cindy breathlessly ran in and grabbed Kate's arm.

"Kate, you need to call Tyler immediately. The number's back on your desk. Didn't you see it?" Cindy gasped. "He's been calling all morning, but he finally just told me what's going on."

Cindy sat down in a free bistro chair to catch her breath.

"It's your dad, Kate. He's in ICU in Dallas. He had a heart attack this morning."

Kate burst from the café and crossed the street to the blare of car horns. She dashed up the stairs two at a time in her heels. She searched the desk for the hot pink Post-it note, finally moving the basket to reveal the unfamiliar phone number. She rifled through her purse for her cell to place the long distance call. Cindy and John appeared in the cubicle doorway as she punched the buttons.

"This is Kate Lawrence. My father's there in ICU. Tyler Hawkins has been trying to reach me. Could you put me through to wherever he may be? … Yes, I'll hold."

Kate shuffled through the papers on her desk and handed documents to Cindy as she waited.

"Cindy, take care of these for me and make me plane reservations on the earliest flight that will give me time to go home, pack a bag, and still get to the airport in time to go through security. John, I don't know how long I'll be gone, but I really have to go."

Cindy took the papers, nodded, and scooted off down the hall. John nodded his consent.

"I'll go get our lunch packed to go, Kate. You need to eat something on your way."

Kate tapped her pen nervously as she listened to the elevator music on the other end of the line. Finally, the music ceased and a crackle indicated that someone was on the phone.

"Kate? It's Tyler. Thank God you finally called me back. I thought it would require an act of Congress."

"How's my dad?"

"He's resting right now, and they're doing some tests to see how much damage has occurred. He's alive, Kate, and he has good doctors looking out for him as well as the Great Physician."

"Cindy's making plane reservations now. I'll be there as soon as it's physically possible. I can catch a cab from the airport or rent a car. Just stay there with Dad." The tears began to flow unbidden once the stream of words had escaped her lips. "What about your ordination Sunday?"

"Don't know anything yet, Kate. Just come on, and I'll keep a watch on the situation and on your mom. Turn on your cell phone, so I can reach you though!"

Cindy rushed in with a scribbled itinerary.

"Tyler, looks like I'll be getting in late tonight. I'd better go if I'm going to make this flight."

Kate dutifully switched on the phone to find all the messages waiting for her on her screen. She gathered her belongings together, but she felt as though she was all thumbs. She grabbed the fruit basket and headed down to the parking lot. John waited by the black Beemer and handed her a Styrofoam container with her lunch. At the last second, he hugged her.

"Good luck. Call us and let us know any news."

Kate nodded as she revved the Beemer and screeched out of the reserved slot. She arrived at the townhouse in record time and threw clothing at the suitcase. A nightgown, a robe, the cowboy jeans and white lace over vest shirt, shorts and tee shirts, and bagged her black suit, in case. She changed into the yoked denim skirt and pink western blouse. The skirt drooped on her, so she grabbed a belt from the closet and cinched it around the waist. Her fingers grazed Tyler's wool jacket hanging in the closet.

Hospitals can be cold, she thought as she grabbed it out and wrapped it around her. The jacket was large on her in June, but now it felt huge. She felt the pain of her disease, but shoved it aside once again as she finished the packing and then hurried off to Dulles.

***

"Katie! Katie!" Tyler called out as she appeared from the jet way.

She ran into his arms, and he enclosed her in them.

She felt so frail, as though a hug could crush her. He held her close. Had she been this thin in June?

He noted that she wore the clothes she had worn to Medieval Nights on their last night together. They were at least a size too large for her. His concern shifted from the father to the daughter.

"How is Daddy?" Kate brushed away the sudden tears. "And how did you know which flight I'd be on?"

Tyler grinned and gave her another careful squeeze.

"I called Cindy back and got your itinerary. Rev. Ryan's doing well. They may move him to a step-down unit tomorrow. He's waiting on your visit. Let's grab your bags and head out to the hospital. Then we'll find an all-night restaurant. I bet you haven't eaten a bite all day."

"Part of a croissant, a grape, and a banana from a fruit basket. The stir-fry was tempting, but I left it on the counter at home," she confessed.

Tyler walked along with her in his exaggerated lope and went to get the truck while she waited for her bags at the luggage carousel. It was after midnight by the time they were on their way to the hospital.

***

"I just can't believe that he's in the hospital, Tyler." She speared a bite of omelet at the Waffle House. "He's always been so strong. Always so dependable."

Tyler stretched his arm around her and held her snug in his embrace.

"You know how bad I wanted you here for my ordination, but I never wanted you here under these circumstances."

"What do they plan to do?"

"Your father seems to think he can preach an ordination sermon from a hospital bed by Sunday evening and the other members of the council seem to agree." Tyler hesitated. "There's something else you need to know, Katydid."

Tyler's serious tone startled Kate. She laid down the fork and twisted around in his embrace.

"My appointment papers arrived yesterday. It's official. I'm your dad's replacement at Mission Mesquite. And they've accepted your dad's retirement papers as of January 1. I guess they feel it's important to go ahead and ordain me. That way when they commission me before Christmas, I'll be the real McCoy."

Kate ate in silence.

"What's up? What did I say?"

"Nothing," she responded. "I think the day has caught up with me. Could you take me back to the trailer?"

***

Friday dawn came too soon. Tyler dropped off a ticket to the rodeo for her. Kate drove her mother's cantankerous station wagon back and forth to the hospital to bring her mom fresh clothes and food, and flowers for the patient. The hospital personnel moved her dad to a step-down unit as promised and continued to assess the damage and plot a rehabilitation plan.

Kate fell asleep holding her father's hand while her mother had a lunch break. She awoke to the sensation of her hair being stroked back behind her ear and a light kiss.

"Mom?" She roused drowsily.

"No," said the deep voice. "It's Tyler. Go on back to sleep. You look like an angel."

Kate stretched and realized she'd was covered with the wool rodeo jacket.

"How long have you been here, Tyler?"

Her dad stirred and hoarsely replied, "Long enough to watch you nap for nearly an hour. Neither one of us had the heart to wake you." He chuckled his usual deep chuckle, but coughed a rasping cough at the end.

"Daddy, shall I get a nurse?" She jumped up, alarmed.

He waved her off as he coughed.

"I'm okay, Sweetheart. You go on and go to the rodeo. I'll be fine, and your mother will be here as soon as she has her a nap at home."

"She went home?"

Tyler nodded. "I finally convinced her to leave when she saw the two of you sound asleep. I took her home. I'll follow you to Mission Mesquite, so Miss Sarah will have transportation when she wakes up, and you can freshen up before the show."

Kate agreed. Back at the trailer, she hopped into a hot shower, and donned fresh rodeo appropriate clothes.

***

Kate walked to the arena from the trailer park in time to participate in the evening barbecue. She grabbed a plate and watched the server mound it up with dripping meat and vegetables. Snagging a Coke, she found a seat in a corner by herself. Kate surveyed the crowd from her corner.

Some of the folks were this evening's participants. Some were fans of the cowboys. Many were children full of excitement with barbecue sauce dripping down their chins. Kate grinned at the rodeo subculture displayed before her. They were almost a different country altogether, like France or Spain, to the world in which she lived. She smiled and cocked her hat back, feeling like a double-agent or a diplomat to a new country.

As she watched the crowd, Kate saw a tall curvaceous woman with long black hair stride in wearing too-tight jeans with fancy cowboy boots and a formfitting plaid shirt. The woman caught the attention of all the men in the room. She walked with a swagger and flipped the black glowing tresses behind her ear. Kate smiled as the men in the room gave a collective sigh. Behind her stood a cowboy with a black hat hiding his face. Her smile turned upside down when the cowboy turned to face the woman, and that woman kissed him longingly.

"Tyler?" Kate gasped.

Chapter 11

Tyler felt the blood rush to his face. Five years ago, he would have kissed Tina back just as passionately, but he was a different man now than the one he'd been then.

"Guava stain." Tyler wiped her lipstick from his lips. "It never was my color, Tina."

"Ah, but you wore a lot of it in those days. Don't tell me you've forgotten, Ty-ger?"

Tina sashayed her hips in a pout. She placed her hands on his chest and traced them down to his waist. Tyler held her hands firmly at his waist for fear of her next move.

"Ty-ger, we are still engaged, you know. I never did give back the ring."

Tyler held her hand up to the light. The diamond splintered the light into a million tiny rainbows all around the eating area.

"Just because you wear this ring doesn't mean that the promise it once meant still holds true, Tina. You are the one who left when I needed you. I'm not the same man you agreed to marry five years ago. We are not engaged. Besides, I've found someone else."

"Naughty, Ty-ger." She knocked his hat to the ground. "But I'll win you back just as soon as you take me back to our house, and we ..."

***

Kate saw the rock on her hand and knew with a sinking feeling who the mystery woman must be. She jumped to her feet and wound her way through the crowd.

"Well, Tyler, I was wondering when you'd join me for dinner." Kate handed him his hat. "I see you've found a new friend. Kate Lawrence." Kate extended her hand and tried to smile.

Tina took her hand with the diamond-studded left hand and dropped it swiftly. Tina moved to close Kate out of Tyler's sight, but Tyler slid around her with a lurch and grabbed Kate around the waist for support. He grinned down at her, but Kate with a shake of her head and a tense smile let him know he was in trouble.

"Charmed, I'm sure. Tyler and I go way back. He's my fiancé, though he's trying to wriggle out of that just now. Just 'cause I've been on the road for five years doesn't mean my heart has changed, Ty-ger."

She growled a low purr at Tyler.

"Katie, this is Christina Martinez. Tina, this is Katie, the love of my life."

It was hard to tell who was more shocked, Tina or Kate.

"Well, Katie darling," Tina purred, "just remember who has the ring. Watch me barrel race this evening, Sweetheart, and then you decide who deserves to be the wife of the best all-around cowboy and lover in Texas."

Tina flipped her hair into Kate's face as she turned to accept the offers of any number of men willing to give her a seat beside them. Kate's blood boiled at the insinuation that she wasn't enough woman for Tyler. She was not too pleased with Tyler's public announcement, either. Kate shoved his hand from her waist and stalked back to her meal in the corner. Tyler limped over to her table and sat down awkwardly across from her. One of the servers brought Tyler his food and Coke.

"What? What did I do?" Tyler pleaded with hands outstretched.

"Ty-grrrr, the best all-around cowboy and lover in Texas, whatever could you mean?" Kate mocked Tina's accent. "And what is this 'love of my life' stuff? Don't you think I should have known something about that if you plan to make it public knowledge? How long has she been hanging around Mesquite?"

"She turned up just after fourth of July. She's been all over me since then."

Kate's eyebrows raised.

"Oh, is that so? Does your ordination council know that you're the best lover in Texas? Do they know about your shameless fiancée? And that you've been leading on another woman on the side? This trip is about to get more interesting than I ever dreamed. And to think you're the man who plans to take over my father's work. You had better just chill out, Ty-grrrr."

With that she dumped his Coke in his lap and stomped out of the barbecue area. Diners applauded the impromptu entertainment. Kate looked back and saw Tina smile a seductive smile and blow Tyler a guava-stained kiss. Tyler rose and swept the ice and soda from his soaked jeans. He headed toward Kate as swiftly as possible, creating a jarring lurching movement which drew more snickers from the crowd.

"Katie! Wait up, Katie!"

Kate was almost to the gate when she was stopped by the crowd entering the Arena for the evening's performance. She had less success than a salmon swimming upstream, so Tyler finally caught her around the waist and turned her around.

Tears poured down on her cheeks and sobs escaped from her choked chest.

"How could you?" Kate blurted out. "How could you not tell me she was back in your life? How could you have … intimate relations with that, that woman?"

Tyler pulled her close, and Kate collapsed into his chest and cried freely. He guided her to a bench beside the rodeo shop and fished a bandanna out of his back pocket. She mopped up her tears and hiccupped as she began to breathe normally. He put his arm around her thin shoulders and pulled her close to him. She didn't fight him.

"Katydid, I never wanted to hurt you. Don't you see? I had already told her you were here and that I wanted you to meet her. She put on that whole scene for your benefit to try to put a barrier between us." He sighed. "I guess it worked, too. I was going to tell you that we'd been lovers, but it never seemed like the appropriate time to share what a cad I'd been in my life before I met Jesus. I told you I had a woman every night. Once I met Tina, I had Tina, every night."

Kate felt so nauseated she felt like she could vomit. The idea of that woman and Tyler, in bed, doing … well, that!

How could she ever compete with Tina? The thought came to her mind unbidden. And how could she ever give herself to him after he's … given himself to so many?

Tears started to flow once again. Tyler held her tighter, but she broke free from his embrace.

"Don't touch me. Don't even touch me, Tyler Hawkins. You may be the next reverend of Mission Mesquite, but I will never let you touch me again!" She shouted at him as she tried to escape from the bench.

Tyler caught her hand and pulled her down into his lap. She squirmed at his touch and at the intimacy between them.

"Katie, I do love you. What's in the past is forgiven by God. Won't you forgive me, too? I didn't know you then. I didn't accept God's laws then. I'm a new man now. Chaste. A spiritual virgin, just like you are no doubt a physical virgin. That sexual relationship is in the past." He whispered in her ear. "Forgive me, Katydid. You are the only woman that I will wait for. You are the one I want to share a wedding night with. Without you, I will be alone, forever."

Kate searched his eyes for some dishonesty, some lack of earnestness to reject his plea. What she found was a smoldering passion and sincerity. She slipped from his grasp as a rodeo administrator tapped him on the shoulder.

"Time to prepare for the evening's events, Tyler."

Tyler nodded assent and grabbed Kate's hand.

"Stay for the performance. We'll talk afterwards. Please. Tina wants to destroy us. Don't let her succeed."

She nodded and wiped her face with his bandanna.

"Having trouble with your little girl, Tyler?" asked the sassy voice. "What you need is a real woman who knows how to please you in all the right places."

"I don't need what you're selling, Tina. Go get ready to ride your pony and leave me alone," Tyler snapped.

He drew Kate to him and kissed her firmly on the lips.

"Don't forget that." He tipped his hat to her and then strode away.

Kate looked at Tina and saw glowing black coals in place of her eyes.

"This ain't over, Sweetheart. You don't know everything." Tina followed Tyler to the contestants' area.

Kate found her ticket stub in her jeans pocket and sat on the bench staring at it.

Should she stay, watch the show, and be snubbed yet again by the lovely Tina or leave and play into the hands of the competition? In the world of diplomacy, one never gives in on the first round. As a diplomat, she should give Tyler the benefit of the doubt and also extinguish the enemy.

She flicked the ticket stub as she thought and finally decided.

"Section A, Box 1, Seat 20." She spoke to no one. "I never give up my cards, Tina. I always play the full hand."

Kate found her seat and settled in for a full night of entertainment. When Tyler took Jake on a trot around the arena, he grinned at her and tipped his hat. She waved his bandanna to him like a lady of yore to her knight. It was a tournament but of a different nature. Tina scowled at her as she took a lap during the parade.

***

"Next we have the barrel racers!" called the announcer. "And our first competitor is the woman to beat in this circuit. She's been racing in another circuit for the last five years but decided to return to Mesquite to show us how the barrels should be run. Watch close, she's lightning fast; Tina Martinez on her Paint Horse, Lightning."

Kate scooted to the edge of her seat to catch her rival in action. Tina streaked into the arena at a full gallop. With black hair flying beneath her brown cowboy hat, Tina headed Lightning toward the barrel on the right, circled it cleanly and gracefully, and streaked toward the barrel on the left. The horse turned around the second barrel as though made of rubber and shot off toward the final barrel. Tina pulled the horse's head around the third barrel and started him on a gallop before they even cleared the third barrel. The electric eye counted her time. The crowd gasped.

"The time to beat is Tina's!" shouted the excited announcer. "She knows how to ride like lightning on her horse, Lightning."

Kate sank back in the chair.

"She's very good." Kate spoke aloud to no one.

"In fact, I bet she's very good at other things as well." The man in the next seat replied to her remark.

"I'd sure like to have the opportunity to find out," replied his friend.

Kate felt the blood rush to her face at their implication and turned away to look for Tyler. He sat tall and concerned on Jake as the next racer entered the arena. He seemed unaffected by Tina's ride and only busy doing his job. As she looked at him, he caught her eye and grinned. She grew hotter under the collar and looked away.

"And the best time for barrel racing goes to Tina Martinez's ride on Lightning," crowed the announcer. "Come on back tomorrow night, folks. Saturday's contestants will need to beat Tina's time tomorrow night. If they can't best it, Tina will win the prize money again!"

The crowd went wild as Kate sank back into her seat.

What chance did she stand with Tyler when Tina's such a good rodeo person? And when did she start wanting Tyler for herself anyway?

She shook her head to rid it of the crazy thoughts bouncing around in it.

She's not the woman I need at Mission Mesquite. Kate heard the quiet voice clearly in her heart. *The woman I need at Tyler's side is you, Kate Lawrence.*

Kate held her breath until she was sure there were no more revelations to be heard.

"God?" She whispered amidst the roar of the crowd. "Was that you?"

Chapter 12

Once all the festivities were completed, Kate walked around the arena to the horses' area, knowing she'd find Tyler there and afraid she'd also find Tina with him. As she entered the corral area, Kate found Tina wrapped around Tyler's body like a python. She caressed his hair and kissed him.

"Please, Tina," begged Tyler. "Please just leave me alone and find someone else. My heart's spoken for and I don't live the lifestyle we used to live. Surely after all these weeks you've seen that I'm different."

Tina shamelessly caressed his body as he attempted to release her grip on him.

"Oh, sure, you're different," said Tina seductively. "But if you had a real choice in a woman, you'd kill to have what I'm offering you tonight. I was yours once. I'm only giving you back what's rightfully yours still."

Tyler gasped as she traced a finger in an erotic zone. He forcefully shoved her aside. Tina laughed a little laugh.

"You know you want me, Tyler. Forget little miss goody two-shoes and come back to me. Let's pick up where we left off before your accident."

Kate perched on the fence as she watched the wrestling match before her. Tyler seemed truly embarrassed by her overt sexual actions, yet she could tell he was also very tempted to give in to her wiles. The struggle was not just physical; it was also spiritual.

"Ty-ler." Kate called to him playfully in as seductive a voice as she knew how to conjure. "Aren't you going to take me out to the hospital to visit Daddy?"

Tyler and Tina both spun around in surprise. Tyler blushed with embarrassment while Tina bleached in visible anger. Tyler escaped Tina's clutches and wiped lipstick from his mouth and cheeks with a handkerchief.

"You are a lifesaver, Katydid," Tyler whispered to her as he kissed her lightly. Tina's perfume wafted over him above the smell of the horses and manure. "I don't know what I'd do without you. You're a Godsend."

Kate allowed him to help her down from the fence. She made a great show of hugging him chastely and returning his kiss.

"I know." She smiled up at him. "You owe me."

He laughed, and they left the corral hand in hand. Tina spit into the dust.

"I'm not through with you yet, Mr. Hawkins," she called after him. "Or you either, Miss Lawrence."

***

The Dallas expressway was frantic even though it was nearly midnight. Tyler and Kate rode in silence to the hospital with the strains of a country-western station in the background. As they reached the hospital lot and parked next to her mom's station wagon, Tyler reached across to Kate to stop her from opening the door.

"I meant what I said, Katydid. You are the love of my life. I don't want or need Tina in my life. She represents everything ugly about my past life."

Kate looked at him carefully.

"But you do want what she has to offer; any fool could see that much."

Tyler rested his head against the back of the truck cab.

"It's almost like a drug addiction, Katie. I know sex with Tina is destructive to me. I know it's not God's will for my life. Nor is it compatible with my ministry here." Tyler struggled to explain. "But it's definitely seductive and tempting. I admit it. I've had trouble resisting her ever since she's arrived in Mesquite once again. And she sure turned up the heat tonight for your benefit."

"So I see," Kate replied wryly. "I guess that makes me chopped liver in the seduction arena, huh?"

Tyler turned in the seat to face her.

"Hardly," Tyler replied huskily. "I'm even more attracted to you, in so many other ways, Katie. But unlike Tina, God is teaching me to master those desires for a special occasion - our wedding night."

Kate's heart leapt in her chest. The look on his face was of pure desire. Warning bells sounded in her head as her heart pounded.

"I think I'd better go check on Mom and Dad. Thanks for the ride, Ty-ger." She teased him lightly and jumped from the truck before he could touch her and discover her desire for him. "I'll see you tomorrow morning when you come to pick up the kids for horseback riding at Green Pastures. I'll drive Mom home tonight."

Tyler smiled, noting her reaction to his pronouncement.

"Call me if there's anything you need, Katydid. You know the number." He spoke darkly and winked.

She nodded and ran into the hospital lobby.

***

Tyler returned home to a dark house. He parked in back and came up onto the deck to reach the kitchen and bedroom and avoid the empty front of the house.

"It would feel so much emptier tonight without Katie here to fill it," he said aloud as his boots thudded on the deck timber. "Oh, Katie, would that I could bring you home some night soon."

He opened the unlocked door to the kitchen and flipped on the overhead light. The fan turned lazily into motion. Tyler dumped out two prescription capsules, turned on the faucet and filled a glass with water. He drank it slowly, taking the pain medication with the draught. He stretched to his full height, touching the ceiling and then flipped off the light. He stripped off his shirt on the way to the bedroom and dumped it in the basket as he reached the bathroom. After brushing his teeth and stripping down to his briefs, he climbed between the cool cotton sheets. As he stretched, he touched something, someone, in the bed. He rolled over urgently and flipped on the night-stand lamp.

"Hey Ty-ger, 'bout time you got home." The naked woman with ebony hair purred in the bed beside him. "Think you can resist me now?"

Tyler jumped from the bed as though it was on fire.

"Get out of my bed!" He cursed inwardly at the pain in his hip and the fire in his loins. "Get out of my house and out of my life, Tina!"

She smiled a lazy catlike grin as she stretched in the soft yellow light.

"You don't really mean that. You really want me just like I want you."

Tyler grabbed the comforter from the bed, snatched his clothes from the laundry basket as he lurched past the bathroom, and carried it all off to the den. In the den, he dressed hurriedly and lurched out to the truck with the comforter. He drove out to the corral and bedded down in the stall next to Ariel and Asher. He could hear Tina's shrill laughter as he left the house in his dreams the rest of the night.

Chapter 13

"Katie, call Tyler while I take a shower and let him know about your dad's test this morning," Her mom called from the bathroom.

"Okay, Mom." Kate hesitated and then dialed the phone.

"Hello?" A sleepy female voice answered.

"Oh, I'm sorry, I must have the wrong number." Kate apologized to the unknown voice while a nagging fear caused the hairs on the back of her neck to raise.

"Are you looking for Tyler Hawkins?"

Kate froze in the process of hanging up. "Yes?"

"Oh, he's already gone out to the barn to check on the horses. Can I tell him who called? Or shall I guess, Kate Lawrence?"

Kate slammed the receiver down on phone. Conflicting emotions warred within her. Finally, reason reigned, and she called the corral.

"Green Pastures, this is Tyler. How can I help you?"

Kate steeled herself to keep from crying. "Tyler, it's Kate. Do you know there's a woman at your house?"

Tyler kicked the side of the stall. "You mean she's still there? What gall!"

"Indeed, what gall." Kate repeated the words softly. Suddenly she understood; Tina had gotten what she wanted after all.

"No, Katie, don't get the wrong impression. I didn't sleep with her last night. I slept here, in the barn. She was in my bed when I got home last night, and I left her there and slept in the barn."

Kate was silent. She wanted to believe him. Her head said that what he said was unlikely. She heard Asher and Ariel whinny in the background.

"Katydid, are you there? I didn't sleep with her; I swear on all that's holy. My commitment is to you, to the Lord, and to Mission Mesquite."

Kate found her voice at last.

"Daddy's having a test this morning, so Mom and I are going to the hospital in about half an hour. Hope you and the kids have a great time with Tina."

Kate hung up on him as he was trying to say something else. She didn't want to hear anymore. She didn't want to hurt anymore. She didn't want to cry anymore.

***

When Kate turned into her dad's room, Tyler was sitting at the edge of the bed in deep discussion with him. Kate turned around immediately and walked back into the hall. Tyler jumped to his feet and wrenched his hip. He started off after her once the pain subsided. He found her staring out the window in the visitor's waiting room.

"Katie."

He tried to put his arms around her, but she shrugged him off.

"Katie, please, listen to me. I didn't …"

Kate whirled around to face him.

"I don't want to hear anymore from you, Tyler, about why that woman was in your bed. I don't want to hear you tell me about how you want her body, but want to marry me. I don't want you to tell me the things I want to hear, but hurt me when you can't deliver on what you've said. I can't stand anymore rejection based on sex. I will not have sex with you before we marry, any more than I'd have sex with Doug before we were going to marry. I may die an old maid, but at least I'll have been an honest old maid who held onto whatever values I had left. I don't need you or Mission Mesquite. I have an important job that I'm very good at and I'm going back to."

Tyler started to speak, but Kate hushed him.

"No, you listen to me for a change, Mr. Hawkins. I'm here for my father, not for your pleasure. I'll stay until my father is better, and then I'm out of here. End of story. What happens to you, Miss Tina, and Mission Mesquite is none of my business."

She felt a tug at her heart but tried to ignore it.

"Katie." Tyler twisted his hat in his hand. "Please don't do this. Please don't throw us away over the conniving of that woman."

"Then throw her out of your life and out of your house, Mr. All-Around Best Cowboy. Don't tell me you can't take some responsibility for the fact that she's in your bed. Being a Christian doesn't mean being a wimp. Stand up for yourself, Tyler. Be the man God wants you to be. And don't call me until you can tell me you are through with Tina, once and for all."

Kate turned her back on him and watched the sun rise above the skyscrapers downtown. When she turned around, Tyler was gone. She collapsed into a stuffed hospital chair in the sunlit room.

God, why? Why now when I've told him to go away, do I find that I love him?

***

Tyler drove out to the trailer. He picked up the noisy, excited children in the old van marked "Mission Mesquite" and drove them out to the corral.

"Joe, take care of this bunch. I have something to do, and Miss Sarah's at the hospital with Rev. Ryan."

Joe nodded and helped the children onto their horses while Tyler rode Asher back to the house. As he galloped up to the house, he saw the red sports car he'd missed the night before parked in front of the porch. When he entered the kitchen, Tina sat at the table watching TV, drinking coffee, and smoking a cigarette. She wore his burgundy bathrobe and her hair was a tangle.

"Put out the cigarette, Tina."

"Ah, lover. You finally return to finish what we started last night."

She blew a cloud of smoke into his face. He waved it away with a cough, snatched the lipstick stained cigarette from her lips and drowned it in the sink. As she started to light another one, he grabbed the lighter from her and trashed it.

"Ah, come on, Ty-ger, you know I got to have my cigarette with my coffee in the morning."

Tyler turned off the TV and dumped her coffee down the drain.

"That's just one reason I don't want you in my house. Get out, Tina. Give me back the engagement ring. Leave me alone."

Tina laughed. She stood up against his chest.

"What's wrong, Sweetie? The barn not so great a place to sleep? Or is it that your little girlie has her shorts in a twist over me spending the night in your bed?"

Tyler grabbed her by the shoulders and marched her toward the bedroom.

"Hey, I'll go willingly to your bed; no need for this military march stuff, Ty."

"Take off my robe. Put on your clothes. Leave this house. Leave the ring while you are at it." Tyler shoved her into the bathroom, threw her clothes in after her, and shut the door.

"Can't we at least talk about this?"

"No!"

"But what if I want to get saved like you? Don't you have to try and save me, Tyler?"

Tyler thought about Tara. Fear welled up inside him. How could he ever hope to change this woman without losing Katie? Was she capable of repentance?

"You can talk to Rev. Ryan. He's in the hospital today, but he's supposed to be out tomorrow to preach my ordination service."

Tina opened the bathroom door dressed in her jeans and western shirt from the night before.

"You? A reverend? You've got to be kidding." She laughed aloud. "So, no more sex for you, huh? No more beers or women, except little miss goody two shoes."

Tina tossed the ring to him. He lurched to catch it in mid-air.

"Don't fool yourself, Tyler. What would I want with a cripple like you anyway? You'd just slow me down. Nobody can do that. Your God can't do anything for me that I can't do for myself. Just remember when you bed down your sweet-as-pie-Katie-doll that you could have had a real woman instead of a beginner."

Tyler pointed to the door and bit his tongue for fear of the words that would come out of his mouth if he spoke. Tina sashayed through the empty hallway, boots clicking on the wooden floor. She turned as she opened the door.

"Looks like an empty house without me, Tyler. Call me if you get lonely, so I can turn you down."

Tina slammed the door and all the windows in the house rattled. Tyler finally let out his breath with a sigh. He heard the car rev and roar off, spinning gravel all over the lawn.

Tyler opened the door and watched the spray behind the red car as she sped toward who knew where next. As long as it was out of his life, he could live with that. He went out onto the porch, then slumped down into the swing and began to pray. The smell of Katie's perfume overwhelmed his senses from the old blanket he kept on the porch. Katydid's favorite spot. He pulled the blanket to him and inhaled its scent. When she was here, this is where he'd find her. If he ever needed her, this is where she'd be.

***

Kate walked into the arena outer hallway with her dad, freshly released from the hospital and stubborn to be here for his cowboys, and her mom just in time to hear the announcer name Tina the winner of the barrel racing prize money. They walked on to the participants' area where her dad was greeted warmly by all the cowboys and cowgirls. Tina snubbed them as she brushed past by with her check.

"This ain't over, sister." She hissed at Kate as she passed by. "You and Tyler don't know everything, ya know."

Kate refused to satisfy her with an answer, but a warm glow told her that Tyler had done just what she'd told him to do.

"What was that all about, Katie? When did you meet Tina?"

Her dad put his hand on her mom's and hushed her as Tyler entered the corral walking straight to Kate.

"Can we talk?"

Kate nodded, and they went out into the night away from the hoopla. Tyler helped her up onto the fence rail and then climbed awkwardly up on it himself.

"Forgive me, Katie, for asking you to forgive the impossible."

Kate nodded. "That's my business. Smoothing over the mistakes of others."

"No, I mean it, Katie. I never expected Tina to come between us because I didn't think she was a problem for me or for you. I was wrong. I still don't know what she wanted from me. She made it quite clear this morning that I'm less than desirable. A cripple."

Kate turned to him and placed her hand on his knee. "That's not at all true, Tyler. I find you desirable."

Though it was summer, a cool night breeze blew. Kate pulled the rodeo jacket up around her shoulders.

"I've got something to show you, Katydid." Tyler pulled Tina's engagement ring out of his pocket. "I want you to have this. Have it reset however you like. I can't use it."

Kate hesitated and then took the ring. It was several sizes too big for her fingers. They laughed.

"Are you sure? This diamond is worth a fortune."

"You're worth more to me, Katie. So much so that I'd like to give you this, too."

He pulled a black box from another pocket in his jacket. He flipped open the tiny box to reveal the spectacular twin marquis diamond that shimmered in the street lamp light.

"Will you consider marrying me, Katydid?"

Kate hopped down from the fence and leaned against it.

"I don't know, Tyler. I'll consider it, but I can't give you an answer right now. So much has happened in the last few days, I don't think it would be fair to you or to me for me to decide tonight."

Tyler hopped down off the fence and circled her waist with his strong arms. He held her tight, but she didn't struggle to get away from him.

"I love you, Katydid. I'll wait forever for your answer. Keep both rings. When you're ready, wear the one I bought for only you."

"I think I love you, too, Tyler. But I'm so afraid of living this Mission Mesquite lifestyle. I never wanted to marry a minister. It scares me."

Tyler turned her around in his arms and kissed her tenderly.

"Don't be afraid. If this is what God wants, then he'll help us do the right thing."

Her parents found them there under the street light. Kate caught the wink her parents gave each other. She pulled away from Tyler's embrace.

"Hey, you two, time we got back home. Tomorrow's a full day, what with service in the morning and ordination and the reception in the evening."

They held hands on the way back to the Mission. Once her parents had entered the trailer, Tyler kissed Kate good-bye, then he whispered into her ear. "Until tomorrow."

***

A brilliant sun greeted the day. Kate dressed quickly and went out to get the Sunday paper on the drive. Sleeping on the front porch was a little bronze boy with straw-colored hair.

"Good morning," Kate whispered into the little boy's ear. "Wake up, it's a beautiful day."

The boy stretched and rubbed his bright brown eyes. He looked around frantically. "Where is she? Where's my momma?"

Kate took the frightened little boy into her arms. He threw his brown arms around her and began to cry.

"What's your name, Sweetheart? How old are you?"

"Tyler Miguel Hawkins. Momma calls me Miguel. I'm four and a half years old."

Kate pulled the boy away and looked into his eyes.

"What's your momma's name, Miguel?"

"Tina Martinez. She's a barrel racer."

Kate clasped the child to her chest and rocked him. Her mother came out onto the porch to find tears streaming down Kate's face and the boy's face as well.

"Mom, call Tyler and tell him to get over here now. Tina was pregnant when she left him five years ago." Tina's words echoed in her head, 'You and Tyler don't know everything'.

Just as her mom was rushing into the trailer, Tyler's truck bounced into the driveway and screeched to a halt. Tyler lurched toward the porch with a letter in his hand. He climbed the steps and came to the place where Kate sat holding the boy.

"Are you my daddy? Momma said I'd meet my daddy this morning if I just waited on this porch. But I fell asleep. You look just like this picture I got of my daddy."

Miguel showed Tyler a crumpled picture torn from a rodeo program of himself five years ago receiving the gold belt buckle. Tyler opened his arms to the small boy, and Miguel scrambled up into his muscular arms. Tyler didn't speak but held the boy tightly.

Finally, he answered the boy's question. "I got a letter from your momma this morning telling me you'd be here this morning. She tells me that I'm your daddy. I never knew you were born, Miguel. I wish I had known before today."

"Momma said I get to live with you now 'cause she's gonna take Lightning to a new rodeo place."

Tyler nodded his head.

"That's what she said in her letter that she wants for you. I guess we'll have to make you a room at my house."

"All right!" Miguel hugged him tight and wiped away his tears. "When's breakfast? I'm hungry as a bear!"

Tyler laughed. "I bet Grandma Sarah can find you something, Miguel."

Miguel scrambled down from Tyler's arms, took Kate's mom's hand, and entered the trailer in search of sustenance. Tyler sank down onto the porch step nearest Kate. Kate wiped her tears and read the letter Tyler offered her.

"So she says she's out of your life, and she's left you Miguel to remember her by?" Kate exhaled the breath she hadn't known she'd been holding. "And gave you legal custody papers at that. How handy."

She waved the documents at Tyler. Then she folded them up and stuffed them back into the envelope.

"Congratulations, Tyler. It's a boy," Kate stood up from the porch and headed down the stairs.

Tyler struggled to stand to follow her.

"Stay with Miguel. He's already had one parent abandon him today. I'm going for a walk. Tell Mom and Dad I'll meet them at the Arena in time for worship."

***

Tyler banged his fist on the porch rail as he watched her walk down the driveway. Miguel stuck his head out the door.

"Daddy? Grandma Sarah wants to know if you want eggs, too. That's what I'm having."

Tyler scooped the tow-headed boy up in his arms and tickled him until he laughed out loud.

"Of course. If that's what you're having, that's what I'm having, too. We're family now."

***

Kate saw them drive up in the old van. Tyler and Miguel climbed out together, and Miguel sprinted across the parking lot to meet Kate.

"Tyler tells me you're the Katie ladybug, or something like that. He says he wants to marry you so we can all three be a family. Why don't you want to stay here and marry us?"

Kate squatted down to receive the small bundle of energy into her embrace.

"Miguel, my job is in Washington, DC. Do you know where that is?"

Miguel shook his head solemnly.

"That's where the President of the United States lives, Miguel; and it's a long way from here. For me to move out here requires giving up my whole life back in Washington. I want to make sure it's the best decision for all three of us."

Miguel nodded. "It is, Katie ladybug. Daddy loves you; he told me so! And you sure are nice. I want you to come live with us, too."

Kate kissed his brown cheek.

"Maybe someday, Miguel." He hugged her tightly around her neck and then broke free of her embrace to grab hold of Tyler's hand and drag him off to see if the animals were up yet. Tyler shrugged and allowed himself to be towed away. Her parents laughed at the small boy's energy and curiosity.

"What do you think, Katie?" Her dad grasped her elbow. "Think you can handle two men of indomitable spirit?"

Kate ignored his question. "I have tickets to return to Washington tomorrow. You seem to be doing okay, and there's a lot on my desk right now."

"And Tyler?" asked her mom. "What about him and Miguel?"

Kate shook her head. "I can't think about that now. I need some space to think and pray about it. Miguel complicates the whole picture even more than before. Whatever I decide to do must consider Miguel as well as Tyler."

"I understand, Katie. I'm glad you'll be here tonight for the ordination council, though."

"Well, I don't understand that at all. Why is the mission board ordaining a man who had an ongoing sexual relationship with a woman who was not his wife? Oh, wait. He also has an illegitimate son who conveniently shows up on the day of ordination. Who holds him responsible for an ungodly lifestyle? Didn't you teach me that a minister's lifestyle must be beyond reproach?"

Her dad caught her hand and pulled her onto a bench beside him. Animal sounds and smells punctuated the air. "Only God makes that decision."

Her mom rushed over to them. "Dad's just home from the hospital. Don't stress him. We can have this conversation another time."

"So some people just get a pass on their behavior. God just loves some people more than others." Kate jumped up from the chair. "I'll be packing while you get ready to celebrate the sinner you're elevating to sainthood. In fact, I'll get a room at the airport hotel for tonight. You needn't bother worrying about me."

Kate took off across the Arena lot to the trailer park.

When she arrived at Mission Mesquite, she slammed each door she came to. They never locked anything 'so anyone can come in and pray'. When she came to her 'special guest room', she slammed that door twice.

"They're always trying to package me in a neat box. And if the box I want doesn't fit the one they pick, then my box is wrong. Maybe my box doesn't want to be in Dallas or anywhere near Mission Mesquite."

She threw the suitcase on the bed.

"I'm not following 'God's will for my life', but they can embrace a man who lived an ungodly life until, oh, four and a half years ago."

She grabbed the clothes from the closet, hangers and all and slung them onto the bed. She pulled clothes from the hanger and threw the hangers back into the closet. She continued to mutter as she folded and deposited clothes into the suitcase.

After a while, Kate sat on the edge of the bed. As her head of steam dissipated, the tears began.

***

Kate heard her mom enter the trailer and each of her footsteps as she came down the narrow hall then rapped on the door.

"Katie? Are you okay?"

Kate slammed the door to her closet. "I'm just great."

Silence punctuated the other side of the door. "What about grace? What about forgiveness?"

Kate slammed her suitcase closed and snapped the locks. "Where was the grace and forgiveness from you and Dad when I was growing up?"

Her mom pulled open the door. "Are we having this conversation again? I thought we were talking about Tyler and Miguel."

Kate collapsed on her bed and let out a deep breath. "Yes, we are talking about Tyler and Miguel."

Her mom sat beside her and took her hands. "Katie, all of us are human, whether we are saved or unsaved. We make big mistakes that affect our lives. God forgives the sin, but sometimes the consequences follow us."

"Miguel."

"Yes. And not Miguel's fault."

Kate stood and gazed at the Dallas skyline out her window. She closed her eyes and pictured the sweet brown boy. Not his fault. But how could she ever see Tyler the same? It was one thing knowing he had sexual experience. Miguel was a constant reminder that she could never be Tyler's first.

"Stay. Come to the ordination. Forgive and extend grace.

***

The ordination went off with just a few inquiries into the origin of Miguel and the change in his life from drinker and carouser to minister of Mission Mesquite. The men from the association placed their hands and blessings on Tyler's head. Miguel sat between Kate and her mom and asked a million questions about what was going on. When Tyler stood after the ordination, his face glowed. Kate's heart jumped and knew what the right thing to do would be. She just wasn't ready yet to give up on her life in Washington. Tyler and Miguel would have to wait.

Everyone then crowded into the Mission van for a reception at Green Pastures. Kate ended up driving her mom's car filled with food for the reception. Tyler drove his truck with a newly acquired car seat for Miguel.

"Set out these mints in that dish and the nuts in this other one." Her mom created her favorite punch while giving directions. "Set those plastic forks near the napkins."

More cars drove up the gravel road to the makeshift parking lot.

"How many people are coming?" Miguel watched out the front windows. Tyler swept him up in his arms.

Kate smiled. Tyler would make a great father if he didn't make Mission Mesquite his only focus.

As the party and the noise grew, Kate slipped away with a cup of punch out to the porch to her favorite place, the swing. God always seemed close when she was there.

"I don't know if I have enough grace and forgiveness in me to do what You want me to do." She spoke her prayer aloud as though God sat beside her. "I said I would never marry a preacher, especially a missionary."

"And yet here's one who loves you, who's asking you to do just that. How do I overcome that title?"

Kate startled to see Tyler standing before her. "It's not proper to listen to other's conversations."

"It was out loud on my porch swing." Tyler sat on the swing beside her. "Still, how do I overcome the title 'Reverend' to win you as my wife?"

"Be the man who loves and cares for his family as a first priority from God." Kate rose from the swing. "Tell my mom I'm taking her station wagon back to the Mission. Good-bye, Tyler."

Chapter 14

As the party wound down, Tyler found Miguel on the porch swing. What was it about that swing? He carried Miguel into the house as he slept in his arms. He nestled the boy down among the pillows on the couch in the den. The phone rang, and Tyler rushed to answer it.

"Yes? … Yes, this is he. … I see. … Nothing else you can do? … But don't you think he should know where his mother is? … I understand. Thanks for your help, Chief."

Tyler hung the phone up quietly and limped over to the kitchen cabinet for his pain medication. He took the capsules and then pulled an envelope of papers from his pocket. One paper granted him full custody of Miguel. One paper granted him the title of Reverend Tyler Hawkins. What a bizarre day it had turned out to be. The phone rang again.

"Hello?"

"Tyler, it's Kate."

"Katydid, am I glad to hear from you. We've not had any time to really talk since this morning. Are you okay?"

"Tyler, I'm going back to Washington tomorrow morning."

Silence hung between them except for the static buzz on the phone line.

"Well, of course, you need to tie up loose ends before you can come back." Tyler's heart skipped a beat.

"Tyler, I have a job to do there. I have a life there. I need to go back and live it."

"You're saying 'no'."

"For now. Tyler, I can't say 'yes' yet. And Miguel only complicates everything. He's so sweet. And you'll be a great dad for him. I'm just not sure I'm ready to be his mom. And Tina may come back. That would be awkward."

"Is this what God wants you to do, Katie?"

Kate's answer was silence at first.

"Tyler, I think I know what God wants. But I need to do this first."

"Katie, be careful. It's dangerous to go about doing something other than what God wants you to do."

"Duly noted, 'Reverend' Hawkins." Kate's voice was strained. "When the time's right, we'll talk about marriage again. You've got enough adjustment with Miguel in your life now."

They said good-bye, and Tyler hung up the phone. Miguel called out in his sleep, and Tyler went over and sat beside him on the couch. He stroked his blond head and shushed him back to sleep. When he was sure he was asleep, Tyler covered him with an afghan and turned off the light.

As Tyler was stepping out of the shower, the phone rang once more. Tyler wrapped a towel around himself and lurched to get the phone before it woke Miguel.

"Tyler, it's Tina. Did you get my gift?"

"If by gift you mean Miguel, yes, I got him. What do you mean by just dropping him off at Mission Mesquite like some kind of donation?" Tyler felt his anger and his volume rise with each word he spoke. He reminded himself to be quiet for Miguel's sake. "Tina, why didn't you tell me about Miguel before now?"

Tina was quiet and a choked sob escaped across the phone line.

"I wasn't sure you'd want him complicating your life, Tyler. The man you were then, well, I loved you. But you weren't too patient with helpless things. And you didn't like things spoiling your plans. And you had big plans, Tyler Hawkins."

"I was selfish. Is that what you're trying to say, Tina?"

"But in a really sexy way, Tyler. I loved your 'take charge attitude' and your big way of living. I found out I was pregnant with Miguel the day of your accident. I was afraid to tell you because I thought you'd tell me to get rid of it."

Tyler groaned thinking of the man he'd once been.

"It's okay, Baby. That's just who you were. And I loved you anyway. But once I saw you were hurt bad, and that you might not recover, well, I just figured I'd have to take care of me and my child. Besides, I figured you'd turn mean on me."

"Oh, Tina. Was I really so terrible?"

"Well, like I said, I figured it was me and Miguel. You had enough to worry about. Who'd have guessed you'd find religion? I still can't believe it. But I figure it's time Miguel had one parent with his head on straight, even if your leg's not."

"Tina, I'm sure you've done a good job taking care of Miguel, in your own way."

Tina laughed. "You're way too kind, Ty. You know what the rodeo circuit's like. Being on the road and practicing, I paid more attention to Lightning than I did to Miguel."

Tina stopped and another sob trickled down the telephone line.

"Anyway, you're settled and sweet, and you got a good girl. Miguel deserves family. Not an RV park every night with a sitter he ain't never seen before and won't see again."

"Tina, why didn't you tell me earlier this summer."

"I wanted to see if you still wanted me. To see if we had any future. And when I saw what kind of man Jesus turned you into, well I loved you better than before. But I'm not the right girl for you now. Your Kate is a better match for the life you are destined to live now. And Miguel will be the better for me giving him to you."

"He misses you, Tina. He's wondering why you just left him."

Tina broke down in wrenching sobs.

"Tell him … that it's because … I love him … so much. And tell him … his daddy … is a good man … and to be good for you and Katie. I'll send him postcards and gifts. And I'll call some."

"And you'll be back to see him whenever you're here in Mesquite, right?"

Tina sniffled. "Yeah, if that's okay, Ty."

"It's fine, Tina. I'll tell him, unless you want to tell him yourself. He just climbed up here on the bed with me."

"Is it Mama?" the little boy asked shyly.

Tyler nodded and handed him the receiver. Tyler went to towel off and put on a robe while Miguel talked to his mom. When he walked back in from the bathroom, Miguel was stretching across the bed to hang up the phone. Tyler caught him as he tumbled toward the floor.

"Mama said you're a good man and to be a good man like you when I grow up," Miguel said softly. Tears glistened in his dark brown eyes. "She said she'll call and write me. Will you read me her letters until I'm big enough to read, Daddy?"

Tyler hugged him close and whispered into his ear. "Of course, little man. I'll help you out however I can."

"Can I sleep in here tonight, with you?"

Tyler laughed. "Tonight, yes. Tomorrow let's find you a bed and furniture for your own room, okay?"

"Okay."

Miguel climbed into the big bed and snuggled down between the sheets. Within moments, he was sound asleep. Tyler dressed appropriately and snuggled in beside him.

***

Tyler roused the child early.

"Hey, Miguel. We're going to go see Katie off at the airport. Wake up and get dressed."

Miguel rubbed the sleep from his eyes and frowned.

"Katie ladybug is going away, too?"

"Just for a little while, Miguel. Before you know it, she'll be back because that's what God wants for us and for her. He just has to convince her of it."

Tyler combed the mass of unruly blond hair into a windblown order while Miguel put on the clothes he'd worn yesterday.

"And we'll need to get you some more clothes, pal. Don't you have anything else to wear?"

"Yeah, but they got stolen in the washing place Saturday. Mama said you'd buy me more."

Miguel hugged Tyler around the knees. "You ain't gonna leave me, are you, Daddy?"

Tyler picked up the little boy and hugged him. "No way, no how. As long as I have choices, I'm not leaving you. And if I have to leave you, I'll be coming right back to you. Promise."

Miguel flashed a bright smile and wriggled down from his grip. He hit the floor running and headed for the kitchen.

"I'm hungry, Daddy. Do you have Cheerios or Fruit Loops?"

Tyler grinned and shook his head. Tyler followed his son to the refrigerator.

"The grocery is our next stop after clothes, Miguel. How about toast and jelly until we can get to McDonald's later this morning?"

Miguel whooped and hugged him briefly as he started opening doors looking for bread and condiments.

***

Kate hauled her belongings out to the station wagon. Her mom followed her to the car while her dad waved from the front porch.

"Rest, Dad. And don't worry. Let Reverend Hawkins shoulder some of the burden. It's his job, too."

Kate jumped into the front seat before her dad could respond. She smiled and waved energetically until they escaped the trailer park. Then she sighed and slumped down into the seat.

"You want to talk about it, Katie?" Her mom glanced over to her. "Sometimes it helps. God can talk through other people's advice, you know."

"I don't need advice, Mom. I know what I'm doing. I also know what I need to do, but I can't do it now. I have other things I want to do with my life before I'm stuck being a housemaid for a man and a child. I mean, look at me! Do I look like the motherly type? Tyler and Miguel need to get to know each other before there's another person in the picture. If God wants me here, He'll give me a big sign."

Her mom was silent for a few miles. "Maybe He already gave you the sign, and you weren't looking."

"What sign?" Kate was distracted by the early Monday morning Dallas traffic.

"Well, you are the one who found Miguel before anyone else. Tina left because she realized that you were the one Tyler needed in his life. And Tyler gave you the ring. What more of a sign can you ask for?"

It was Kate's turn to be silent. As they finally turned into the entry for Dallas-Ft. Worth airport, Kate turned to her mom.

"I'm almost late for this flight. Just drop me off at the entry." Kate cleared her throat and continued. "I need the sign to say it's safe, Mom. I need to know it's forever and that I can be a parent for this child without the urge to fly off to Europe. I don't want to leave Miguel to do what I feel God wants me to do after I've committed to be his mom. Don't take this wrong, but years of boarding school were not particularly nurturing. Teachers and house parents are not the same as your own parents. I don't want that kind of life for any child in my responsibility."

Kate watched her mom bite her lip and try not to cry.

"I love you, Mom. But I needed you all those years, and you weren't there."

Kate hugged her mom and jumped from the vehicle. She grabbed her bags from the back of the wagon and handed them to a luggage handler at the sidewalk kiosk.

"Kate, I'm so sorry." Her mom called out the open window. "We never meant to hurt you. We only wanted you to have a good education."

Kate tipped the handler and leaned back in the window.

"I know, Mom. Let me use the education you gave me. God will make it clear when I should change to the mommy-track."

"You could do both." Her mom's eyes pleaded with her. "Don't walk away from God's plan, Katie."

Kate wiped the tears from her face and blew her mom a kiss.

"It'll be okay, Mom."

Kate hurried into the terminal leaving her mom to drive back to Mission Mesquite alone.

***

Kate sat at the gate reading a discarded *USA Today* as her flight was delayed for another fifteen minutes. She heard the sound of running little feet, but shrugged off their importance to her. Suddenly, a small brown face with tousled blond hair appeared above the newspaper.

"Miguel. How did you get here?" Kate knew the answer was probably limping behind him.

"We thought we were going to miss you, Katie ladybug." He dived into her lap, crackling the newspaper into a mass of wrinkles. "But we got here just in time."

His brown arms wrapped around her neck and squeezed tight.

"You can't go." Miguel stage-whispered into her ear. "Daddy will be so sad when you leave, and I need a mommy while mine is away from me."

"He's right, Katydid." That familiar deep voice chimed in. "We need you to stay."

Tyler sat down in the chair whose back adjoined hers, leaned over and kissed her on the cheek. Miguel laughed and ran around to jump into Tyler's lap. People around the waiting area all watched her response. She felt the deep red flush from her toes up.

"I can't stay, Tyler. Not now. I'm not ready to give up my life for the life you represent. Maybe sometime …"

"Soon?" Miguel asked loudly. "You'll come back next week?"

Kate struggled to refold the newspaper and finally crammed the mess into the adjacent chair. She walked over to the huge panes of glass and watched the airline activity outside while tears slid down her cheeks.

Miguel sat in the seat vacated by Kate. Tyler appeared, reflected in the pane, and wrapped strong arms around her.

"It's okay, Katie. Take your time. We'll be waiting. Come back when you're ready."

Kate turned in the circle of his arms and sobbed into his chest.

"We are now ready to begin boarding Fight 393 for Atlanta with continuing service to Dulles. First class and passengers requiring additional time or with small children may board at this time."

Kate struggled free from his embrace.

"Don't make this harder than it already is, Tyler. I think love you. I just have to finish up the things I need to do before I settle into being a preacher's wife and mother. Understand?"

Tyler nodded and kissed her with passion.

"Finally, three ticks. I love you, Katydid. Call me when you need me, and I'll come. No matter what."

She nodded and embraced him. She then walked to Miguel and picked up him up from the seat and hugged him. Tears glistened in Miguel's eyes, too, as she handed him to Tyler. She picked up her carry-on bag and boarded the flight, waving back as she walked down the gateway.

She sat in an aisle seat because she couldn't bear to see that little boy waving good-bye. How they got through security to the gate she'd never know.

"Excuse me, Miss?" The flight attendant handed her a tissue. "Is there anything we can do to help?"

Kate hadn't even realized she was crying. She took the tissue and shook her head.

"Thanks."

***

After the chaos of the Atlanta airport and the bumpy flight to DC, Kate was glad to grab her bags and head out to a taxi since John had driven her to the airport. In the back of the cab, she texted her mom, dad, and Tyler that she was safely in DC.

***

Kate opened the mini-blinds in her office in the State Department. It was early, very early. It was her favorite time of day to come to work. The frantic pace of foreign diplomacy hadn't yet begun. She had slipped into the building practically unseen, which was a blessing. She was tired of explaining her relationship to Tyler. Tired of explaining her reasons for not going to Texas permanently. Tired of fingering the black box in her purse with the fabulous marquis diamond. Tired of struggling with God. The sun rising over the Potomac made her squint, so she turned back to her desk.

She pulled the satchel from her seat and eased into the rolling chair, adjusting the skirt that swam around her waist, cinching the belt another notch smaller. She flipped on her computer and checked e-mail. Four messages from Tyler. One from Dad. One from Mom. And a slew of messages, all marked urgent, from Stefan at the French Embassy. She looked down at the picture of a happier Kate, Tyler, Mom, and Dad in Dallas from May. She glanced at the small Bible on the desk. She reached for it, caressed the leather cover, but drew her hand back to tap the computer keys to retrieve her mail.

Dearest Katydid,

It's early afternoon, and I'm thinking of you. I wish you were with me. But, hey, no pressure! Not even a little boy who asks about the Katy ladybug all the time. We both need you in our lives, Sweetheart, not in Washington. Let the French take care of themselves. The rodeo went fine last night. A kiss and hug from Miguel and me. Maybe I should bring Miguel to Washington. Every American kid needs to visit DC sometime.

Yours always, Tyler

The second and the third sounded about the same. No pressure? Right. Kate sighed. This situation is intolerable for everyone. He could show up any moment with Miguel and demand that I return with them to Texas. But he won't. He said he wanted me to choose to come.

A vision of Tyler riding up on Jake into her office and swooping her up in his arms flitted across her imagination. She giggled in the quiet office space. For the first time in her entire life, she knew exactly what God wanted her to do. The signs were clearer than any of the traffic signs she read on the way to work in the black Beemer.

Chapter 15

Saturday morning at the Hawkins house required a large spread: biscuits and gravy, eggs and bacon, and grits. Tyler dished out a sampling of all of it for Miguel. As he placed the small bowl of grits next to Miguel, the doorbell rang.

Before Tyler could stop him, the small boy had raced to the front door ahead of him. Miguel peered through the art glass side panels to ascertain the visitors' identity.

"It's the mailman." Miguel was always excited about mail.

Tyler opened the door.

"Mr. Hawkins, I need you to sign for a registered letter."

Tyler signed the appropriate place, and the mailman went on his way.

"What is it, Daddy? Who sent you a special letter?"

The small boy jumped around his feet in anticipation. Tyler leaned down and picked him up. "It says it's from your mom, Miguel. Let's go check on breakfast, and then we'll open it. Okay with you?"

"Don't send me back to my mom. I like it better here. And when Katie comes back, we'll be a whole family."

Tyler ruffled Miguel's hair. "Nope, you are staying with me, like it or not."

Miguel threw his arms around Tyler's neck. Tyler buried his face in his back and smelled the blue sky and the warm grass that little boys are made of.

***

When breakfast was over, Tyler and Miguel climbed up into the jumbo recliner in the den. Tyler turned the TV on and adjusted the channel to cartoons. Miguel was quickly entranced while Tyler opened the letter and read it.

Dear Tyler and Miguel,

If you've received this letter, it means I lost the last rodeo. I brought Miguel to you because I had ovarian cancer. I knew the time was coming when I could no longer care for our child.

You already have the custody documents. I've enclosed Miguel's social security card, his birth certificate, and his passport.

If there's anything left in my estate at the event of my death, my lawyer will liquidate everything and send it to you to help with Miguel's care. If you want my horse, call my lawyer (his card is enclosed) to arrange transport.

Don't seek me out, arrange a funeral, or allow Miguel to see my body. Help him understand why I won't be by to see him. Find a way to tell him that I was really sick and died. My lawyer is handling the details of my cremation and scattering my ashes.

The biggest mistake of my life was leaving you when you needed me most because I needed you to be Miguel's father from the beginning. It seems to have worked out okay for you. Katie seems like a good lady. She'll be great as Miguel's new mom. Good luck with your missionary work – so hard for me still to imagine, Ty.

So here's one loose end tied up.

Loved you until the end,

Tina

"Why are you crying? Was the letter sad?" Miguel put his hands on Tyler's face. "Don't cry, Daddy. God will fix it all up."

Tyler smiled. He'd only been Miguel's daddy for a few months, but he already understood that God 'would fix it all up'.

"Let's go for a ride, little dude. There's something I want to tell you, but I want to do it someplace special."

Miguel jumped out of the chair. "Great!" He went in search of shoes while Tyler tried to compose himself.

Once Tyler thought he could speak, he called the lawyer on the card.

"Wharton and River." The voice seemed so far away. "How can I help you today?"

Tyler cleared his throat. "I'd like to speak with Mr. River concerning the final affairs of Tina Martinez. I'm Tyler Hawkins."

"Just a moment. I'll see if Mr. River is available." A symphony blared from the phone.

Miguel came back with his shoes. Tyler put the phone on speaker, so he could have both hands to tie Miguel's shoes.

"Why don't you go out and swing on the front porch while I make this phone call?" Tyler hugged the boy then pointed him to the front door. "You wait for me on the porch."

Miguel nodded and headed toward the front door. About the time he had closed the door behind him with the accompanying slam of the screen door, the music stopped.

"Mr. Hawkins, I figured I'd be getting a call from you today, what with the registered letter and its contents. How can I help you and Miguel?"

"Is it too late to have Tina buried on my property?"

The silence on the other end was palpable. "She was quite insistent on this point, Mr. Hawkins. She had no desire for Miguel to be part of her death and final arrangements."

Tyler composed himself. "I have a five-year-old who has been abandoned by his mother. I think it would bring him comfort to have her buried in the family graveyard on my property. I know it brings me comfort as an orphan to have my parents there."

"I will consider it. I'm afraid she may already be cremated."

Tyler clenched his fist and breath. "Then perhaps you could bring the cremains here for burial. I had planned to marry Tina. I built my house for her. We have a child. Surely you can find a way to bring her home."

The voice on the other end of the call cleared his throat. "I'll see what I can do."

Tyler relaxed. "Thank you. Call me when you can have her remains brought here, and I will do whatever I need to do to prepare a place for her. Oh and yes, I want her horse."

After he hung up the phone, he realized he should have discussed it with Katie. He heard the swing creaking on the porch. He placed a call to DC.

"Is something wrong?" Kate answered Tyler's call, concern edged her words. "I received your note about Tina. What happened? How's Miguel?"

"Caller ID is a wonderful thing, isn't it? She left Miguel with us because she was dying of cancer. I'm afraid I just did something without talking to you about how you might feel about it."

"What could that be? We're not married yet. We're barely engaged."

"I just made arrangements to have Tina buried on Green Pastures, so Miguel has a physical marker for his mother. I'm hoping it will make him feel less abandoned."

Silence ticked the moments by.

"Katie, are you there?"

"*Oui, monsieur. J'es ici.* I'm just trying to process what you're saying. It's a lot to take in, Tyler."

"Please understand, Katie. I would never marry her now. I'm a new creation in Christ, and she probably died without Him. I know you had a rocky time with her this summer, but she's still Miguel's mother."

Kate interrupted his onslaught of words. "It's fine, Tyler. If it's good for Miguel, how can I say no?"

Tyler smiled to himself. "Have I told you how much I love you?"

"And I you, my love. Gotta go though, I'm in a meeting and the director is unhappy with me for a) having my cell phone ring and b) actually having a conversation on it. *Au revoir, mon ami.*"

As he hung up the phone, the door opened; and Miguel called out for him. "Daddy! Are we going or not? I'm tired of swinging."

Tyler rushed to the door, swooping up the boy under one arm. "Here we go."

Tyler negotiated the steps with a giggling boy under his arm, plopped him in the passenger seat of his ATV, buckled him into the child safety seat, and headed across the pasture to the stable to pick up Asher.

***

"Why'd you name him Asher, Daddy?"

Tyler lifted Miguel onto the big red horse in front of the saddle, then boosted himself into the saddle behind him. Tyler clicked to Asher, and they started out across Green Pastures.

"Asher is a Bible name, Miguel. It means happy."

"Is that in the big, black book you read every morning?"

Tyler nodded. "That's the Bible, son. God's word."

"Was Asher an important person in the Bible?"

"Asher was the son of a man named Israel. Israel had twelve sons who became the beginnings of the twelve tribes of Israel." Tyler hugged the child snugly against him.

"Who was Israel?"

Tyler laughed. "The man of a thousand questions, I see. Israel used to be named Jacob. He had a twin brother named Esau."

"So why'd he get another name?"

Tyler remained patient. "God renamed him when He changed Jacob's life following a wrestling match. God won, but Israel's hip was hurt, and he limped the rest of his life."

"Like you, Daddy. Is that how you got hurt, too?"

Tyler looked down at the blond head below him. "In a way, yes."

They rode in silence briefly. Tyler guided the gentle horse through the shady creek path.

"Daddy, can God heal your leg?"

"Absolutely. If He wanted to, Miguel, He could. Will He? I don't know. Bible people don't have perfect lives."

Tyler galloped the horse across the prairie to his favorite shady "thinking spot" by the old stump. He helped Miguel down from the horse. Miguel ran over and climbed up on the stump.

"Is there a Miguel in the Bible, too?" asked the little guy.

Tyler thought hard. "Well, no Miguels, but there is a very special person in the Bible named Michael, the English equivalent. He and his brother, Gabriel, are the archangels for God. That means that they are God's messengers."

Tyler wandered over to the small graveyard near the stump. His parents' headstones slumped in the Texas soil adorned with wildflowers.

"Well, then." Miguel placed his small hands on his hips. "When I have a brother after you and Katie ladybug get married, we'll have to name him Gabriel. That's Spanish as well as English."

Tyler smiled. "I'm not so sure Miss Katie wants to be called 'ladybug', Miguel. And I think Katie would like some say in what we name a child. What if it's a girl?"

"Well, then we call her 'Gabrielle.' Momma always said I was her little angel."

Tyler swept him up in his arms and lifted him up over his head. Miguel giggled as he swung him back down in a lurching arc.

"There's something here I want you to see. These are the graves of my mom and dad, Miguel. This was my dad's land. I bought the rest of the land around this lot so I would own it all. They would love to have known you. I wish I had known them."

"You didn't know your parents?"

"No, they died when I was nearly as small as you. They're your grandparents."

Miguel looked solemnly at the cold granite stones.

"What about Grandma Sarah? And Papa Ryan?"

"They're Katie's mom and dad."

Miguel went up to the stone marked 'Cherry Hawkins' and hugged the stone. Then he hugged the second stone marked 'Esau Hawkins.'

"You're missing knowing me, Grandma and Grandpa."

"The letter this morning was from your mom." Tyler was unsure how to continue.

"She died, too, just like your mom, didn't she?"

"Yes, how did you know?"

"She's been sick for a long time. When she said she was taking me to my daddy's, I sorta knew she was getting sicker."

"You are wise beyond your years, little boy." Tyler gathered him into his arms and they wept together.

Chapter 16

The week had flown by with a multitude of catastrophes to navigate. The paperwork on Kate's desk required completion, so she was at the office on Saturday too. She read through all the email that had come in since Friday evening.

An email message from Tyler popped onto the screen. All it said was, "Tina's ashes arrived and were interred."

"Lord, you know it's not easy for me to surrender to this. You know how I feel. It's a dirty trick to put the man I love in a missionary place of service. I know, I know. I know what you want; I just can't do it now."

"What can't you do, Kate?" John settled into the Queen Anne chair in the corner of her office. "My experience with you is that you can do just about anything you want to do."

Kate startled and pressed the sleep mode button on her monitor.

"Good morning, John." Kate cleared her throat. "It's nothing."

John searched her face as though looking for some affirmation of her assertion. Finding none, he frowned and walked over to the window to see the sun rise into its place in the Washington skyline.

"Well, Kate, I have news for you. I knew I'd lose you sooner or later. You've been requested specifically to fill an open position at the US Embassy in Paris. Your dual citizenship is an asset as is your friendship with Monsieur Dremond. Stefan is returning to Paris to be a grand muckity-muck in their Ministry of Foreign Affairs. He asked for you directly. Of course, we'll need your answer directly."

Kate felt swimmy for a moment. The dream of her life. A position in Paris. Then reality clicked in. Without Tyler or Miguel. Red flashing neon stop signs exploded into her brain. But how could she turn it down? They could wait a little longer for her to fulfill her dream, couldn't they? They were soul mates; he'd have to wait for her. How long could it be, six months, a year, two? Then she'd resign and return to Dallas.

"Yes! When do I leave?"

"The movers can pack up your townhouse at the end of the week. We'll put you up in the furnished official residence. We'll store your unnecessary things while you are out of the country. Pack your clothes and necessaries, and we'll ship them for you. Let's have you in Paris by the beginning of business next week."

**

"Daddy, have you checked your computer for a letter from Katy ladybug? Maybe she'll come back today."

Tyler lurched to the refrigerator for the milk to pour on Miguel's Fruit Loops. He glanced at the clock. Running late again, he swore softly to himself. It took so much effort to begin the day with Miguel – kneeling at the tub was especially painful. His leg burned these days with pain.

Probably just arthritis. What do you expect from a broken-down cowboy?

He felt the sadness then. The loneliness and sadness came when he thought of life and ministry without Katie. Two ticks. How much longer would he wait for the last tick?

"Forever." He spoke it aloud because it was a commitment, and it was real.

Miguel climbed on the stool and placed his hands on Tyler's face.

"Daddy, forever is a long time. We won't have to wait that long for Katy ladybug, will we? I'll be grown up by then."

Tyler laughed and picked up the little boy in his arms and held him tight.

"In God's time, Miguel. God's time is different than yours or mine. But His plan is already in action, boy. You wait and see."

Am I promising something I can't promise?

He set the boy down in his seat and winced as pain shot up his bad leg and into the injured hip. He reached for the pain capsules earlier every day. And they didn't last as long either, he noticed as he read the prescription label. He popped the two capsules and made a mental note to schedule an appointment as soon as possible. But right now he had to get the two of them out to Mission Mesquite and the crew of rodeo folks that made up his flock.

As he picked up his hat, the computer winked at him. He sent Miguel out to the pickup and clicked the Internet connection open. Sure enough. A letter from Katie.

Dear Tyler,

I have great news! I'm being transferred to Paris at the end of the week. This posting has always been my dream. Don't deny me this pleasure. I promise that when I return in 6 months to a year, I'll be ready to decide. Wait for me. Hug Miguel. Tell Mom and Dad the news. I'll give more info later. Call me tonight before they disconnect my phone.

       Love,

       Kate

Tyler's hands shook as he closed the Internet connection. The pain in his leg throbbed as did his head and heart. He jammed his hat on his head as strode to the pickup where his motherless son waited.

***

Rev. Ryan was on the porch as the gravel spun out from under the pickup. Miguel jumped from the truck and ran into the arms of the older man.

"Papa!"

They snuggled in a tight embrace as Tyler struggled from his truck.

"You get mail from Katie this morning?" Tyler labored up the pressure treated steps to the mobile home. "Says she's headed to Paris for six months or a year."

Miguel jumped down from Rev. Ryan's grasp. 'Papa' swatted his rear end as he ran to find Grandma Sarah.

"I got that message, too. Don't let her go. I got a bad feeling about this. Go stop her, Tyler. We'll keep Miguel. Junior Cantu can ride pickup with Stan this weekend. Don't let my daughter make this horrible mistake."

One look in Rev. Ryan's eyes told him a million thoughts that passed behind them.

"I can't make her come back with me, Ryan. She's got to come on her own. I promised her no pressure."

"Darn it all, Tyler. She's running from God, not just you. What if it's like Tara? What if you could save her, but you don't?"

Tyler dropped into a lawn chair on the porch deck. Pain filled his brain.

"I'm sorry, Rev. Ryan. Maybe I will go to see her off. Maybe she'll talk herself out of it."

Tyler struggled to his feet. "Can I use the phone?"

The men bustled in, slamming screen door behind them. Miss Sarah rushed up to the tall young man and hugged him ferociously. Miguel piled onto "Grandma" for his own hug and ran off to watch cartoons. Tyler made two phone calls after the hugs and salutations: one to his doctor and one to the airline.

***

The taxi pulled up in front of the Georgetown address behind the moving and storage truck. Tyler paid the fare and struggled out of the back seat of the yellow car. He grabbed his bag from the trunk and slapped the trunk closed. The car pulled away from the curb and out into the busy Washington streets. Tyler struggled up the walk and steps to the propped open door. He rapped sharply and called out. A burly man answered and told him the lady was upstairs.

Tyler climbed the stairs carefully, wincing at each riser. When he reached the top of the staircase, he rubbed the offending leg briskly to calm the screaming nerve endings. He rounded the top of the landing and caught sight of Katie amidst boxes of clothes and bric-a-brac. She was thinner still since he'd seen her after Rev. Ryan's heart attack. And she looked so sad for someone pursuing her dream. The stereo blaring covered his clomping entrance as he slipped his arms around her and held her tight. She turned in his embrace.

"Tyler." Their lips met in a violent crescendo of need. They hugged each other desperately.

"You didn't even ask me." Tyler looked directly into her eyes. "Shouldn't I be included in this decision process?"

Alarm crossed across her face. "But I had to decide … we're not married … I have to do what's right for me …" The excuses stuttered from her lips. He kissed her to stop the babble of words.

"How can I help?" He pushed himself away. "I'm not here for the wherefores and how-tos. I'm here to see you off and make sure you really will come home to me someday."

Katie assigned him a task, and they set about working in an uncomfortable silence.

***

Sunday morning came too quickly. Tyler and Kate found themselves saying good-bye in yet another airport, each holding tickets for opposite directions.

"Do you have the ring I gave you?" Tyler ended the awkward silence. At Kate's nod, he continued, "Will you wear it as a promise to return to me someday?"

Kate's heart broke, and she began to cry wracking sobs. "I shouldn't go at all," she gasped out. "I should be getting on your plane instead."

Tyler shushed her. "Only when you have finished following this dream will you be truly mine. Will you wear my ring, Katydid?"

Katie nodded and fished the worn black box from her purse. Tyler opened the box and removed the marquis diamond from its interior. He slid the ring on her finger. It wallowed on her tiny hand.

"You've lost more weight, Katydid. Get this resized in Paris. Or wear it on a chain until you're back up to fighting weight. Don't forget to eat. Write me. Come home to me."

The flight announcement interrupted their moment. They kissed and embraced again. Tyler was afraid to crush her in his bear hug, but also afraid to let go. The final boarding call caused Kate to wriggle free from his embrace.

"I love you, Katydid. You owe me one more tick."

"Tyler, can't you hear my heart ticking for you?"

With that she kissed him lightly, picked up her carryon, and ran to the gate. She turned to wave good-bye; he sagged, in great pain, into an airport seat. He covered his eyes with his large hand while the tears coursed down his face.

Chapter 17

The ringing phone disrupted the dream Tyler was having of Katie. *Two o'clock A.M.? Who would call so early? Katie?*

He made a grab for the phone on the nightstand and knocked it to the floor. Reaching for it he nearly fell out of bed with it. Fumbling it, he finally answered.

"Katie? Is it you?"

"Bon jour, mon ami. It's a beautiful morning in Paris, my love. I can see the Arc de Triomphe, the Tour Eiffel, and the Promenade from the balcony of my State Department apartment. The only thing lacking is you."

Tyler yawned. "And sleep, Katydid. Did you forget about the time difference?"

"I'm so sorry, Tyler. I was missing you and wanted to share. Go back to sleep. I need to finish getting ready anyway."

"By the way, I'm going to the doc finally about my hip and leg today. Just to check in because I'm taking too many pain pills." He left off the part that might include surgery. "No worries; just information."

The line went silent except for the international crackles and pops. "Is something wrong, Tyler?" Concern edged the words.

"'Course not, sweetheart. Just checking in." Tyler grimaced at what was almost a lie. He expected to need surgery, but he'd not have her flying from Paris to hold his hand.

"Let me know how it goes, okay?"

"Of course, Katie. Just making sure I can stand at the front of the church when you're coming to be my bride." *Not a lie, exactly.*

"We're not quite there yet, Tyler. Hey, someone's knocking at the door. I should see who it is. Au revoir, sweet man."

With that she was gone. Would he ever get back to sleep now?

***

"Un moment, si vous plait." She hurried to open the door.

"Thought we could ride in together this morning." Doug leaned on the doorframe holding a red rose.

"What are you doing here?" Kate trembled. "Why are you following me?"

"Sweetheart, when you put in for this position a year ago, we had planned to be married by then. In fact, I had to request separate housing because they had us in the same apartment." He held out the rose. "Perhaps there will be time to iron out our differences while we are here and so far from a certain cowboy."

Kate grasped the ring on the chain around her neck. "I'm in love with that cowboy, er Tyler. He makes me better."

Doug smirked. "If by better, you mean fatter, you've got me there. Lucky I'm here to supervise your bread and fat intake. The French do so love their pastries."

"You are cruel, Doug."

As she went to slam the door in his face, he grabbed the edge and came into her tiny space. He handed her the rose and crushed her hand around the thorny stem.

"Come, come, darling. We're in Paris, the romance capital of the world. Give us a chance."

Kate grimaced as the thorns dug into her hands. As soon as he let go of her hands, she pulled the rose out and threw it back at him. "Almost time for work. Best take this rose for a French woman who can be bowled over by an American. I'm not buying nor am I interested."

At that she yanked the marquis diamond from the space at her heart. She dangled it for him to see as it turned and caught the light and splintered the sunlight into a million rainbows across the apartment's walls.

"I'm taken. Find someone else."

Doug backed away. "If you were really taken, you would not be here, in Paris, without him. Mark my words. Absence may make the heart grow fonder, but the one who is present reaps the benefits."

Kate pointed at the door, too angry to speak. Doug held up his hands and backed away. His rose lay on the floor, wilted and broken, just like Kate's soul.

Once she was sure that Doug was really gone and not lurking in the hallway, she pulled on her sweater and bounded down the stairs and into a fairyland called Paris. So much to see and do while she was there. She reached for the ring on the chain around her neck. *I'll do it all and then come back to you, Tyler.*

The brisk September breeze greeted Kate as she reached street level. As always, the noise and bustle on the street was at cacophony level, tweedle-y gendarme sirens, rumbly motorcycles, high pitched mopeds, parents walking children hand in hand to school. Revolution-era tall apartment buildings stood on every street with monuments winking between. She breathed in the cool September air and headed to a quaint little bistro for coffee and croissant, to go, so she wouldn't be late on her first day. *Was there anywhere more amazing than Paris? Unless it was Versailles or Mont St. Michel?* The bells from Notre Dame rang out, alerting her to continue to her destination without losing her head to her imaginings.

***

Tyler pulled his shirt on and buttoned it over the scars on his chest. Dr. Waters pushed into the room and stuck x-ray film into the clips on the light and flipped the switch. The x-rays showed the repairs on Tyler's shattered left leg. The second set Dr. Waters arranged below the first set came from the yellowed film envelope. They showed a twisted shattered leg from the original injury. A third set he held up to the examining room overhead light.

"Well, doc? What's the scoop?"

The doctor regarded him seriously over his half-moon spectacles. He sighed and went back to the film in his hand. Tyler struggled to sit up straighter to peer at the film. It all looked like metal and shattered bone to him. Dr. Waters pulled the original film from the examining light and replaced it with the latest x-rays. Only then did he sit on the rolling chair and give his patient his full attention.

"Here's the problem, Tyler. You saw the original x-rays, and these are the x-rays after surgery. We reconstructed the leg as best we could to give you maximum mobility and pain management. Remember that we told you it would never be perfect, and it would never be pain-free."

Tyler nodded solemnly.

"The problem," the doctor continued as he stood to indicate the place on the film, "is this area around the hip. You see that the pins in this area have shifted since surgery. There's also a shadow in this area that indicates some type of growth. My guess is scar tissue. The growth is probably shifting the pins. The nerves in this area are very irritated by the metal and tissue growth. That's where I'd guess the pain is originating."

He circled the area with wax pencil and sat back down to face his patient.

"And? What happens next?"

The doctor shook his head. "Surgery is my suggestion. At the very least, we can shift the pins back into place, examine the growth, and perhaps soothe the nerve endings, giving you some pain relief. At the best, we can remove the tissue causing the obstruction and restore the original construction."

"And the worst case?"

"The worst case is a malignancy, cancer. Hard to tell what it is without looking at it. You've got too much metal in the leg to make an MRI possible. Going in surgically is the optimum course of action."

"When? Remember, I have a son to look after now, too."

"Tomorrow. If it's cancer, we can't wait to find it and stop the growth, or you could lose the whole leg. Will Rev. Ryan and Miss Sarah keep Miguel?" Tyler's nod urged him to continue. "Then go home and get him settled and return to the hospital with your things. Don't know what kind of recovery you can expect until I know what it is. Make sure Joe knows you'll be gone, so he can tend to the ranch."

After the flurry of paperwork and arrangements at the clinic, Tyler drove home to the big, empty house. A call to Rev. Ryan settled arrangements with Miguel. A call to the arena removed him from the docket for the remaining rodeo. The computer winked at him, and he checked his mail.

Dear Tyler,

Paris is beautiful in September. My apartment is in the embassy area and is furnished in old French antiques. I brought your wool jacket with me because I hear the nights get very cool. I ate at an outdoor bistro last night and sipped cappuccino among the art students from the university. I felt younger and freer, yet lonelier as the young couples strolled off arm in arm. I thought I heard a katydid tonight on my balcony with FRENCH DOORS! I saw the stars amid the lights of the city and realized they shine much brighter in Texas. Perhaps because you are there. I miss you already. Is it too late to change my mind and come home? Yes, for a few months anyway. Take care and tell me all that goes on with you and Miguel, so I feel like I'm at least in the same world with you.

Adieu,

Kate

Tyler paused over the reply button and thought over the wisdom of telling her everything. After all it could be nothing. It could be a simple adjustment. Not telling the whole truth was the same as telling a lie, right? Perhaps it was better to say nothing.

Dear Katie,

Don't be alarmed if you don't hear from me for a little bit. I have some business to attend to that will take me away from home and my computer connection. You needn't worry. If it was a big deal, I'd tell you. Imagine those French doors lead to my bedroom. Pretend I'm as close as your balcony. Don't give up on our dream just because we're far apart. I'll always love you. Come home when it's time to come home.

Love,

Tyler

He then fired off an e-mail to Rev. Ryan to tell him not to tell Katie of the surgery unless it became a bigger deal than he hoped it was. He turned out the light, turned off the computer, and headed for the hospital.

***

"Mr. Hawkins, wake up. The surgery is over, and it's time to come back to us."

Tyler opened his eyes groggily and stared into the face of the recovery room nurse. He moved to look around, and pain shot up his back and down his leg.

"It's a good thing when I feel pain, right?" He grimaced as the pain recoiled through his body. "At least, I'm not paralyzed."

The nurse hurried away to read the chart as Tyler drifted back into drugged sleep. When the nurse returned, Tyler awoke long enough to see the hypodermic before it eased relief into his pain-wracked body.

The next time he came to, he was in a regular room with Rev. Ryan sleeping in the chair in the corner. He tried to move, but found it difficult amidst the IV tubing and monitors. He flashbacked to that horrible night when the accident had first happened, but the peace of God and morphine reassured him. His dry mouth was almost as annoying as the tubing. He rang for the nurse.

"Mr. Hawkins, can I help you?" The pretty young nurse poked her head into the room. "Do you need pain medication?"

"How about some water? I'm mighty dry."

"Ice chips may be the best I can do. I'll check."

"Thanks." Tyler tried to clear his throat.

Rev. Ryan stretched in the vinyl chair. "Welcome back to the land of the living. I thought I was going to be alone all night. Good grief, it's already 4 a.m."

"Guess the rodeo's long over by now. Seen my doc yet?"

"Just briefly. He said he'd be by early this morning to talk with you about the results. You sure I can't let Katie in on this, so she can at least pray?"

Tyler shook his head and found himself in a swell of dizziness. The nurse returned with ice chips and a plastic spoon and charged Rev. Ryan with feeding them to Tyler. Tyler dozed between spoonsful and incoherent chats until sunlight filtered in through the hospital drapes. The night nurse came in to take his vital signs and check on his alertness, so she could inform the next shift. Soon meal carts rattled through the hall with cheery disconnected voices calling, "Good morning" as staff entered each room with a hot tray of food.

"Go home, Rev. Ryan. They pay folks to watch over me here. I'll let you know after the doctor comes by. You can send Stan or someone to pick me up when they release me in an hour."

"Yeah, right." Rev. Ryan dodged the large lady with the hot tray as he left the room.

Dr. Waters followed the tray lady into the room.

"Hungry yet?"

Tyler nodded and raised the lid to see broth and Jell-O. He scowled and covered the tray once again. "How about eggs and bacon?"

"We'll see if we can arrange that after we talk. The good news is the growth looks like scar tissue, but we're having it analyzed by pathology to be sure. And I removed all of it. The other good news is that the nerve endings are healthy. I replaced the pins and realigned the hip joint."

"And the bad news?"

Dr. Waters cleared his throat. "Rodeo days are over, Ty. There's arthritis covering everything we've done. I'd tell you not to ride anymore, but I know you'd ignore me anyway. I'm firm on the rodeo. It's someone else's turn to pick up. You can pray with the participants, watch from the stands like the tourists, sign autographs, do color commentary, grill barbecue, or something. No more pick up riding. I also think you need to consider wearing a brace on the left leg to give you more support. Limping around has probably spurred the scar tissue growth and shifted the pins. I want the leg supported, or I'll see you in a wheelchair shortly. You choose."

Tyler closed his eyes and prayed. When he opened them, Dr. Waters stared earnestly at him.

"Well? Any arguments?"

Tyler shook his head.

"Good. I want you at rehab this morning. The prosthetics guy will be here at 11. I'll check the dressing and release you in a day or two if you promise to be good at rehab. That includes daily visits to the hospital for a couple of weeks. Might be good if someone else drove you for a while until you get used to the brace. Dallas traffic will kill you. You think the bull was bad. You should see the lady I just sewed up in emergency today."

The doctor signed the chart and whisked out of the room.

Tyler whistled a long, low note. "Crippled. Disabled. Handicapped. Retired from rodeo. Can it get worse?" He peeked at the cool beef broth and melting Jell-O. "It's worse." He reached for his Bible, tangling the IV tubing and monitors, and turned to the 32nd chapter of Genesis to reread the account of Jacob's struggle with God.

The ringing phone interrupted his doze, and the Bible slipped from his hands into the floor with a thud. It took Tyler a minute to clear the post anesthesia fog and realize just what had wakened him. He struggled to reach the phone and managed to knock it off into the floor beside his Bible. In exasperation, he reached for the nurse's signal and jabbed it repeatedly until a young aide came flying into the room.

"Answer the phone! And pick up my Bible and untangle these dad-blamed tubes."

He could hear the long-distance crackle as the nurse plucked the phone from the floor, but his foggy temper didn't catch the warning.

"Hello," she said, flustered. "Yes, ma'am, it is. ... Of course, I will."

The blushing nurse untangled the IV tubing and phone cord and handed the receiver to Tyler.

"Hello." Tyler growled into the phone. "Can't a crippled man get any peace? What do you want?"

The overseas chirps and crackles punctuated the silence on the other end. Dread and regret washed over him.

"Who's there?" He knew the answer before it came.

"Tyler, it's Kate. How dare you not tell me you were having surgery? I thought you cared for me. Is this what you do to the people you care about, Mr. Minister of the Lord? And what do you mean crippled man? What is going on?"

Tyler took a deep breath and began coughing. The aide struggled to help the big man sit upright. Pain shot through his body causing him to catch his breath and start coughing all over again. A nurse rushed in to help the aide. The phone slid back onto the floor. Frantic cries came from the receiver as it hit the floor. Once Tyler had recovered his composure, the aide picked up the phone. The nurse snatched the phone from the young girl.

"May I ask who is calling?" the nurse inquired gruffly. "Mr. Hawkins has only been out of surgery overnight and is still not fully awake. Can I redirect your call? Or would you rather call back later after he has had time to sufficiently awake?"

Tyler could hear Kate's reply.

"No, I will not talk to anyone else. I don't care if he's in a coma. That man is my fiancé, and I will speak to him now."

The nurse checked his condition and then handed the phone back to the aide.

"You will stay here until this conversation ends. If necessary, hang up this phone."

The aide nodded nervously and propped the phone back up next to Tyler's ear.

"Calm down, Katydid. I'm okay. I just have dry throat and mouth from the breathing apparatus. Where are you?"

"I'm in Paris, you twit. Because you didn't think it necessary to tell me what was going on so I could fly in. What did you think you were doing?"

Tyler leaned toward the aide. "Go on. I think this should be a private conversation, if you know what I mean. I think I get to eat crow for breakfast. Sorry about yelling at you."

The aide blushed and scurried from the room. Tyler could hear the nurse yelling out reprimands at the young girl. Tyler made a mental note to send her flowers later with a sincere note of apology.

"Tyler? Are you there? What do you have to say for yourself?"

"Guilty as charged, milady. I only hoped not to worry you for no reason, Katydid. And I was right; it's not that big of a deal. How did you find out?"

"Rosa called me. Joe told her you were having surgery and not to tell me. Smart woman found my number and called me anyway." Katie's voice cracked, and he could hear her tears begin. "I've been worried sick knowing you didn't want me to know. That meant it was really serious, or you'd have used that as an excuse for me to fly to Dallas."

Tyler tried to adjust his position in the bed and scooted onto the fresh incision. He yelped into the phone, which had two effects. First, Kate sobbed out loud, and second the nurse rushed into the room and tried to take the phone away from the cowboy.

"I'm okay, lady. Help me get situated without pulling my stitches loose, and I promise we can all get over this melodrama. The call is from Paris from my fiancée. I will get out of this bed and dump what's on my tray in the floor if you hang up that phone."

The nurse eyed him carefully and finally helped him adjust the bed and his gown, so that his wound was protected from further trauma while the transatlantic minutes added up on Kate's phone bill. When the nurse was finally satisfied that he wouldn't pull out his stitches, or have a stroke, she gave him back the phone and left the room.

"Katydid, I'm finally situated, and the Iron Maiden has gone back to her base station. Here's the lowdown. The pins were out of alignment and some scar tissue was gumming up the works in my hip. It's all taken care of, and I'll be discharged as soon as I prove that I can walk in rehab. Everything's fine."

Kate sniffled and coughed. "Take care of yourself, cowboy. I'm expecting to see you doing pick up duty when the rodeo reopens next spring."

"Is that a promise? You called me your fiancé. You'll be here in the spring?"

"No promises about timetables, Tyler. You just get well. Sorry to cause so much more trauma, but I sort of went off when my Mom and Dad wouldn't tell me anything."

Tyler felt sleepy suddenly. "Listen, Sweet Love. I need to lay back and sleep now. I'll call you from home when I get there. Might be a week or so. Tell your dad we talked."

"Good bye, Tyler."

Tyler struggled to reach the nightstand with the phone and finally hung up. He drifted to sleep with a smile. She really was mad. She really cared. And she'd be home in the spring. She called him her fiancé.

Chapter 18

"Rehab. It has such a promising tone. Like you'll actually be glad to be here." Tyler grumbled as he had the brace fitted to him, finally cinching about the torso. "Feels like I'm being saddled."

The physical therapist Joy patted his knee. "It will be better, Mr. Hawkins. It just will take time and effort."

"Neither of which I have the luxury nor willingness to expend."

Joy helped him to his feet at the end of a set of vertical bars. He took a few steps leaning heavily on the bars.

"Good. Now try it standing straight up without depending so much on the apparatus."

Tyler grumbled under his breath. "If I thought I could do it, do you think I'd be leaning on the 'apparatus'?"

Joy touched his arm gently. "I understand you have a fiancée in Paris who may be home by spring. She'd want to see her cowboy whole and standing erect at the altar, wouldn't she?"

He wanted to swear a blue streak. Before he became a Christian and a minister, he would have. How dare she dangle Katie as a carrot? What does she know about this upside down turnover relationship? He stood as straight as he could, as straight as the incision and bandages would allow. He would do this thing, not only for Katie and Miguel, but for the Lord, so he could serve Him all the rest of the days of his life.

And he would tell her everything, even send a picture. He owed her full disclosure. Besides, how could he expect accurate appraisals from Paris if he wasn't sending her the same?

"Joy, could you take my picture with my cell here at the parallel bars so I can send it to my fiancée?"

***

It was early Paris time when the email from Tyler arrived in Kate's inbox. Kate was up; she still hadn't fully adjusted to the time difference.

Dearest Katie,

I'm enclosing a pic of me at physical therapy with my new supporting character, the full leg brace. I know that phone call went poorly, but it was so good to hear your voice, even when you're yelling at me.

Full disclosure: Doc went in to readjust the pins and scrape out scar tissue from my perpetual limp. I have a long miserable incision laid along the old one, and it's not too pretty either. Doc wants me to wear the full leg brace all the time. Not sure if I can get it under a tux, though. Bet I could do without it for one wonderful day.

Are you eating? Enjoy the food. After all it's the gourmet capital of the world. You can eat it all and still come back at a healthy weight. I promise to love you no matter the label in your clothing. Your self-esteem should not be linked to the number on the scale or the tag on your clothing.

I love you, Katydid. Nothing will change that. Come home to me well and happy.

Yours forever,
Tyler

***

Would that it was all as simple as Tyler believes. She ignored her tummy rumblings and left early for work. It was just a few blocks, and she needed the exercise to work off all the bread and croissants she'd already indulged while in Paris. No more of that nonsense. Easy to say that gaining weight won't matter. Besides, Doug was always at her elbow to remind her how much it matters.

When she reached the US Embassy, she took the stairs to her third-floor office. No reason to indulge in the elevator. Stairs would keep Paris off her hips.

Kate hurried into her cubicle as the clock in the hall struck the hour. She flipped her poncho onto the back of her chair and wrapped the scarf around the hall tree like garland around a Christmas tree. Plopping into her chair she spun around until she saw the interoffice envelope from Stefan on her desk. She grabbed it on her slower last rotation and opened it.

"Oh my goodness!" Kate waved around the contents. "Tickets to fashion week in Paris!" A note fell out of the envelope as well.

Dear Kate,

All work and no fun is not the *vie de la Francaise*. Go to the show. Buy something extraordinary to wear to the rounds of endless receptions you'll be forced to attend. May as well buy one amazing runway demo. Then you can 'knock your cowboy dead' when you go back to him.

Stefan

Kate dumped the envelope again to determine that he had not also provided his credit card to purchase such a creation.

"Find a mouse, Kate?" Doug leaned against the desk, peering over the reasons for the excitement. "Something from the French secretary?"

"No. Yes. Not your business. Please leave." Kate hurried to stuff all the tickets and the note back into the brown envelope.

"Fashion week tickets? You truly will hate yourself if you go, my dear Kate. All the runway models are smaller than you. The size 2 and 0 ones are the heavy ones. You'll find it difficult to buy anything in your size now."

Kate bit back her reply but found herself shudder at his remarks. She knew they were poison for her just as if he was feeding her cyanide. "Get out, Wormwood."

"Just trying to help, *mon chere*." His grin was not a friendly one. "Your cowboy may say he likes meat on your bones, but he is not French."

Kate gasped at his insolence. She picked up her phone. "Calling security to have you removed from my life, Doug."

"Too funny. You know that's not even possible. I work here same as you."

Once Doug had finally left her office, Kate examined more closely the contents of the brown envelope. Two passes to the fashion show, a backstage pass, an entry pass to the demo sale, and a blank check signed by Stefan Dremond. Who could go with her? Who did she know, besides Doug and Stefan?

Kate's secretary put her head into the office. "*Mademoiselle*, I have a few phone messages for you. Several are from your Tyler Hawkins. He seemed anxious to speak with you."

"Thank you." Kate took the slips from her. "Hey, Arianne. Monsieur Dremond has sent me passes to the fashion week finale show the first weekend in October. Want to go with me? I might need some fashion advice because I also have instructions and cash to purchase a gown."

Arianne did a happy dance in the office. "Oh yes, yes, yes, yes. I would be so excited to go with you, Mlle. Lawrence."

"Then you should really call me Kate. How many times did Tyler call?"

"I stopped counting, uh, Kate. You should probably call him first." Arianne pointed to Tyler's picture on her desk. "Is this him? He is *tres magnifique*."

Kate took a good look at the picture as well. "You have no idea. He is quite handsome, but there's so much more to him."

After Arianne left, Kate used her desk phone to call Tyler.

"This is Reverend Tyler Hawkins. I am not available. Leave a message …" Kate refused to leave another message, so she pulled the phone from her ear to hang up.

"Don't hang up, Kate. I'm here. I'm here." The disembodied voice reached Kate before she disconnected. She put it on speaker instead.

"Tyler, I have maybe ten messages saying you called. Is everything okay?"

"No. You're not here with me." Silence from Kate spurred Tyler to continue. "Miguel has his birthday on October 1. He'll turn five. I want to do something special. Have any ideas?"

Kate smiled. "You are making multiple international calls to discuss a birthday gift?"

"Well, you'll be his mom someday soon. I thought you should be in the loop."

Kate laughed at him, his sentimentality, his ever presence in her life despite the distance.

"The very best thing you can do for Miguel every day of his life is give him you. Take him for pizza and playtime at the park. Buy a radio-controlled car, plane, or boat and share it with him. You can never give him enough love, Tyler. Simply be there with him. And when you are called to minister or whatever, be there for him as well. Don't put him second."

***

After work, Kate walked to Notre Dame. The size of the place made her feel small indeed. The intricate stone carving made her in awe of the work man had done to adore, venerate, and worship God. What had she done to praise Him? She'd turned her back on Him. She'd acknowledged His plan for her life then said, 'Okay, but let me play a little longer.'

The darkness and coolness of the cathedral drew her in. Once her eyes adjusted to the candlelight and the fading sunlight through the stained-glass windows, the beauty of the place caused her deep wonder. Hundreds of years of men constructing and maintaining this sanctuary led to this moment that made Kate catch her breath. The farther she drew into the apse, the more the holiness of the place struck her. An evensong service was beginning, so she took a seat toward the back in one of the wooden folding chairs.

Kate realized that the folding chairs were set over the tombs and memorials in stone of those important enough to be buried in the cathedral. Not an American custom, properly grim. Perhaps they reminded the congregants that life is fleeting, and it could be one of them under their feet one day.

Kate breathed in the incensed candle-smoky air. This visit wasn't her first to Paris, nor to many of the sites. In boarding school in France, field trips to Paris, Versailles, and other important venues were part of her education. But as a student, she'd not taken the time nor the interest to truly experience these places. She allowed the choir's selections to wash over her. Peace with God. It had been so long. But she was halfway around the world from His will for her. That needed to change soon.

Before she knew it, the service had ended. Tourists and congregants alike rummaged around for their belongings and spoke to one another. The silence was gone, and it was time she went home and resolved the evening meal issue.

On the way back, she stopped at a bakery for fresh French bread and at a deli for cheese and meat. By the time she reached the state department apartment, she could see the Tour Eiffel sparkling like a

Christmas tree. She bounded up the stairs. Why wait for the elevator? She could use the exercise. She searched in her purse for her keys until she reached the door and saw it. A dozen rose stems with the blooms removed and dying on the mat. The card was from Tyler. The damage was undoubtedly by Doug.

Kate stalked down the hall to Doug's apartment and pounded at the door.

Doug answered and gave her a knowing smirk.

"Why did you destroy Tyler's flowers?" Kate's heart pounded in her chest to the point that it hurt. "Why are you being so cruel? I loved you once. Do you hate me so much?" Her breath was labored. Was she having a heart attack?

"Come in. I'd love to discuss those issues with you. Besides you don't look well."

Kate spun on her high heel and hurried back to her home. Darned if she'd have a heart attack at his door. She stepped over the mess on her doormat, plucked Tyler's card from the ruins, and slammed the door to her apartment. She threw the meat and cheese into the fridge and put the bread on the counter. How could she eat anything now?

The card read, "Thinking of you. Wishing you were here forever. Love, Tyler and Miguel"

That's when the tears sprang from her eyes, and she slumped onto the worn couch. No sooner had she relaxed into the couch than a knock sounded at the door.

"Doug, why don't you just give it up?" She threw open the door.

An impossibly beautiful man stood at her door. Blond and lanky but muscular, he reminded her of the warrior elves from the *Lord of the Rings* movies. He held out his hand to reveal several red rose petals.

"I believe you missed these." The man took her hand and pressed the petals into hers. "Landon. I've seen you at the embassy. I'm also with the US State Department. If I told you what I do there, I'd have to kill you. I heard the fight with your boyfriend. The walls here are frightfully thin."

"Doug is not my boyfriend. Come in."

Landon stepped over the rose disaster to enter the apartment. "When I saw this explosion on your doorstep, I thought it was a silly prank. Your reaction told me it was nothing of the kind. Instead it was an evil act. Am I right?"

Kate motioned for him to have a seat on the kitchen bar stool. "I have fresh bread and meat and cheese. Would you like anything?"

He laughed. "No, the bistros are so amazing; I'm eating my way home one bistro at a time." He patted a flat stomach as though he'd put on weight. "Perhaps you could join me one day."

Kate smiled, but her tummy rumbled at the thought.

"I just came over to see if all was well. Are you well?"

Kate nodded. "I will be. It's sweet of you to come over to check on me."

"Then I'll be gone so you can get some relaxation and sleep. See you at the embassy."

"Thank you again. Which apartment is yours?"

"C, right next door, Kate. Nice to meet you, mademoiselle."

She closed the door behind him and latched the chain. She returned to the couch and wrapped her comforter around her.

Chapter 19

When she awoke or revived, which she was not sure of, it was still dark, two a.m. She roused herself from the couch, kicked off the black work heels, and grabbed her phone. She padded to the door to take a picture of the mess before she cleaned it up.

Opening the door, she only saw one lone petal remaining. No evidence remained of Doug's cruelty. Did Landon clean it up? She took a picture anyway. It was time to file a complaint against him, with the embassy, with the gendarme, if necessary. Tyler was right. Doug was never going to just leave her alone, plus he was escalating in cruelty.

She sliced two very thin slices from the loaf of bread she'd brought home after being at Notre Dame. So very long ago, it seemed. She plopped them in the toaster and then found a butter packet in the fridge. While she waited for the toast to pop up, she called Tyler.

When he answered, she nearly burst into tears again.

"Anyone there? Katie?"

"I'm here, Tyler. I needed to hear your voice." Her voice sounded choked. She attempted to clear it.

"What's wrong, Sweetheart? You've been crying."

"Oh Tyler, he cut up your roses and left them on the mat." The dam of emotion broke then as tears flooded her resolve.

"Do I need to come there and beat him up?"

Tyler's joke and chuckle had meant to lighten the mood, but it served to create a new sobbing. He was silent while she tried to regain her composure.

"Are you okay, Katydid? Did he hurt you physically too?"

She wiped her face with the back of her hand while trying to locate a tissue, napkin, cloth to stem the salty stream.

"No, of course not. Though I'd love to hold you now, beating him up would be a ridiculous use of airline price and time. I miss you so much. I thought I was having a heart attack last night. Guess I survived after all."

"Are you eating, Katie?"

"I bought meat, cheese, and bread last night." Not exactly the answer to the question, but true all the same. "I'm making toast as we speak."

The toasted French bread finally popped. She hurried to spread the butter on it while it was hot.

"Take care of yourself while I'm not there to do it for you."

"I'll try. I just needed to hear your voice this morning. Hug Miguel for me. Talk to you soon."

She hung up before he could ask anything else that she'd have to lie about. She took a tentative bite of the toast. She ate the rest of the toast hungrily, then wrapped up the bread and put it in the freezer among the population of other partially eaten loaves of bread.

A knock on the door caused her to slam the freezer door. Kate tiptoed to the door and peered through the peephole. Landon. She swept open the door with relief.

"I was so afraid you'd be Doug. I just was not up to that this morning."

"Glad to allay your fears, fair maiden. May I escort you to the embassy? I have a car." He bowed then flashed her his million-dollar white smile.

"*Mais bien sur*. Let me grab my things." She picked up her purse and briefcase, a wrap, and an umbrella. "Ready as I'll ever be, Sir Landon."

"My steed awaits, fair one."

At street level, Kate began to laugh. "Your 'steed' is a '64 midnight blue Mustang. It's beautiful." She ran her hand along the fender.

"It's Caspian Blue. An original color in 1964." Landon opened the door for her, and she slipped into the blue glove leather bucket seat.

"Car guy? Did you restore her? Why did you bring it to Paris? Not a great driving city with all the mopeds." Kate closed her eyes and experienced the feel and smell of the car. "It's wonderful, Sir Landon."

"My grandfather bought her new and kept her in the condition you see today. He gave her to me when I turned twenty-one on the condition that I maintain her the way he did."

The muscle car engine roared to life, and Landon led her onto the streets of Paris.

"Lucille really is like a mighty horse, you know. Eight cylinders under the hood is more power than it needs, and frequently I feel I'm reining her in."

Kate closed her eyes to enjoy the ride and to avoid watching their progress through the congestion of pedestrians, mopeds, motorcycles, and tiny cars at rush hour.

***

"Wake up, Kate. We're here. You must not have slept much after we met."

Kate jerked awake. "I am so sorry, Landon. I didn't intend to sleep."

"It's okay. We're at the embassy now."

Kate jumped out of the car with her head spinning. Why was she in a car with a man she didn't know? Where was she? Oh, the Place de Concorde.

"Are you alright, Kate?" Landon gripped her elbow and turned her toward the Embassy on Avenue Gabriel. "It's this way."

She pulled her elbow away and straightened her jacket. "I'm capable of walking down the street to work. In fact, most days I do walk it from home."

"Hey, it's cool, Kate. No problem." He held up his hands like a shield. "Didn't mean to ruffle your feathers. Just trying to help."

Kate's head still hurt. "You should know that I have a, well, a fiancé in Texas. He was best All-Around Cowboy in everything a few years back. And he has real steeds, thank you very much." She pivoted on her heels and nearly fell. Not the exit she had planned.

Kate showed her badge at the embassy gates and headed for the Chancery across the cobble-stone courtyard. She nodded to the statue of Ben Franklin. Since cellphones were not allowed in the building, she stored her purse and electronics in the employees' secure locker room.

As Kate headed toward her office, Carol, the receptionist, called out to her.

"Who was that blond hunk in the Mustang you rode in with? Had you spent the night with him? Does he work here?"

"Shhh." Kate hurried across the lobby, lanyard and badge swinging. "Yes, Landon works here somewhere, but he wouldn't tell me where. His apartment adjoins mine, and he rescued me from a difficult situation last night. He just offered to chauffeur me in this morning."

"I for one have never seen him before." Carol sifted through some messages and handed her a few. "And I see everyone. It's my job."

Kate shrugged. "All I can tell you is he said he'd have to kill me if he told me what he does at the embassy."

Carol fanned the remaining messages and her blouse. "He is one handsome honey, Kate. Maybe he's MI6."

"Attached to the US Embassy? I don't think so." Kate turned and took the stairs to her office while perusing the phone messages. Three from Tyler, one from Doug, and one from Stefan. Shouldn't messages received at work be related to work?

As she reached the third floor, the exit door flew open, nearly catching her in the face.

"I caught you!" Doug reached out and grabbed her from the brink of falling down the stairs.

"Are you trying to kill me now?" Kate stepped off the top step into the landing. "What are you doing?"

"I went by your cubicle, and you have a visitor. I knew you often take the stairs."

Kate pulled his hands off her.

"Who warrants all this drama, Doug?"

"The head of Embassy Security is there in your office. What did you do?"

Kate put her hands on her hips. "You should be the one examining yourself."

She pulled open the fire door leaving Doug on the landing. Nevertheless, she felt shaky as she rounded the corner to her desk area.

"Landon? What are you doing here? Can I help you with something?"

Kate plopped into her chair and kicked off her heels. Luckily, she kept black flats in her desk drawer for days like today.

"I am checking on you to see if you got in okay." Landon stood and stretched. "You had a rough night and an unsettling morning."

"Doug said the head of security was after me." Kate laughed. "That's a frightening thought."

Landon laughed. "I am the head of security. And I've added Doug to my list of suspicious individuals. I care about your safety, Kate. He seems dangerous. Here's my card. Put my number in your phone. Call me if you need anything."

"Hoping it won't come to it. Thanks for looking in on me. I'm fine." Kate waved Landon off. "See you later, neighbor."

"Want a ride home later?"

"No, I'll walk this evening. Enjoy your bistro surfing."

Landon nodded and headed back out into the hallway.

Kate sighed. *What a day; and it hasn't even begun.* On cue, her desk phone started ringing. She put Landon's card in her purse to add to her cell phone at the end of the day.

Chapter 20

Tyler hefted the box onto his better hip and struggled out to the truck. After depositing the box, he hobbled back into Mission Mesquite.

"What else can I do, Rev.?" Tyler looked around the nearly empty trailer. "I hate to be displacing you. After all, I won't be living here."

Rev. Ryan handed him another box, this one clearly full of books. "Retirement is an opportunity for some well-earned privacy. We're just around the bend, so we can answer any late-night calls while you're getting Miguel up and ready. You can take over when you get here."

They'd set up a video doorbell to ring on both of their cell phones. Any emergency could be handled swiftly.

Tyler hustled the box out to the truck while Miguel played with the trailer park dog. "Be careful, Miguel. That dog may change his mind about you."

Miguel grinned. "This dog loves me. I call him 'Rodeo.' Good name, Daddy?"

Tyler slid his hat back on his head and hooked his thumbs in his belt loops. "Yes, it's a good name. But is he a good dog?"

"No worries, Daddy." Miguel threw a stick that Rodeo chased.

No worries. Tina's pat phrase. No doubt he'd heard it plenty in his short life.

"Tyler, I need your height to reach something on the top shelf."

"Yes, ma'am. Miguel, come out of the road and help Grandma Sarah."

Miguel dropped his stick and ran into Tyler's arms. Tyler brought him up to sit at his waist and squeezed him tightly. Then he stood him down on the walkway where he ran into the trailer and slammed the screen door.

Miss Sarah had already captured the squirming, giggling brown boy.

"We have something for you, Ty. Go on, open it." Rev. Ryan handed him a comic-page-wrapped box with a stick-on blue bow.

"Open it, Daddy. Do you need me to help?"

"Let Daddy open it by himself. You can open your presents next week on your birthday."

Tyler grinned. He took off the bow and ripped the colorful newsprint. He opened the box and pulled out a desk plate on a mahogany holder. He read the name plate aloud. "'Reverend Tyler Hawkins, Pastor; Mission Mesquite.' That is so amazing."

Miss Sarah picked up Miguel. "Come put it on your new desk."

Tyler walked into the designated Pastor's Study and discovered a new wood desk with a fresh manager's chair. "How'd you pull off a new desk and chair without me noticing it?"

"We had help; come out, guys." Rev. Ryan slid the closet open.

Miss Sarah laughed as rodeo stunt men, clowns, and performers piled out of the sliding door closet. They all piled on the big man in congratulations on his new office. Miss Sarah snapped pictures as Miguel piled on too.

"We need to send these pics to Katie. A little decorum, men."

Miguel scrambled through the scrum to Tyler's lap. The big men stood, perched on the desk, stood behind Tyler, and knelt in front. Miss Sarah had to go into the small hallway to angle her camera phone to get all the men in the picture. After the flash, Tyler was at the center of a firestorm of congratulations.

"Grandma, Grandma, let me see the pictures before you send them to Katybug." Miguel ran to Miss Sarah and pulled on her skirt.

"Fresh chocolate chip cookies in the kitchen, boys."

The trample of feet shook the mobile home.

"I'll leave it to you then." Rev. Ryan closed the door, leaving Tyler alone in his office.

"Well, Lord. Here we are finally. When Miss Sarah sends that picture, will Katie rebel? Will it send her into a tailspin? Will it send her home to me?" With forehead in hand, he continued, "Be with her tonight. I know you can protect her. Help her to make wise decisions. Make one of those decisions to come back to me. I can't do this alone."

***

Kate met Arianne at a little bistro prior to the final day and night of Fashion Week. The dress she'd chosen after discarding half her closet on the floor was still not what she would have worn if anything else in her closet had fit. All of it hung too loosely on her frame. Tyler would have a fit if he saw her now.

The waitress set the salad, dressing in a cup to the side, in front of her. She set a plate of roast beef and vegetables in front of Arianne. Then she set a basket of baguettes in the center of the table between them.

"May I get you something more, Mademoiselle?"

"You may refill my coffee. It's not your business what I eat or don't eat." The waitress left looking perplexed

Kate shoved the bread basket closer to Arianne. "And don't you start either."

"But all I see you eat are salads. You have lost a great deal of weight in the time you have been in Paris. I hear the things Doug says to you. He is not your friend, Kate."

"I do a lot of walking to see as much of Paris as I can while I'm here." Kate stabbed the naked lettuce with a fork and knife to cut it into tiny pieces. "Doug is my ex-fiancé. I am aware of the toxic advice he gives. But even a broken clock is right twice a day."

She focused on cutting the iceberg wedge into increasingly smaller pieces. She ate three bites and sat back satisfied. Arianne split the baguette releasing the aromatic steam from its center. She spread both pieces with the whipped butter that had arrived with it.

"Sure you wouldn't like part? Bread is the staff of life, *n'est-ce pas?*" Arianne held out one half of the bread.

Kate took the bread and ate it hungrily. An extra mile on her walk tomorrow and the steps to Sacre Coeur.

When Arianne had eaten every bite and Kate's salad appeared to have been through a cross-cut shredder, they paid the bill and headed to the fashion district for the evening's entertainment.

***

As they walked into the hall, the energy of the place excited Kate. Whirling colored lights, back beat driven music at an unholy decibel range, and the chatter of celebrities and glitterati caused her heart to pound and her head to ache.

Arianne grabbed her arm. "Look! Isn't that Stella McCartney?"

Kate nodded as she grabbed onto a folding chair for support.

"Ladies, do you have your passes? If not, I need to ask you to leave."

The usher held out his hand and looked ready to wave security over. Kate brought the passes out and handed them to the over-dressed usher. He almost looked disappointed that he didn't get to show authority over them. Instead he directed them to a dignitaries' box. Then he handed back the passes, which were signed by Stefan.

"Kate, we're sitting in the Director of State's seats." Arianne clapped her hands and pedaled her feet. "I can't believe it. What did you do to get such seats?"

"Not that!" Kate was indignant. "Stefan was ambassador to the US while I was at the State Department. We've eaten a great deal of rubber chicken dinners and drank a lot of watered down drinks before both being posted in France."

Arianne blushed the color of the red Ferraris Kate saw racing through the streets. "I didn't mean anything inappropriate. Really I didn't."

"I believe you. Shush, it's starting."

The lights suddenly dimmed, and the music dropped to a background level. A spotlight shone in the eyes of the Master of Ceremonies. The show began. Impossibly thin, even wraith-like, tall models strutted and sashayed down the catwalk in swirling fabrics and impossibly high stiletto heels. The audience oohed and aahed at the fashions by celebrity designers. This show was to be the best of the best. Kate watched for something that would fit her body as well as her personality. Most of them were inappropriate for state affairs.

Arianne helped her watch with "what about that?" or "what about this?" sprinkled throughout the show.

Kate saw the dress before Arianne. Flashes from all the cameras confirmed her opinion that this could be the best of the show, save the unveiling of the prerequisite wedding dress. The black lace formed a yoked bodice, lined from the yoke to the floor. The lace fit snug at the top and gradually widened as it fell to the floor in shadowed puddles of black lace and light. This was the one. Definitely a special occasion dress. But would it fit?

***

Once the show was over, Arianne and Kate went back stage with her passes and joined the crowd bidding on the 'gently used' dresses for charity. The bidding prices were more than she'd ever consider spending on a dress. Fortunately, the crowd had thinned by the time the black lace dress came up for bidding. The others in the room were there for the last dress, the wedding dress, so Kate could buy it without much competition using Stefan's check.

"I can't believe you got a designer original tonight." Arianne helped Kate put the dress in the car Kate had borrowed for the occasion. "You'll look beautiful in it, Kate."

"I just hope it actually fits or has some fabric at the seams to let it out."

Arianne caught Kate by the wrist. "Are you kidding me? Have you genuinely looked in the mirror? You are every bit as thin as any model we saw tonight. You need to eat."

Kate wrested away from her. "That's my business, girl Friday."

They didn't speak on the way home. Kate dropped Arianne at her apartment and then drove the borrowed car through the dark streets. A sense of foreboding prickled the hairs on the back of her neck. Arianne was right. She couldn't keep losing weight. But she didn't want to eat except for the bread, which she really shouldn't eat.

Bread is the staff of life, Kate. You cannot serve Me if you destroy the temple in which I dwell. Yea, though you walk through the valley of the shadow of death, I will be with you.

The voice was as real as if God was sitting in the passenger seat beside her.

Chapter 21

Miguel climbed into Tyler's bed early October 1. Tyler felt his presence but kept his eyes closed to see what he would do.

"Daddy, are you asleep?"

Tyler grunted and rolled over.

"Daddy, is it my birthday?"

Tyler did his best fake snore.

"Daddy? Is my birthday party today?"

Tyler rolled over and pulled him into his arms. Miguel giggled and tried to break free. Tyler held him tighter and tickled him.

"Daddy, are you awake now?" Miguel struggled and giggled.

"Yes. To all your questions."

Miguel threw his arms around Tyler's neck. "I knew it would be today."

Tyler hugged him. "Happy birthday. How old are you now?"

Miguel stretched out his hand and counted the fingers. "Five!"

"That's right. We've lots of things to do today to celebrate. How about Mickey Mouse waffles?"

Miguel pulled back and gave him a puzzled look. "How do you make Mickey Mouse waffles?"

"You buy a Mickey Mouse waffle maker."

Miguel's squeal could have been heard down at the barn. He bounced out of the bed and ran to the kitchen. Tyler followed with his slower pace. Pajama morning it would be.

Tyler turned on Saturday cartoons for Miguel. He started a waffle then dialed a Paris phone number.

"*Bon jour.*"

"This is Tyler Hawkins."

"*Oui, monsieur.* How are you today? It is morning there, *n'est-ce pas?*"

"Any word on my girl?" Tyler nodded to Miguel as he squealed and pointed at Wile Coyote being bested by the Road Runner, again.

"She and her assistant are going to the last night of fashion week to buy a design original in the charity auction."

"How is she?" Tyler flipped one waffle out onto a plate. "Is she well? Is Doug out of the picture?" He started another waffle.

"Kate continues to lose weight. I tried to entice her into my bistro project, but she refused. Perhaps she does not want to be disloyal? She did mention that she was 'effectively engaged,' whatever that means. Tonight Kate's out with her assistant Arianna. Dremond gave her tickets to the Fashion Week finale. I loaned her my car so she wasn't wandering Paris at night."

"Thanks. I can't tell you how much this means to me."

"Aah, a knock at the door. This is probably Kate returning the keys to the car."

"Ok. Just keep Doug away from her, if you can, without overstepping your authority. Continue to watch her for me while we're apart. I appreciate your help, Landon."

Tyler hung up after the conventions of saying good-bye to the Head of the US Embassy Security. He flipped a second waffle onto another plate.

"Birthday waffles, hot off the griddle."

Miguel came running to the breakfast bar.

***

Kate waited for Landon to open the door. She could hear his voice, as though on the phone with someone.

"Ah, Kate. Back from the fashion show so soon?" Landon opened the door to admit her.

Kate stayed in the hall. "I'm just returning your keys. Thank you so much for the loan of your spectacular steed. It would have been tiresome to carry this dress through the streets of Paris." She held up the swaddled black lace formal. "Something for the rounds of Christmas receptions."

"You were successful in buying the dress of your dreams?" Landon motioned for Kate to enter the apartment.

"I can't stay, Landon. Especially in a man's apartment in Paris."

Landon leaned against the door frame. "But I am only offering decaf Irish coffee between friends. I would not take advantage of you. Remember, I'm sworn to take care of you."

Kate smiled. "Irish coffee, definitely decaf, sounds wonderful. I don't think my fiancé would approve. And I don't want to be tempted to have more than a coffee."

Landon grinned. "I could bring the coffee to your apartment, if that is more preferable."

"Hmmm. Okay. I'll try on my dress for you and get your reaction. I'm terrified it's too small, and I'll not have enough fabric to let it out." Kate made a face.

"I don't think you should be afraid of that. Why don't you go put it on while I make the coffee?"

Kate nodded and headed toward her apartment door. She heard Landon's door close as she stuck the key in the lock. Was it wrong to have a male friend over for coffee and a fashion show? Would Tyler be threatened by Landon?

***

As Miguel and Tyler pulled up to the corral on the ATV, the van from Mission Mesquite was also pulling up. Rev. Ryan jumped out of the driver's seat hurried to meet Miguel.

"Happy birthday, buddy." Rev. Ryan opened his arms to catch Miguel as he ran to him with open arms.

"Papa! You came for my birthday." He wrapped his arms around his papa's neck.

"Wouldn't miss it for anything. How old are you?"

"Five." Miguel held out his hand with all his fingers outstretched.

Tyler surveyed the scene, his son with Papa Ryan, Miss Sarah opening the van to release its bevy of excited children. Joe and Rosa were leading the horses into the corral for their weekly exercise. Could any man be as blessed as he was? Katie was the missing piece. Tyler was trying to leave that to God since he could do no more to affect that in Paris.

"I know, Lord, I keep taking it back. I do have faith that You will do the work in Katie to bring her back to me. Just show Your love to her; let her know I love her and want her back." It wasn't the first time he'd prayed that prayer. Probably wouldn't be the last time either.

Once the riding lessons were finished, Rev. Ryan and Miss Sarah loaded the children into the van and drove them up the winding drive to the 'big house'. Tyler followed on the ATV; Miguel rode with the other children and Katie's parents. He really hoped the guys had done the decorating he'd asked them to do and fixed the chili with much less spice than they'd normally do. After all, these were children.

He rode the ATV to the deck and entered in through the French doors to the family room, so he could see the look on Miguel's face when he walked in.

"Stan, Cantu, how's it going?"

They shook his hand and gestured to the folding tables covered in bandana fabric. Each place had a small cowboy hat, candies, and cupcakes. On a side table, presents were piled. Crepe paper and balloons festooned the ceiling.

"Wow, you guys did a great job." Tyler whipped out his phone and took a picture of the scene for Katie.

The children came running in with Miguel at the front. Tyler took pictures of his reactions to the transformation of his home. The other children cried out in delight and ran to find their space at the tables. As Tyler was snapping pics, Miguel spotted him and ran to him.

"Daddy, I never had a party before. It's beautiful. Did Mr. Stan and Mr. Cantu help?"

Tyler took him into his arms and hugged him tight. "Yes, they did the work before. We'll probably do the work to clean it up."

Miguel wiggled free and gave knee hugs to the other cowboys. "Thank you for making my party."

The cowboys served the children chili, hamburgers, corn chips, and soda. Children's laughter filled the lonely house. Tyler leaned against the wall watching his son, HIS SON, enjoy the attention and mayhem. If only Katie was here, then his world would be complete.

When the feast had concluded, birthday present unwrapping time came. Tyler's friends passed out small gifts – small Legos cowboy and horse sets – while Miguel opened presents from Miss Sarah and Rev.

Ryan, Katie, and Tyler. Without specific planning, the three gifts created a child-sized pro rodeo outfit complete with hat, chaps, vest, and boots. In addition, Rev. Ryan had made him a stick pony. Miguel allowed the children from the mission to play with the stick pony, but he was wearing the rodeo apparel.

As the children loaded up into the van with Miss Sarah and Rev. Ryan, Miguel shook each child's hand and thanked them for making this birthday better than any he'd ever had. Tyler was proud of his son's manners, clearly imparted by Tina with no input from himself. After all, he'd missed almost 5 years of Miguel's life.

***

The first weekend of October was also the Pro Rodeo Finals. The arena had been quiet since the end of August. Some rodeo folk made the Mesquite trailer park home when the season had ended. Others had moved on to new stomping grounds. For the Finals, though, the best had assembled once again at the Mesquite Arena.

Tyler stood awkwardly and stepped into the circle of cowboys and cowgirls. They gathered closer around Tyler for him to lead in prayer. The men and women removed their hats. Several requests were made quietly. Tyler removed his hat and cleared his throat.

"As you know, my Katie is in Paris. She's been there coming up on two months. The longer she's there, the worse my gut feels about her being there."

"Afraid you're going to lose out to a Frenchman, Reverend?" The new man laughed after his quip.

"Call me Tyler, if you don't mind. No, it's not about her affection for me. It's about her well-being that I'm concerned. She hasn't said anything when we talk or in her letters. But there's something wrong. Just pray for her, please."

The group closed in tighter and took a knee. Tyler led in the prayer time before the Finals at the Mesquite Arena. As he finished praying, Rev. Ryan clapped him on the shoulder.

"I know what you're talking about, Tyler. I've felt it, too. She's on edge, overtired, anxious, drained. Maybe we need to put an end to this nonsense and bring her home."

"No, I promised to give her this time before requiring a final answer to my proposal. I also promised to let the answer be hers, not a manipulation. She doesn't want to be a minister's wife, Rev. I think she loves me but not what I represent. Only God can change that. I'm waiting for Him to do His work in her. But I'm also very worried."

The two men prayed together specifically for Katie before the announcer called the parade participants to their horses. Then the show began; Tyler moved stiffly to the spectators' area, leg brace still balky with each step. Miguel waited there with Katie's mom.

"There you are, Daddy. I was afraid you'd be too busy to watch the rodeo with me and Grandma Sarah." Miguel wore the rodeo gear in a child size, making him a near carbon copy of Tyler.

Tyler swept the boy up into his arms and hugged him tightly. "I promise; I will never be too busy for you. If I am that busy, you will go with me, so you won't be alone."

He placed Miguel back in his seat next to Miss Sarah. "If I ever need to be gone a long time, I think Grandma Sarah and Grandpa Ryan will be there for you until I get back."

"Where are you going, Daddy?"

"I bet I'll need to go to Paris to bring back our Katydid."

Sarah nodded. "I think so too. Miguel, you are always welcome in my home especially whenever your daddy has to be away."

Chapter 22

Dawn awakened Kate from a restless sleep. She had tried on the dress for Landon, and it was too big. Not only was she alarmed, but it seemed to upset Landon as well. That wakeup call had kept her up half the night. She needed to regain control of her situation. She could baste the seams, so she could wear the expensive black lace dress until she could let it back out.

After dressing in her running outfit, she looked in the fridge.

She poured the last of the orange juice and vowed to visit the grocery before dinner. She checked the pantry, no food in there either. She'd stop for coffee at her favorite shop and get a croissant.

Once she began running toward Montmartre, she passed the coffee shop completely. She only stopped when she got to the steps to Sacre Coeur. Kate's heart pounded, and she could barely catch her breath. A man stopped and touched her shoulder.

"You okay, lady?"

"Not sure. Was headed to the church." She wheezed and coughed.

"My advice is to take the funicular today." The man ran on, leaving her stranded.

Kate shook her head; that only left her dizzy. She sat down on the curb, feeling nauseated. A car pulled up next to her, and the door opened.

"Can I give you a ride?"

Kate looked up into Doug's sneer. "No. I'd die here first than get into the car with you."

"Looks like you're getting close to doing that all on your own." He slammed the door and sped off.

Kate thought she heard laughter amid the engine roar. "Nice, Doug. And to think I agreed to marry you once. Why aren't you here, Tyler?"

Kate was determined to climb the steps to Sacre Coeur. She could hear the *chantons* of the sisters of Sacre Coeur. Perhaps she'd climb the steps a section at a time, then she'd stay for the mystique of the Mass.

The service had already started when Kate stepped into the cold, dark cathedral. While gasping for air, she found a seat near the back. The liturgical music enveloped her. No one seemed to notice or care that she was in her running gear. She closed her eyes to calm her heart and to open her spirit to the adoration of the Lord.

When the service ended, Kate stood but the room spun. She sat back down but knocked over chairs in doing so. She drew the attention of some of the congregants who rushed to help her. They helped her up and out to the fresh autumn air.

"*Non, ne nécessaire pas.*" Kate waved off their insistent pleas to help her.

Kate took her cellphone out of its arm holster. Thank God she'd put Landon's number in before this morning.

"Landon, I'm stranded at Sacre Coeur. Can you come and get me?"

"Of course, Kate. I'll be right there. I just stepped out of worship as well."

After a few moments, a gendarme pulled up beside her. "How can I help you, *mademoiselle*? Do you need an ambulance?"

"No, officer. I have a ride home coming soon. I'll be fine."

The priest joined them on the curb. "*Mademoiselle, ce va? Américaine?*"

Kate blinked at all the concern shown her. "*Ce va. Oui, je suis Américaine.*"

"Then let us speak English. I am Father Francois." He took her hand. "You do not look well. I called the gendarme and ambulance for you. Won't you let them check you over?"

"*Merci beaucoup*, Father, but here is my ride now. I promise to take this seriously, but right now I just want to return home. I ran too far this morning."

"What are you running away from? God has a great work for you to do in a different place. Why are you in Paris?"

Kate yanked her hand back as though from a fire. "What do you mean?"

"Only that it is clear that you are out of place, *n'est pas*? You have another place, another duty to fulfill. This man is not your true rescuer either."

The blue Mustang pulled up, and Landon leapt from the car. He took the steps 2 and 3 at a time. Kate stood tentatively leaning on the Father Francois.

"What happened, Kate?" Landon took her arm to steady her. "Father, can you help us to the car?"

"*Mais bien sur.*"

The two men steadied her on each side as they took the steps carefully. When they reached the car, Landon helped her into the passenger's seat.

Landon shook the priest's hand. "I'll be sure she gets home. The US Embassy physician can look at her tomorrow, if necessary. We both work there."

The priest made the sign of the cross over Kate. "Be well, young lady. Do not be any longer distracted from your true calling, Kate. God loves you and so does your fiancé."

"Thank you, Father, for your reassurances. I am building courage to face what God seems to be calling me to do."

Landon closed the door once Father Francois stepped back away from the car.

"That was freaky." Kate pulled on the seatbelt. "It was like he was psychic."

"Is there something you want to tell me? We are friends, aren't we?" Landon threw the Mustang into gear and roared away from the church, down through Montmartre, over the bridge under which the famous cemetery resides. "Tell me about this great work the priest spoke about."

"My fiancé Tyler is the pastor of a cowboy church at Mesquite Arena, in the Dallas area. It's the same mission church my parents have been running until my dad's heart attack." Kate fidgeted with her sleeve. "I grew up a missionary kid. It wasn't easy, and I swore never to be involved with God or missions when I grew up. Until I met Tyler, I'd had no problem keeping my oath. I know what God wants, and I want Tyler as my husband; I'm just having trouble letting go of my fear."

"That's where the anorexia comes in." Landon continued looking at the street while Kate gaped in terror. "By the way, I'm picking up food on the way back to the building. No ifs ands or buts, lady, you will be eating lunch with me today."

"How do you know about the anorexia?"

"Head of security. I scan everyone's files when they come to Paris. If there's a discernible weakness of any kind, I know it, flag it, and make sure it can't be exploited." Landon glanced over at her as they stopped at a traffic light. "You've been on my radar ever since you arrived. Doug's another reason why you came into my area of concern."

"Why is that?" Kate crossed her arms, feeling like a scolded schoolgirl.

"He made such a fuss the first day he was here about being placed in your building instead of the one across town."

"Wait! Doug told me we were slated for the same apartment."

Landon shook his head while he parked in front of a shop. "I'll be right back with food. You stay put."

Kate nodded, and Landon hurried into the store. Doug had lied to her. Not the first time, mind you. The sudden chill that ran down her spine had nothing to do with the autumn breeze blowing in the open car window. Was she in danger?

Landon returned with a feast – chicken salad on croissants, chips, fruit, ham sandwiches, sodas, and chocolate pie. After parking the car, Landon helped her up to her apartment then went back for the food.

Kate set out plates, utensils, and napkins. She slipped back to the bedroom to change into leggings, instead of the jeans that didn't fit, and a baggy sweater. Then she hurried to the door to help Landon with the food.

Chapter 23

Life had become routine. Tyler knew what he did as pastor of Mission Mesquite was important as was raising and loving Miguel. Without Katie, though, all seemed tedious. On this October day, he was alone at the trailer/church. Miss Sarah had dropped off oatmeal cookies, and he'd made coffee for anyone who might drop by. Truth was he'd eaten too many cookies and drank too much coffee. And it was only 10 AM.

Katie would be getting off work about now. He called Paris.

"Tyler! This is a pleasant surprise. I was thinking about you. You must have heard me."

"How are you, Katydid?"

"Went to Sacre Coeur for church Sunday. I bought a CD of the Chantons of the Sisters of Sacre Coeur. Not sure it's your kind of church music though."

"Chantons? Is that like the chants of the Gregorian monks?" Tyler swiveled in his desk chair. "Not sure the rodeo folk could take much of that."

Katie's laugh across the miles soothed his soul.

"Probably not. But they might like it, you never know. You sound like a fuddy-duddy."

Tyler scowled. "Do people still use the word 'fuddy-duddy' or is it code for something else?"

She laughed again. "I want to tell you about the strangest thing that happened at Sacre Coeur. The priest there was some kind of psychic. He told me to quit running from God and from the future He wanted me to have."

"Katie, we don't call men of God psychic. We say they have the gift of discernment. Will you listen to his advice?"

The line went silent.

"Are you there, Katydid?"

Snaps and crackles. "Yes, Tyler, I'll listen to him. But I want to wait until spring. Let me experience Paris in the spring."

Time to change the subject before he made her cry again. She knew what God wanted. That was enough for now. "Making any new friends? Find a frock at the fashion show?"

"Yes. The head of security, Landon. I think I mentioned him before. He picked me up after services, and he stopped for the best chicken salad I've ever eaten. It had grapes and Craisins on a fresh croissant. We sat on the balcony and enjoyed the autumn weather."

Tyler knew he should say something about his own conversations with Landon, but he was afraid his good intentions would cheapen her trust in Landon and in himself.

"What's this Landon guy like?"

"Don't get jealous; he's just a friend. I'll send you the selfie we took on the balcony."

In point of truth, Landon had sent him pictures of her and the selfie from his own phone. Guilt twinged his heart. "That would be great. I need a new picture for my wallpaper."

"One favor, Tyler. Don't use it for dart practice."

Why would he ever do that? "Of course not. Are you eating, besides your Sunday balcony meal? You look too thin, Sweetheart."

"I'm fine."

Tyler could hear her defenses raise in those two words. "I love you, Katie. Send me a pic of you in your new dress."

"I love you too."

A crash at the living room door alerted Tyler to a ministry need.

"Someone just crashed into the living room. Gotta go minister."

"Talk later." And then she was gone again.

Tyler's frustration was put on the back burner as he raced to the living room. There he found a man, bleeding from a chest wound, on the floor. Tyler grabbed the landline and called for an ambulance while he gathered clean kitchen towels to stem the flow of blood.

"Sir? Can you hear me? I'm Tyler Hawkins, pastor of Mission Mesquite. Who did this to you? What's your name?"

The man mumbled. Tyler leaned closer to the man's lips.

"Only place I knew to come. I'm Bobby Carpenter. Cantu did this."

"Bobby, stay with me. Did you say Cantu did this?"

The man nodded. The ambulance and police sirens became audible.

"There must be some mistake, Bobby."

Emergency responders broke into the mobile home and took over from Tyler. Before he knew what had happened, the ambulance was pulling away, and the police were him asking questions.

"Detective Paul Rodriquez, Reverend." The Dallas PD detective held out a hand and realized Tyler was covered in the victim's blood. "Did you know the man?"

"No, he said he was Bobby Carpenter." Tyler wanted to wash the blood off his hands.

"He was talking when he came into the Mission?" The second detective scribbled in a notebook. "I'm Detective James Kellan. Did he tell you what happened?"

"No, he didn't tell me what had happened." Tyler really didn't want to answer the next question. He rubbed his hands on his jeans.

"Please don't do that. You may have critical evidence on your hands." Rodriquez waved one of the forensic team over. "Test for GSR and DNA. You know the drill."

"Am I a suspect?" Tyler's voice quavered. The room spun around him. "All I know about it is what he said to me. He came here because we're a Mission. I guess he needed spiritual solace."

"That may well be, but you know we have to examine all the angles. Did he also tell you anything about who shot him?" Kellan continued his furious scrawl.

"Yes, he named an assailant."

The forensic team took swabs of his hands, blood and all. Probably find evidence of the half-eaten BLT on his desk.

Detective Rodriquez glared at him. "Well, who'd he say shot him?"

"I can't divulge that without asking some questions myself."

"You do realize you can be charged with impeding an investigation here." Rodriquez jammed his hand into his trench coat.

"I can't divulge that information until I have a chance to check the story with the one accused."

The forensic officer finished dabbing at his hand, then took a cheek swab, "…to rule you out." She handed him a sanitizing wipe to clean his hands. "We'll need your bloody clothes, too."

Detective Kellan followed Tyler to the guest bedroom where he kept a change of clothes 'for such a time as this'. The forensic tech took the bloody ones and put them in an evidence bag.

Kellan looked up from his notebook and twirled his pencil between his fingers. "If you know something, you need to tell us. It could be his dying declaration, Reverend Hawkins."

Tyler pulled on a Paris t-shirt from Katie and jeans. "As the recipient of the declaration, I'm his priest; his confession could be protected under the law."

"Yes, I'm sorry; but the blood on your carpet tells me that whatever he said is relevant to the investigation."

"He said 'Cantu did this.'" Tyler sat down on the edge of the couch. "My pickup partner at the Arena is Junior Cantu. Yes, I'll call you if I learn anything more about the situation."

Detective Rodriquez handed him his card.

Finally, the police followed the ambulance to the hospital to gather more information. As soon as they were gone, Tyler used his cell to call Cantu.

"You've reached Cantu. I ain't answering the phone right now. I might be saving somebody's life. Leave a message, but that don't mean I'll call you back. Beep!"

"Call me, Cantu. It's Tyler. You know where I am."

The puddle of blood soaking into Miss Sarah's carpet demanded his attention once the forensic team was done dusting for prints and trying to find every possible human fluid in the living room. He'd head over to the hospital once Rev. Ryan came over after lunch.

***

Monday morning. Kate drug herself from bed. The woman in her mirror looked tired and frazzled. Even her auburn hair looked frazzled.

"Ugh. Mondays in Paris are no better than Mondays in America."

She readied for work. The half-eaten chicken salad croissant became breakfast but made her nauseated. She dressed and hurried the few blocks to the Embassy.

Arianna met her with a sheaf of messages. "Many from your Tyler. Have you lost your cell?"

"Yes, Arianna, I turned the sound off after my last phone call with Tyler."

"That sounds very bad, Kate. Did you quarrel?"

Kate turned on her heel on Arianna. "I'm so tired of people commenting on my weight. After Tyler turned my lovely afternoon into something about what I ate, I was uninterested in anything he had to say on the subject."

Arianna cringed as though she'd been hit. "I'll go back to my desk. Let me know if you want to go out for lunch."

"Lunch! You think I need lunch?"

Arianna scurried away. Kate covered her mouth with her hand. "Oh, God, keep me from being cruel or difficult." She knew she was on the slippery slope. She tried never to be rude to anyone on purpose.

Sifting through the messages, most from Tyler were marked urgent. She picked up the phone to call him when Landon stuck his head into her cubicle.

"Morning, neighbor. Did you get your invitation to the Pre-formal Informal?"

"I did. I have no idea what it's about, and it's in St. Denis." Kate looked up and smiled. "I planned to decline."

"No, you mustn't decline. It's the best event all year." Landon sat in the chair beside her desk. "It takes place prior to the holiday round of formal receptions and the endless dinners at every embassy in town."

"Exactly why I thought I must decline." Kate popped up her laptop and turned it on. "Why would I choose to attend a party I don't have to go to?"

"Because it's just us – Americans in Paris, McCullough called us. We come in American dress, jeans and sweaters or whatever. We hang out around a fire pit, roasting marshmallows, making s'mores, and cook hot dogs and hamburgers on the grill. And we talk to one another in English instead of French. We play board games, enjoy wine, and relax."

"Is there also apple pie?" Kate's tone was lighthearted though certainly sarcastic. "Not sure I can come if there's no apple pie, Landon."

"I guarantee you apple pie, milady." Landon stood to go. "I'll be your chauffeur for the evening; only say you'll come."

"Sounds like an offer I cannot refuse."

Landon's fist pump and his "Yes" sounded as he left the cubicle.

Kate shook her head. It was time Landon got back to the States when hotdogs and s'mores are a major draw for an evening out. As she searched through the interoffice mail to find the invitation so she could RSVP, she knocked a card onto the floor. She picked it up and opened it.

The card read, in childlike tracing of letters, "We miss you." On the front was a child's drawing of Tyler and Miguel. On the inside, it said, "We're not a family without you." The picture showed a woman in a rocker with Tyler and Miguel around her. She had a baby on her lap, too. An arrow pointing to the baby said "Gabriel." Behind the happy foursome was the trailer with a cross on the top, obviously Mission Mesquite. She turned the card over. Written in child script was 'Love, Miguel' inside a lopsided heart. And he'd drawn a crown at the bottom as though it was a Hallmark card.

Unbidden tears coursed down her cheeks. If only the future was as clear to the adults as it was for Miguel. "No pressure, huh? Dirty pool using a child like that."

Her email came up finally. The message from Tyler was frightening. Someone had been shot in the trailer park, and they'd come to the mission for help. Not only that, but he'd named Cantu, one of Tyler's best friends, as the shooter. How could Tyler help, much less minister, in that situation?

Kate looked at the clock. Six hours behind would make it two AM. Would he still be up? She would in a similar situation. She emailed Tyler to be safe.

"Are you up? Want to Skype?"

She continued sorting her mail, waiting for the beep that meant she had a message. When it came, she called Arianna and asked her to hold her calls.

The message read, "Yes, Yes!"

Now would be a great time for an office door, but this situation was an emergency. She logged on and rang Tyler's computer. He answered immediately.

"Katydid! Boy, I am so glad you suggested this. We can talk almost face-to-face."

"Good to see you too." In fact, her heart ached at seeing him.

"You look thin, Love. I know it exasperates you for me to mention it, but I want you to live long enough to make it back, safe and sound, under my roof."

"How's Cantu?" Changing the subject was always a good life saver. "What's happened with the gunshot victim?"

His smile fell. "In the hospital. Cantu's in jail. They haven't found the gun yet. I think they suspect me too."

"Oh, Tyler. Wish I was there to hold you close." She realized she meant it. Paris was not what life was about for her. She needed to go home to Texas.

Tyler looked into her eyes, with nearly 5000 miles between them. "What do I need to do to make that happen?"

"Listen, these next weeks will be pretty crazy with the holiday receptions all over embassy row. Let me think on it. Would Christmas be too soon?"

She smiled at his reaction. Her heart jumped nearly as high as he tried to jump. In the end, he whooped, then missed the chair and fell in the floor. A small blond boy climbed into the chair.

"Katie Lady! I'm so happy to see your face. Daddy misses you something awful."

"I got your card today, Miguel." She held it up, so he could see. "I have a serious question for you. Who is Gabriel?"

"That's yours and Daddy's new baby. Gabriel was an arch-angel just like Michael. It's only right that my brother be Gabriel."

"What if it's a girl?" Kate snarled her lip at him. "We don't need no girls, do we?"

"Just you, Katie, Mama." Miguel looked like he would weep. "If we have another girl, we can call her Gabrielle.

Suddenly he was removed from the chair and replaced by Tyler. Then Tyler pulled his son onto his lap.

"Sounds like the two of you have been making big plans. I'd like to be part of the brainstorm sessions, too."

Miguel opened his mouth, and Tyler placed a hand over it. "Of course, you will. When you come back to us. Meanwhile, this little child needs to be put back to bed. Can you wait?"

"No, I'm at work. Later? I'll be home by noon your time. Will you be at the mission?"

"Until noon then." Miguel threw Kate a kiss as did Tyler.

Kate threw them a kiss back, then closed the screen. She reached for the tissue box on the corner of her desk to stem the tide of tears that coursed down her face. She never expected the sobs that came with the tears. How would she ever make it until Christmas?

The phone rang on her desk. She sniffed back her tears, then answered as calmly as she could.

"Hey, tomorrow, let's go early to St. Denis and tourist around before the informal. Have you ever seen the cathedral at St. Denis?"

"Landon? Yes, I went when I was in boarding school. I'm sure it'd be good to see it again as an interested adult. What time do you want to leave?"

"Let's go early, see the sights, and have lunch. We can enjoy the entire day."

Kate agreed, if for no reason than to get him off the phone, so she could blow her nose properly.

***

Tyler walked out of the dim light of the Jack Evans Police headquarters in Dallas. He squinted against the sun and pulled his hat brim down farther. He checked his cell phone for the time. He was not going to be back at his computer for the noon Skype session. He quickly sent a text for Katie to find when she picked up her phone from her locker.

As he was putting the phone back in his pocket, it rang.

"Tyler Hawkins speaking. How can I serve you today?"

"It's Landon. Thought I'd let you know that Kate will be unavailable all day into the evening tomorrow. She'll be with me in St. Denis, then we have an embassy function."

"You do remember that she's my fiancée, right?"

"I'm here, and you're not. If she prefers my company, that's her choice to make, right?"

"I thought we were working together to keep her safe. I can't believe that you are attempting to date my fiancée. Is that what she wants? Have you made your intentions clear to her?"

Tyler bobbled the phone as he attempted to get into the cab of his pickup.

"Sorry, repeat what you said."

"No, I have not declared myself yet. I promise I will not treat her the way Doug has in the past. I will treat her as a princess because that is what she is to me."

"Now here, here." Tyler turned the key that brought the truck to roaring life. "She's my fiancée."

"Should you have allowed her to come to Paris? Should you have created an 'effectively engaged' status with her? I think you've left her on the market. She doesn't even wear your ring."

"That's because it's too big. She wears it around her neck on a chain. I saw it today when we Skype-d."

A text came in from Katie.

"I need to go, but this conversation is not over, Landon."

"Later then." Landon hung up.

Tyler called Katie.

"Tyler! What do you mean we can't Skype now? I've been looking forward to seeing you all day."

Tyler put the Bluetooth in and pulled out of the parking lot.

"I know, Katydid. Me, too. Cantu was arrested this morning. The victim still claims Cantu shot him. If the guy dies, I'm going to have to testify to his 'dying declaration'. That'll put Cantu in prison for murder on my word."

Frustration, desperation, exasperation. All these words fit his mood. Hitting the dashboard would just mean replacing the dashboard though.

"I'm missing you so much. I'm thinking of resigning effective January 1. What would you think of that?"

Tyler smiled. "I'd like that very much."

"What's the deal with our child being named Gabriel?"

Tyler laughed. "I told Miguel that his name was the same as the archangel Michael and that Gabriel was the other archangel. He said his brother or sister would need to be Gabriel or Gabrielle."

Silence on the other end. "Katydid, are you there?"

"Yes. Full disclosure. Anorexia comes with a price. Damaged heart, damaged reproductive capability. If that's a deal-breaker, let me know now."

The sob from 5000 miles away nearly broke his heart.

"We have Miguel. As long as I have you, all will be fine."

Choked laughter on the other end of the phone. "You are ever the optimist, aren't you?"

"No, Katydid. I have hope and faith. 'Now faith is being sure of what we hope for and certain of what we do not see.' Hebrews 11:1, I am sure that God has brought us together. I have faith that you will come home to me." Tyler took the exit ramp off the highway and headed to Cantu's trailer to comfort his family. "I'm just about to Cantu's trailer. Call me before you turn in tonight. I love you, Katydid."

"And I you, Tyler. *Au revoir.*"

She was gone. Never had 5000 miles felt so far away. Paris may have well been Mars.

Tyler climbed out of the truck and walked up to the shabby little trailer with flower boxes blooming with hardy pansies. He knocked at the door, which was promptly opened by Cantu's twelve-year-old son, Jorge.

"Hey, Rev. Tyler. Did you know the police took Papa away?" The boy looked as though he'd been crying. "I know Pa; he'd never do no murder."

"Agreed." Tyler stuck out his hand and was enwrapped in a bear hug. "It's not fair, nor is it right."

Elena, very pregnant with child number six, entered the room from the kitchen.

"Tyler, they took him away from us. No way would Cantu shoot someone." She hugged Tyler as well. "Besides, someone stole that gun he had."

"Do you know the victim, Elena?"

At the question, Elena broke into tears and sat on the edge of the couch in the tiny living room. "Bobby Carpenter, right? Yes. I was engaged to him for a time. Until I met Cantu. Bobby and me, we fought all the time. He always wanted to control me – who I was with, who was on the phone, where I was going. I'd had enough of the abuse, so I walked out."

"How'd he take that from you?"

"Not well." Elena slumped back onto the tattered couch with a fresh set of tears. Tyler sat down next to her. "Cantu came along, and he treated me like a princess. He's rough 'round the edges and talks a mean talk, but he's a decent man."

"A good man." Tyler encouraged her to continue.

"I fell in love with Cantu. But that was twelve years ago. I can't see no reason for Cantu to kill him or for Bobby to say Cantu done it. That's all water under the bridge."

"I'm so sorry. When's this baby due?"

"Just after Christmas. Hoping he comes before January 1, so we can claim him on our taxes. But now Cantu's in prison." Another flood of tears began. "You're his friend, Tyler. Help him."

"I'll do what I can." Tyler hugged Elena and stood up from the sofa. Tyler stopped to peek in the playpen at the youngest playing with blocks. "This must be Joaquin. What a big boy you're getting to be."

"Papa, Papa, Papa." The boy began to cry.

Tyler reached in and pulled the child into his arms. "It's okay, Joaquin. We'll get Papa home as soon as we can, little boy."

The boy threw his arms around Tyler's neck and drooled down his shirt. Tyler rocked him side to side. Soon Joaquin's breathing was steady and slow. Tyler laid the sleeping boy down into the playpen.

"You are good at that, Tyler. You need a few of your own, you know." Elena smiled at him. "When you get your girl back in the USA, you will have many babies, too."

She handed him a spit cloth, and Tyler wiped at the damp spots on his neck and shirt. "We'll see, Elena. Let's get Cantu home before I have a house full of babies."

Chapter 24

Saturday dawned bright even though it was also chilly. Kate scurried around the apartment trying to prepare for tourist-ing as well as the "informal".

"Camera, sweater, rain poncho, snack food." She muttered to herself as she searched for every item and stuffed them in her backpack.

The knock at the door caught Kate by surprise. Landon or Doug?

Doug had already called that morning to announce his willingness to go with her into St. Denis, so she wouldn't be alone. She'd informed him, "I won't be alone. Thanks anyway."

Kate peered through the peephole to ascertain her caller. She swept open the door.

"Hurry in out of the hall." She pulled Landon in and closed the door swiftly. "Doug has already called to lobby for 'date' status for tonight. I do not want to accidentally run into him in the hallway."

"As long as you're not hiding from me, I can go with that." Landon gave her a gentle hug. "Are you ready? The Mustang is raring to go."

"I've almost got it all together." Kate started a tote bag with a blanket. "Do we need to take the Mustang? The Metro 13 runs out to a stop just across the street from the Basilica. Could someone pick us up in town and take us out to the party?"

Landon crossed his arms. "Sure, we could do that. I'll go back to my place and make some calls."

"You don't mind, do you? You seem irked."

"No problem, Kate. Whatever you want is fine. But if we take the Metro, you should leave some of this stuff here." He left to secure alternative transportation to the party.

He was right. With a sigh, Kate dumped the tote and the backpack to reconsider the load. As Kate was sorting and repacking, she felt arms reach around her into a hug. She jumped, flinging the hugger off. She turned to find Landon in the floor.

"I can see that sneaking up on you is a bad idea." He stood and brushed the imaginary dust off. "Ready to go? Derrick, the embassy limo driver will pick us up about four at the Basilica."

Kate and Landon stepped out onto the Parisian street from behind the tall doors of the apartment complex. The air was crisp and full of life; motors, sirens, people, and birds created the cacophony of the city. They walked arm in arm carrying two backpacks, one with picnic lunch, one with items for the party.

Hurrying across a busy street, Kate and Landon disappeared into the Champs-Élysées-Clemenceau Metro stairway. The echo-y silence surrounded them the deeper they descended. Kate felt her hearing had been muffled. At the B1 Mezzanine, they used the fare machine to purchase roundtrip tickets to St. Denis on the Line 13.

After slipping their fare cards into the turnstiles and retrieving them after allowance into the station, they attacked another set of stairs leading deeper into the underground cavern. They came out on the B-2 platform. A train whooshed into the station with bells and announcements signaling its arrival. Waiters rushed the doors, barely allowing riders to escape the cars. Kate's heart raced as she hurried to make the train. Landon grabbed her arm.

"Not our train." Above the din, Landon yelled and pointed to yet another grand staircase going even deeper underground. He grabbed her arm and pulled her away from the Line 1 subway.

As they descended the third set of stairs, Kate's heart began to pound and her vision to cloud. She grabbed the railing and closed her eyes. *Not here, not now.*

"What's wrong?" Landon hugged her to him.

"I'm dizzy, is all." She pushed him back from her. "I'll be fine. The trains run every six minutes. If we miss the next one, we can await the one after it."

"I'm not concerned about the train schedule, Kate. I'm concerned about you."

Kate opened her eyes to see Landon's face.

"Can you make it the rest of the way? Should we go back? Do I need to call for emergency assistance?" His eyes were full of worry.

"Go on down. Give me a minute. I'll be there."

"At the landing take the northbound stairs for Line 13."

She waved him off. "I think I can find it. It's a really big train." Kate didn't mean to be snippy, but Landon was giving off a Doug-vibe, managing, overbearing, too much concern. He made her feel trapped, almost claustrophobic.

Landon took her backpack to lighten the load for her and headed down to the landing. "It's not much farther, Kate. You can do this."

Kate nodded but a wave of nausea accompanied her motion. It was coming again. The very thought of the hospitals and doctors and her parents hovering over her made vomiting a real concern. Had she even eaten breakfast this morning? Clearly, she needed to get off the steps, or she'd be trampled by the continual tide of humanity seeking a weekend out of the city.

During a gap, she stood and used the railing to steady herself down to the landing. Two more sets of stairs. Northbound- toward Asnières - Gennevilliers-Les Courtilles or Saint Denis - Université (Miromesnil) or Southbound – toward Chatillon - Montrouge (Invalides). She crossed to the Northbound steps and made one more descent under the city.

Landon waited at the bottom of the stairs. Kate dodged the hug he clearly planned to give and found a seat on a metal bench. She breathed deeply and willed her heart to return to a normal beat.

People milled around waiting to begin their northbound adventure. Some had suitcases. Some bicycles. Some stared into the tunnel while others watched the sign indicating the time of the next arrival.

The sound of the train's arrival pulled all to the side of the tracks on the B3 platform. It arrived just as the sign indicated and began the countdown, six minutes, until the next train. Landon picked up both backpacks and offered a hand to Kate. She took it, and they entered the train just before the doors began to close.

Kate rummaged in her backpack for the granola bars she'd packed. She offered one to Landon and quickly ate hers. Just hungry; don't forget to eat. Tyler would be unhappy to know this had happened. But he'd still love her.

***

The train headed under the city, stopping at each of its thirteen stops, finally arriving at Basilique de Saint Denis. Most of the travelers had disembarked before this next to last stop on the Line 13 train. Kate and Landon climbed the stairs to the surface. When they reached street level, Kate felt like she had emerged into a medieval village in the midst of the modern as she faced the Basilica.

As Landon rattled off facts about the significance of the building, the kings and queens who'd been entombed there, and the architecture, Kate closed him out and felt the presence of God in the empty, hollow sounding building.

"Kate, do you hear anything I'm saying?" Landon's voice finally broke through her reverie.

"Some of it, yes. Forget the facts for a moment and feel the presence of God." Kate closed her eyes and felt the sun as it streamed through the stained glass. "It's beautiful."

When she opened her eyes, she saw Landon with his hands on his hips. "I was saying that the French call this the 'necropolis Royale'."

"The city of the dead royals. Got it." That's all he saw. Even as her soul was awakening in the cathedrals of worship, Landon's was closed. He felt nothing.

"Tourist guidebooks call it the Westminster Abbey of France."

Kate laughed. "Been there. Dark and gloomy it is. Look, this building is full of light."

When Landon started rattling on about the stained-glass windows, Kate shut him out once more. She could buy a tour book in the gift shop. While she was in this place, she waited on God to speak to her, just like her parents had taught her. Tyler could appreciate this sanctuary. And he would join her in silence, sit in the wooden folding chairs and hold her hand while they each prayed. Christmas would not come too soon. It seemed that once she had made her decision, time had dragged by at an *escargot* pace.

When she looked up, Landon was motioning to her like a cathedral traffic cop. She sighed and went over to see his great find.

"You're missing it, Kate. We're here to see the sights. Here's the effigies of the kings and queens. Their remains were dumped out and buried in a mass grave next to the church."

Kate scowled and raised an eyebrow. No, he was the one missing it.

"Because of the Revolution. Honestly Kate. You act like you're not even interested now that we're here."

"I promise to listen to you, but know that when God talks, His voice will be the only one I hear." Kate was surprised herself by the words she'd spoken, but also satisfied that they were, in fact, truth. She smiled.

Landon looked at her like she'd had a stroke. She took his arm and went with him into the crypt to see the funerary art of the ancient kings and queens and the resting place of the Bourbons: the Dauphin (who would have been Louis XVII had he lived), Louis XVI, Marie Antoinette, the actual Louis XVII, as well as other family members.

After they'd explored every nook and cranny, with Landon reading the tour book to her, Kate was thrilled to see the sun and feel some autumn warmth.

***

It had turned into a beautiful day for a picnic at the nearby park. Kate ate more than she had planned, to Landon's delight. They talked and enjoyed what had to be the last day of sunny, warm weather of the autumn.

Derrick arrived with the embassy limo to whisk them and several others to the pre-formal informal. The site was the administrative conference hall of the Université de St Denis. The hall was outfitted to mimic a Great Hall in one of many European castles. Velvet couches on cherry turned legs, chairs fit for kings, and rich mahogany tables greeted them. A massive chandelier illuminated the hall and sparkled as the crystals turned in the central heating

"See, now aren't you glad you came, if for no other reason to see this place."

Kate nodded in agreement.

Her coworkers arrived sporadically; each guest added snacks to the tables until they groaned. The chatter was fun and light. Wine flowed freely, though Kate abstained since she knew that at her current weight, she could easily overindulge and be sorry later.

Doug was there as well. He kept his distance, but he clearly wanted Kate to see him. Even the thought of him made her shiver. She pulled on her Aran sweater.

When the chit-chat had reached a decibel level, the Ambassador stood and raised her glass.

"To you who work diligently day by day, without recognition, solving the world's problems behind the scenes. I know it's not Christmas yet, but please enjoy the party as a gift to you all. I appreciate each of you. You make the USA look good and help me sparkle. As we enter the season of parties around the government center, remember that you represent those whom most of you will not see during the holiday time. I understand your sacrifice. I know you've worked hard to get a position in Paris. To all of you."

"Hear, hear." The response rippled through the crowd while glassware clinked.

"And now, my friends, we will play our annual party game: 'What adventure did you have when you were posted in Africa?'"

"I'll start. I'm Joanie. When I was posted in Africa, I was stationed in South Africa..."

Kate slunk back to a far wall to be hopefully unnoticed. Her memories of her time in Africa were ones she tried to keep hidden from herself as well as others.

Chapter 25

The Ivory Coast, 2009

The wheels screeched, and the plane bucked as Kate landed at the airport in Abidjan, Cote d'Ivoire.

"We're finally here." She didn't even realize she'd spoken it aloud.

The woman in the seat next to her twisted in her seat to see out the window over her. "Indeed. We have arrived. Is it your first time to Cote d'Ivoire?"

"Actually no. My parents are missionaries here, since I was ten."

"So, you are going to visit them?" The woman's brilliant smile punctuated the question.

"Of course, I plan to see them during my two-year posting here." Kate was careful in choosing words. She was unsure how much of the 'mission' was meant to be shared.

"You are missionary as well?"

"In a way. I am here in support of 'The US Mission to Abidjan.'" All her worldly goods had been shipped except for a suitcase and her carryon. "I'm looking forward to sharing this mission with them."

After going through customs, Kate waited for her bags among the throng of people speaking French, but also tribal dialects. It felt like home, the sounds of Ivoirian languages and the dazzling colors of the costumes on the many darker faces.

Kate slung the carryon over her shoulder and manhandled the larger suitcase off the revolving belt.

"Here, let me help with that." The tall man in a linen shirt with rolled up cuffs grabbed the handle and read the baggage tag. "Kate Lawrence? I'm Doug Hastings. I'm tasked with taking you to the embassy."

"But, my parents are coming to get me. I don't start work until day after tomorrow."

"Plans change, Kate." He stalked ahead of her

"Has someone notified my parents?"

Doug gave her an impatient look. "Your parents are the ones who contacted the embassy. They are unable to tear themselves away from the 'mission field' to pick you up. I'll take you to the apartments, and you can get settled."

They couldn't even come to get her at the airport. Some things don't change.

***

The phone rang later that evening while Kate was unpacking her belongings.

"Hello? Kate Lawrence here."

"Kate! It's so good to hear your voice. Have you eaten?" Her dad's voice sounded like nothing had happened. "Are you there?"

"Yes, Dad, I'm here. I'm not very hungry. The guy who picked me up took me by the market to pick up groceries. I've eaten some. Besides, I have unpacking to do."

She could hear the disappointment across the phone line.

"Could I come get you for church in the morning then?"

"I don't think so. I'll be fighting jet lag. I can't believe you couldn't come and get me at the airport, Dad."

The pause was audible. "Well, God's work comes first, Katie. You know we're all to be living sacrifices."

"Of course. Gotta go." Kate hung up before he had the chance to reply. But she really didn't care. Tears streamed down her face.

***

Kate rode along in a Jeep over the rough dirt road to a village on the outskirts of Abidjan with supplies to feed the villagers. Dressed in what appeared to be standard uniform, Kate wore a white linen shirt over a tank top and khaki capris.

The wind gusts and dirt swirls from the road blew through her hair, making it a mess. She pulled a Scrunchi from her hip pack and pulled her hair into a ponytail.

"You should take off that cross, Kate." Doug yelled over the noisy travel. "We can't be the missionaries. We are emissaries of the US government. We promote religious liberty. We can't be seen to promote a specific religion."

The cross was one her parents had given to her when she first went away to boarding school. Kate had rarely been without it around her neck since. She unhooked it and carefully placed it in a zippered pocket inside her pack.

"We'll be distributing food and water because this village is very impoverished. You'll see agricultural diplomats out in the fields. You'll see others giving health classes. Just do the job you are supposed to do."

Kate was excited for this chance to serve in the villages, like her parents had always done. She considered her work a 'mission' as well. She was pretty sure too that her parents would choose to differ with her about that.

As her team pulled into the village, the Jeep was surrounded by smiling children. Doug stopped the Jeep and grabbed Kate's arm.

"Don't take anything from them. Don't give them anything either. We're not here to interact. We're here to provide sustenance only. I'll be watching you."

Though the temperature was hot, Kate shivered. Others started unloading the rice, milk, and water.

"Katie!"

Kate turned to face the shout. It was her dad, running toward her. She opened her arms and hugged him.

"Daddy, so glad to see you finally. Is Mom here too?"

Another set of arms grabbed her from behind.

"I'm here; I'm here."

"Lawrence, come help set up the distribution line!"

"Gotta go. Can we meet at lunch? Or after work, could you take me back to Abidjan?"

They nodded and let go of her. She ran off to help her team.

***

At the end of the day, Kate went back to her parents' mission home. She helped her mom prepare a native meal of cassava and groundnut stew washed down with precious Coca Cola. A slice of chocolate pie made the meal feel almost like home.

After the dishes, they sat on the couch in the living area.

"Katie, you should come and work with us at the mission. We do the exact same things you did today, but you can share the gospel."

Her father reached out for her hand. Kate took it back

Kate shook her head. "I don't want to work for the mission. I can do the exact same thing without having to share the gospel or having to hand out Bibles or attending multiple worship in all the villages here. My work with the State Department is a mission. I'm proud of my work."

"What's wrong with sharing the gospel and attending worship? Didn't we teach you to love those things?" Her mother looked as though she'd cry.

"Actions speak louder than words. When the USA sends people to distribute food and help provide clean water, the message is that the USA cares about the needs of people."

"Those same things say that God cares about them." Her father shifted closer to her.

"Exactly my point, Dad. God can serve them in many ways. I can serve them in God's name without having 'Christian' attached to my service." Kate stood. Anger coursed up through her like hot magma. "What did sending me away from 'Christian service' say? What about the times you were in the States, and I was still left at boarding school? What about all the parents' days you missed?"

Her mom sniffled, making Kate that much angrier.

"We sent care packages. We were at graduation, both in France and at the American University. We were at the hospital when you suffered that bout of anorexia." Her mom snagged a tissue and wiped her eyes. "We always love you."

"Actions speak louder than words, Mom. Dad, can you drive me back to Abidjan now before it gets any later."

Her father stood. "I'll get the keys."

***

The ride back to the capital was silent. In the shadows, Kate saw her father working his jaw. He was angry, too, and trying to find words to say that weren't angry. He'd always been that way, stuffing down his anger, trying to say the Christian thing instead of the honest thing. Kate had decided long ago that saying what you think is better than living a lie.

"Dad, just say what you're trying not to say."

"You hurt us when you say things like you said tonight. We did what we felt God wanted us to do."

Kate laughed. "You always blame everything on 'what God wanted'. Surely being parents to your only child is something God wanted. Instead you sent me away, for eight years of boarding school and 4 years of college. Twelve years is half my life. I thought serving in the same country would be a good two years to reconcile with you."

They bumped over the same road she'd come on. It was just as jolting and dirty as it had been that morning. The headlights were the only light on the road. Abidjan glowed in the distance. This time together had ended in disaster. Kate had hoped for better.

The mission van pulled up to her apartment complex.

"Dad, I have chosen my life career carefully. Look up Mark 9:28-41. I can serve God, in His name, and still work for the State Department. I'm in Cote d'Ivoire for two years. I'm sure we'll have opportunities to cross paths. Thanks for dinner and the ride home."

Kate got out and slammed the door. That's when the tears started.

When she entered the lobby of the complex, Doug was sitting there.

"Did I miss curfew or something?" Kate wiped away her tears.

Doug shook his head. "No, but I'm responsible for you when we're out in the field. I had to know you were home safe and sound. Are you okay? You've been crying."

He stood and came close. "I have a shoulder to cry on if you like."

Kate walked into his open arms.

St. Denis, Pre-formal Informal, present day

"Kate, come back to us. It's your turn. Tell us a story from your time in Africa."

Kate came back to the present with everyone watching her.

"My time in Cote d'Ivoire was a mixed blessing. I was able to serve alongside my missionary parents. I met Doug. I served in the US Mission to Abidjan as an emissary of the USA. That about sums it up."

"Aah!" The group rolled their eyes as if on cue. "Tell us a specific event."

"Doug and I got engaged there. But that's over now. What do you want me to say?"

"Next."

Kate escaped the room to a patio as the next person told about being charged by a rhino. Landon slipped up behind her.

"Not easy being a missionary kid, eh?" Landon draped an arm around her shoulders. He smelled of too much good wine.

Kate shrugged him off. "It was a hard time. I learned more about myself and my parents and our relationship. I somehow got engaged to a narcissistic, manipulative, obsessive jerk. What more can I say?"

Landon placed his arms around her. "I'm here now. I can take care of you if you'll let me."

Kate shoved against him to get away, but he only tightened his grip on her.

"Stop. You know I'm engaged to Tyler."

"But what you don't know is that I'm Tyler's informant. I keep him informed on your well-being."

Landon tried for a kiss; Kate escaped his grasp and hurried back into the main room. She located Derrick, the limo driver.

"How soon can you take me into Paris? I need to leave now."

Derrick checked his watch. "The party's not over till midnight. I can drive you in now and still be back in time for anyone else who needs a ride back."

"That's great. Let me grab my backpack."

Chapter 26

The trailer park at the Mesquite had hosted the Cowboys of Color in mid-October and the Arena Cross performers in November. Thanksgiving to Christmas the temporary population included crafters and sellers for the Holiday Shopping Expo at the Arena. Tyler wandered the aisles along with the thronging masses. As he went from booth to booth, he gave his card and an invitation to stop in to see him. He also picked up interesting doodads along the way.

"How much for the shawl?" Tyler fingered a teal knitted lace shawl. Miss Sarah would love that.

He handed the woman running the booth the $40 she requested, then gave her his card. "I'm Tyler Hawkins. I'm the pastor at Mission Mesquite, near the entrance to the trailer park. If I can help in any way, please call or come by."

The lady pocketed his card and handed him a plastic bag with the shawl.

Next he came to a wood worker's booth. On display was something called a remote 'boat'.

"Excuse me, can you explain this to me? A remote boat?"

The man looked eager to help Tyler. "Yeah, yeah, yeah. This is a place to park all the remotes in your living room. Then they don't get lost. Like a Noah's ark for remotes, if you will. Only $20."

Tyler reached for a twenty in his wallet. "That would be perfect for Rev. Ryan." He handed him the cash and his card. "I'm the pastor at Mission Mesquite in the trailer park. If I can help, call me or come by."

The man smiled as he handed him a box with a 'remote boat'. Then he turned away to sell to someone else. Tyler shrugged and moved on.

Another wood worker had pop guns armed with marshmallows. Something fun for Miguel. He also ordered a multi-colored striped tepee with PVC support poles. Miguel would love that too.

At another booth, he found a quilted tree skirt. Someone would actually be living in the house who wanted to celebrate Christmas and the birth of Christ. He needed to step up to that challenge. Tyler had pretty much ignored decorating for Christmas and spent the time with the Lawrences instead of being alone.

A lady selling beaded bracelets and necklaces talked for thirty minutes about how much she missed her family at Christmas, but she and her dog would just keep traveling. Tyler bought some matching beaded jewelry for stocking stuffers for Katie, whom he really hoped would be home for Christmas.

He'd bring Miguel back sometime later to help him pick out gifts. Tyler also hoped he could minister to some of the people who'd received his card. Christmas was the perfect time to accept Christ as Savior.

Tyler turned his collar up and pulled his hat on against the stiff cold wind. He'd decided to walk across the parking lot. The problem with that now was that after he'd stood and walked for hours, he would need to walk back across the lot with his treasures. Luckily the tepee folks would deliver it to the mission, so he didn't have to drag that back with him. He shivered in his leather jacket.

When Tyler approached the mission trailer, the police were waiting for him.

"Reverend, I have a warrant to search your trailer. This includes under the trailer." Detective Ed Brown had been on the case since that horrible day of the shooting.

Tyler took the paper with a frown. "What do you hope to find?"

"Sorry, we can't tell you that. We're working a hunch." Brown called out to the officers standing around the trailer, "Ok boys! Go to it."

The blue uniformed men begin ripping the skirt from around the trailer.

Tyler was restrained from entering the trailer while the search was conducted. The cold seeped into his leg and hip through his blue jeans, particularly where the metal of his brace touched. The ache not only touched his disability but also his heart. If the police were back at the crime scene, they had a good idea what they were looking for.

"Okay if I sit in my truck, detective?"

The man turned on him with a sneer, then remembered Tyler's leg brace. "Yeah, whatever. Just don't leave."

Tyler climbed into the truck and cranked it on to provide heat. Cantu was still in jail with no bond on Tyler's testimony because the victim had named Cantu as his assailant. It ate at him that one of his closest friends suffered innocently. And he knew Cantu was innocent. But how could he help when Tyler's word held him there?

Lord, stop this witch hunt and free Cantu. Help the police find something that ultimately sets him and me free from this nightmare. Your will be done.

As he finished the prayer, he heard one of the searchers cry out that he had found something. As he watched the scene, a man emerged from under the trailer with a gun. Turning off the truck, Tyler left the warmth and headed toward Brown.

"I think you need to come with me to the station for more questioning, Reverend. You're under arrest for concealing a murder weapon."

Another man handcuffed him then bumped his head and twisted his bad leg trying to get Tyler into the back of the squad car.

Tyler glanced at the clock on the dashboard and added six hours to acquire Paris time. Katie would be at the French State Reception at the Louvre tonight.

***

After hours of interrogation followed by stifling boredom in a holding cell, Tyler had finally fallen asleep – only to be awakened by the noisy cell door being unlocked and opened.

"You can go Reverend. The fingerprints on the gun exclude you as one handling it."

"Go figure." Tyler's tiredness fueled snippiness. "A man bleeds onto my carpet, the church's carpet, asking for help, but you thought I'd shoot the guy and blame one of my best friends.

Brown greeted him in the lobby. "Sorry about the inconvenience, but we've got to check all the angles. By the way, your innocent best friend is the registered gun owner. Just saying."

Tyler turned away to avoid the blast of anger he felt rising in him. He gathered his belongings and signed that he'd received them. He slowed his breathing, then turned to face the detective. "What about his fingerprints? Suppose they're all over the gun and no one else's?"

"Not supposed to comment on an open investigation. By the way, don't disappear."

Tyler tipped his hat to the man and left the precinct. Rev. Ryan was there to pick him up and take him to the prison where Cantu was being held. As Cantu's religious guides, Tyler and Rev. Ryan had access to him just about anytime they went.

After passing through security and handing over personal items, they went to the bank of kiosks with telephones and waited for Cantu to be escorted to the visitors' area.

Cantu arrived in his prison wear. His smile at seeing them gladdened Tyler's heart. Both men quickly grabbed the receivers.

Cantu spoke first. "You gotta have some good news for me. You know I didden do this shooting."

Tyler nodded. "There's both good news and bad news, friend. They searched under the mission and found your gun then arrested me. Haven't got the ballistics back, but my fingerprints were not on it. They let me go."

Cantu's smile vanished. "Thought you said there was good news. No offense, dude. Glad you're not rotting in a cell too. How does this help me?"

"How did your gun get under the mission?" Rev. Ryan spoke into the shared handset.

"I told the cops and you that it went missing; guess it was stolen from my trailer."

Tyler shook his head. "Someone has gone to a lot of trouble to frame you. Who is your worst enemy? I can't see this being a coincidence."

Cantu rocked back in the seat causing the guard to draw nearer.

"The dude who died was my worst enemy. See the problem? He tells you I shot him. You have to testify that he told you that. When he recovers, they better make him tell the truth."

"Well, there's the other bad news. Apparently the search occurred 'cause the dude died." Tyler could sense the feeling of drowning in the man across the glass from him.

"Where's God now, preacher man? God know I didden do this murder. They gonna up the charges now, ain't they?" Cantu stood and the guard shoved him back down with a warning. "Am I ever gonna see my children or my wife again?" Tears streamed down the tough man's leathered brown face. "You gotta help me."

The guard looked at his watch, signaling the time was nearly up.

"Let's pray." Rev. Ryan prayed aloud for God's mercy and revelation. At his 'Amen', the guard hung up the phone; and Cantu shuffled back to his cell.

Tyler was anxious to get the skirting back on the mission but was more eager to get back to Miguel and hold him tight. First, though, he'd need to go visit Cantu's family.

Chapter 27

The powers that be in the French Department of State prided themselves on hosting the first and best holiday soirée of the season. The Louvre as a backdrop to the party was a stroke of brilliance.

Kate dressed in the altered black lace gown. She was excited to wear it and to show it to Stefan. She turned in front of the mirror, and the room spun with her.

She caught the bedpost on the way down. *Oh God, help me to get through tonight. Don't let me embarrass the ambassador nor Stefan at this Christmas reception.*

Derrick and the limo from the US Embassy arrived on the dot and drove swiftly and smoothly through the Parisian traffic. A French usher gave her a hand out of the car and escorted her to the elevator to take her down to the subterranean lobby of the museum. She entered the lobby under the glass pyramid which punctuated the ancient buildings in the courtyard of the Louvre. Guards stood watch to protect the treasures displayed in this most sacred holding place.

The black lace swished as Kate walked in and greeted many diplomats from every embassy in Paris. Stefan was a puff pastry in its element tonight. Pastry? Why would she even think of that? She picked up a glass of Perrier water and avoided the hors d'oeuvres table. The bite size desserts encouraged guests to eat one of each kind. Kate could not bring herself to taste even one of them. She circled the room, greeting diplomatic acquaintances, before getting into Stefan's receiving line, as everyone was expected to do. Perhaps she could slip away to see Mona Lisa, who hung all alone on her own enormous wall.

"There you are, Kate. You chose well at the show, I see."

"Have you seen your bank account yet? It was a very generous offer that I plan to repay." Kate hugged the man who had been her friend in Washington.

"*Ce n'est nécessaire*. Can a friend not gift a friend with a lovely dress, which looks extraordinary on you?" Stefan kissed her hand.

"Not in politics, I'm afraid. Someone will think I'm your mistress and spread all kinds of rumors." Kate smiled. "But I do love the dress and thank you for your encouragement to spend the money."

"You look wan my dear. Most people here speak French or brought their own embassy's interpreter. Spend the evening enjoying the Louvre and all the compliments on your new gown."

Kate nodded and moved on so the receiving line would not stagnate. She'd not had time to spend at the Louvre. While the evening would in no way provide enough time to see all the treasures contained within, she'd find the most precious while she had the opportunity. She picked up a guide from the docent's desk and located the most popular exhibit, the Mona Lisa. Then she'd find the sculpture: David, Venus de Milo, Winged Victory. She'd be able to see others on the way.

"*Excusez moi, mademoiselle?*" The docent handed her a museum picture book. "You will want this as a souvenir, even if you do not want to walk all the galleries. They are free this evening for Monsieur Dremond's guests."

Kate took the book and flipped through its colorful pages. "Thank you so much. Could you point me toward the Mona Lisa?"

The docent showed her on the map where the gallery was located and which set of stairs to use. With the map and the picture book, Kate headed out to find her treasure for the evening. The map, however, was hard to follow and instead of the paintings she found herself amid sculpture. In fact, she found herself in front of Venus de Milo. Every sculpture was amazing. She was alone among the sculpture; some more lifelike than some politicians she'd encountered. In the dim galleries, alone, her sense of safety was challenged.

"You've seen too many Dr. Who Weeping Angel episodes." She spoke aloud to no one to reassure herself. "As magical as these stone people are, I need to find my way back to the reception. " Maybe it was too many *Night at the Museum* films.

The ceilings were fantastic. But looking up as she went made her dizzier. The lace swished as she walked through the empty rooms and halls. Where were the rest of the guests? Who would pass up the opportunity to stroll the Louvre without the crowds of tourists taking pictures that they weren't supposed to take?

She spun beneath a beautiful ceiling, then gasped for breath. Kate found a bench on which to sit down and recover her equilibrium. She took off her black patent killer heels for they were most definitely killing her feet tonight. Her feet had become so bony. Kate rubbed her soles.

After checking her watch, Kate decided she had lingered too long. The soirée would be winding down soon. The map made no sense no matter how she turned it. She headed to the end of the hall and down a set of stairs. The Winged Victory of Samothrace at the juncture of several stairways greeted her. She had no idea how to proceed. Were they turning off the lights on her? Why was it so dark?

***

"*Mademoiselle? Mademoiselle Lawrence?* We've been looking for you."

When she opened her eyes, she was lying in a clump at the base of the Winged Victory of Samothrace. Guards stood all around her.

"Monsieur Dremond is beside himself with worry."

She heard a guard relay the message, in French of course, over his radio.

"Can you stand, mademoiselle?"

She still had cobwebs for brains and tried to clear them. But shaking her head created more dizziness. "I don't think so, monsieur."

The guard helped her to her feet and then scooped her up in his arms. He carried her down all the steps to the subterranean level under the glass pyramid. He set her on her feet. "Are you, how do you say, okay?"

"*Merci beaucoup*, monsieur, for the lift."

Stefan hurried to her side along with his wife, Marie. "We were so concerned when you did not return."

Marie took her in her arms. "We are so glad you are okay."

When Marie released her, Kate felt the room twist and turn before her. She caught the edge of a side table and swung herself onto the adjacent bench. She closed her eyes and prayed she wouldn't black out again.

What is wrong with me? Why am I losing it? Have I done this again?

Stefan moved quickly to her side. "Are you okay, Katerine? You look pale and frail."

"Ambassador, I may have a case of the flu coming on. Please forgive me for inflicting myself on you this evening."

"Kate, we have known one another for three years. In that time, you have always been delightful. That is why I asked your Secretary of State to assign you to the US Embassy here in Paris." He knelt beside her. "But there's something dreadfully wrong with you, *chérie*. Please see my personal physician in the morning."

"*Non, Secrétaire*. There's a physician at the embassy for US citizens to see." Kate held her hand to her suddenly aching head. "It's truly nothing."

Stefan grasped her hand and raised it to her eyesight. "Kate, you're nothing but skin and bones. It's more than nothing. You're wasting away in front of us. I can't bear to see you so ill and believe that I am responsible."

"You're hardly responsible, Secrétaire. I am an adult."

"Nevertheless, I'll have my driver take you home now. I will check with the American doctor in the morning. Your health is more important than a week of diplomatic parties. And please call me Stefan. We are much too close to stand on mere formality."

While Stefan summoned the driver, Marie sat down beside Kate and patted her hand. "You must let Stefan care for you. He is quite fond of you."

"Oh, Marie. There's nothing inappropriate going on between us." Kate turned to face her. "I will pay him back for the dress."

"Nonsense. Who do you think came up with the idea for you to go to the fashion show, purchase a dress, and think to send a check with you? Men have no clue." Marie laughed. "You are of great importance to him and so to me as well. Please enjoy the dress with my hearty well-wishes. When Stefan is happy, I am happy. *Comprend tu?*"

"*Merci*, Marie." Kate hugged her.

Stefan hurried to her and easily picked Kate up off the sofa. He carried her to the car and bid her adieu.

Chapter 28

Derrick and the car came for Kate the next morning and took her to the embassy medical office.

The nurse silently weighed her, took her blood pressure, temperature, and pulse. Kate felt too tired to converse and break the silence. She undressed at the nurse's command and lay down on the crinkly paper under the paper gown. She drifted to sleep in the few moments before the doctor entered the room.

"Kate Lawrence? I'm Janet Crumb, the embassy doctor. I had your medical records faxed from Washington. Secrétaire Dremond is quite concerned about your health. What seems to be the problem?"

Kate sighed and struggled to sit up to talk with the doctor. The doctor waited patiently for her response.

"I'm dizzy a lot. I've lost some weight. I'm never hungry. I'm lonely. I shake sometimes. My head aches at times. And I'm sleepy all the time. My heart races sometimes, but not often. It could be a bad bout of the flu."

The doctor listened intently, reviewed the faxed pages, and reread the information the nurse had scribbled down on the page. The doctor sat down on the chair opposite the examining table.

"Or anorexia again, Kate? Are you refusing to eat? Vomiting what you eat? Exercising too frequently?"

Kate's eyes flew open in alarm. When had she eaten last, besides coffee, diet soda, or carrot sticks? She couldn't think of anything else for days. She pictured the refrigerator at her apartment - it was empty, she knew, except for frozen half-eaten baguettes. She breathed with difficulty as the fear grew within her.

"It's okay, Kate. We can still help you, but first I want you in the hospital for the next day or so to run some IVs and get you some concentrated nourishment. Then I think we need to send you back to the States to a hospital there. You're no good to anyone here in your condition. Is there someone I can call for you?"

Kate broke down into tears. The doctor snagged a tissue from the box in the room and handed it to her. When she collected herself, she stood shakily from the table and looked into the full-length mirror behind the screen. She removed the paper gown and looked at the frail, bony body before her with the engagement ring hanging on a chain.

"Tyler. Call Tyler Hawkins. He's my fiancé. And he will tell my parents."

"Give Mr. Hawkins's number to the nurse. I'll talk with him while you're being transferred to the hospital. Is there someone here who can pack up your things?"

Kate shook her head. There was no one in Paris that she'd allowed into her life. She was truly alone here. Only God had been here with her, when she'd looked for Him. She'd forsaken everyone who cared for her by coming to Paris. And turned her back on God's will for her life. No, there was nothing for her here in Paris. And it had nearly killed her. Maybe still would. The blackness closed in on her again.

***

"I have a person to person call from Paris, France, for a Tyler Hawkins, *si vous plait.*"

Tyler rubbed the sleep from his eyes.

"This is Tyler. Katie? Is that you?"

"Your party, mademoiselle," the operator intoned.

"Mr. Hawkins, this is Dr. Crumb at the American Hospital in Paris. I have Kate Lawrence under my care here. She told me to call you concerning her condition."

Tyler sat bolt upright in the bed, fully awake now.

"What's wrong with Katie? Why didn't she call me herself? Should I catch a plane there?"

Miguel ran into the room, rubbing the sleep out of his eyes, and climbed up into the bed with Tyler. Tyler pulled him to his side.

"Relax, Mr. Hawkins. Kate is here to receive vital fluids and nutrients. We plan to send her to Walter Reed in Washington in a day or so, as soon as she can travel. Her secretary will be packing up her apartment. Where shall we ship her things?"

"What's wrong with Kate?"

"Severe malnutrition and dehydration caused by anorexia."

"I'll be there as soon as I can get a flight, doctor. Don't ship her or her things until I can get there."

"I'm not sure that's necessary, Mr. Hawkins. We can take care of things here. She'll need you in Washington later this week."

"I'm coming today, Dr. Crumb. Tell her I'm coming for her."

Tyler slammed the phone and jumped from the bed, collapsing into the floor. He bit back the curse from his lips.

"What's wrong, Daddy? Is it about Katy ladybug? Will she die too?"

"No, Miguel. If I can keep that from happening, with God's help, she will not." He crawled across the floor to the chair and pulled himself upright. "Still it is a very good idea to pray for her, son."

He dressed quickly, including the brace. He called the airline and scheduled a flight leaving Dallas-Ft. Worth in two hours. Then he called Kate's parents.

"Rev. Ryan. It's Tyler. I don't have long because I need to get to the airport."

"What's up, Ty?"

"I'm headed to Paris to bring our girl home. Can you come and get Miguel? Go ahead and bring the kids over this morning anyway; Joe will be here. I'll not be back for services on Sunday either."

"Calm down, Tyler. Tell me what's wrong."

"It's Katie. She's ill in Paris, and they're preparing to send her home. I'm going to her now. I'll bring her back to us, Rev. Ryan. Just keep praying."

Tyler hung up the phone before his mentor could protest. She was his; he would care for her. He threw clothing in a satchel and lurched toward the pickup and the airport after Joe came to keep Miguel. On the way to the airport, Tyler left a message for Detective Ed Brown that he had to go to Paris, France; not sure when he'd be back.

***

The smells of hospital lunch wafted through the ward. It nauseated Kate as she took in the aroma. The IV continued to pump life-giving fluids into her collapsing veins. But she was alert, and the room wasn't spinning any longer. The nurse cheerily carried in the tray and uncovered the hot food.

"It smells divine, *n'est pas*? Try to eat today, mademoiselle."

Kate nodded. The headache started again.

"Can I have a Tylenol chaser, nurse?"

"*Mais bien sur*. The headache's back, is it? I'll check the chart. Meanwhile, you must try to eat. Your secretary has brought your nightie, so you can get out of that horrible gown. I hear you may have company later."

The nurse brought the bag to her side and pulled the nightgown and robe from it. She bustled out of the room, and Kate heard her cheery voice in the next room. An aide came in to help Kate change into her gown and robe through the tangle of IV tubing.

***

It was dark when Tyler crept into her room. He gasped. She looked skeletal. Machines whooshed and beeped. He dragged the chair over next to the bed. She startled at the sound; her whole body quivered. His ring hung from a chain around her neck, looking massive in comparison to her emaciated face and body. He gently took her hand and kissed it.

I'll not leave her side, Lord, not if I can help it, for the rest of my life. Just spare her life.

He laid his blond head on the bed beside her. "Don't give up, my Katydid. You still must give me that final tick." He fell asleep beside her.

Tyler was awakened as Kate's body began to seize. Alarms blared as the crash cart veered into the room. He was shoved to the side as the medical trauma team went to work to restart her heart.

"Give us the room, *monsieur*. Go for *café*. We'll do what we can for her. Pray; her life is in God's hands now."

Tyler entered the hall and realized tears were streaming down his cheeks. He needed to call Rev. Ryan and Miss Sarah. But what could he say? He wandered down the hall, alone, where he didn't speak the language and his reason to live was possibly dying.

Lord, save her life if for no other reason than I need her to do the work you have called me to do. He had no more words. Tyler prayed for the Holy Spirit to intercede for him.

"*Excusez-moi, monsieur?*" A petite nurse touched his arm. "Can I help you?"

"Point me toward the chapel, please."

He stumbled behind her to the place of sanctuary in this building of life and death. She opened the door; he entered and found a seat at the back. Then he wept. For his leg, for his son, for Tina, for his Katie. Surely God wouldn't take her away from him now.

Chapter 29

A nurse found him there just after dawn's first light.

"*Monsieur* Hawkins?" She handed him a box of tissue. At his nod, she came and sat beside him. "I want to give you a status report on Kate Lawrence. She is stable at the moment. As you know, we had some excitement when her heart decided to go out of rhythm. The problem with anorexia is the damage poor nutrition does to the major organs. I wouldn't say Kate has, what do you say, got out of the forest?"

Tyler nodded. "You mean she's not out of the woods."

"*Exactement.* Especially after a second severe bout of the disorder. There's damage from the previous bout and new or worsening damage from this last bout." She placed her arm around his shoulders as he sobbed. "All can be okay with faith, *n'est pas?*"

Tyler gasped and felt a hot flush. A nurse should not have to tell him this. *Thank you for sending someone to me to remind me to look up.*

"One more thing, *Monsieur.* She is awake and asking for you. We moved her to ICU, but you can go in to see her. You traveled a long way to be at her side. Please, she needs you there now."

Tyler stood stiffly, then picked up his satchel.

"You can leave your luggage in the ICU lounge. There's also a very comfy couch you could rest on in there. Let's not have to admit you too. Come with me."

Tyler smiled and followed the little nurse. *Thank you, God, for a positive outcome today. Your mercies are new and fresh every morning. Keep Katie in your strong hand. Amen.*

***

In ICU, a low hum pervaded the senses. Machines whirred, and IV pumps pushed life-giving fluids. Oxygen whooshed in and out of some patients. It was almost hard to find his Katie amidst all the machines and tubing. He gingerly took her hand.

Her eyes were closed, but he heard her faint voice whisper, "Tyler."

"I'm here Katydid. I'm never leaving your side for any length of time again. You and I are better together than apart."

She nodded. "Yes, for forever. For whatever God has planned. Tick."

Once again Tyler found tears streaming down his face. "I love you, Katydid. I'm taking you home to Green Pastures when you are able to travel."

"Can a chaplain perform the wedding here? In case ..."

"You will make it back to Green Pastures, girl. Don't you want to wait until then?"

Kate shook her head. Her auburn tresses lay tangled and lifeless on the hospital white pillows. She opened her eyes and stared into his eyes. "If you love me, marry me now. Then when we go home to Green Pastures and Miguel, we don't have to ever be apart again."

Tyler stood and kissed Kate. "Yes, Katydid, I'll locate the chaplain and see what can be arranged. Is there anyone in Paris you'd like me to call?"

"Stefan at the French state department. Staff at US Embassy. Not Doug or Landon." She smiled. "Gotta sleep now."

Once Tyler was sure she was asleep and not in danger of cardiac arrest or seizure, he set about making the arrangements she wanted.

***

The hospital information desk sent Tyler to find the trains into Paris and the US Embassy. Upon arrival at the embassy, he walked past the bronze statue of Benjamin Franklin and between stone pillars topped with American eagles. The white building, with its guards and fortified fence looked formidable. Tyler entered after producing his passport to the guards.

"Can I help you, sir?" The receptionist continued typing while waiting for his reply. "Do you have an appointment? You can't be seen without it."

"Um, I need help arranging a wedding…"

"Oh, sir, you should just forget that now." The receptionist stopped typing and stared up into Tyler's face. "One of you has to be living in Paris for at least 30 days and then you have to post banns for 10 days. You can't just fly in from the US to have a French wedding."

"You don't understand. None of that really matters because she's been working here for the last 4 months. And she's in the hospital in ICU right now."

"Well, the civil ceremony must take place in the town hall in the neighborhood where she is living." The lady pointed her pen at him. "The consulate has no dealings with the marriage laws."

Tyler stammered and sputtered and clenched his fists. What could he say to get the answers he needed?

"My fiancée is Katie Lawrence."

The bustle in the entry hall came to a halt suddenly. People from every corner converged on Tyler, all asking how Kate was doing.

"Did someone mention Kate?" Doug appeared from nowhere into Tyler's view. "How's she doing?"

Tyler didn't really think; he just acted. Before he knew it, Doug was on the carpet with a bloody nose. Guards parted the crowd to take Tyler into custody.

As the guards were laying hands on him, an authoritative man appeared in the circle.

"Did you mention my Kate, *monsieur*?"

"My Kate, for now and forever, sir."

"*Mais bien sur, monsieur*. Forgive my misspeak; Kate would have given me more grace in the English. You must be Tyler Hawkins, her knight on horseback that I've heard so much concerning." He waved the guards off and extended his hand. "Stefan Dremond, *Secretaire de France*."

Tyler extended his hand but realized it held Doug's blood. "Please excuse me, sir." From the assemblage, a handkerchief appeared out of nowhere. Tyler wiped his hand and then shook the Frenchman's hand. "I have heard only good things about you except for one."

Stefan looked perplexed. "And that is…"

"You took my Katie away and allowed her to nearly die without me present."

As Doug began to rise from the floor, Tyler turned on him again. "And you, with your vile tongue took advantage of this opportunity to allow old demons to surface. Those demons almost killed her last night."

"What is all the fuss here?" A well-dressed lady pushed her way into the center of the crowd. "I'm the ambassador, Jane Hartly."

"Tyler Hawkins, ma'am. I'm Katie Lawrence's fiancé."

"Is she well? She gave us quite a scare." The ambassador shook Tyler's outstretched hand.

"She coded last night, but they were able to bring her back. She's in ICU. I just came here to find out how to marry her while we're here."

Stefan stepped forward. "It would be my pleasure to help with that. Come with me." Stefan led him back out on the street, directed him into an official car, and took him to Hotel de Ville, the Paris town hall.

***

The regulations were daunting. Since Kate had been living in Paris longer than thirty days, they'd have no problem there. Next the banns needed to be posted in the town hall ten days before the wedding. Tyler arranged for the posting while he was there. Kate would not be well enough to leave the hospital before then anyway.

Passport copies, the residency paper (vouched for by Stefan), the celibacy paper (stating neither was married to anyone else), and the application for the civil marriage certificate. Finally, the paperwork was done.

"No religious ceremony can be held until after the mayor marries the couple at the town hall in a civil ceremony." The clerk stacked and stamped the paperwork Tyler had signed. That stipulation meant bringing Kate to the massive edifice known as Hotel de Ville. No matter the wisdom of the mayor coming to the hospital, what Tyler had hoped to accomplish. No, Kate would have to be strong enough to go to the mayor.

"May I give you a ride to the hospital, Tyler? I would love to give Kate my best wishes."

Stefan gestured to the waiting car. Tyler stumbled on the irregular stones in the sidewalk and caught himself against the car door.

"I think the lack of sleep is finally catching up to me, Stefan. Perhaps your driver could take me to a hotel near the hospital."

"*Mais bien sur*, Tyler. I know just the place."

Chapter 30

"*Bon jour*, Kate." The nurse threw open the drapes. "Today you have a great adventure. Today is the day your cowboy comes to take you to the Hotel de Ville to get married."

Kate had been awake most of the night contemplating this very thing. She'd even made a trip to the bathroom with the IV pole to see just what his bride looked like. Not a pretty sight, though better than two weeks ago.

"Come, come, mademoiselle. Why are you crying?"

Kate reached up and touched her face. She hadn't even realized that tears were streaming down her face.

"I look horrible, Madelaine. I just look horrible. How can I wed Tyler looking like this?" The tears and sobbing began in earnest then. "And it is all my fault. I should not have come when I knew, I knew, what God wanted me to do. If I had only not been wayward and headstrong, I could be the blushing bride Tyler deserves. Instead I look like a victim of the Holocaust. Even my hair …"

Madelaine sat on the edge of the chair beside the bed. "Kate, you have visitors who are waiting for you to eat your breakfast. They will help you feel more beautiful. I have heard their plans." She patted her hand. "You will see; it will be okay. I have seen the way Cowboy Tyler looks at you. To him, you are beautiful, outside and inside. All he wants is to take you home as his wife."

Kate hiccupped in the midst of a sob and accepted the warm washcloth from the nurse. As she finished washing away her tears, her breakfast tray arrived. Eat it, Kate, her inner voice chided. You must if you hope to go home with Tyler.

"You eat as much as you can, cherie. I will let your entourage know you are awake." With that the spritely nurse whisked out of the room.

"My entourage?" Too late for the nurse to hear her.

Kate picked at the eggs and bacon, French bacon not American. The croissant was tender and flaky. The coffee was not standard issue - instead it was her favorite mocha from the coffee shop around the corner from the Embassy. Stefan must have arranged that. Not only did it taste good, but it warmed her all the way to her tummy.

Nurse Madelaine returned and propped her up in the shower, call button within reach, after removing her IV. A basket of fragrant shower gels, shampoos, and conditioners stood at the ready with a poufy scrubby.

Her favorite robe had materialized on the hook on the back of the door. After carefully toweling off, she shrugged into the pink Turkish terrycloth. Holding onto the safety bars, she opened the heavy door to the sound of slumber party style giggles.

"Oh, my entourage." She reached out to Cindy and hugged her close. "You came all this way?"

"Well, you did promise I could be maid of honor at your wedding. Hard to do that in DC when you're in Paris, don't cha think? Look who else is here."

Looking around the room, she saw friends from the US Embassy, the French State department, ladies from her apartment building, and her mom.

"Mom." Tears started afresh.

Cindy lent her strength to help her across the room.

Her mom hurried to her side and clasped her in her best 'mama bear' hug. "You didn't really believe I would allow you to get married without me and Daddy being here, did you?"

"I didn't know you'd come all this way. I've made a mess of it, Mom. The doctor says I might not even be able to have children now." Kate trembled, and her mom helped her back to the bed.

"Now the resident hairdresser will be up in just a few minutes. Cindy picked out flowers. Stefan's wife Marie found a beautiful dress we hope will fit and a lovely veil with a tiara."

Her makeover began with a fresh haircut to cut away the lifeless, malnourished hair and shape up the hair that hadn't come out in clumps. Cindy worked on some fresh makeup, purple eyeliner with mauve shadow and a hint of white sparkle under the brows and at the inner corners of her eyes. A high drama mascara accentuated her eyelashes. A moist mauve lip gloss and powdery blush completed the makeup.

The silvery white lace dress was loose but beautiful. A white satin ribbon took up the slack with tail ends that flowed down the back of the dress. Freshwater pearls accented with garnet beads, Kate's birthstone, graced her throat. Silver dangled earrings hung from her earlobes.

"I can't believe it." The mirror held a different Kate than the one she'd seen for that last month. "Thank you so much. You are all wonderful."

"Don't you dare cry and mess up your makeup, Kate." Cindy helped her over to the big recliner. "Rest now that you are a picture fit for the Louvre. We'll take you to the town hall around nine."

"But, what about shoes? I can't get married barefoot, can I?" Kate's insides trembled, and she wished she could climb back into bed. But Tyler would be waiting for her at La Hotel de Ville at nine. He'd waited so long already. She couldn't possibly put him off any longer without losing him. Perhaps she could sleep in the chair until the doctor came.

"Kate, I have exactly what you need for today. Tyler sent these over for you. He said you don't have to wear them, if you don't want."

Sarah handed her 2 large shoe boxes labeled 'Laredo Boots' in the perfect size from the day they had bought her cowgirl duds. The style name on the first box said 'Miss Kate'. The brown and teal leather boots inside were suede. A note inside the box from Tyler read, "Because that's what the kids who come on Saturdays will call you."

She opened the second box marked 'Tattoo' and gasped. It held crushed white leather with a silk screened black 'tattoo' on the front. Tyler's note in this box read, "For the sophisticated cowgirl's wedding, if you choose to wear them." She slipped them on. Like Cinderella in the tale, they fit her perfectly. This was the life she was choosing.

***

Tyler slipped into the tuxedo pants he'd bought and had altered earlier in the week. He'd never owned something so fine and well-fitted. Then he strapped on the cursed leg brace, muttering epitaphs to no one.

"Everything okay over there?" Rev. Ryan sat on the hotel bed flipping channels on the TV. "There is nothing on cable in English. What's the point?"

Tyler walked over and sat down next to him. "Any advice about marriage, Dad?"

"Every wife is right, even if she's wrong." They chuckled at the joke. "Seriously, make sure Kate feels your love all the time. This anorexia stuff takes a great deal of control and understanding. And it could still take her life, "

"I witnessed a seizure and heart attack last week on the first day I arrived. It was a sobering experience. It made her all the more precious to me, sir. When she can be released to be flown back on the hospital flight, I intend to go with her. And if I can swing it, I'll have that flight go straight on to Dallas."

Tyler slipped on the custom-tailored vest and jacket. Fit like a glove. Even with the brace on. He combed and styled the blond hair, that should have had a haircut in the midst of preparation, but he was not the focus and never would be. After God, his Katie would always be the focus of his world. Miguel and he would make it so because they both needed her.

***

When Dr. Simmons arrived, he took Kate's vitals and read the chart without comment. His brow furrowed. He closed the chart.

"Despite Dr. Crumb's okay, I think this excursion is ill-advised, Ms. Lawrence. However, I do understand your desire to wed given your health status and your presence in Paris. I'll give you the day pass under the condition that you return promptly to the hospital, IVs and all, once the wedding has concluded. The honeymoon must be postponed until you are released from care. Understood?"

Kate nodded. "When can I be transferred to the States?"

"Probably within the week, as long as you suffer no setback due to the day's frivolities." He scrawled his illegible signature across the day pass and in the chart. "No physical exertion. No 'play'. No extreme emotional occurrences. Wheelchair required. Be sure you eat lunch and are back here for dinner. Nurse, order a tray for Mr. Hawkins so he can be sure to bring her back on time. I am not pleased with this adventure. Do not misunderstand; you are still not well. Don't take my permission for license, young lady."

"I understand, Dr. Simmons." Kate looked into her lap. She'd done this to herself. She hadn't trusted God or Tyler. If she had, she would be on Green Pastures, riding Ariel, mothering Miguel, and keeping a healthy weight. She'd thought Paris was her dream come true, but instead it was her personal nightmare.

She felt a gentle touch on her chin raising her eyes to Dr. Simmons's eyes.

"You look lovely. Mr. Hawkins is a lucky young man. Remember not to give in to negative thoughts. That's just as important in your recovery. Look up. God has shined his face upon you. Look at your friends and family who are here to support you. You will win this battle when you turn your thoughts on God and your groom. I was stern because reality is also an important factor in your recovery. Don't jeopardize it so you can go home."

His kind eyes triggered tears. She nodded.

Cindy rushed across the room with tissue. "Oh no, you don't. No crying. You'll ruin your make-up."

Nurse Madelaine glided into the room with a wheelchair festooned with glittery crepe paper and balloons. "Your car is here. Ladies, there's room for all, compliments of the nursing staff."

Her mom looked out the window. "It's a stretch limo with the trunk open for the wheelchair."

The group piled out of the room in high spirits; Kate laughed despite her tears and Cindy's remonstrance.

***

Tyler paced in front of the Hotel de Ville. It was past nine o'clock. Where were they? Where was Katie? Had she relapsed? Had she decided not to marry him?

Rev. Ryan leaned against the brickwork. "You won't be getting them here any faster wearing a path in this sidewalk. You should sit, rest; the rest of the day will be challenge enough."

Stefan laughed. "He's not wrong, *n'est pas*? I know Kate. She will be here. She can be distracted, but you can count on her. I will miss her in Paris."

At that, the limo pulled up in front of the ancient town hall. Tyler rushed the vehicle, but Rev. Ryan held him back.

"Go inside and tell the mayor we are finally ready. You aren't allowed to see the bride just yet."

Tyler muttered under his breath while he and Stefan headed back inside the Hotel de Ville.

***

With Tyler gone, her dad opened the limo door as the chauffeur pulled the wheelchair from the trunk. He reached in to help Kate out of the car.

"Are you ready, baby girl?" Tears formed in his eyes. "You look beautiful. Better, you look better, as well."

The limo driver brought the wheelchair around and steadied it as Kate transferred to it. Cindy helped her arrange her dress and set her cowgirl wedding boots on the foot pads before rolling her up a ramp into the town hall. After getting directions to the mayor's chambers, they rolled off with Kate's 'entourage' in tow.

As soon as Kate saw Tyler waiting for her, she cried out to Cindy to stop. Cindy stopped the chair, and Kate attempted to stand up.

"I'll not go to my wedding in a wheelchair. I'll walk to Tyler of my own accord."

Everyone around her yelled out for her to stay in the chair. She stood with great effort anyway. When she took her first step, she crumpled to the floor of the mayor's chambers.

Tyler was by her side in a heartbeat.

"What are you doing, Katydid?"

"I don't want to be wed in a wheelchair." Tears began again in earnest. "I want to come to you on my own power."

"Would you compromise by allowing me to carry you to the place you need to be?" He asked in a whisper.

"I'd like that. Help me stand upright too."

Tyler grinned. "I can hold you up too."

With that he swept her up in his arms and carried her to where the mayor stood waiting. Tyler set her down on her feet then looped an arm around her to hold her upright as the mayor spoke the wedding in broken English and unintelligible to Tyler French.

Kate and Tyler looked into each other's eyes. They paid little attention to the Mayor until he said, "Well? Do you take her to be your wife?"

"Yes, I do."

Kate, understanding the mumbled French, didn't miss her opportunity to say the same. "I do."

"I now pronounce you man and wife in the eyes of the French government."

Tyler pressed Kate upon him. "I have waited a long time for this day that I can call you my wife." He kissed her again, a deep, passionate kiss.

The entourage and onlookers cheered.

Chapter 31

The rental car and limo stopped in front of Chez Richard.

"There's been a mistake. Chez Richard is not open during the day."

Tyler picked her up and placed her in the wheel char.

"For a price, they will fix us an elegant meal and even music."

Tyler rolled Kate in her festooned wheelchair to the head table next to his place. He was the man she loved and who loved her most. It was balm to her soul; it made her whole. Every touch he gave her made her stronger. Every kiss thrilled her. Kate needed him as much as she needed food to be well again. The ring on her finger linked her to him forever. It was loose today, but she was sure he would help her regain the good weight she needed to live.

As the group finished eating, Chef Richard himself brought in a three-tier wedding cake.

"Oh, Tyler, you have done everything to make this the perfect day."

He helped her stand to cut the cake. He took a piece and placed it in her mouth. "This bite is only the first of the sweet things we'll taste for the rest of our lives."

Kate gave him his bite. "Sweet things forever."

When all had had plenty, the group squeezed into the limo while Tyler took Kate in his rental car to the hospital.

"How long can you stay in Paris?"

"As long as my wife is here. Not going to leave you now that you're mine. I'll fly back with you whenever they give the go ahead." Tyler reached across and took her hand. "You have made me the happiest man in the world, Katydid. Thank you for letting me in."

"It's what God wanted. He told me so before I left for Paris." Kate squeezed his hand. "I love you. God knew what was best for me. Wish I'd done it straight away instead of after ruining my health."

Tyler kissed her hand. "No regrets. This is the time God is giving us."

"Where's Miguel? Don't Mom and Dad usually keep him?"

"Tom and Rosa have him. No worries, Mrs. Hawkins."

Kate smiled. She felt a wave of dizziness. Why couldn't they have a normal bridal night? *Never mind, God, I know it's my own fault. But I could ride next to Tyler into the sunset and beyond.*

***

When they reached the hospital, Kate was asleep. Tyler lifted her from the passenger seat and placed her in the wheelchair. He insisted on being the wheelchair driver up to her room.

The entourage had arrived before Kate and Tyler. While they'd been gone, someone had decorated with white crepe paper and red roses. The decorations and the effects of the champagne lunch lent a festive air to the room. When Kate and Tyler entered her hospital room, the entire hospital may have heard the exclamations. Within moments, the head nurse charged into the room.

"This is a place of healing, not a private party room. You must all leave at once." She waved her arms like she was shushing pigeons away from a park statue. "Mr. Hawkins, you may stay, but you must not have any wedding night activities. You understand, *n'est-ce pas*? Doctor's orders."

Tyler nodded and lifted Katie from the chair and placed her in the bed. Nurses came to hook up IVs and heart monitors. He drew the large recliner up next to the bed. He hardly even noticed that the rest of the wedding party had exited, leaving them alone on their wedding night.

***

Tyler woke as Nurse Madelaine slipped in and pulled back the drapes.

"Good morning, ma'am." He straightened up while pain shot down his leg and up his back. "Note to self, sleeping bent over will hurt in the long run."

Madelaine chuckled. "How did she sleep?"

Tyler shrugged. "All I know is that every time I tried to pull away to lay back in the chair, her hand tightened on mine to keep me here." He stood with great agony.

"Doctor is thinking on sending her to Walter Reed this week, if all is well after yesterday's excitement." She noted the details on the machines that beeped continuously and monitored vital signs. "Vitals are good, *Monsieur* Hawkins. Doctor will be in this morning. Perhaps you'll be home for Christmas."

As Madelaine swept out of the room, Kate stirred. "Tyler?"

"I'm here, Katydid." Tyler sat stiffly on the edge of the hospital bed. "Never going to be far away ever, if I can help it."

"Did the nurse just say I might be sent to the States this week?"

Tyler gathered her in his arms. "Yes, and then home as soon as possible."

As he leaned in to kiss her, Tyler's cell phone rang. He gave her a quick peck, then pulled his phone from his pocket. "Tyler Hawkins."

"Tyler, this is Joe. You're not going to believe this."

"What's wrong?"

"The police and that detective are here searching the big house and the stables."

"Got a warrant?"

"Yeah, I wouldn't let 'em on the property without it. They're none too happy you're in Paris either."

"When they leave, give them my cell number. They should already have it. Look as though you are the most cooperative person ever. Tell them the doc thinks Katie can travel sometime this week. I'll be happy to speak with them then or now on the phone."

Joe mumbled something Tyler couldn't quite make out.

"What's that, Joe?"

"I said, maybe you should stay in Paris. I swear they got the look of a posse with a hangin' rope."

"Just be cooperative, Joe. I'll be home soon, God willing." Tyler ended the call and put his phone away.

"What's happening now?" Kate's small voice entered his ear canal. "Is it Cantu?"

Tyler hugged her with intensity then relaxed his grip on her. "The police want to question me again."

Kate's face furrowed in worry. "That can't be a good thing, can it?"

Tyler shook his head. "It may mean that they've released Cantu. But now they have no other suspect."

A knock at the door alerted Tyler and Kate that they had company.

"Hey all! Not too early are we?" Rev. Ryan and Miss Sarah entered. "We're on our way to the airport and to sweet Miguel in Dallas."

After hugs all around, Rev. Ryan and Miss Sarah left them.

It was mid-morning when Dr. Simmons came into the room.

"I think I have good news for the newlyweds. I'm sending you to Walter Reed this afternoon. The ambulance is on its way to take you to the airport." He turned to look at Tyler. "You should go check out of the hotel and bring your luggage. Once they get here, they'll be ready to go."

Tyler kissed Kate and hurried down the corridors into the morning light to get to the hotel across the intersection from the hospital.

When he returned, the EMTs were there loading Kate and her things into the ambulance.

"*Monsieur* Hawkins?" At Tyler's nod, the EMT gestured to the bench beside Kate. "Welcome aboard, *monsieur*."

Tyler threw the overnight and the tuxedo suit bags into the back and climbed in next to his wife.

Chapter 32

"We're on our final descent into Andrews. Be sure our passengers are secure for landing. Operation Home for Christmas accomplished."

After a flurry of activity, the medical personnel sat and seat-belted themselves.

"An ambulance is waiting for us, Katydid." Tyler peered out the window. "It also looks like a squad of black SUVs are here to greet us. That's not good."

Kate was still strapped to the gurney. "What do you think it is?"

"Trouble with a capital T. FBI perhaps. Probably about Cantu and the guy who bled out on our carpet." Tyler held her hand. "Whatever happens when we land, remember I'll be back to you. Four days until Christmas."

The wheels screeched as the medical transport plane landed. After taxiing to the ambulance, the back descended so the medical personnel could wheel Kate to the waiting ambulance.

Tyler grabbed his two bags and followed her. Two men in suits approached him.

"Reverend Tyler Hawkins? FBI. We need you to come with us for questioning, after leaving the States during a murder investigation where you are the only witness and the sole suspect as a result." The man in a black suit handcuffed Tyler and led him to a black SUV.

"Tyler!" Kate struggled to sit up to see him.

"It will be okay, Katydid. I'll be at the hospital as soon as I convince these men that I'm innocent."

Tyler was helped into the SUV, and the caravan pulled off the tarmac with the ambulance behind them until it left the caravan to head to Walter Reed while the SUVs continued into DC to FBI headquarters.

***

Once in the building, the agents removed the handcuffs and allowed Tyler to move about freely as though he was just visiting. They all went to a conference room, and the agents offered Tyler coffee and doughnuts.

"I don't understand. You pulled me away from my ill wife. You handcuffed me and drove me through town like I was a criminal. Now you offer me refreshments. What is happening here?"

The younger agent smiled. "I'm Agent Taylor. When you left the country, the Dallas police made it FBI business to take you into custody."

"But I was in constant contact with the US Embassy in Paris. Someone could have easily talked to me there. Most of them were at our wedding yesterday, wait two days ago."

The grizzled older man sipped his coffee. "Agent Davidson. Relax, Reverend Hawkins. You are a material witness in the murder investigation in Dallas. As such, the DPD wants you available. I believe they told you not to leave the country."

Tyler straightened up as best he could after the transatlantic flight in his braces. "He told me not to disappear. Many people knew exactly where I was. My wife, fiancée then, had a medical emergency in Paris. She needed me more than the DPD did. And as I said, the US Embassy knew where I was the whole time I was in Paris. You see, Kate Lawrence Hawkins was a diplomat there."

Agent Davidson shuffled some official looking papers. "Yes, but Dallas PD was anxious, so they sent out an APB and involved the FBI."

"Am I free to go? I need to be with Katie until she's able to go home with me."

"That's all well and good, but we have an extradition order from Texas to send you there ASAP." Agent Taylor bit into a doughnut, and the glaze flaked off all over his dossier. He blushed and swiftly hurried to the trashcan to sweep the sugar flakes into the trash. "Sorry about that."

"I can't leave her. You can question me here. What's different since I left? We're hoping to be home with my son for Christmas. Can't it wait until then?" Tyler rubbed his wrists where the handcuff had rubbed marks. "You treat me like a fugitive, now you tell me you need to separate me from my ill wife because Dallas PD has their shorts in a wad."

Agent Taylor laughed.

Agent Davidson picked up his folder. "Let me have a chat with DPD. I'll see what we can work out."

Tyler was left alone in the conference room, worrying what was happening with Katie. Only four days until Christmas. Would they both make it to Dallas in time for Christmas with Miguel?

***

Tyler strolled into Kate's hospital room. She was napping so he sat in the chair by the window. Soon he had fallen asleep as well.

He woke when someone touched his knee.

"Sir, are you Reverend Hawkins?"

He looked up into deep brown eyes. Then the nurse consulted Kate's chart.

"The doctor will swing through here on his way home and wants you to be available then. Are you able to stay until six or so?"

Tyler nodded and cleared his throat. "Of course, I'll be here. Where else would I be if not with my wife?"

The nurse giggled. "Newlyweds, I hear. I always thought Paris would be a wonderful place to get married."

Tyler rose stiffly and hooked his thumbs in his belt loops. "You don't want to do that. Trust me. Unless your fiancé lives there or you plan to move there, the regulations are nearly impossible to meet. Katie had already been there three months. And she knew the Secretary of State in France. Otherwise we would have had to wait until we were back in the US of A."

"Really? So much for my dream wedding. So Kate works for …"

"The State Department." Kate's voice floated into the conversation from her bed. "At least for a little while longer. Tyler. You're here."

"I'll leave you two alone. We've ordered a good dinner for you both, so it should be up in just a little while." The nurse smiled as she left while closing the door.

Tyler sat gingerly on the edge of the bed and took Katie into his arms.

"I'm so glad to see you. What happened with the FBI?"

He kissed her. A long passionate kiss. If only they could finally get home.

"Nothing happened with the FBI. I ate doughnuts and drank a gallon of coffee while they talked to Dallas PD. They didn't even have the courtesy to take me here. I had to hail a cab." Tyler gave her another kiss. "Basically, they have no good suspects. They've still not released Cantu and got nervous that I'd not return."

Katie put her arms around his neck and pulled him in for another kiss.

"How I've longed to be in your arms. You are better than any medicine they could put in this IV. I'm even hungry, I think."

Tyler picked up a hospital menu from her tray. "hat's this good dinner we're getting?"

Kate plucked the menu from his hands. "Steak, potato, and broccoli. Yeast rolls and strawberries. Iced tea."

"In a hospital?" He was sure that could not be a good thing.

"Now be nice. Apparently they have an arrangement with a local restaurant to provide a special meal for special events. Homecoming wounded and their families, for example." She took each of his scarred hands into hers. "We came in on the VIP flight. We qualify."

Tyler looked into her eyes. "You seem perky. Something going on I should know about?"

She gave him a curious face. "You have to wait to talk to the doc. Dinner should be soon, but I'm so hungry. Could you find a bag of chips, cookies or something?"

"Seriously?"

"I am so serious, Sweetheart." Kate's plea melted his heart.

"Okay then, but I won't be gone long."

***

After Tyler left the room, Kate lay back in the bed and closed her eyes. Home. Funny to think that she pictured Texas on Green Pastures land as home. So many years she had felt homeless, living in 2 year increments wherever other people sent her. Now she needed to be well enough to go home with Tyler to Miguel and, yes, her parents. So much to repair, so much to take in, so much to look forward to.

The rap at the door drew her attention.

"Come in. Did you find M&Ms?"

"Hey, I promised to replace those M&Ms, but you moved to Paris, remember?" Cindy popped her head around the door. "Safe to come in? Nothing inappropriate going on, is there?"

"Girlfriend!" Kate's voice squealed. "I know it hasn't been that long since the wedding, but I'm so glad to be in DC."

Cindy ran into the room and hugged Kate after they negotiated the tubing and wires. She climbed up in the bed with Kate.

"You're not coming back, are you?"

"Texas and Miguel are waiting, if I ever get out of the hospital."

"Now that's what I wanted to hear. Let's get this happily ever after on track." Tyler entered the room with arms full of snack food.

"Did you buy the whole snack machine?" Cindy grabbed a bag of Cheetos as it fell from the stack. "I see the attraction to the cowboy now. He can sure rustle up a batch of snacks."

Tyler dumped the vending machine output onto the hospital bed.

"What sparks your interest, milady?"

While Kate was mulling over the selections, Doctor Anderson sauntered in.

"I'd love to hear the answer to that, Kate. I assume all this means you feel hunger?"

She grabbed a packet of soft chocolate chip cookies and nodded. Kate had a momentary struggle about whether to wait until the doctor left or eat the cookies now. The cookies won.

Doc Anderson laughed. "Your dinner will be delivered soon, so I wanted to pop in to share with you my prognosis of care."

Cindy got off the bed. "That's my cue to go." She snagged a bag of white cheddar popcorn, hugged Kate and Tyler, then scooted out the door.

"So?" Tyler reached for Kate's hand and sat in the chair next to the bed.

"My Parisian counterparts did an excellent job caring for you, Kate. Therefore, I see no reason why you can't go home for Christmas. To do that, I need you to sign this form to release your files to a colleague in Dallas who can continue your care as an outpatient." The doctor brandished a pen and the File Release form, which Kate signed immediately.

"I want you to stay the night just to be sure this gourmet feast doesn't mess with your digestion. Then you can travel tomorrow morning. Work for you?"

Kate's mouth was full of cookie. She nodded.

"I'll take good care of her, Doc." Tyler rose awkwardly and shook the man's hand.

"Here's Doctor Stephenson's information. Be sure and schedule an appointment for right after Christmas." The doctor handed Tyler the card. "Kate, this isn't your first rodeo. You can't do this again. You nearly died in that hospital in Paris. Your body started shutting down. Do you understand the gravity of your condition?"

"Yes, sir. I do understand." Kate paused, afraid to ask the question on her mind. "What about children? Will I be able to get pregnant and carry to term?"

"Some of that depends on you. Some more of it may be physical."

Tyler shook his head. "What do you mean?"

"Often female athletes train their bodies so hard that their reproductive processes stop. They no longer have periods because they no longer ovulate because they don't have enough fat on their bodies. You haven't had a period in a year. In order to have a baby, you must ovulate."

"If I gain an appropriate amount of weight, I should be able to ovulate?" Kate hugged herself. "It's not that simple, is it?"

"The complication is that you may have destroyed your ability to ovulate or the ability to keep a pregnancy." Doctor Anderson paused. "Then there's the pregnancy. You have spent a lot of years trying to look thin. Pregnancy requires an appropriate weight gain."

Kate began to cry. "You're saying I'll have to gain a significant amount of weight in order to be able to get pregnant and more in order to carry the child."

"I'll send you a recommendation for a psychiatrist. You are not well, Kate. You will never have a normal relationship with food. Tyler may help you, but you need to change how you think about food." Doctor Anderson took her hand. "You can be as well as possible if you stay the course."

Tyler ripped a tissue from the box beside the bed and handed it to Kate to wipe away her tears and whispered in her ear. "We have Miguel."

She nodded.

"Dinner!" The sing song voice of the person carrying two trays into the room disrupted the conversation. "VIP dinner for two."

"I'll write the discharge orders for tomorrow morning. Stay the night, recover from jetlag, and have sweet dreams, Kate." Doctor Anderson took her hand. "You have a whole new life in front of you. Enjoy it."

Kate nodded and tears flowed again. He squeezed her hand and left the room.

***

After the enormous and delicious steak dinner, Tyler climbed into bed with Kate and held her while she fell asleep. The nurse who came in first thing to complete discharge protocols found them wrapped in each other's arms.

Chapter 33

Three days until Christmas. That's all Kate could think about while they waited to board the plane. Tyler had insisted on a wheel chair for Kate and pre-board cards for them both.

"Don't worry, Kate." Tyler patted her arm. "I bought some good things at the holiday craft fair for Miguel and your parents. Christmas will come no matter. 'It came just the same … It came without ribbons! It came without tags! It came without packages, boxes or bags! … Maybe Christmas … doesn't come from a store. Maybe Christmas … perhaps … means a little bit more!'"

"You're seriously quoting me Dr. Seuss?" Kate punched him in the arm.

Tyler laughed so loud the other waiting passengers turned to see what was going on. "I was reading it to Miguel. Don't blame me. It was a gift from your parents."

"This is a boarding call for flight to Dallas. At this time, we'll be boarding our pre-boards."

***

The plane began its final descent into the landing pattern.

Kate eagerly watched out the window. "It's snowing, Tyler. It really is snow."

The wheels touched down with a screech and a discernable slide before grabbing the pavement.

"I can't believe it's finally our wedding night." Kate turned and faced Tyler.

"And we have a child. Who finds it easy to come into the bedroom and slide into the bed."

"Hmmm. Awkward." Kate kissed him. "Then we just have to be sure he's tired enough to sleep then. And feels safe having a daddy and a mommy in his house."

The attendants came to get Kate first with the wheelchair, and Tyler hauled the carry-on bags for both of them. When they got into the terminal, Tyler tipped the attendant and handed Kate her bag. Then Tyler pushed the wheelchair in his jagged gait.

"I could walk, you know." Kate twisted to see Tyler's face. "You don't need to be in pain to keep me from walking."

"Stay in the chair until we get to the baggage area. I'm hoping we have a welcome home group that can help us."

As they exited the secure terminal area, Kate saw Miguel, running for all he was worth toward them. Instead of running into Tyler's arms, however, he jumped into her lap and hugged her around the neck.

"Is it okay if I call you Mama now? I'm so glad you are well enough to come home and to marry Daddy."

Kate's tears rolled down Miguel shirt collar. "Of course, you can call me Mama. I'm so glad I could come home too."

Soon the rest of the delegation surrounded the wheelchair. Stan took the wheelchair away from Tyler.

"Sorry I couldn't be the best man at the wedding, but I can rescue you from his wheelchair pushing." He headed for the elevator to go to baggage claim.

The rest of the crew headed down the escalator.

"Tell me what's going on with Cantu." Kate waited until after the elevator doors closed to ask Stan. "There's something Tyler's not telling me."

"Not much to tell. Cantu's still locked up. Tyler's testimony is keeping him there."

"The FBI met our plane from Paris and took him into custody."

Stan's eyes widened as he squatted next to the chair. "Hadn't heard that part. They didn't extradite him?"

Kate shook her head. "Tyler talked the FBI out of it, then the FBI reached some kind of consensus with DPD."

Stan took off his ten-gallon hat and ruffled his hair. "That is not good news. DPD is going to feel humiliated and will exact some revenge, I'm afraid."

Just then the elevator doors slid open. Tyler was waiting there.

"I'll get the van so Miss Kate doesn't have to walk far." Stan stood and wheeled Kate to the baggage carousel. Then he got the keys from her dad and left.

"What's that all about?" Tyler bent down as best he could. "What did he tell you?"

"Cantu's still in jail. He's afraid DPD will be ready to arrest you since the FBI did not comply with the extradition order." Kate's voice trembled as she spoke. "Guess it's not quite time for happily ever after."

"Hey, stop that worry, wife." Tyler took her hand. "If God be for us, nothing can be against us."

"Tell DPD that." Kate put on a smile for the crew trying to guess which luggage was theirs.

Chapter 34

Everyone piled into the Mission Mesquite van leaving the airport wheelchair behind. When the van pulled up to the big house at Green Pastures, the Dallas Police Department had three cars with flashing lights in front.

Miguel jumped from the van and ran over to the patrol cars. "Are you here to welcome my dad and new mama home, too?"

Tyler climbed out of the van, stiffly. "No, Miguel, this is not a welcome home tribute. Is it, officer?"

"No, sir, I need to take you into custody." He at least looked apologetic.

"Tomorrow is Christmas Eve. Can I come by tomorrow early and settle this up with the chief? I'm not going anywhere. My wife and son are here. There's nowhere else I'd rather be."

"I'm sorry, sir. The chief was quite determined to see you as soon as you landed."

"What's going on now?" Katie clung to Tyler's arm.

"I'm sorry, Katydid. They want to take me into custody now." He bent down a kissed her. "Hopefully I'll be back by morning. Rev. Ryan can you come down to the station once everyone gets home."

"You bet. And you can start calling me 'Dad'."

Tyler handed Kate the keys to the house and allowed himself to be cuffed and put into the back of the patrol car. He had to look away when his Katie began weeping.

***

Kate's knees gave out as the patrol cars pulled away, and she ended up in a heap on the cold ground. She couldn't catch her breath between sobs and the tears.

Why, God, would You take him away when we're finally where You want us to be? After all it has taken for me to obey You. Is this some kind of cruel joke? And two days before Christmas?

Miguel piled up into her lap with arms around her neck, holding on tight.

And then the answer came as clear as though whispered into her ear. *Cantu's family deserves to have him freed for Christmas as well.*

Oh, Lord, be merciful to me a sinner. I am selfish and short-sighted. These sins have kept me from my parents and from my husband. Help me put away my pride and care for Tyler's, our, son while You work to clear Cantu's name and put away this situation. If I had come home sooner, Cantu could have been free before now. Forgive me.

"Mama Katie?" Miguel brushed back her hair and put his hands on her cheeks. "Daddy will be back before Christmas 'cause God always brings him back. Come in the house and see the surprise me and Grandma Sarah and Grandpa Ryan did while you were on the long plane ride home."

Kate smiled and wiped away her tears. "You're right, Miguel. We must go in and sleep so we can have a proper Christmas Eve tomorrow. And Daddy wouldn't want to miss Christmas, would he?"

"No way!" Miguel jumped up and pulled her up.

Kate looked around at their friends and family. Joe and Rose had joined the group without her notice as well. "We should go in for hot chocolate, if we have any. Will you stay for a little while?"

Nods and 'yeses' indicated the group's agreement, and all headed toward the big house with Miguel pulling Kate leading the way.

The door was unlocked, so Kate didn't need Tyler's key after all. When they entered the dark foyer, Miguel let go of her and ran for a step stool. He set it beside the wall and flipped the light switches. A Christmas tree in the front room lit up to oohs and aahs from all.

"Oh, Miguel. It's beautiful. There are even packages under the tree."

"I'll start the hot chocolate." Her mom hurried on to the kitchen as Miguel led Kate into the front room.

"Look, here's my favorite ornament. It's Santa kneeling at the manger where Jesus is." Miguel pulled the ornament from the low limb and handed it to Kate. "Grandma Sarah told me all about how Jesus came as a baby. She said that's what Christmas is all about."

Kate kneeled beside him. "Yes, even Santa bows down to Jesus."

Miguel solemnly placed the ornament back on the branch.

"Look, here's a package to you from Grandma Sarah and Grandpa Ryan." Miguel handed it to Kate. "I helped wrap it. I know what's inside. You'll like it. Want to know what it is?"

"Yes, will you tell me?"

Miguel laughed and ran back toward the kitchen. "Nope, you gotta wait till Christmas, Mama."

Kate knelt before the tree a little longer, then she rose shakily to go help in the kitchen. As she stood, she realized that on the far wall was a folding table groaning with presents wrapped in white and silver with crisp bows. Wedding presents. Lots of wedding presents. Kate blinked back the threatening flood of new tears. *You are so good, Lord. Don't let me forget to praise you for every good and perfect gift.*

She found her dad lingering at the hall entrance to the front room.

"Not sure what your mom is doing in your kitchen." His statement was punctuated by banging pans and loud shouting. "Perhaps we should mosey back and find out." He held out his elbow, and she looped her arm in his.

In the kitchen, friends had gathered around the huge farmhouse table. On it sat a three-tier wedding cake adorned with silver bells and marzipan holly leaves and berries. Kate's tears began afresh.

Her mom was making hot chocolate for the crew.

Kate snagged her arm. "I can't cut that cake without Tyler."

"Of course, you can't. Luckily we also made *petit fors* we can enjoy just the same." She showed Kate a tray of individual-sized cakes, each decorated with a holly leaf. "When Tyler returns, the two of you can cut the big cake or wait until we're together for Christmas."

Her mom handed her a tissue from her pocket, then hugged her. "It will all be okay. They can't hold Tyler for being a witness, even if they don't have other suspects."

Chapter 35

Once all the guests departed, Kate sank back into Tyler's recliner. The whiff of his aftershave and manly scent lingered in the chair. She could almost imagine him holding her as she lay back, exhausted from her travels, Tyler's arrest, and the impromptu reception of guests.

"Want to watch Rudolph?" Miguel stood beside the chair.

"Isn't it time for bed? Tomorrow will be Christmas Eve." One look into his deep brown eyes made it hard to take a stand on Christmas Eve Eve. "Sure, but I don't know how to operate Tyler, er, Daddy's video equipment." The tower of devices loomed in the corner next to the TV and a media shelf with an impressive collection of DVDs and Blu-ray disks. Too many buttons, remotes, and other possibilities.

"It's okay, Mama Katie. I know how to do it. Daddy teached me."

"Taught you."

"Yes, ma'am. I'll do it."

In no time, Burl Ives in snowman form filled the screen singing the famous Rudolph song. With Miguel occupied, Kate drifted off to sleep.

***

Detective Rodriquez led Tyler to a conference room and uncuffed him.

"Did you really have to do this today? In front of my family and friends? I thought this had been all worked out when I was in DC yesterday." Tyler rubbed his wrists where the cuffs had rubbed them red.

"We still want to settle this case before Christmas, if possible."

Detective Kellan joined them and closed the door. "I'm sure Cantu would like to get out of jail for Christmas. Don't you?"

"I'm not sure why he's in jail to begin with, frankly. You found Cantu's gun thrown under the Mission. You checked fingerprints. Mine weren't on it. Cantu's were, but you also found other prints. Whose were they?"

"Some were the victim's."

Tyler fell back in his chair. "The victim's hands were on the gun. On the barrel or the grip?"

"The grip. We've just got the forensic information. The lab had to separate the prints on the handle to determine who else had left prints." The older detective sat across from Tyler while the younger lounged against the glass.

"So why do you need me again?" Tyler leaned forward and looked the man straight in the eye. "I have nothing to do with the shooting. The man just stumbled into the Mission, which is normally unlocked. Bled out all over the carpet. Said 'Cantu did this.'"

This time Rodriquez leaned back, stunned. "'Cantu did this.' Not Cantu killed me or Cantu shot me?"

"Right. What are you thinking, Detective?"

"We've been looking at this all wrong. We need to go down to the prison to speak to Mr. Cantu about Bobby Carpenter. Do you want to come with us, Reverend?"

Tyler grabbed his coat and slung it on. "You bet I do."

The three men headed for the detective's car. Tyler sat in back, but at least he wasn't in handcuffs this time. They fought early morning Christmas Eve last minute shopping traffic.

While the detectives navigated traffic, Tyler called Katie's phone.

"Tyler? When will you be home?" She sounded sleepy, and the Rudolph song was playing in the background. "I think we slept in the den with Rudolph on continuous play."

"We are headed out to talk to Cantu. Pray that he will be cooperative. I think we've finally figured out this mystery."

Tyler could hear the doorbell ring.

"I think that's Mom and Dad. They wanted to come over on Christmas Eve for dinner and to read Christmas stories and such. They're so excited to have a grandchild at Christmas."

Tyler smiled in spite of himself. "I hope to be there for dinner. Tell Miss Sarah to save me dinner. I love you, Katie."

Tyler hung up and noticed that snow was drifting across the windshield. *Is there any better time than Christmas?*

***

Cantu sat chained to a table across from Tyler and the detectives.

"Merry Christmas, old friend. Thanks for nothing." Cantu sneered at Tyler.

"I never wanted you here. You should know that."

"I hope you're taking care that my Elena and our children have Christmas since I'm here on your word." Cantu's long black hair shaded his face as he stared down at the shackles. "I didn't do no murder."

"Which I have contended from the start, Junior. Listen to what we have to say. We got a writ to release you on your own reconnaissance for Christmas, but you got to cooperate." Tyler placed his hand on the man's shoulder. "Ask your questions, Detective."

"Reverend Hawkins tells us that Bobby Carpenter was your wife's fiancé prior to your relationship. Were there hard feelings when Elena broke up with Carpenter?"

Cantu laughed. "What you think, man? Elena is a fine catch. I let her catch me instead. Bobby Carpenter was trash. He beat her. I wouldn't let that go on."

"When Elena left Carpenter …" Detective Kellan tried to get Cantu to say the magic words that would put the whole case to bed.

"He was angry, sure. I'd have been too if someone blew into town and took my woman." Cantu sniffed and rubbed his nose. "He couldn't get her back. He came to the wedding."

Tyler sat in a chair. "What happened then?"

"He said 'Elena was pregnant with his baby'. I said, 'No, man, that baby's mine, and you know it.'" Cantu nodded at Tyler. "Sorry, Reverend, it's just what happened."

"Can't say a word about it." Tyler thought of his son at home with his wife and all he wanted was to be home.

"Anyway, he speaks up when the preacher says, 'Anybody have a reason?' and Bobby says, 'I do.'"

The chair legs scraped the concrete floor as the detectives drew closer to the table.

Rodriquez leaned forward. "This is really important, Cantu. What'd he say? Where's he been since then?"

"This ain't gettin' me nowhere. I may as well go back to my cell and sing "Silent Night.""

Cantu started to motion for the guard. Tyler grabbed his arm. "Wait. We're coming to it. Be patient. Elena wants you home for the birth of your child."

Cantu settled down. "He say, 'I get you real good someday when you not expect it.' I broke his nose and left him in the dirt outside Mission Mesquite. Guess that's what he did."

"Where's he been? What's he do?" Tyler prodded him.

"He hung out at the rodeo. Couldn't ride right after a broken arm one night. Played the clown for a while, then just disappeared." Cantu sneered. "And good riddance, too, until he showed up this summer. Hung around with the groupies. Pathetic drunk."

Tyler nodded, and the detectives smiled.

"That's it. Kellan, go give this to the clerks and paper pushers, so we can get this man home in time for Christmas." Rodriquez stood and adjusted his belt buckle.

Cantu's face puckered up in question. "I don't understand."

Tyler punched Cantu's arm. "He killed himself with your gun and implicated you in his death."

"Yep, case closed. Suicide."

Tears squeezed out of the tough man's eyes. "I can't forget what you done here, Rev. And here, I been blamin' you for this mess. Forgive me."

"No problem. Just glad it worked out for the best.

Once the paperwork was done, hours later, the detectives dropped Cantu at the trailer park and Tyler off at Green Pastures.

Chapter 36

Mayhem reigned in the big house as Tyler entered the front room. Lights, presents, and the pine aroma assaulted his senses. The front room was a Christmas peace island amidst whatever was happening in the kitchen.

As he rounded the corner into the bright space, Miguel jumped out of his seat and yelled, "Muggins! Grandma, I got Muggins on you."

"That can't be, Miguel. There must be some mistake."

Tyler leaned on the wall and watched Miss Sarah hem and haw while Rev. Ryan helped Miguel unload most of his stack of numbered cards onto the various piles around the table.

Katie looked up, and he put his finger to his lips. She smiled. Could any man be any better blessed?

"Daddy!!" Miguel padded across the floor in his footed pajamas. "I knew you wouldn't miss Christmas. 'Specially with Mama Katie here."

Tyler scooped the boy up as he flung himself at him. The wall steadied Tyler as he lifted him into the air. "What Christmas traditions need to happen before the child needs to go to sleep?"

"We've got a big cake, but Mama Katie wouldn't let them cut it without you." Miguel squirmed down from Tyler's arms and pulled him to the table to show him.

"That looks like Christmas wedding cake to me."

Miss Sarah stood from her seat and hugged him. "And so, it is."

"Getting a little late for cake, buddy. How about milk and cookies for Santa? Then let's read the Bible about Jesus' birth. After that, you need to settle in for a long winter's nap."

Katie wrapped her arms around him. "Did you see the snow? Did you have anything to eat? Do you need to go to bed?"

"I'm fine, Katydid. Let's find some Christmas cookies for Santa. Are there Christmas cookies, Grandma?" He raised his eyebrows. "Then we'll read the Christmas story about Jesus."

Miguel ran from the kitchen, then returned with his favorite ornament of Jesus and Santa.

Joe and Rosa made their excuses and slipped out as Tyler settled into his chair with a worn Bible. Miguel scrambled up into Tyler's lap.

Miss Sarah produced Christmas cookies and a glass of milk, and she sat next to Rev. Ryan on the couch. Katie found her seat in the rocking chair.

"Luke 2, 'In those days Caesar Augustus issued a decree that a census should be taken of the entire Roman world'."

"Daddy, what's a census?"

"He wanted to count all the people."

Miguel nodded. "I can count but not that high."

Tyler hugged the boy. "" (This was the first census that took place while Quirinius was governor of Syria.) And everyone went to his own town to register. So Joseph also went up from the town of Nazareth in Galilee to Judea, to Bethlehem the town of David, because he belonged to the house and line of David. He went there to register with Mary, who was pledged to be married to him and was expecting a child.'"

"Wait, Daddy." Miguel wiggled out of Tyler's lap and rushed over to the child-friendly Nativity set. "Look, Grandma Sarah gave me this." He gathered Mary and Joseph and the manger with Baby Jesus into his arms. Then he climbed back up into Tyler's lap.

"This is Joseph. This is Mary. And this is baby Jesus; just like the ornament with Santa."

"That's right, Miguel." Tyler continued reading. "'While they were there, the time came for the baby to be born, and she gave birth to her firstborn, a son. She wrapped him in cloths and placed him in a manger, because there was no room for them in the inn.'"

"Look, Mama Katie, this is a manger." He held up the crèche from the Nativity set. "And on this orn'ment. Mama Katie. When will baby Gabriel come?"

Katie smiled. "We don't know yet. We must wait and pray, too."

Tyler winked at her.

"'And there were shepherds living in the fields nearby, keeping watch over their flocks at night. An angel of the Lord appeared to them, and the glory of the Lord shone around them.'"

Miguel procured some sheep and some shepherds, and returned to Tyler's lap. "Here they are, Daddy." He ran back and got an angel, then rushed back to Tyler's arms.

"'Suddenly a great company of the heavenly host appeared and saying, "Glory to God in the highest, and on earth peace to men on whom his favor rests"'."

"Read more." Miguel wiggled in Tyler's lap, causing Tyler to wince.

"'When the angels had left them and gone into heaven…'"

Miguel held up the angel and flew it back to the nativity scene, then he returned, bouncing into Tyler's lap.

"'…the shepherds said to one another, "Let's go to Bethlehem and see this thing that has happened, which the Lord has told us about'."

Miguel held up the shepherds. "These guys?"

"Yes, 'so they hurried off and found Mary and Joseph and the baby who was lying in the manger.'" Tyler tousled Miguel's hair. "And it's time for bed, sleepy head."

Rev. Ryan came and picked up the sleepy child. "You didn't realize it was the interactive version of the Christmas story, did you?"

"Lots of things happen I didn't realize would happen." Tyler struggled to his feet. "Come on then, children must head for bed or Santa won't come."

Miguel climbed out of his dad's arms and plodded up the stairs to his bedroom. Tyler pulled himself up the staircase to kiss his son goodnight.

***

Kate helped her mom with the cleanup of the impromptu party.

"I'm so glad you're home. Really home." Her mom hugged her until she couldn't breathe. "What are you doing tomorrow?"

"Opening lots of presents by the look of the front room." Kate laughed. "I'm more worried about tonight's 'party'. You know, Tyler and I haven't had a wedding night yet. I'm nervous."

"There's no need to be nervous. You love him and he loves you."

Her dad entered the kitchen. "What are we nervous about?"

Kate and her mom turned to him and said, "Nothing."

"I can see I need to give the two of you space."

Kate's mom dried her hands on the Christmas hand towel. "Actually, Sweetheart, we need to get going to give the newlyweds some private time."

"Oh, that kind of private time." Her dad blushed to the roots of his gray hair. "Yes, we should get going. Glad you're doing so well. Don't overdo it. Give us a call when you want us to come over to open packages."

Tyler lurched into the kitchen and grabbed Kate from behind. "We're having a decent breakfast before company."

"They can come for breakfast, can't they?" Kate turned in his arms. She fluttered her eyelashes. "After all they're family."

"Yes, of course, whatever you want, my love."

After walking to the door, hugs and kisses were exchanged all around.

"Finally, alone in our own home." Tyler leaned and kissed her.

"I think an early bedtime is a good idea." Kate took his hand to lead him to the bedroom.

"That's a great idea, but we have a teepee to put up before Miguel comes down on Christmas morning." Tyler gave her a helpless grin. "Then the parents can lay down for a long winter's nap. But then, Miguel is going to up at the crack of dawn."

"Very well, lead on to the Santa chores." Kate allowed herself to be pulled to the den. "Afterwards, you're mine."

"Can't wait. Get the lights while I get the teepee out of hiding."

Kate shut off the tree lights and checked the kitchen for lingering tasks. Once all was ready for the morning, she turned off all the lights but the den.

Tyler had pulled a multicolored teepee out from behind the couch. The PVC pipes were already in place. He held it in place while Kate pulled the fabric wrapped supports into position.

"Wow, where did you find this? It looks homemade." Kate pulled the final pole into place. "Miguel is going to be thrilled. You make a good Santa."

"Got it at the holiday craft fair at the arena." Tyler grinned. "I think that makes all done. I can finish wrapping your parents' gifts before breakfast."

"Will you take me to bed now, husband?"

"It would be my distinct pleasure, wife."

They walked to the bedroom arm in arm. Kate shook but hoped he wouldn't notice. After all, he was going to share all of his very self with her. Still it gave her pause.

While he was in the master bath, Kate drew out the negligee Tyler had bought her in Paris. She slipped out of the clothes she'd worn since Paris, ugh. She looked in the mirror. She'd not yet gained enough weight to do it justice. Her body still looked too thin and ill; she guessed it'd have to do. She slid between the cold, clean sheets.

"Need in here before I cut the light?"

"No, but probably later. Leave it on."

"Are you sure you wouldn't just like to sleep? I'd understand you'd like to wait."

"I couldn't have you till now. You're not getting out of it." Kate still shivered under the covers. "Warning; my fingers are ice cold."

Then he came to her, without his braces, without a stitch of clothing. His scarred, warm body slid under the covers, and his muscular arms pulled her to him. They kissed.

Soon the negligee was on the floor.

"I thought we'd never get here." Kate said as he kissed her neck and shoulders.

"I always knew we would." His mouth claimed hers.

Chapter 37

Something woke Kate. She rolled over and looked at her phone. 5:30. She strained to hear and identify the sound. Tyler snored as he turned over in his sleep.

Kate slipped from the bed and into her tank top and pajama pants. She crept from the bedroom out to the living room with the tree. Then she tiptoed to the den. Kate snickered behind her hand.

Miguel was curled up in the teepee with a blanket.

"Mama Katie, look what Santa brought." He yawned. "I found it and slept here the rest of the night."

Kate crawled inside the teepee with Miguel. He came into her arms. She threw the blanket over them both. Then they both fell asleep.

***

Kate was awakened with a camera flash. Miguel jerked and began to cry. She held him and rocked him back and forth.

"Mean Daddy." Kate scowled at him.

Tyler blew her a kiss and took another picture.

"You guys don't want to waste Christmas morning sleeping, now do you?"

Tyler laughed as Miguel ran for the living room and the tree. Then he reached into the teepee and pulled her out in an embrace. They kissed.

"Merry Christmas, Tyler."

"The best of Christmases, my Katydid."

A shout from the living room told the adults it was time they hurried up. Kate ran away from Tyler.

"Not fair. Crippled cowboy card. I'm playing it now, wife."

Kate laughed and ran into the living room where it looked as though the packages had multiplied even after she and Tyler had retired to bed. She flipped the switch that turned on the lights on the tree. It was only 6:30 by the clock on the mantel. How could he have done all this in only an hour?

"Mama! Look at all the presents!" Miguel held his face in amazement. "Never did I ever have a Christmas like this."

He ran to her and threw his arms around her legs. "You know what I wish?"

Kate thought she knew. She sat down beside him and pulled him into her lap. "What do you wish on this lovely Christmas morning, Miguel?"

"I wish Mama Tina was here to see this beautiful room full of Christmas."

His tears fell onto her shirt as she hugged him.

"It's hard when people we love can't be part of our lives anymore. Your Mama Tina loved you. When she knew she couldn't be part of your life anymore, she made sure to bring you to your daddy." She snuggled him close. "And lucky for me, that made you part of my life too."

"I'm glad too. And Mama Katie, I love you so much." His juicy kiss left her cheek damp and mingled with the happy tears she cried.

He hugged her again and then jumped up to join Tyler in the 'room full of Christmas.'

Chapter 38

New Year's Eve. Kate couldn't believe that so much had happened since her arrival in the States. Christmas had been a raucous open house affair with visits from Mission Mesquite friends who wished them happiness and shared the Christmas wedding cake with them.

She took a bite of the lower tier she'd cut this morning. Early for cake, but so good. The twinkle lights around the ceiling were all that was left of Christmas, giving way to the New Year's Eve wedding reception this evening. Her mom had made a second cake anyway for tonight, with sparkling cider and wedding reception necessaries: nuts, mints, cucumber sandwiches, and whatever else her mom ran out to buy.

Wedding packages remained unopened on the table tempting her to pick at the wrappings. They planned to open them tonight during the reception. Kate wandered back through the quiet house to the den and the big plush recliner. While Tyler and Miquel slept, she enjoyed her cake and quiet time with God.

"'For I know the plans I have for you, declares the Lord'." Kate read the verse out loud from Jeremiah. "'Plans to prosper you and not to harm you. Plans to give you hope and a future.'" She bowed her head. *Thank you for bringing me home, Lord. Help bring me back to You, so I can be your servant alongside Tyler as he ministers for You.*

The doorbell brought her out of her prayer. She pulled her kimono on over her tank top and pajama pants and rushed to answer before the guys were awakened anymore. She peeked out of the sidelights to see who was there, then opened the oak door.

"Mom?"

Her mom burst into the house with her arms full of bags and boxes. "Aren't you all up yet?"

A parade of semi-recognizable people followed her mom into the house carrying boxes and bags of décor. Kate pulled her silky kimono tighter over her tank top and pajama pants. Each person ducked their heads and mumbled 'Morning' or 'Miz Hawkins' as they passed.

When the last person and stuff had entered the house, Kate grabbed her mom. "What is going on? It's just 8 a.m."

"Why, Katie, we're here to decorate for the reception tonight. You hadn't forgotten your wedding reception is tonight? I also need to put together the reception wedding cake."

"That's still twelve hours away. We still have breakfast, lunch, and dinner before then."

"I hope we have enough time. We should have started yesterday."

Kate heard her cell phone ringing. "Whatever, Mom." She threw her hands up and went in search of her purse.

Yanking the phone from her bag, she saw the caller ID was 'US govt.' "Kate Lawrence… er … Hawkins."

"Kate, so good to hear your voice. It's John, slaving away in an empty office while others take the day to party."

Kate ducked inside the office space Tyler was creating for her. "I think the party is at my place. What can I do for you, John?"

"Right to it, okay. I've been calculating your sick leave, honeymoon leave, and vacation. Before I can close the books on this year, I need to know if you still plan to work for the State Department now that you're married and relocated to Dallas."

The patter of little feet scurried into the office and launched themselves at Kate. Kate backed into the office chair and pulled Miguel into her lap.

"Not sure what that would look like, John. What are you suggesting? My life is here now." Kate hugged the little boy closer.

"I'm sure you're aware that there is an Honorary French Consulate in Dallas. You are a Foreign Service Officer. As such, I can make a transfer to Dallas take place. You would be an independent contractor of the

State Department working at the Honorary French Consulate. Your friend, the French Secretary Dremond himself, approved this post. You can pick and choose the times and venues that you work. What do you think?"

"Do I have time to think about it?" Kate cringed as she heard the sound of breaking glass in the kitchen.

"Close of business today. Probably 1 p.m. ET by the look of the office. This is a great opportunity, Kate. We don't want to lose you."

"I'll call you back later, John. I need to include Tyler in this decision."

They hung up, and Kate snuggled with the still bed-warm Miguel.

"Mama, why are so many people in the house?" He took her face in his two hands and gave her a juicy kiss.

"There's a party tonight, and Grandma Sarah wanted to be sure to have everything ready. Why don't you go see if she'll pour you a bowl of cereal while I wake up Daddy?"

***

Tyler lay in bed. No way anyone could sleep through whatever was happening in his house this early on New Year's Eve. His freshly pressed tux hung on one closet door while Katie's white lace dress hung on the other. He already regretted agreeing to this reception.

Stirring in the bed brought fresh pain to his leg and hip. Overcoming inertia always meant taking on the pain of movement.

Katie slid back into the bed beside him. "Morning, love."

"What in the world is happening in my ... our... house?"

"Mom and a battalion of helpers are here to decorate, cook, and arrange a new wedding cake for this evening." She kissed his forehead.

Tyler groaned as he moved over to her and captured her in an embrace. "Guess that means it's time to get up."

Chapter 39

Kate helped Tyler with the studs in his tuxedo shirt, and Tyler tried to tie the sash in the back of the lace dress. Kate took the ribbon away from him and adeptly created the full bow required.

"Girl training." Then she slipped on her wedding boots.

Sounds from the front room had steadily increased as they had finished getting dressed. The knock on the door made Kate jump.

"Are you ready? It's time."

"We'll be right out." Tyler buckled the brace over his waist and secured the cummerbund in place. "Ready, Katydid?"

Kate took his arm and realized she was trembling. "Ready as ever, Reverend."

Tyler wrapped her in his arms. "I know what that word means to you. I am yours, your husband, your lover, your fellow journeyer with Christ. Don't allow that word Reverend to separate us. I love you, desperately. You are my life partner in whatever it is God gives us to do."

They kissed.

The knock on the door was sharper this time. "Come on, you two. People are waiting."

"Are we good then, Katie?" At her nod, he wiped away the single tear that fell down her cheek.

As they entered the living room, they were handed flutes of sparkling cider. Everyone crowded into the front room while some trailed into the hallway.

"Ahem." Her dad cleared his throat. "It is my consummate pleasure to introduce my son-in-law and my daughter for the first time on U.S. soil, The Reverend and Mrs. Tyler Hawkins."

After the cheers subsided, he continued, "Long life to you both. A happy marriage. A productive ministry together. A family full of love. Hear! Hear!"

Glasses clinked. Tyler entwined his arm with hers and drank fully from his glass as well as from her eyes. Her eyes just wouldn't stop leaking.

After the toast, the crowd queued up as a reception line from the living room and back into the kitchen where her mom served the New Year's wedding cake. Once the crowd had dispersed to eat New Year's appetizers and cake, Kate escaped onto the porch swing with a blanket around her.

"Reverend. God, it's really not fair. I said 'Never!'" Kate flashed back to the argument she'd had with her mom before she left to work at the State Department.

"Never will I have the life you've chosen. I will not have my life controlled by whatever crisis God plants in my road. I want my husband to be home when he's home, not attached to a pager that sends him off in the middle of the night to minister to unknown persons for however long it takes."

Her mother had replied, "Never say never, Katie. God delights in changing us to do His will. He takes our never and makes it someday. Then our never becomes reality."

She wrapped the blanket closer around the lacy dress and pulled her wedding boots up under her. Yep, another 'I told you so' coming soon. *Lord, I know what I've signed up for. It pleases You to see me conform to Your will. I accept it, even though fearfully. Thank you for Tyler and Miguel and whatever blessings You may give.*

***

Kate's grandfather clock in the foyer chimed the half hour at 11:30. Tyler was in discussion with a young man from the mission.

"Find your sweetheart and fill your glasses. Only thirty minutes until the new year," Katie's dad called out, brandishing more bottles of sparkling cider.

Tyler ended his conversation for now and set out in search of his wife. He found Miguel, out of bed, in his pajamas, with Grandma Sarah wrapped around his finger. A bellyache portended there. Katie was nowhere to be seen, not even in her office where she had accepted John's Foreign Service Officer position in Dallas.

The clock chimed the three-quarter hour.

Finally, he opened the front door and found her wrapped up on the porch swing.

He sat down beside her. "A little cool for porch swing sittin', Katydid."

Katie offered him a corner of blanket, and he slid in next to her.

"Your dad will want to showcase our first kiss in the new year. Our first year as husband and wife. That's okay, isn't it? You're not having second thoughts, are you? Talk to me."

"Never about you, Tyler. Just needed to talk about stuff with God."

Tyler pulled her up and folded the blanket. "We'd best get in there then. Time is almost up."

As they entered the house, the countdown had already begun.

"There they are, Reverend and Mrs. Tyler Hawkins."

At the stroke of midnight, as chimed by the clock in the hall, Tyler and Kate kissed. As they kissed amid the hoopla, Tyler's phone began to vibrate. Kate's head drooped.

"I've got to check this." He pulled out the phone. "It's Cantu. They've been in a wreck on the way to the hospital to have their child."

"How can I help?" Kate's eyes pleaded with him.

"I bet the other kids are home alone, Katydid. Your mom and dad will crash here with Miguel." Tyler kissed her again.

"Okay, let me get my bag and tell my parents what we're doing."

Chapter 40

Kate lay in the porch swing, enjoying the warm sun. She dozed as she swung lazily, wrapped up against the early spring breeze. What a journey it had been, the coming home part. In this very swing, Tyler had called her Katydid for the first time. Now all of it belonged to her.

Tyler carried two mugs of mocha onto the porch. "Isn't it a little chilly, sweetie, to be on the porch in the swing?"

Kate reached for one mug and made room for him in the swing. "Thank you. No, it's really lovely. This swing is my favorite spot here." She took a deep drink from the mug. "Well, besides our bedroom."

"Ah, yes." Tyler's face reddened. "Probably not necessary information for the congregation."

"Well, I think they're going to guess that anyway as I begin to show." Kate looked at him for his reaction.

Tyler's puzzled look gave way to joy. "You mean …"

"Yes, our second angel, Gabriel or Gabrielle, is conceived and due in early November, if all goes well."

Tyler's whoop of excitement could be heard all the way to the barn.

Sign up for Forget Me Not Romances newsletter and receive a special gift compiled from Forget Me Not Authors!

About the Author

Diane E. Tatum began writing in grade school with short mystery stories, a play performed by her sixth-grade class, and a dictionary of supernatural beings. High school found her writing serial fiction with her friends, including developing characters and plot lines through hand-written notes. Her first book, *Gold Earrings,* is an outgrowth of a short story written in a high school creative writing class. More historical Christian novels are in the works; most are part of an  historical series. *Mission Mesquite* is a contemporary novel inspired by the Mesquite Rodeo in the Dallas area.

Diane has written many assigned pieces for Lifeway, including curriculum, devotions, and assigned articles for leadership magazines. She has also branched out into freelance publication including poetry, leadership articles, a story for teens, and helps for parents. In addition to her writing career, Diane taught middle school language arts for 11 years. She has worked as a church youth group leader and worker since 1981. She also serves as adjunct professor of English at Motlow State Community College.

She is loved and supported by her husband, Ken, and their 2 sons and daughters-in-law. Her four young grandsons are a joy to them all.

Bible Study/Book Club Questions

A continuing theme in *Mission Mesquite* is knowing the will of God. How did people in the Bible hear God?

Enoch - Genesis 5:18-24

Noah – Genesis 6:9-7:5

Abraham – Genesis 11:31 – 12:9; 22:1-19

Jacob – Genesis 28:10-21; 32:22-32

Joseph – Genesis 37:5-11; 45:1-15

Moses – Genesis 3:1-4:17

Joshua & Caleb – Joshua 1:1-9

Deborah – Judges 4

Samuel – 1 Samuel 3

David – 2 Samuel 11:1-12:15

Daniel – Daniel 1:8-21; 6:1-23; 9:20-23?
Nehemiah – Nehemiah 1:1-2:8
Mary – Luke 1:26-38
Joseph – Matthew 1:16-25
Peter – Acts 10
Paul – Acts 9:1-19
John – Revelation 1:9-20
Each of these people heard God in different ways. Match these ways
with the way they heard God's word to them.

A. Some spoke with God!

B. Some saw angels.

C. Some prayed and felt His guidance.

D. Some had dreams or visions.

E. Others had God bring them his messages through other people.

Most knew that God would not violate His own Word. So, not only
did God share His plan, but He also caused people to know His Word
and helped them apply His Word to their situation.

On Pentecost after Jesus ascended into heaven, the Holy Spirit came
into the lives of believers to be a Comforter & Counselor. Some
Christians think the Holy Spirit acts like a conscience, giving guidance to
Christ followers.

How has God spoken to you?

What is God speaking to you about now?

In *Mission Mesquite*, why does Kate have such a difficult time
hearing and doing God's will?

Have you ever found yourself in a situation that caused you to run
away from what seems God's will?

In *Mission Mesquite*, Tyler's past is not exactly pure. How can he expect to be God's pastor at *Mission Mesquite*?

How is God's forgiveness also at work with Kate?

Has God forgiven you for attitudes or actions as well?

How has God's forgiveness impacted your life?

Enjoy the first two chapters from Diane's contemporary romantic suspense *Kudzu Sculptures*!

Kudzu Sculptures
Chapter One
Moving to Daelin

Daelin, Georgia, is one of those towns where everybody knows everything about everybody else. Built on the side of a mountain, people can look down into other people's windows and patios. It's a wonder the town needed a newspaper. But if they hadn't had a newspaper, Dorie wouldn't have a job.

Dorie Hudson came to Daelin on a summer day, a ten-hour drive from her midwestern home, fresh from journalism school at Virginia Tech. Would the deep South be the same as home? Dorie drove her azure compact car into the town square past Confederate statues and a tall stand of foliage covering all the trees at the edge of town. It looked like a herd of elephants linked trunk to tail. It made her smile.

Behind the square rose the mountainside, dotted with elaborate Italianate homes, ivory and ebony dominoes waiting for a certain breeze to cause a chain reaction down the slope. She passed the *Daelin Beacon* newspaper office in the strip mall in front of her townhome complex.

The lights were still on, so she pulled into a spot and went in. A bell rang on the glass door as Dorie entered. She saw a man in the editor's office and poked her head in.

"Hey, Mr. Andrews. I just got into town. Thought I'd pay respects to whoever is still here on Friday evening."

"Glad you're in Daelin. Monday, eight A.M. We're excited to have you here. That cleared desk is yours. Appreciate it now 'cause by Monday it might be interminably cluttered."

They both laughed, and Dorie made her exit for her loaded down car and the townhouse she rented sight, unseen.

Dorie pulled into the parking spot labeled "Reserved for 1246" and popped the trunk. Before Dorie had fully climbed out of the car, a red-headed woman ran up to the car, grabbed her, and hugged her tightly.

"Your license plate says Virginia! I love Virginia! Were you a Virginia Tech Hokie?"

"Graduated in May." Dorie wiggled out of the lady's grasp. "I'm Dorie Hudson, the new Lifestyle Editor at the *Beacon*."

"Trudy Jakes was the editor before you. She moved out to Atlanta, to better things, I guess." The lady squinted into the lowering sun. "By the way, I'm Hilde Behan."

Dorie laughed. "Good to know, since we already hugged."

She grabbed a box from the trunk, and Hilde grabbed the suitcase.

"I live next door. We're going to be good friends, I reckon. Being the Lifestyle Editor, you'll need to know all the gossip. I'm plugged into the Daelin grapevine. I'm your best source."

The Daelin grapevine? Oh my! Dorie smiled and took the suitcase from Hilde after opening the door to her townhome. "Thanks so much. I have much to do before I sleep. We'll have coffee soon."

Hilde took the hint and withdrew from Dorie's front door.

Dorie peeked behind the front curtains waiting for Hilde to get her mail from the unit mailbox and go into her townhome before Dorie went to the car for another box of essentials, like the coffee machine. Whom would Hilde tell about meeting her on her grapevine? She seemed nice enough on the outside. She'd better watch what she said around Hilde.

She set up the K-cup coffee machine on the counter. Two mugs on the shelf and her coffee singles in her rotator next to the machine, making breakfast essentials handy. If only she had half and half in the fridge.

Grocery store run on the horizon soon. She went about unpacking her sleeping bag, pillow, nightie, and toothbrush. The moving truck would be at her place in the morning with the rest of her things.

When the moving truck arrived promptly at eight AM, Dorie was sitting on the first step drinking her first cup of coffee. She didn't have many things, but what she did have was precious. Her grandmother's armoire. A dresser from her Aunt Sue. A retro blast from 1950 steel table and chairs from Aunt Mindy. The new queen bed she'd purchased on Memorial Day furniture sales. More boxed stuff from college and home.

Sunday morning, Dorie woke up in her own bed, running late before she ever started. She fixed a K-cup of coffee and hurried to get out the door for church. As she came off the stoop, Dorie bumped into a large man holding a cup of coffee as well. Coffee sloshed over his chest.

"Oops! I'm so sorry!" said Dorie.

He drew a handkerchief from his pocket to clean the coffee from his dress shirt and tie. As she attempted to help him, he brushed her hand away. "You've done enough already." He smelled of coffee and the outdoors. "You must be Dorie Hudson. The neighborhood is abuzz."

"How? I literally just got here."

"You met Hilde. I'm Ross Johnson." The morning sun shone through his ginger hair and formed patterns in his well-trimmed beard. "I'm right next door at 1248. Hilde's at 1244. She activated the 'Hilde alert system' last night."

"'Hilde alert system'?"

"She called her grapevine. She thinks you're perfect for her favorite bachelor." He frowned and removed his tie, dripping with coffee. "That'd be me, by the way."

Dorie covered her mouth and felt hot blood rush to her face.

"Where are you rushing off to?"

"I planned to visit First Church." Dorie's heart skipped a beat.

"I gotta change my shirt. If you want, you can ride with me."

Dorie felt a thrill. "Yes, that would be great."

She waited outside his townhome looking at the big green nursery truck with the sign, "Johnson's Nursery and Service". The step up into the cab was huge. *Not a good day to wear a tight skirt and high heels.*

When Ross emerged from 1248, he offered his hand to stabilize her as she climbed up into the cab.

When Dorie and Ross arrived at the church, Ross helped her down from the big green nursery truck. A man at the door offered her a program for worship and directed her to the fellowship hall for coffee and doughnuts. Since she hadn't eaten, she picked up a glazed one and was eying a Boston cream.

"Here she is now! You really must meet Dorie."

The voice was Hilde's. She was dragging a man across the fellowship hall. Ross had slipped away in the crowd like a spirit, leaving her to handle Hilde by herself.

"Meet Mayor Goldstein. Not only is he mayor, he's the head deacon of the church. He's even done baptizing and leading in the Lord's Supper."

"Call me Sonny." He gave her the 'glad hand' as she juggled coffee and a doughnut. "So, you'll be reporting on our fair community? Trudy Jakes was a close friend."

Hilde coughed at the comment.

As quickly as they'd come, they disappeared into the crowd.

The organ's music began, inviting the stragglers to come for worship. Dorie gulped the hot coffee and ate most of a doughnut before trashing the rest. She hurried to the sanctuary, slipped into a pew next to Ross, and tried to focus on worship. Familiar hymns helped her feel at home in this unfamiliar place.

Chapter 2
The Kudzu Situation

The alarm went off at five on Monday. Dorie ran fingers through her bobbed auburn hair. Lots of time to get ready to drive into the strip mall in front of the complex. If only she knew which box held her hair dryer and straightener. After a frenzied search, she settled for the self-drying frizzy look, a bagel, and coffee.

She pulled up to the *Beacon*'s offices at 8:01. *Rats, late on the first day.*

At the ringing of the bell on the door, Mr. Andrews voice called to her from the back of the office. "Nice of you to join us, Ms. Hudson. The news waits for no man or woman."

Dorie threw her things on the desk that was empty on Friday, but now held a mountain of paper in her IN box. Grabbing her portfolio and pen, she hurried to the conference room in the back of the office. Applause greeted her.

"Our new Lifestyles Editor, Dorie Hudson, from someplace cold in the Midwest. Talk to her later." Mr. Andrews was all business. "Dorie, you're covering the town council meeting tonight. We go to press on Tuesday evening. Get info on the kudzu situation."

Dorie nodded, scribbling away on her legal pad. Two of her new coworkers were talking in a low whisper.

"Have you heard from Trudy?"

"Not a word. You know, she and the mayor, uh-huh."

"No! Sonny's a good Christian married man."

"Well, he's a man."

Back at her desk, Dorie Googled 'kudzu'.

> "They are climbing, coiling, and trailing perennial vines native to much of eastern Asia, Southeast Asia, and some Pacific islands…. The plant climbs over trees or shrubs and grows so rapidly that it kills them by heavy shading" (Wikipedia.org).

The kudzu situation. What is that all about? One of her search results showed a scene like the elephant sculpture she'd seen on the way into town. She started an article about kudzu. She felt kinship with the plant, transplanted from somewhere else.

It was standing room only in the stuffy town council room. Dorie stood in the back, so she could watch the townsfolk and their reactions.

"Let the meeting come to order." Mayor Goldstein was a short, stout man with a disagreeable toupee, Dorie noted. "First on the agenda is Ross Johnson with a bee in his bonnet again."

"Mayor?" A timid woman raised her hand and cleared her throat loudly.

"What is it, Sue?"

She shrank into herself at his bellow. "We haven't done the minutes nor the financial report."

"We'll waive all that this month."

Ross stood stoically at the podium in the center of the room. Finally, the mayor waved the gavel toward him.

"Ross, what is eating you *this* month? Say your piece."

"That kudzu is getting worse, and it's suffocating the trees at the road into town. Every year, the town has me kill it. Why is this year different, Sonny?"

"It's like throwing good money after bad." The mayor rolled his eyes.

"This isn't about money. We can't replace old growth loblolly pine. The kudzu must be removed before the stand of pines is dead." Ross's face grew redder, matching his hair.

"We all know who gets the money for saving the trees, don't we?"

"I'd do it for free, if you'd let me."

The two men bantered while the town watched, like it was a tennis match.

"Sorry, Ross, the town has already ruled this issue dead. I see no reason to revive it."

The mayor banged his gavel to dismiss Ross from the podium. A buzz went through the crowd. Ross muttered as he went to his seat at the back of the room. Dorie caught his eye. He nodded to her.

Like that, the 'kudzu situation' was forgotten to tackle the big question of buying another golf cart for the town maintenance staff.

Two hours later the town hall discharged its citizenry. Dorie grabbed her bags and headed for the Java Coffee Shop to tackle the rough draft of her article. After she'd awakened her computer, she ordered a coffee and received a Wi-Fi code. She found a table in a back corner.

"Here ya go, Darlin'." The barista set her double shot mocha in front of her.

After a sip of the life-giving fluid, she Googled Ross Johnson. Only info about his business popped up.

She took another sip and felt his presence at her left shoulder, so close she could smell his woodsy aftershave.

"Can I help?"

Dorie calmly closed the window on her laptop and felt the heat flaming her face. "Yes. I don't understand the whole kudzu issue."

Ross smiled. "You and most of the town. I'll get a cup and join you."

Dorie watched him walk across the café. His ginger hair curled at his collar. The sleeves of his red plaid shirt were rolled up to his elbows, accentuating his broad shoulders and muscular arms. Jeans and boots completed his clothing. She turned around, so she wouldn't be caught looking. She typed in the questions she had about kudzu. The questions she had about him she did not record.

Ross returned to the table and scooted the chair out. "What can I tell you about kudzu?"

"Why is there a big conflict over kudzu."

"Andrews gave you this assignment right out the gate, didn't he?" Ross shook his head. "You know that's a test?"

Dorie nodded and then sipped her coffee to give him time to organize his thoughts.

The barista brought his coffee and stroked his arm as she turned to go. "Enjoy, Darlin'."

Ross reddened at the attention and mumbled something affirmative. He then cleared his throat and continued. "Kudzu is not native to the

United States. The vine creates a beautiful façade, but it kills whatever it covers." Ross paused to drink his coffee.

"Why is the mayor so torn up over destroying a parasitic vine?"

He shrugged. "Every year the town gives me a contract to kill the growth of kudzu. It's just about impossible to kill completely. This year the mayor decided not to attempt it." His face began to redden. "Why is he willing to allow an old stand of Georgia pine to die?"

Dorie typed his answers. "It's going to be okay, right?"

He banged his fist on the table. "It's not okay! The pine trees are suffocating, and I am legally restrained from saving them."

Dorie closed her laptop. "Legally restrained?"

He tossed an official document from his wallet across the table to her.

Dorie considered the document. "Over kudzu? What if I go see what's under the vines tomorrow morning? My story isn't due till three."

Ross finished his coffee. "I'll drive you to the easiest place in. I just can't get close enough to touch the kudzu. What time do you need to be at the *Beacon*?"

"I'm investigating my story, so whenever."

Ross stood. "I'll drive you over at seven A.M. Bring a camera. I want to see what's in there."

"It's a date, um, sure, I'll be ready."

The door jangled as he left. She watched his big green nursery truck drive past the café's doors.